The Horsecaller: Book One

a novel

Candace Carrabus

Witting Woman Works
publisher@thewitting.com
www.thewitting.com/WittingWomanWorks.html

Ordering information:
Quantity sales. Special discounts are available on quantity Purchases by corporations, associates, and others. For Details, email the publisher at the address above.

ISBN-13: 978-0989605700
ISBN-10: 0989605701

Cover design by Faye Rice
Cover images by
© Wojtek Kwiatkowski Equine Photography
© leafsomen | Dreamstime

This is for Robert

RAVER

To Austin —
the true horse-caller
of this world.
Candace
7/4/13

From the Crone Prophecies...

The ground will not shake from sacred hooves,

nor the wind carry a proud whinny,

nor warriors smell sweet horse breath

for two hundred and twenty-two courses.

But before the horses leave forever,

a new Horsecaller will come

along dark, unused paths.

··· 1 ···

LAST, RECKLESS hope. It was the only thing keeping Leinos standing in a driving rain staring into the spiraling mouth of the Ravery. The blurry opening grew larger by the moment. Yesterday, the portal had been no more than obscure myth. Today, terrifying truth. At his shoulder, his lifelong friend, Pheeso, who hated rain, gawked at the mysterious threshold, his lips set in a thin line and his face bloodless.

Two strides farther on, third-degree sage Vraz and high crone Sebira gazed at the yawning maw of the Ravery with fascination, not fear. Soon, they would dive into it. Or through it. No one knew for certain what it held or where it led. They risked everything on very slim chance. The downpour slicked the crone's thin white hair against her head. Rain splashed off Vraz's already bare crown. Sebira waved her arms through the air, coaxing the Ravery open. Tiny flames shot between her fingers and the vortex.

"If this is the mouth," Vraz shouted over thunder and wind, "there is no escaping an exit through its ass."

The comment did nothing to calm the pounding in Leinos's head. Wherever they landed, Sebira intended to keep the portal open while Vraz searched that other place for the one they desperately needed. The high crone made vague references to a dream, a message received, and the certainty they would find the Horsecaller on the other side.

Leinos clapped a hand on the sage's soaked shoulder. "Someone has to be first," he said. "And when it spits you back out here, you will bring a Horsecaller. You will be heroes."

If the Ravery returned them, Leinos thought. If the murky legends were true. If, indeed, the Ravery was a gate, and one that worked both ways.

It had to be.

Pheeso backed away. "Maybe this is the ass end," he said. "But I am too pissing old to stand in a cold deluge waiting for a deranged sage and a mad crone to make up their minds."

"Our minds are made, old man," Sebira said. "The Horsecaller is there. We merely await the Ravery. It fully opens only at the height of the storm."

With a grunt, Pheeso pulled the sodden hood of his cloak farther over his eyes, leaned against the broad trunk of a tree, and feigned sleep.

Blue light crackled through the clearing, and a clap of thunder nearly knocked them off their feet. Leinos held his ground and watched the Ravery swirl faster, sparks appearing at the center.

The familiar scents of wet dirt, wool, and leather were

swept aside by a fusty combination of burning hair and rotten eggs. The storm darkened the morning to an unnatural green dusk, but he could still see the Ravery's edges growing larger, obliterating the sheer rock face behind it.

The sage's head barely reached Leinos's chest but Vraz stood stave straight, facing the unknown. He was old, but it was hard to tell with sages. And Sebira? Ancient. The last of the living to know a horse. Her eyes gleamed with excitement. Cirq would never be able to repay them for what they were about to attempt.

"It is not too late to say no," Leinos said.

Vraz's shoulders hitched almost imperceptibly beneath his cloak. "You have already tried everything else," he said. "Your exact words were, 'it is our only hope.'"

True, not that Leinos needed reminding. If they failed, Cirq ceased to exist. He held Vraz's intense gaze a moment, then nodded and stepped back.

Sebira stretched her hands toward the center of the spiral and got sucked in like spit going down the drain. Vraz grabbed the hem of her cloak and followed. The Ravery shrank on a watery whoosh and snapped shut with a hiss. Leinos and Pheeso jumped.

The thunder and wind stopped, and the clouds tore away. They were left standing in silence.

··· 2 ···

LAUREN GALLAGHER dumped a wheelbarrow full of manure and studied the sky. Wind shredded the remaining clouds, and bright sunshine lit autumn's wet leaves like a million tiny mirrors.

The storm had been brief and intense. Nothing like fall in New England. Taking a deep breath of the crisp, newly washed air, she whispered a brief prayer of thanks. The busy training stable was closed, and its owner, her brother Steven, had taken the day to visit their mother in the nursing home.

Lauren had the place—and the horses—to herself.

One more stall, and she could ride. This was her favorite time, after a downpour, when all the wood's colors stood out in vivid relief, and the earth smelled of freshly sliced mushrooms.

Pindar enjoyed a good gallop, and Steven had said the stallion needed work, his way of asking her to put the horse through his paces. Steven didn't get along with the quirky gray, but Lauren loved him.

She sifted through the last stall's bedding, tossing manure and wet wood shavings into the wheelbarrow, and wondered for the umpteenth time how she—an indifferent scholar—had ended up writing computer code, and Steven—brilliant in college—got to play with horses all day.

Then she remembered her husband, Darren. Her ex-husband as of this morning. Who she had fallen in love with long before she knew what love was, and who didn't like horses. An accountant who'd crunched more than numbers with his young assistant. She'd found him working late. In the conference room. *On* the conference room table with his assistant. Such a tired old story.

She didn't like the feeling thoughts of him conjured up. As if she'd been punched in the gut. Especially today, when she should be celebrating a new beginning.

She stabbed the pitchfork into the deep bed of wood shavings flinging horse poop around the stall, making more work for herself. But that was okay, because she loved being with the horses, loved everything to do with them, including flinging horse poop.

For that, she was thankful. Thankful that when her marriage fell apart, it made sense to also leave the firm where they both worked. To walk away from the pain.

Darren was like "Hydracode"—the kind where one fix results in two more bugs. The kind that can't be fixed. She, on the other hand, was more of a "Reality 100 failure"—a program that does exactly what is asked, but when deployed, it turns out the original problem was misunderstood. A completely useless program.

No more. She'd ditched the unfixable code and was in the process of rewriting her own program.

The prospect of being in her late forties, single, and jobless had worried her at first. Then, she'd rediscovered horses and riding. She'd always helped Steven with his web presence. Now, she worked for him full time. Suddenly, she hadn't minded being single again.

Except for sleeping on his couch. She loved her brother and even got along with her sister-in-law and enjoyed her two very loud nephews, but she needed to get her own place, and she would, as soon as she could afford it.

Life had become predictable again. No more surprises.

She tilted the last barrowful down the hillside. That's when she saw the odd man striding out of the woods. Odd, if only because he'd obviously been walking in the storm.

He wore a long, hooded cloak. The shiny cloth reminded her of a school of fish with their multi-hued scales, moving together as a unit, turning and banking, bright one moment and fading in the depths the next.

As he gained the base of the hill, he pushed back his hood, shook out long, gray hair, and laughed.

She tried to think if she'd ever seen him at the place where her mother lived. There were a few there who'd lost touch with reality. But he didn't look familiar. An unsettling feeling crept up the back of her neck, like a damp fingertip tracing her spine.

She left the wheelbarrow and sprinted to the barn to call the police, but he slipped in front of her before she could enter the office.

"You." Celery green eyes stared from under bushy black brows.

Impossible for an old man to cover so much ground so quickly. Her heartbeat kicked up and she went cold. "How'd you do that?"

"You," he said again, not accusing, but as if in recognition and with a hint of surprise.

She took a step back. Why, on the one day she was here alone? She smiled in an effort to look harmless. But not helpless—she still held the pitchfork. "We're closed. If you come back tomorrow, my brother will help you. Actually, he's just on the other side of the barn," she lied.

His pale eyes and how he looked too happy to be soaking wet made her nervous. He smelled like a combination of the worst greasy spoon and a wet dog. Jack, the barn's resident black Labrador, chose that moment to trot around the corner. The big dog came to her side and pushed his nose under her free hand. He looked at the stranger curiously, but didn't growl. That made her feel a little better.

The stranger stared at the dog with wide eyes, shifting his walking stick into both hands. His cloak lifted on a breeze she didn't feel. Jack wagged his tail. She trusted Jack, but after the old man flew up the hill like that— okay, she hadn't seen him fly, but how else?

She went into the office, making sure Jack followed, acutely aware the stranger could have stopped her. The stick he carried was taller than both of them and tipped with a metal point. The hands that gripped it were gnarled with age, but not frail.

He studied her through the wire panel, like she was an insect, like he could see inside her.

Without taking her eyes off him, Lauren kept hold of the pitchfork, cradled the phone against her shoulder, and reached for the coffee pot. If necessary, she would throw the hot liquid in his face. Why she felt so threatened by him, she couldn't say.

His cloak shifted from orange to red to gold like flames licking the inside of a blacksmith's forge. It captivated her, and for some reason, she didn't dial 911. He smiled kindly. She instantly relaxed, feeling as if she'd known him her whole life. No, that wasn't right. If he could get up the hill as fast as he had, could he manipulate her thoughts?

"You have nothing to fear from me," he said, his voice rolling into her like hot cocoa on a winter's day. "I am Vraz. Can you show me a horse?"

No accent she could place, but an odd lilt. Something was off. Lauren put the phone in its cradle and poured a cup of coffee, glad to see her hand shook only a little. With a breath, she steadied herself. She'd had years of experience concealing her true feelings.

"You want to buy a horse?"

"In a manner of speaking, yes. And a rider to go with it."

She stifled a bubble of nervous laughter. "We don't sell riders."

"Ah. Just a horse, then."

No joking with this guy. Lauren put her coffee down

and took a steadying breath.

"What sort of horse are you looking for? Pleasure or competition?"

The bushy brows pushed together as if he'd never considered it. "Courageous," he said. "Strong. A leader. One who listens well and gathers others to him."

Sounded more like qualities to seek in a job applicant than a mount. She sipped her coffee and thought of the beautiful gray stallion, Pindar. He was strong and courageous, if a bit reckless at times. She'd never been able to resist him, and they communicated well. She hadn't thought of it that way before, but it was true.

Steven would like nothing better than to sell the gray. She should have bought him for herself long ago. But Darren didn't like horses and the divorce had left her short of funds. Another of the little surprises she'd discovered in the wake of the sinking ship of her marriage. Her ex had spent much of their savings entertaining his girlfriend.

Her brother would let her pay for the horse over time, but he needed an influx of cash, too.

Badly.

The six-year-old horse, Pindar, was his most valuable asset.

She left the office and walked down the barn aisle toward Pindar's paddock, Jack the dog padding along beside her, the old man following closely. Steven would never forgive her if he heard they'd had a customer, and she hadn't shown the gray.

"Is this horse for yourself, or are you looking on

someone else's behalf?"

"Not for me, no."

"For a child?" A stallion wouldn't be an appropriate mount for the inexperienced.

"Certainly not," he said as if she'd suggested the moon were pink.

She hesitated at his incredulous tone. "Okay, well, I can show you what we have, and if you see any prospects you like, then you'll bring the person who'll be riding the horse, right?"

A momentary pause, then, "Of course."

They stopped just inside the back barn doors. Lauren watched Pindar cropping grass at the far end of his enclosure. Sunlight glinted off contours of sleek muscles beneath his smoky coat. She'd turned him out after the storm, so he was dry. He stamped a foot, bringing attention to his perfectly clean limbs. A little thrill tingled through her. He'd been a steady friend all through her crappy marriage and messy divorce. The one who always listened and made her laugh.

Could she part with him?

She looked at Mr. Vraz. "What's your budget?"

He'd been gazing out at the horses in the paddocks and pastures with a look of wonder and delight. "They are all so beautiful," he said, his tone wistful.

Beneath the strange cloak—she itched to pinch a hunk of it—his loose dark green leggings and matching shirt looked like they were made of felted wool. Small wonder he smelled like a wet dog. Suede boots reached to mid-calf. A wide leather strap crossed from shoulder to hip and supported a messenger-style pack. All looked hand made and expensive. And the walking stick—quarterstaff —that's what it was, judging by the rest of his getup. He could have stepped out of the local Renaissance fair. If it were May instead of October.

"Budget?" he asked.

"Yes. What can you afford?"

He dipped his chin to his chest as if this were the deepest question he'd ever pondered, then looked her steadily in the eye.

"My life would not be too much."

... 3 ...

"AT LEAST it took its rotten stench with it," Pheeso said as he and Leinos stared at the place where the Ravery had been but a moment before.

Leinos rolled his shoulders, but the effort did nothing to release the tightness gathered there. He built a fire, heated water for tea, and they hunkered down to wait.

And wait they did.

Three days of pacing, working out with their short staffs, and fitful sleeping passed before he asked, "How long can we stretch our provisions?"

"We agreed to wait six days," Pheeso said. After a small pause, he added, "You know we can make what we have last ten days—or more—if needed."

Leinos resumed pacing. How long should they wait? Cirq had little time left.

"It will not matter," Pheeso said, reading Leinos's mind as he often did. "We might as well stay here if they are not to return. Soon, there will be nothing to go back to."

He threw a pebble at a stone wall that ran through the

woods. It pinged away into the trees. "All this time keeping a secret Horseguard ready, for what?" The older man crossed his arms over his chest. "Queen Naele will never approve, especially not a Raver."

Leinos eased to the ground next to his lifelong guardian and friend and stretched out his long legs. He'd never seen Pheeso look so haggard, and he expected he himself looked no better. He sighed. "We have to try, even if the queen does not agree. I cannot allow our country and our people to die."

Pheeso looked at him with sadness. He did not bother to comment. They both knew the queen was one of a majority who had long ago ceased to believe the horses necessary for Cirq's survival.

"Death is happening whether or not you choose," Pheeso said. "The next harvests, if there are any at all, will feed but a fraction."

Even before their rich soil had died, the people had begun to wither, and fewer and fewer babies were born each season. Leinos's own mate and two children had faded to nothing in his arms. The light in their eyes had winked out, and none of his strength had mattered.

Cirq needed her horses, whether the queen liked it or not.

"This will work," Leinos said. "It has to."

It was what he always said.

"No one wants the horses."

It was what Pheeso always said.

"We will convince them."

Pheeso grunted. "Leave me out of it."

They did not argue but sat in a comfortable and comforting silence grown from a lifetime of living, fighting, and laughing together. Though Leinos did not remember when last they laughed.

A hand of time passed. And another. The day's light weakened, and they dozed.

A queer tingle lit in Leinos's chest and brought him awake. He pressed his hand against the unfamiliar sensation. Then a pat of moisture landed on his cheek. He looked up.

A sharp wind drove heavy clouds across the setting sun, and another raindrop hit him in the eye. The ground trembled with a roll of thunder. He jumped to his feet, dragging Pheeso with him.

The Ravery began to open.

4

LOTS OF people—mostly teenaged girls—said they'd die for a horse. Or at least give their kingdom. Lauren decided Mr. Vraz meant his life savings—which could be anything. She'd leave the haggling to Steven. Showing a customer a couple of horses would keep her mind off her sorry life.

She turned her attention to Pindar. As usual, with his finely honed sixth sense, he lifted his head and looked for her before she said a thing. Steven insisted the horse was too smart for his own good. But the stallion was worth a lot. Steven and his family needed that money to keep the farm and themselves afloat.

"C'mon," she said more softly than Pindar could hear with a breeze blowing between them.

He whinnied and trotted over.

"How did you do that?" Mr. Vraz demanded.

Lauren crossed to the gate, feeling more confident the moment she had Pindar by her side. She decided for another try at humor.

"I could tell you," she said as she returned with the horse, "but then I'd have to kill you."

Mr. Vraz stepped back and took up a defensive stance with his stave.

"Whoa." Lauren held her hands out toward him. "That was a joke."

He relaxed but still looked wary. She snapped Pindar into crossties, deciding the sooner she saw the backside of this caped weirdo, the better. She gave the horse a quick brushing, saddled and bridled him, and led him into the sand-filled riding ring. If Steven sold Pindar, he'd be able to pay overdue bills and build an indoor riding arena. The incredible horse for a building. Hardly seemed a good trade.

If only…

Dark clouds gathered again in the distance. They'd have to hurry. No rain had been predicted, but it looked like another downpour was on the way just the same.

"I had hoped we could walk," Mr. Vraz said.

"Walk?"

"Yes. Together. Along that trail." He pointed his stave at the dirt road he'd arrived on, right toward the coming weather.

Lauren swung into her saddle and settled. "That's not a good idea."

He couldn't see the horse work if they were walking down a trail together. "As it is, with this weather, you'll have to come back another day if you want to see any other horses."

Mr. Vraz locked eyes with her. His turned dark green, not unlike the color of the sky. "There is only now."

A twinge of doubt twisted her gut. Maybe how the horse moved out in the open was exactly what he needed to see. Lightning flashed behind the clouds, followed by a rumble of thunder.

"Nope, bad idea," she insisted.

His brows lowered, almost obscuring his eyes. "It is a very good idea," he said. "And we must hurry."

Lauren tried to tear her gaze from his, but couldn't. She heard herself say, "Okay."

The stranger began walking.

She and Pindar followed him through the gate, down the hill, and into the storm.

... 5 ...

LEINOS STILL gripped Pheeso's arm as the Ravery quickly grew to twice the size it had been when Sebira and Vraz went through. In the moment between the first drop and gaining their feet, rain soaked them to the skin. Lightning flashed without break. Thunder rattled the branches overhead. Wind whipped their leather cloaks in all directions and scooped barrels of dead leaves into the air. These caught the swirling edge of the spiral making it appear even larger.

They leaned into the squall. Pheeso slung his arm across his eyes and turned to yell into Leinos' ear. "It circles in the opposite direction as before."

Leinos nodded, unable to look away from the raging swirl. Yet his cautious nature held sway. "What if it is not them?" he shouted to Pheeso.

What if we have invited some new and worse plague upon Cirq?

Without another word, the two men took up positions behind two trees flanking the entrance to the clearing. Both nocked arrows into their crossbows.

The center of the Ravery bulged and exhaled the horrible smell again. A sound emanated from it, like thunder, but deeper still, as if bellowing from far beneath them. Leinos had stood his ground against many foes—seen and unseen—and he would not turn tail to this. But every drop of blood pounding through him feared it was not the wise ones coming through.

The portal continued to stretch. Something small and solid emerged from the center as if pushing a membrane, impossible to make out between the lightning flashes and churning leaves. All at once, a very large object exploded through and flew past them.

Leinos shook water from his eyes. The creature was moving away fast so all he could see was the powerful thrust of its hind end and a flick of silvery tail.

Hind end? Tail?

He and Pheeso exchanged a startled look. The Ravery still spun, but their attention was riveted by what had already emerged. In the next lightning flash, they could see a rider atop a large beast. The magnificent animal slowed, stopped, turned. Leinos' breath caught in his chest. By goddess, it was a horse. He'd seen enough statues and paintings to know.

The rider pushed her sodden hair back and looked around. A woman. A woman who could be goddess incarnate, but not the Horsecaller. The tiny spark of hope in his chest flickered out as surely as their fire had been doused by the cold rain. The horse pranced forward, shaking his head and snorting. Leinos straightened, and the horse stopped an arm's length away.

He could touch it, if he dared.

The woman on it spared him a glance, missing nothing.

"What the hell?" She vaulted to the ground.

Leinos noticed she wore strange attire that fit her like a second skin. *Was she real?*

He could touch her, if he dared.

"Where are the wise ones?" Pheeso asked.

A ripping sound came from behind them, and Vraz tumbled out, landing flat on his face in the mud like a great hand had tossed him through a window. Sebira followed, gracefully settling on her feet.

Leinos helped Vraz up without comment.

The sage rose, brushed off some of the heaviest bits of mud, and beamed. "We did it."

"Her?" Leinos gestured toward the woman. He started to say she could not be, but the unfamiliar woman stared beyond them to where the Ravery had begun to shrink.

"No!" she shouted.

She launched herself toward it, dragging the horse along. Had Vraz just said he had done it? Could he mean…? Leinos stepped into the woman's path and caught her. She thrashed and twisted, stronger than he expected, landing a kick to his shin before he pinned her legs between his. Still, she fought, almost knocking him off balance, pummeling him with her fists and writhing against him. She elbowed his head and yelled to be let go.

The Ravery squeezed shut with a sigh.

"No," she said again, this time an anguished whisper.

The wind died and the storm broke up, just as it had

before. The last pale rays of daylight illuminated them through the dense forest.

Her garments were thin, their hearts pounded together, her tense curves molded to him, and quick breaths stirred the hair on his neck. Little by little, her body went limp, and still he held her tight, telling himself she might try to escape again. She carried the Ravery's stink with her, but her own scent teased through, fresh as a cool morning. An intense urge to keep hold of her overtook him. He stroked her back and whispered into her ear.

"You are safe, *k'varo risa*."

She pulled back, still in his grasp, and looked at him, brown eyes wide, generous lips slightly apart and scarcely a fingertip from his. She had high cheekbones and a stubborn-looking chin, but it was her mouth that stole his concentration.

What was she? *Horsecaller? Goddess?*

Woman. With his blood still roaring with fear and elation, he could have laid her on the soggy ground and taken her right there.

"What did you just call me?" Lauren demanded.

He blinked as if snapping out of a spell and eased her feet to the ground.

Her arms had twined around his neck and her body melted to his like a lover.

The question had came out harsher than she'd intended, Lauren thought, but she'd never been able to control that sharp tone when she was livid or terrified or frustrated. All of which she usually avoided. All of which quivered through her right now.

She noticed the others staring and felt a blush creep up her neck. Pindar stood near, motionless, breathing steadily, though she'd dropped the reins. She took them. She'd been in a daze since mounting him outside the barn to follow the odd old man in the multi-colored cape.

Somehow, Mr. Vraz had led her and Pindar through the woods to where an old woman waited, then forced them down the "rock drop," a stone embankment in the northwest corner of the farm. In a driving rainstorm. Insanity. But where they landed was not the sandy creek that cut through that area. It was a heavily forested glade the likes of which she'd never seen.

And the smell. Foul. Small wonder their mother had always forbidden them to go to that part of the farm as kids. She never explained why. But this was some other place, even though the same storm had been raging here as it had where she started. Or was it another time? No, not possible.

Was it?

"You," she said to Mr. Vraz.

He inclined his head. "Third Degree Sage Vraz at your service, Lady Horsecaller. Welcome to Cirq."

Two other heavily cloaked figures bowed to her, the man who had grabbed her and one other, older. Good God, were they holding crossbows? *Friends of Mr. Vraz.*

She pushed her hair out of her eyes and wondered absently what had happened to her riding helmet. She frantically searched the area for any familiar landmark. The trees were truly enormous with trunks that at their base were big enough to hide a truck and six-horse trailer.

Where was she?

"I am High Crone Sebira," the aged woman said. "I also extend welcome to you, Lady Horsecaller. You come at a time of great need. There is no time to waste."

Come? Kidnapped, more like. "This is your fault," Lauren said to the sage, ignoring the others. "How'd you do it?"

"Ah," he said with a smile. "I could tell you, but then I would have to kill you." The smile faded. "No joke."

The one who'd held her bowed again and said, "I am Leinos, Supreme Guardian of Cirq. We apologize for the poor quality of this reception but welcome you to our land."

Part of Lauren's brain registered that beneath his drenched exterior, the man was handsome and fit. He'd held her tight without hurting her, had somehow comforted her despite being a stranger, even though running into him had been like running into a wall. He'd rubbed her back and said a few words, some in a language she didn't recognize, yet felt familiar, like the echo of a dream.

He was about her age with short-cropped dark hair shot with silver. A jagged scar ruffled his right eyebrow, and his nose had been broken at least once. Just like Mr. Vraz, he smelled of wet dog, but also of leather and pine. The barest trace of a certain kind of smile lingered in his copper colored eyes. She felt her gut tighten in response.

Not the time for that.

"I am Pheeso," the older man holding a crossbow said,

dropping to one knee.

"Guardian of the Supreme Guardian. Welcome."

She looked from one to the other, fighting competing urges to laugh and cry.

"And your name, Lady Horsecaller?" Leinos asked.

Lauren's clothes were soaked and she was getting cold. Her feet squished inside her boots. Pindar rested his chin on her shoulder and breathed warm air down her neck. It felt good and grounded her enough to play along until she figured out how to get home.

"I am Lauren Gallagher…of…what is Cirq? Is that your country?" Leinos nodded. "…of the United States," she finished, feeling ridiculous. She yanked off her gloves and stroked Pindar's velvety nose with her fingertips. "This is Pindar."

"He is magnificent," Leinos said before turning to Vraz. "Are you sure? How can the Horsecaller be a woman?"

"I am sure," Vraz said.

"Oh, yes," Sebira said at the same time. "Thank the goddess. Very sure. She is the direct descend—"

A sharp gesture from Vraz cut her off. "Not now."

"But—" Leinos began.

"Think on the meaning of this, Guardian." The old woman took a step closer to him. "A woman Horsecaller. From the goddess herself."

"No," Lauren said. "No, no, no. I don't know what that means, but I'm not it."

"You are," Vraz said.

Crone Sebira smiled and nodded, entirely too smug.

Lauren changed tactics. She already knew the futility of arguing with the odd man in the multi-hued cloak. Clearly, this old woman was no better.

"Can you repeat what you said to me before?" she asked the good-looking one. He, at least, had displayed a small measure of skepticism that she was what they said she was. Which she wasn't.

He hesitated a fraction of a second before answer, then repeated what he had said. "You are safe, *k'varo risa.*"

She'd been anything but safe wrapped in that man's arms. "And what does that mean?"

The Supreme Guardian radiated power, perhaps enough to protect an entire land, but at that moment, he all but shuffled his feet in discomfort. "It is from the old language. A term of endearment, I believe, for a horsewoman. Forgive me if I insulted—"

Lauren waved him off, unconcerned with appearing rude. "I need a minute," she said.

She led Pindar several yards away to the edge of the clearing where tree trunks formed a dense wall, her brain in overdrive as she glanced over her shoulder to where the others stood watching. She positioned Pindar so that he blocked their view.

Vraz had messed with her mind somehow and brought them here, she was sure of it. And the old crone had a hand in it is well. Sages and crones. Honestly. Whatever else they were capable of could probably be done to her with or without a horse in the way, but she felt better with the big gray's solid body in between.

Implausible though it seemed, she had to face the

reality that she was in a different place. She hadn't been everywhere on Earth, but no place she'd ever heard of or seen in a documentary had trees like the ones surrounding her. Not only could she have parked Stephen's truck and six-horse trailer behind each one—with room to spare—but their trunks were smooth and black as the calves of her riding boots. They soared so high above, she couldn't see their tops, and they were naked except for a few tiny green buds.

But it wasn't spring. Not where she'd been a short while ago, anyway. It had been fall. And it had been morning, not dusk. She moved closer to one of the giant trees and scraped at the bark. Real. For a moment, she'd had a wild hope this was some sort of crazy hoax or a bad dream.

Lauren had always been good at analyzing situations and acting quickly to resolve challenges—at work anyway. It was how she kept her life on an even keel—stomping down molehills before they became mountains. If only she'd recognized Darren for the mole he was…

She'd immediately known the swirly thing had been some sort of portal and tried to get back through it before it closed, but the big guy—the one who called himself Supreme Guardian—had stopped her. Clearly, they planned to keep her here against her will.

Yet, they were giving her time to think. They hadn't tied her up. They'd been polite, deferential even. It was too much to take in, too many shocks for one day…one hour. She had no frame of reference.

Or did she?

What the Supreme Guardian had called her sounded

like 'cavallerizza,' an Italian word for rider, not that she spoke Italian. Her mother had called her that whenever she fell off a horse or didn't bring home a blue ribbon from a show—rare as that was.

And, she had to consider the hush-hush family history, stories reaching back generations of an ancestor and his prized horse vanishing in a storm in that same forbidden corner of the farm. Stories her mother told in bits and pieces that never made sense. Stories of a great-great-grandfather who had been a spooky-good horseman, a man whose blood ran in her veins. Stories that ended with a line about him returning some day to claim his own.

No, she thought with a shake of her head. Impossible. Those were tall tales used to scare kids into doing what they were told. *Granpa Enzo will get you if you don't clean those stalls. Better treat your horse right or Granpa Enzo will come for you…*

Lauren sucked in several deep breaths of cool air. Everything else might be different, but one thing was the same. The wet ground smelled of freshly sliced mushrooms, of home. But she wasn't home. Not even close. She buried her face in Pindar's warm neck, forcing the fear back down her throat. She would not cry. She'd done enough of that over the last few months.

Branches breaking overhead brought her up short. A large object landed with a thud, rolled a few feet away from her, and unfolded until it towered over her. She squinted into the fading light, determined not to be shocked again today.

Before her, a creature stood on two thin, yellow legs each completed by three long claws. Stumpy wings covered in short, red feathers stuck out from its plump body. Its squat neck supported a large, round human-like head that looked as though it might topple off. A spray of the red feathers topped a face with a thick beak, mottled skin, and glowing orange eyes. It looked like an experiment to breed human with ostrich gone horribly wrong.

The nasty taste of burning rubber spread over Lauren's tongue as the bird-man's wings retracted, and spindly, scaled arms replaced them.

"Oh. My. God."

She pushed Pindar back and looked for the others. Hadn't they seen?

Her heart jumped into her throat. If this was all a weird dream, it had just become a nightmare. "Help—" she started, but little more than a croak came out.

Just like in a nightmare.

Another creature dropped, then a third, each pausing to adjust its wing-arms. The awful things threw back their heads and howled.

That was enough for Pindar. He reared and jerked her off her feet. She heard the others shouting as she swung from the reins like a helpless doll and slammed into a stone wall, but hung on. She would not let go of her horse.

"Guardian, save the Horsecaller," Sebira yelled. "We will hold them."

Monsters crashed through the trees, coming from all

directions. The burning rubber smell grew stronger. Lauren gagged and coughed. A loud hissing ended in a solid thwack, and the bird-man closest to her thudded to the ground, a short arrow sticking out of its skull.

She had to get into the saddle, but her legs refused to support her. Pindar scrambled back, feeling for a way out, hind end knocking into trees. She stumbled to her knees trying to keep up and grab a stirrup.

The others surrounded her. Leinos reached her side at the same moment a bird-man jumped on her. Sharp claws sliced through her leather boots, gripped her ankles, and jerked upward. Burning pain screeched into her brain, freezing her in place.

Leinos hauled her up by her arm, knocking the monster's head clean off with a swipe of his stave. "Get on," he ground between clenched teeth.

She forced herself to kick the horrible creature away. More bird-men encircled them. For a moment, she'd thought they'd get away, but the sun had set. It was dark, there were too many, and her legs had turned to wet noodles.

Pindar dragged her a little farther, out of her protector's grip, and her free hand found a stick on the ground. She closed her fingers around it and whacked the feet out from under the nearest monster. It sprang right up. Suddenly Pindar stepped forward, ears flat, teeth bared. He reared and struck the bird-man down, stomping it beneath his sharp hooves.

The Supreme Guardian grabbed her waist, threw her into the saddle, and swung up behind her.

"Go!" he shouted, pointing down a narrow path with his stave. "Now."

Instinct took over. She scrabbled for the reins and clucked. That was all the encouragement the stallion needed. He lowered his head and galloped into the unknown.

Lauren grabbed his mane and didn't look back.

... 6 ...

LIGHT FROM a rising moon illuminated the path. They galloped for minutes, or hours, heads down, quiet. Lauren knew only the fear driving her away from the monsters, the thudding rhythm of Pindar's stride, and the feel of the stranger at her back. The extra passenger didn't bother the horse even though the weight was more than twice what he normally carried. Still, she could feel Pindar growing winded, and she wanted to stop or at least slow, but didn't dare.

She was bothered by their passenger. Very bothered, but she couldn't think about that now. Couldn't think of anything except escaping.

The woods ended abruptly, and the trail continued over flat open ground. Leinos asked if they could stop. *He* was asking *her?*

"Is it safe?"

She felt him nod against her tangled hair, and she slowed Pindar to walk, then halted at the top of a small rise. Behind them about one hundred yards, the huge dark trees were indistinguishable from one another, blending together like splattered black ink spreading over paper. Ahead, the ground sloped toward a river with a bridge leading to a stone fortress. Both a few miles away yet, but clear enough in the bright moonlight.

And the moon.

Well, there were two.

Lauren blinked in wonder at the sight of the twin moons, knowing it sealed tight any arguments about where she was or, more accurately, where she was not. Not that the flying monkeys hadn't been evidence enough. They weren't in Kansas anymore.

Her heart pounded the blood in her brain, jumbling her thoughts about what exactly had happened.

She had to get home. Somehow. Had to get Pindar back to Steven.

For the moment, though, with the immediate danger passed, two moonbeams on her face, and her bones tingling from a hard ride through a mysterious wood with an equally mysterious man, there was no denying what she really felt.

Excitement.

That was wrong, wasn't it?

Pindar's sides heaved. He pawed the ground and snorted. He didn't think it was wrong.

Leinos slid down and turned to her with a smile that said he felt the same exhilaration. He became serious quickly, though, and placed his hand on her knee.

"All right?"

Was he kidding? She stared at him, trying to order her

thoughts. In the extraordinary illumination cast by the double moons, she could see his eyes held kindness and intelligence, and the lines at the corners hinted at a sense of humor. But there was a certain weariness she recognized as well that spoke of a long-held sadness. She had glimpsed that same fatigue in her mirror often enough.

The short answer to his question was 'no.' She was not all right.

"You cannot go home," he said as if able to read her thoughts.

But then, it would be her most pressing concern.

He gave her leg a light squeeze and let go. She wished he hadn't. Let go, that is. He traced one of the slices in her boot made by the bird-man. Strange, she would swear the thing had cut through to bone when it happened but could feel nothing now.

"I have to go home." *Maybe. Eventually*, a voice whispered within.

"Perhaps, but only Vraz can say."

At least he hadn't said *never*. Lauren looked to the line of trees. "Are *they* okay?" Flashes of light shot into the sky from deep inside the wood.

Leinos nodded. "It will take more then a handful of yekerk to slow those three."

"There were more than a handful of those nasty beasts, and those three are...old."

Leinos looked at her sharply, and she expected a rebuke, but he didn't say anything. Instead, he gazed at

Pindar with the same reverence Vraz had when he'd first seen the horses. Pindar flicked an ear in their direction and swung his nose up and down as if in accord, jingling his bit and flapping the reins against his sweaty neck. Of course he agreed horses should be gazed upon in wonder, but Lauren knew the nodding was simply one of his silly habits.

She was glad to have Pindar with her in this strange place. But it was small comfort against the enormity of her situation. She'd been kidnapped, and there would be no ransom. These people wanted her for a reason, but it was clearly a case of mistaken identity.

In her world, she and the horse will have disappeared without a trace. Her family would search for a while, but eventually, their story would be added to the family history. Their disappearance too easily accepted because of it. Another vague secret never to be understood. Unless she could get them home. She had to.

For now, she would deal with what was in front of her.

"May I?" Leinos asked. He reached toward Pindar's shoulder.

Lauren started to dismount.

"No, stay," Leinos said. "We must get you in. I only wanted to touch him for a moment."

"Haven't you ever—?"

"Never."

Never? She looked at his outstretched hand, pale in contrast to Pindar's dark coat. Never touched a horse? Plenty of people she knew had never been around horses, but she couldn't help feeling there was more to it in this case than a lack of interest or time. She nodded.

For the second time that night, Lauren saw hesitation in a man she suspected rarely felt fear or second-guessed his decisions. She couldn't know that about him, not really, yet she sensed the truth of it. She took his hand, pressed it to Pindar's shoulder, and held it there, trying to imagine seeing and touching a horse for the first time.

Leinos spread his fingers against Pindar's damp coat and remained still. Lauren released him and held her breath. The Guardian's knuckles were cut and bleeding, and he hadn't noticed or didn't care. Given his scarred face and disfigured nose, he'd obviously had worse. Pindar turned his big head to sniff the man's elbow, and Leinos smiled. The horse snorted and shook his head.

"You jumped on like you've ridden all your life," Lauren said.

He'd been staring at the big gray as if he still couldn't believe it, but turned his copper eyes to her. "Anything to save you, Lady Horsecaller."

Despite all the rest, her breath hitched in her chest, and she couldn't stop a smile. It had to be wrong, but it didn't feel that way.

He walked on. "Come," he said, and without a backward glance led them toward the river, picking up a long-legged lope that Pindar had to trot to keep up with.

Heavy clouds covered the sky in the direction they traveled and soon obscured the moons as well. By the time they reached the bridge, waves of woozy panic swept through her. Had the bird-man's claws cut deep after all? Hang on, she told herself. One thing at a time. Surely we'll stop soon. Probably inside the fortress.

Which loomed before them now like every evil castle in every princess movie ever made.

Leinos trusted the Horsecaller to follow. She was confused and frightened, but smart and holding up well, showing more concern for the others than herself. Still, he wanted her inside the safety of Raver's Keep where he could tend her wounds. Had she been Cirqian, she would already be unconscious from the yekerk's poison, so perhaps she would not be severely affected. But the sooner Vraz returned, the better.

Artepa met them at the stable. The woman smiled jubilantly at the horse and rider, but assessed Leinos' demeanor with an expert eye. "What happened?"

"Yekerk."

She nodded, bent close, and pitched her voice low. "Who is this woman?"

Artepa had seen many cycles of the seasons and was never one to act surprised or show much emotion, but Leinos could see the excitement in her eyes.

He turned to introduce them just in time to see Lauren slowly swing her right leg over the horse's back and lower her feet to the ground. There, her legs buckled. He caught her before she fell.

She leaned into him. "Can't feel my feet," she said, although she sounded unconcerned and slurred her words.

She started to loop a loose arm over his shoulders, but after it slipped twice, she settled it around his waist.

"You're tall, you know that?"

He and Artepa exchanged a worried look.

"A yekerk cut her," he said. "Help me get her inside."

Lauren groped for Pindar. "No, have to take care of him."

The yekerk's poison was having a strange affect, or perhaps it was the result of traveling through the Ravery. Either way he needed Vraz.

"Get the sage. Now."

Artepa took off at a run.

He shifted one arm under the Horsecaller's shoulders, the other beneath her knees, and picked her up.

"Weeee," she squealed. Her head and arms flopped like limp lettuce. One hand came to rest by his ear. "That was fun," she said. "Can we do it again?"

"What does your horse need?"

"Pindar? He's not actually my horse. I wish he was. He's pretty smart."

"I see. So, we do not need to take care of him?"

"Of course we do. You have a stall?"

Her fingertips brushed his neck. He needed to put her down so he could concentrate. But he would not. He would hold her all night if required. Not that holding her would save her if it were already too late. They should have continued running until they reached the Keep. Foolish to stop, to want to touch the horse when the Horsecaller was injured.

He nabbed Pindar's rein hoping the huge animal would follow him because he was carrying the Horsecaller, and headed toward the nearest stall. Despite standing next to life-sized statues in Lerom, even sneaking a "ride" on one when he was a child, nothing had prepared him for a living, breathing horse. Pindar exuded more raw energy and intelligence than anything he had ever encountered save the most powerful sages.

Feeling that force beneath his body had been incredible. Now, he could not imagine leaping to the majestic creature's back without first asking permission, but in that moment, the urge had been instinctual, as if he had done it a thousand times before. Whether that had to do with saving the woman in his arms, or the horse who dutifully followed after the two of them, he did not know.

Everything changed when the woman and the horse burst through the Ravery. Did Cirq have a future? Had she really come straight from the goddess as Sebira said? The old crone was the only one remaining ever to have seen a horse. She might be the only one living still intimate with their deity.

Perhaps they had a future. First, he had to keep her alive. Where was Vraz? Surely he and the others had killed the yekerk with no trouble. He pushed down an unnerving moment of dread, a feeling he had not known since losing his mate and children. After that, he had become adept at feeling nothing.

"Need to take off his saddle and bridle," Lauren said.

"How do you feel?" Leinos asked.

"You smell nice."

"Indeed. Tell me what to do."

She explained, and he found the right buckles, but it

was awkward while holding her.

"Can you feel your feet yet?"

"Can't feel anything, but I feel great. Did I hit my head?"

"I am going to set you down for a moment."

She hugged his neck. "Must you? Did I mention you smell good enough to eat?"

The next stall had a pile of clean straw in it. All the stalls were always ready. "Indeed."

"Is that all you can say?"

Leinos hoped the poison had simply gone to her head like too much wine, easily slept off. He propped her against the wall, but she lay down and curled into a ball.

"I'm cold," she said.

Leinos removed his cloak and laid it over her, then pulled off Pindar's tack. The horse's legs bent, and for a moment, Leinos thought he, too, had been hurt, but the big animal rolled around and got right back up, shaking straw from his mane and tail, and looking at him as if he expected something. Leinos returned to Lauren and asked what to do next.

"Is he still all hot and sweaty?"

"I do not think so."

"What's wrong with me?"

"I do not know."

She tilted her head to one side and assessed him as Artepa had but a few moments before.

"Just my luck to get snatched to another world and be rescued by someone good-looking but clueless."

"Indeed."

"Honestly. Can't you think of some other answer?" She tried to rise but couldn't. "Help me up. I'll tell you whether it's safe to give him water."

Leinos did as ordered, trying to order his thoughts and come up with a better answer to her next question. She slid her hand down the horse's chest and between his front legs.

"He can have water. And some hay would be good."

Vraz ran in. Pheeso, Artepa and the high crone followed. They all stared at each other for a few moments. Vraz spoke first.

"What is wrong?"

"A yekerk got her legs."

"By the goddess, man, what are doing? Get those boots off her."

"We were—" Leinos rarely felt put on the defensive, but Vraz gestured sharply, not giving him time to explain.

The sage commanded them back into the stall. Leinos told the others to water and hay the horse, then to make tea and find clean clothes for the Lady to wear.

Vraz examined her legs. "Cut them off," he said to Leinos.

"Hey," Lauren said, but without much conviction.

"Your boots," Vraz clarified. "I apologize, Horsecaller. It is the only way."

"No, no, no." She tucked her legs close. "You are not cutting my boots. Pull them off."

Leinos already had his knife ready.

"Put that thing away," Lauren said, wagging a finger at him. "Someone might get hurt." She put her hands over her ankles where the leather was slashed. "Oh. I see. They're already ruined. Damn it. They're so expensive."

Leinos cradled one leg and inserted the knife at the inside of her knee. She winced. He froze. "Am I hurting you?"

She waved her arm in a negligent gesture. "No. I just hate to watch." She flung the arm over her eyes. "So, I won't."

He sliced both boots to the foot and peeled them away. Beneath, the socks were bloody, and her ankles swollen. Ugly gouges marked where each of the yekerk's claws had struck. Lauren peeked under her arm.

"Is it over? Oh, yuck. That looks bad. I'm going to need hydrogen peroxide. Where's the medicine cabinet?"

"I will take care of you, Horsecaller," Vraz said, "but you must remain perfectly still. Do you understand?"

"Sure," she waved again. "I'm not going anywhere."

Vraz touched his finger to the first cut. Lauren yanked her foot away and yelped.

"Are you insane?" She looked wide-eyed from Vraz to Leinos.

"I must draw out the poison, Horsecaller. It should not hurt. You must remain still."

"Didn't hurt. Tickled. Bad." Warily, she replaced her foot in his hand.

At a subtle signal from the sage, Leinos moved closer to Lauren, ready to hold her steady. Vraz began again.

"Yow!" Lauren kicked away and scooted back against the wall. "No way. You have to give me something."

"There is nothing I can give," Vraz said. "I am unsure of how the poison has affected you as it is. I could not risk it. The Guardian will help you."

"Oh, *indeed*," Lauren drawled. She smiled as Leinos narrowed his eyes at her and braced his forearms over her legs.

Again, Vraz began to trace one of her wounds. Lauren bucked Leinos off. The sage grabbed for her, but she thrashed and twisted, landing a kick to his jaw. Straw fluttered around them. Leinos wrestled Lauren until he sat with her arms locked by his under her breasts, and his legs wrapped around hers. They were both breathing hard.

"Do it," Leinos said to Vraz.

Vraz touched her skin.

She braced hard against Leinos' chest, her head on his shoulder, cheek pressed to his. Her whole being strained against him, against Vraz. It took little effort to contain her, but he had to grit his teeth against the feel of her bottom nestled against his groin.

A grunt of effort exited her lips, and Leinos was reminded of a women giving birth. He had not been present when his own children were born, but had assisted others into the world.

"Be still," he said. "It will be done sooner that way."

"He's killing me," she said in a hoarse whisper.

"He is trying to save you."

"Am I dying?"

Leinos's heart clenched tight. His little girl had asked the same question not long after watching her mother and older brother die.

"No," he said, more vehemently then intended. "But I believe you will have the gods' own ache in your head come morning."

She wiggled her hips and he groaned. Vraz smiled at his predicament.

"You're very—" she started.

"With all due respect, my lady, I will thank you to keep quiet."

Despite his tight hold of her, she shrugged. "Just like before, when you kept me from going back through that portal thingy. You were hard then, too."

Vraz chuckled, and from outside the stall, the others laughed. Leinos sighed.

"You're keeping me here against my will," she continued, oblivious, her words garbled. "Do I have any rights?"

Her body began to soften, the fight gone.

"You have all the rights, honor, and power accorded Horsecaller, my lady," he said, though he doubted she heard.

Her eyes drifted closed, and she turned her face into his neck, her breath warming his skin. He loosed his hold, but the raging desire did not abate. If anything, as her body settled deeper into his, the craving grew stronger. Leinos tried to shift out from under the Horsecaller.

"Stay with me," she said, her voice drowsy.

He halted, unsure, painfully aware it was not the first time he hesitated because of her.

"Please," she whispered.

"I will not leave you."

Vraz took a blanket offered by Pheeso. "She will likely sleep for some time," he said, "and remember nothing. But she will fully recover." He tucked the blanket around them.

Pheeso removed the lantern and shut the stall door, a too-satisfied grin splitting his face. Leinos breathed deeply and settled in for a long night.

"I like you," she said so quietly he was not sure he heard right. "Even if you are clueless."

She slid her leg over his, burrowed against his shoulder, and tucked her hand inside his shirt to rest over his heart.

She might not remember, but he would.

... 7 ...

LAUREN HAD a nine a.m. meeting, a report to get on her boss's desk by the end of the day, and a new program to start. Usually, she'd be up early, showered and at her desk in plenty of time. But this morning, she couldn't rouse any interest in getting out of bed. Darren had spooned close, and that was so rare, she would stay for as long as possible. His heart beat against her back, and she sighed in contentment, realizing with the deep breath that she must have dumped her riding clothes right next to the bed instead of in the laundry room where they belonged. Darren would have something rotten to say about that.

She arched her back in a cat-like stretch, and he pushed a healthy morning erection against her.

Not Darren.

"Holy hell!"

She launched herself away from the stranger, sprawled through fragrant straw, and rolled against a hard wall flailing to push dust and hair out of her face and make sense of what was happening. Too many thoughts and images assailed her mind at once.

Pindar whinnied to her from the next stall.

It hadn't been a dream. They'd been kidnapped and there'd been a fight and she'd been hurt and she'd slept with…with the Supreme Guardian. He rose, large and powerful, brushed straw from his leather pants, and folded the blanket, never taking his eyes from hers. Leinos. His name was Leinos. And, oh lordy, she'd never regret sleeping with him, only she'd like it better if she could remember.

"Good morning, Lady Horsecaller."

He reached for her. After a moment's hesitation, she let him help her to her feet.

"Feeling better?" he asked.

A simple question. But today there would be only complicated answers. Pulling herself together, assessing how her body felt, she sought for a measure of dignity.

"Of course. I'm fine." She rubbed her temples, trying to recall how she'd bedded down with this man, feeling fairly certain all they'd done was sleep.

Then why did she feel as if…as if…she'd bared herself to him? If not physically, then in an even more intimate way? His eyes dragged over her, and she felt heat boiling up from her very toes.

From outside the stall, a woman's voice asked if she would care for tea, and Lauren grabbed the excuse to turn away from the awkward moment. It didn't matter. Today, they would get this ridiculous misunderstanding straightened out, and she would go home to her monotonous, uninspiring, small life.

With shaky hands, she accepted a steaming mug from an older woman who had the longest, whitest hair she'd ever seen, wondering from where the rebellious thought about her life had sprung. Small was good, right? Her father had liked to live big, her mother had said. That's why he left them. Big was bad. Small was good. This had held true when she'd been five years old, and it still did.

The woman gave a courteous bow. "I am Artepa, Lady Horsecaller. Together with my mate, Pheeso, I am guardian of the Supreme Guardian. Welcome to Cirq."

"Yes, welcome," said another woman from near Pindar's stall. "I hope your clothes suit. You will need comfort and warmth in the mountains."

"This is Ramela," Artepa said, indicating the younger woman. "I apologize for the intrusion, but Leinos insisted we get you into something warm and dry."

"Oh—" Lauren glanced down at herself. She wore heavy quilted drawstring pants and a long-sleeved wool shirt over some sort of soft undergarments. All baggy, shapeless, and serviceable. She should change back into her own clothes. But she had nothing for her feet, except the thick socks they'd put on her.

"That old battle scar," Ramela said to Lauren, eyes wide. "Tell us about how you got that. You must have gifted healers where you come from to have survived."

Lauren sipped her tea, grateful for the steam, hoping it hid her confusion. "Battle scar?"

The young woman traced a line along her belly.

Lauren went hot all over. Just how thoroughly had

these women inspected her? Had they reported their findings to the Supreme Guardian? Had he been there? A wave of lightheadedness swept through her at the thought.

"Appendectomy," she said, explaining the surgery. Battle scar, indeed. Life in this place would be…bigger.

Artepa nodded but looked dubious. "New boots for you, Lady Horsecaller."

She held out a pair of dark-brown, suede boots with deep cuffs at the top. Gracing the outside edge of each cuff a small horse's head had been carved.

Lauren pulled them on. They fit perfectly. "These are beautiful, but, how?"

"When the Supreme Guardian orders something, it is done," Artepa said.

"Remind me to express my undying gratitude to his Supreme Guardianship," Lauren muttered.

From a shadow in the doorway came his deep voice, a voice that expected obedience. "Readying yourself and your horse quickly will be thanks enough, Lady Horsecaller."

Yes, she needed to get ready. Good, now she could get going. Surely they would take her back to the portal now they had figured out—must have figured out—this was all a mistake.

Oh, but why did she feel such a disappointed tug inside? And such warmth when Leinos spoke to her? She put down her mug and looked for her tack, finding it neatly stacked along with her clothes, but took a moment to check on Pindar instead of immediately readying him.

He munched hay and paused to prod her sides for treats when she went into the stall with him. She ran her hands all over his body, but he was fine, thank goodness. Her brother would be relieved when she returned the valuable stallion to his stable.

Other than a dull ache, her legs felt fine, too. She didn't remember much about the night before, but she knew a bird-man's claws has slashed her boots open, and there'd been a lot of blood—hers—but Vraz had done something to heal the wounds. She supposed she should thank him…

Leinos looked at her over the stall door. "We must go."

"You're taking me to that portal-thing, right?"

"No, not the Ravery. To Lerom, our capital," he answered. "The Queen."

"Am I a prisoner?"

"Not at all, my lady," Vraz said too quickly.

"An honored guest," Leinos added.

"Well, thank you for your hospitality, but I have to go back where I belong."

She tried to look firm without causing offense. One night in this strange place was enough. She had to go home. Because…this was not her home.

Fear wallowed in Lauren's gut. Not only fear of this place, although the attack by the bird-men the day before still cast a dark shadow. There was something else— alongside the fear crouched a deep longing for—what?

Staying? How could she be afraid to go and afraid to

stay all at the same time? Or long to go and long to stay all at once? It didn't make sense. She leaned on the wall as a wave of dizziness swept over her. Conflicting emotions robbed her self control. She prided herself in her control. In her ability to keep things small. This was all too big. And it was getting bigger every moment.

The Guardian joined her in the stall and put a steadying hand on her arm. "Do you need help?"

She shook her head and stepped away from him, breathing deep to regain her composure. He didn't release her. The layers of borrowed clothes became the sheerest silk. His warm hand trapped her arm, his touch a caress that sent shivers of awareness along every inch of her skin.

A young boy squeezed past Leinos into the stall. "Take me with you," he said.

Leinos turned the boy around and gently pushed him out. "No."

"Malek," Ramela said to the boy, shaking her head. "We already discussed this. The Supreme Guardian said no."

The boy peered through the door at them. His tousled blond curls framed earnest blue-green eyes. "Please."

Lauren exhaled hard through her nose before speaking. Some things were the same everywhere. Nobody got to have everything they wanted when they wanted it. "I think he's right about this. You should stay here with your family."

From close behind her ear, Leinos whispered, "Thank you for that hearty vote of confidence, Lady Horsecaller."

His breath fanned her inflamed skin, but did nothing to cool it. What on earth was happening to her? Oh, right, she wasn't on Earth.

Ramela shooed the the boy out of the stall. She produced a large folded garment from behind her back, then shook it out and draped it over Lauren's shoulders. A long, fur-lined cloak swept the ground.

"I made this quickly," she said. "But it will keep you warm. The mountains are cold this season."

Soft fur tickled Lauren's cheek. Around the edges, tooled horses danced and played. The young woman might have made it quickly, but the artistry was exquisite, and it certainly would be warm. Clearly these people didn't know how to take "no" for an answer.

"I can't accept this," she said. *What mountains?* she wondered.

Through the thick leather, Leinos touched her arm and leaned near again. "You insult her if you refuse."

She swatted his hand and he moved away, but a teasing smile played at one corner of his mouth. It made her stomach tilt and left her off-balance, as if the ground had shifted. She grasped Pindar's mane to steady herself.

Belatedly, she remembered her manners. "Thank you," she called as Ramela bowed and left the barn, towing a reluctant Malek behind her. The boy kept his eyes on the horse until he and his mother disappeared around a corner. Lauren knew that feeling. She never wanted to leave the stable, either.

Pheeso and Artepa stood in front of Pindar's stall. Each leaned on a long staff, had a small crossbow hanging from their belt, a pack slung over one shoulder and a quiver of blue-fletched arrows over the other. Their leather cloaks were travel worn and undecorated. Pheeso handed Lauren a second staff he held.

"You will need your own. I made a strap for you to carry it as you ride. When we have time, I will train you to use it."

The smooth staff had substance without weight. Maybe she could learn to use the fighting stick when she got home. That would bring a little spice to her dull existence.

She put down the stick and fetched her tack. While she readied Pindar, Leinos took up his things. The crone was not with them, but Vraz stood near, his cloak glowing softly in the cold morning air. She sensed their eagerness to go. Like Steven's dog, Jack, who whined softly whenever a horse was being tacked up, hoping someone would take him on a trail ride.

Could she dart past them? They wouldn't hurt her but would try to stop her. And if she did get by them? Then what? Could she find her way to the Ravery? What if those flying bird-men were there?

She had to chance it.

"Why the rush?" She tried to sound offhand but fumbled the saddle billets three times before getting the girth buckled.

Leinos settled his cloak before answering. "You must call the horses before it is too late."

"I can't do that." She gritted her teeth, yanked the girth, and Pindar nipped her side. With a soothing murmur to the horse, she insisted, "I'm not your Horsecaller, whatever that is. Why don't you call them yourself?"

"You are the Horsecaller," Vraz said.

The sage. She couldn't trust him as far as she could throw him. He had tricked her into coming here with some sort of mind control. He wasn't using it now, she was fairly certain. She'd gone into a fog the day before after mounting Pindar. The rest was a little fuzzy until they'd landed here. She would recognize that foggy feeling if he tried it again. He would be the toughest one to get around. Could she distract them?

"Our country has been under the subjugation of a king of Tinnis since the conquest," Leinos said. "We need our horses to right the balance of power."

Lauren slipped Pindar's bridle onto his head.

"You want the horses so you can go to war?"

Pindar seemed to follow the conversation, looking from her to the others with his ears pricked. He mouthed the bit, making the hardware clink with soothing familiarity.

The Supreme Guardian stared at her, the force of his will buffeting her like a gust of wind.

"We need them. To live." He paused as if fearing he'd said too much. When he spoke again, his words came slowly, almost a whisper. "We need you, Lauren, if we are to survive. If you leave—"

"It won't come to war if you call them soon," Vraz said, sounding impatient. "Call the horses. You can leave when next the Ravery opens."

Leinos stared at the sage for a long moment, then turned a bleak look to her. There was nothing of the lightness or teasing from before. If she were staying, she'd work to bring that smile to light more often. She pushed all that aside and focused on getting away.

The heavy stall door creaked loudly when she pushed it open. The two men made room and argued over whether she could stay or go. But she already knew the answer to that question. She double-checked the girth as she cleared the barn door, clucked to Pindar as she put her foot in the stirrup, and they were already trotting as she swung into the saddle. She pointed him in what she hoped was the right direction, and booted him into canter.

There were shouts, but she didn't slow. They clattered down a stone-paved street, through an arch, and over a bridge spanning a deep gorge. Finally, dirt—good for galloping. They took off. The others wouldn't catch her.

For a few minutes she savored the feel of the magnificent horse rolling beneath her and settled into it, melding with him as if they were one.

At the top of a rise, she reined him in, remembering when she and the Supreme Guardian had stopped here the night before, when she had seen two moons rising, when he had asked to touch the horse. To touch a horse for the very first time. The wonder in his face when he had put his hand against Pindar's warm neck had sent her back to her childhood, when she had felt that very same way each time she was around the gentle creatures.

What did Leinos mean, they needed the horses—and her—to live? To *survive*. Why had he looked so desolate? Yesterday, before bringing her here, Vraz had said his life would not be too high a price to pay for a horse. But what could she do to help them? It didn't matter. She had a life somewhere else, and people who depended on her there.

Not much of life, and not many people, but…

She heard boots pounding the ground, coming faster than she'd thought they would.

Her heart hammered her ribs and a cold sweat lifted the fine hairs on the back of her neck, a feeling she got when she realized she was making a huge mistake. The thought of leaving made her ill. No, it was the idea of staying.

She urged Pindar forward, but for the first time in his life, he refused her. No, the second time. He'd resisted the day before when she'd tried to pull him through the Ravery. The shock of it took her breath.

She snatched up the reins and kicked him. "C'mon!"

Pindar took a step, stopped.

"I'll leave you here you vile beast," she whispered, knowing she couldn't. She kicked him again, and again, panic closing her throat, bringing hot tears to her eyes. "Please!"

They were nearly upon her. She vaulted off, put all her weight against the reins, then let go and started running.

Leinos tackled her, knocking the wind from her and banging her forehead against the ground. She fought him, knowing she wouldn't win. In a moment, he had them righted, had her cradled in his arms and was stroking the hair from her face and asking if she was hurt.

"Please," she sobbed when she caught her breath, hearing the hysteria in her voice and not caring. "It's too dangerous." A hoarse, unconvincing rasp. "I have to go."

"Shhh," he soothed. "You cannot. It is dangerous for you to try to leave."

"You can't make me stay." But he could. He would. His arms enclosed her like steel bands, but there was gentleness, too, and beneath it all his unflinching will. She had no weapon against any of that.

She'd had her eyes squeezed shut, but she opened them now, not caring how she looked, knowing her nose was red and running and her eyes were puffy, and why was she thinking about how she looked at a moment like this? His face was very close, and in his eyes she saw the hope, a great deal of hope, enough for an entire nation. With a great lurch in her chest, she realized he was the most dangerous element of this place for her.

"This isn't my home." A futile argument. A moot point. Repeating it changed nothing.

He nodded slightly, as if reading her thoughts. "It will be all right. I will protect you."

"You can't."

He couldn't protect her from her own heart, and she couldn't put a name to what she feared. His scent still held that hint of pine, layered now with clean straw and soap. He'd bathed since the night before.

"This isn't my home," she persisted. Her beseeching prayer wouldn't be answered, and she felt herself giving in, but she went on. "I don't belong here."

His coppery eyes searched hers for a long moment. "What if it is?" he asked. "What if you do?"

... 8 ...

QUEEN NAELE of Cirq counted her steps. Fifteen paces from one side of her receiving room to the other. Repeating the exercise calmed her racing mind. If the news sent by Supreme Guardian Leinos were true—

The guards announced Chancellor Seyah. The woman glided in silently, bowing when she reached Naele. Seyah's boots left wet prints across the stone floor from traversing the palace's frozen bridges, and she bore the same pinched look she always did when it was dark and cold and wet. As it had been nothing but dark and cold and wet in Lerom for too many cycles of the seasons to remember, the wan and perpetually annoyed expression seemed to have become irreversible.

It had not always been so.

"Seyah," the queen began with false cheeriness. "You wear the waiting season better than most."

"Thank you, my Queen. I rest and reflect. Even in this season, the palace gardens offer tranquillity. Walking in them is most soothing."

Naele smiled thinly at the banal lie. She had no expectation of honesty from anyone, least of all her scheming chancellor. Should she tell her the news she had received? If only there were someone to talk to. Once— was it really so long ago?—she could discuss anything with Seyah. There had been trust. There had been warmth. Some long-lost feeling threatened to catch in her throat.

Naele breathed past the lump, released it, and reached instead for the iron force at her core. She was queen. No one had said it would be one long fête.

No one had informed her it would be a sentence of solitary confinement, either.

And no one could have predicted the swiftness with which the decline of their country had occurred. The sages and crones had alluded, they had hinted, but never precisely warned.

She decided to skip the niceties.

"I have a message from the Supreme Guardian."

Naele watched Seyah draw to attention. Leinos communicated via messenger only when…never. The potential gravity of the news was not lost on Seyah. The chancellor might be scheming, but not stupid.

"Will you share this news with your chancellor?"

Naele considered. There was a time when she would have let Seyah read the note herself and together they would have puzzled out its meaning over a pot of tea. Now, the weary queen realized she should not have mentioned it. She crumpled the tiny scrap of parchment in her fist and hid it in a fold of her tunic.

Disappointment and malevolence prowled the corners of the chancellor's mouth before she arranged her features into bland indifference.

"I must be gone for…a short time," Queen Naele said. She should not have said a word. Could not shake long habit. Should she stoop to sneaking around in the dark? No. The end might be near, but she would stay in the light until then.

"Lerom is in your hands until I return," she said.

Lust flickered in Seyah's cool gray eyes. Would this be when she made her move? Naele embraced the thought. She welcomed a fight. Even if there was precious little left to fight for.

She waited for Seyah to leave, which her Chancellor did after a fleeting hesitation. Had she wanted to say something but thought better of it?

A memory darted through Naele's mind. The two of them racing through the forest together, young, joyous, their feet barely touching the ground. Golden sunlight sifted by green leaves, the tang of the ocean pulling them down the bluffs to the beach.

She dropped the Guardian's message into the small brazier in the center of the room. The greasy parchment caught, curled, and sent up a thin cylinder of yellow smoke.

There is a chance, it said. *Send them.*

... 9 ...

LAUREN SULKED. She hated herself for it, but couldn't help it. They'd been riding all day

Well, she rode, they tirelessly walked, or jogged, Supreme Guardian Leinos out in front setting the pace, followed by her and Pindar, with Vraz the sage and the other two guardians, Pheeso and Artepa, bringing up the rear.

They glanced over their shoulders and scanned the sky too often for her liking, but no bird-men came. For that matter, there were no birds at all. The barrenness of the landscape matched the leaden sky, as bleak as the look the Supreme Guardian had given her back at Raver's Keep when he said they needed the horses to live.

What did it mean? Leinos never once looked at her or anyone else. He drove relentlessly forward and up. Up into steep, rocky mountains. No one spoke. Saving their breath in the thinner and thinner air of high altitude. They'd barely stopped for lunch, and the meager rations of stale bread, hard cheese, and dried fruit had scarcely taken the edge off her hunger.

For Pindar, there was grain, but not much, carried in several sacks by each of them and strapped behind her saddle. No grass for him to graze, and now a thin layer of dry snow covered the ground. She pulled the hood of her new leather cloak tighter to her throat. Wind flew against them in frigid blasts, swirling clouds of prickly ice crystals into their faces.

Shortly after they started out, she'd tried making another break for it. Pheeso had blocked the path with his massive body and an equally giant glare. But it had been Pindar who again had fought her. Again, she had failed.

What was there to do but sulk? She'd grown bored with staring daggers at the Supreme Guardian's broad shoulders. It had no effect anyway. Each step took them farther from the Ravery and deeper into her conflicted feelings—equal parts fear and anticipation for…what she didn't know.

She wondered about the portal. Was it a worm hole? Physics hadn't exactly been her subject.

If she could make her mind blessedly blank— meditation practice had eluded her as well—she could block out the million ways her body hurt. Nothing had prepared her for this many hours in the saddle, not to mention attacks by weird flying bird-men, or being tackled by a linebacker also known as Supreme Guardian Leinos. She was nearly fifty for Pete's sake. Much too old for this nonsense. Even with whatever Vraz had done to heal her ankles, they ached. Her knees and forehead were bruised. Her seat bones felt like they might poke through her skin. Her back...oh, cataloguing it didn't change anything. Everything hurt. She'd kill for a tube of lip balm.

She had a bad feeling that this night would bring a hard, cold bed on the ground, not the hot bath with mineral salts, candles, soft music, and big glass of red wine she needed.

She huffed out another sigh and sat up straighter. Sulking didn't help. They needed her for something. Who didn't like to be needed? And the something they needed afforded her their deepest respect. Find their lost horses. How hard could it be?

She patted Pindar's neck. He didn't complain. Neither would she.

But good God—or goddess, as her new friends said—it was a long day. Finally, the ground leveled and the wind settled to a mere whine. Perhaps they had reached a pass. They stopped at a large overhang of rock as the last of the day's paltry light gave way to night. It was not quite a cave, but would shelter them from the worst of the elements.

Lauren carefully slid to the ground, knowing her frozen toes would break off if she landed too hard. Painful pins and needles poked her as circulation slowly returned to her feet and hands. She loosened Pindar's girth and exchanged his bridle for a large leather halter she'd nabbed from the barn at Raver's Keep—old, but in good repair. She stroked Pindar's nose wondering about the horse who'd last worn the halter. What was his name? He'd been bigger than Pindar, that much was plain.

"You're having a grand adventure, aren't you boy?" The horse pushed his muzzle into her belly and wuffled softly then rubbed his face against her. She massaged his cheeks and ears and everywhere the bridle touched.

Artepa and Pheeso quickly had a fire built in a stone depression seemingly made for just that, and there had been dry wood stacked inside the shelter. So this was a regular stopping place. As the flames danced illumination along the interior walls, Lauren realized there were places for horses with deep basins for water and feed. She led Pindar to one of these, removed his saddle, and brushed him down using more supplies she'd stuffed in the pack they'd given her. He didn't have a winter coat, would soon be shivering. One thing she hadn't seen at the Keep had been horse blankets.

She slipped the heavy leather cloak from her shoulders and laid it over his back, unsure that would be enough to keep him warm all night. Using the reins from the bridle and the girth from the saddle, she fashioned a surcingle to keep it on him. Before she finished, cold knifed through the remaining layers of her clothes. Deep shudders of exhaustion racked her. She went to the fire.

Someone had laid furs on either side and Artepa was just placing a heavy kettle on a hook above the flames. Lauren closed her eyes. The scent of wood smoke transported her to her brother's cozy living room where her family gathered for Thanksgiving dinner, filling the house with laughter. She basked in the memory for a few moments before asking, "Can I get some water for Pindar?"

"He will be first, of course, my lady," Artepa said without looking up. "Then, tea for us."

"And soup," Pheeso said. He concentrated on slicing something into a large pot.

The sound of her brother Steven's chuckle echoed in Lauren's thoughts. She wrapped her arms around herself and knelt as close to the fire as she could without getting in it, thankful for its heat and something warm to fill her belly, even if it wouldn't be a five-course meal. Tea and soup sound good." She clamped her jaws together to keep from chattering and considered how quickly her needs and wants could be reduced to the essentials.

Leinos came up with more wood. "By the goddess, Lady Horsecaller." He cast furious glances at the other two, picked Lauren up, and slid her between two thick furs. "Did you not see that her lips were blue?"

There may have been more recriminations or explanations, but Lauren fell asleep before she even felt warm.

Leinos gave water and grain to the horse and stood there for a time, listening to him chew. The rhythm resonated deep within him, stamped into his bones and carried by his blood, a gift from generations of Cirqian horse people back to the first Horsecaller

He placed his hand on Pindar's neck as Lauren had shown him, feeling the big animal's throat work and concentrating on the flow of breath. Closing his eyes, he slowed his own breathing until they were in time with each other. The horse accepted his presence, but no more. Leinos did not feel the light pressure he would expect from connection, the gentle hum vibrating up the back of his neck. It had been so long since he had bound his energy with another, had he forgotten how? He had no right to even try with the Horsecaller's horse. Pindar could be blocking him.

Leinos still struggled to believe the woman sharing his fur was the Horsecaller. But if Vraz and High Crone Sebira said it was so, then it was. And soon all Cirqians would be reunited with their horses. The land would be healed by their sacred hooves. Perhaps it was not too late. He would reserve judgment. He would not allow longing to take root.

When they finished eating—which they did in uncommon silence—Leinos banked the fire around the pot and kettle to keep the soup and water warm should the Horsecaller waken. He did not assign a watch rotation because Vraz had surrounded them with an aegis before going to ground for the night.

It thickened the air like clouds rolling in from the sea, the mist that roiled with sighs of the dead. Did the dead whisper of horses? Of fierce gallops through shadowed woods? Of languid days softened by the sun's warmth across a broad back? Did they remember the feel of bare skin against rough-sleek hair?

He could listen, if he chose. If they were near the simmering sea. But they weren't. Instead, they straddled the unyielding hump of the Raver mountains.

The wind had stilled, hushed by the aegis. He fancied the land holding its breath.

Waiting.

Just as the people waited.

Before sliding into their furs, he, Pheeso, and Artepa tucked their cloaks around Pindar and stared at him, his tangible presence nourishing their souls as much as—no, more than—the thin soup sustained their bodies. Hope lit his guardians' eyes, expectation that everything would be all right. They had faith. They had each other.

As magnificent as this singular creature was, he alone was not enough.

The Horsecaller must do her part.

... 10 ...

SIXTH-DEGREE sage, Rezol, stared out into the night toward the nameless mountain that contained his future. Fortunately, his tower's single window faced north. But at that moment, he was not devising new ways to penetrate the mountain's mysteries. It contained layer upon convoluted layer of shields placed there generations ago by a first-degree sage. The same mythological sage had also sealed himself inside to help protect what he had hidden there.

The Absolute.

Or so the story was told.

Then, the story had been forgotten—by most—and a new country sprang up, blithely ignorant of the land's history, of the incredible power beneath them. And blithely ignorant they remained, right up to their despotic rulers, including their current king, Rast.

Rezol pulled his thoughts back. It did no good to dwell on the paltry mental faculties of his benefactor.

Instead, he pondered what might have happened to the yekerk he had sent to the Ravery. Though nearly brainless, the flying creatures were useful. They were dead, of that he was sure, for he had kept a sliver of their small minds in his thoughts always, like bubbles on the roof of his mouth. These had popped, quickly, and in succession.

When the measureless chasm that was the Ravery gaped in his mind like the voracious jaws of the legendary frit, he had sent the yekerk to defend the opening. Chances were slight anyone would come through after all this time. Perhaps they had stumbled into it, back to where they originally came from. No matter. There were always more yekerk, other ways to find information. And now that he had broken the aegis over Raverwood, he would keep the Ravery closed. One less thing to be concerned about.

If the sage leaders in Elaz knew he sensed the portal's activity, if they knew he could open it, they would surely find a way to kill him. The knowledge came as a surprise even though he was well acquainted with what they were capable of.

Rezol would extract the secret tucked so deeply in the mountain no matter how long it took. Then, he would be the one giving orders. First, he would dispatch King Rast. For now, he needed the grasping tyrant as a cover for his real work. Then, he would punish the other sages for what they had done to him, what they had taken from him. A vision of his mate and their baby daughter flashed. He forced the painful memories where they belonged—in the far recesses of his mind—and returned to his earlier ruminations.

Something was happening in Cirq. Flames of sage thought, quickly extinguished, pointed to Raver's Keep. He would send another contingent of yekerk to probe farther inside the borders. Even with Cirq weakened, it was the only place that held any hint of threat so long as the Guardians remained in place.

Tinnis's neighbor to the south, Derr, had long ago eschewed the assistance of sages, and later made the fatal decision to banish all sages and crones. Their country had been in turmoil ever since. He must find the Absolute before they reorganized. They also could thwart his plans.

But Cirq still keep a sage in their capital. Marzak of Lerom was the most powerful sage in service to a monarch, though Queen Naele had little enough left to rule. And Vraz would soon match Marzak in power. Vraz, whom he had once called friend, was unswervingly dedicated to Cirq.

And only Cirq held the key to righting the balance of power: her horses.

He had studied what little had been written about the strange, four-legged animals and knew that with their strength, Cirq could crush his dreams. He had gone to the Bitter Reaches himself, but the confounded beasts had eluded him. Perhaps they could fly. No one could gather them but a true Horsecaller, and there were none of those to be had.

He would make sure it stayed that way.

Whatever it took.

~~~

Thousands of horses stampeding across a vast plain, obscured by a cloud of red dust. Their high-pitched calls echo in her ears, the ground shakes with their pounding. The sky darkens as hundreds of bird-men blot out the light, howling their blood-curdling shrieks.

They sweep down on the herd. Horses scream in terror, whipping their heads around to bite their pursuers. Blood streaks the horses' backs. They begin to waver and stumble.

"No!"

Lauren woke, a heavy weight on her chest. Leinos had thrown his body over hers, had one hand clamped over her mouth.

"Not a sound," he whispered.

She gave a quick nod, and he removed his hand.

"Something is out there." His breath tickled her ear. He spoke on the exhale, barely audible, but clear nonetheless. "Do not move. No sound. Understand?"

He cocked his head, listening to something outside that only he could hear. She couldn't hear a thing, not with her heart pounding blood into her ears like a kettle drum.

She tried to be still, but had to shift, slightly tilting her hips to a more comfortable angle. Her body responded to his against her will—softening, inviting. She kept her eyes squeezed tight as his body answered the call with a sudden, unmistakable hardness. Then, he was gone.

She stared into the blackness and groped around until her hand found the smooth stave Pheeso had given her. She couldn't remember bringing it into the fur, but she scarcely remembered going to bed.

Scuffling made her peek out to see Vraz dragging something large into their camp. He tossed whatever it was at Artepa's feet.

The boy from Raver's' Keep stared at them in frozen terror.

"Malek!" Artepa cried. "What are you doing here?"

It took Lauren only a moment to answer that question for herself. He was there because of her. Malek's teeth clattered together as he glanced from Artepa to Pheeso, then to Leinos, and finally settled on Lauren.

Vraz stood with his hands on his hips, his angry breath clouding like steam from a locomotive. "Not much longer and he would have been a frozen pile of frit dung." He threw Malek's small pack at the boy's feet.

"Please," Malek cried. "Let me stay. I will keep up. The Horsecaller will need help."

Artepa dropped to one knee and put her arms around the boy. "Nephew," she said gently, "your parents forbade this." Her eyes shifted to Leinos. "The Supreme Guardian forbade this."

"The Horsecaller herself forbade this," Leinos added.

Lauren thought *forbade* too strong a word but didn't interrupt.

Artepa gave the boy a swift hug. "We will decide come morning."

The woman picked him up and crawled beneath her fur. Pheeso grunted as he joined them, and Artepa murmured something lulling to him, or to the boy, or maybe to both. Lauren knew a quick stab of homesickness, a longing for her mother that she hadn't felt in a long time. Leinos threw more wood on the fire. Vraz melted into the dark from wherever he'd come. The camp grew quiet.

The next best thing to her mother's soothing voice was a horse. Lauren wanted to check on Pindar anyway, so she shrugged out of the sleeping bag and went to him. He was lying down but got up and nickered softly as she approached, and she instantly felt better. The dream of the horses being attacked by the flying bird-men had left her uneasy, and her nerves were already rattled and raw. Getting yanked from sleep with the Guardian on top of her didn't help. He'd said he would protect her. She guessed he was doing his job. Too well.

"Hey, buddy." Pindar turned his head into her chest, nibbling her shirt with his lips. She noted that everyone's cloaks were either on or under him where they were sure to get damaged by his steel shoes. His water bowl was full and clearly someone had fed him. Their level of dedication to his wellbeing made her smile. "I'm all out of treats, my friend. Maybe I can find something when we get to…wherever it is we're going in such a hurry."

"Tomorrow we will reach Steepside. A village."

Lauren nearly jumped out of her skin at the Supreme Guardian's voice by her shoulder. The man was quiet as a cat.

"Don't sneak up on me like that."

He paused for a moment before saying, "My apologies."

"You don't have to keep apologizing. It doesn't change anything. We've established that I'm not happy about being here, you care only about getting your horses, I'm going to do what I can, and then go home. So, let's just get on with it."

Usually, she was the one to smooth things over and make everyone comfortable. But once again, her fear and frustration had gotten the better of her.

Again, the slight pause. "Indeed."

Lauren could come to hate that evasive comeback. She took a deep breath and exhaled loudly, trying without success to release some of her mounting tension. "Please don't humor or placate me. And let's not pussyfoot around, either. Why don't you just come clean about what's going on here?"

The Guardian placed his hand next to hers where it rested on Pindar's neck, his fingers grazing hers. "He is well?"

She flinched at his touch and the abrupt change of subject. "Yes. Thank you. He is well. But—"

"Then let us return to the fire. You must be hungry. I will answer your questions after you have eaten."

She followed him to the fur where he bade her sit while he poured a cup of tea and ladled soup from the simmering pot. She clasped the warm mug gratefully and let the steam thaw the insides of her nostrils. Oh, how she longed for hot water. Lots and lots of hot water.

He sat next to her with his own cup and arranged the fur around them. Altogether too cozy, but it was that or slowly freeze to death. Reluctantly, she admitted she liked the feel of him next to her. She hardly knew him, and she understood why he'd vowed to protect her, but there was no escaping the sense of safety she felt with him by her side. Something she'd never experienced with Darren.

There were similarities. Both men were tall and handsome, though Darren's features were just-a-little-too-refined, his look too practiced. That polished exterior hid a boorish ego, though. Where Leinos was rough around the edges, so far, he'd been kind and respectful toward her. She'd seen the gentleness at his core. She could get used to that.

Leinos watched Lauren tuck into her soup and waited until she held out her bowl for seconds before beginning.

"What is your most pressing question?" he asked.

She peered through the thin haze above her bowl but answered without hesitation. "What happened to your horses?"

"It was a long time ago—"

"Oh, bloody hell. Isn't it always?"

He stopped, startled. But a smile tipped one corner of her mouth. Good. He had begun to fear she had no sense of humor. Not that he had found anything to laugh at in some time. Nor did he think it made any difference to her ability to call the horses.

It did go a long way toward easing their journey, however.

"Why plod when you can dance?" he said.

"Meaning?"

"Something my father used to say about our choices in life."

She nodded. For a moment, his own questions about her other life crowded out the answers she needed and deserved. Questions like whether she had a mate in that other place. That had to keep. Even though sleeping next to her roused long dormant inquiries of another kind from his body. It would keep.

"So," she prompted with an elbow to his side. "A long time ago in a galaxy far, far away…"

"Ah!" He purposely overreacted to her poke in his ribs, grabbing his side.

She blinked at him, long lashes sweeping gracefully up and down. Her hand flew to her mouth. She was trying not to laugh. "That didn't really hurt…did it?"

He shook his head. Her dark eyes captivated him, and he was overlong in answering. "No, my lady."

She looked away to her soup, seemed to be searching her thoughts for a moment. Finally, her eyes returned to his.

"Please call me Lauren."

"I will grant your wish if you will return the favor."

She nodded solemnly.

He began, "The land of Cirq was settled by the first Horsecaller when he called the horses from their home in the Bitter Reaches."

"Oooohhh. *The Bitter Reaches*. Nice touch."

"You may not think so when you go there. It is a most inhospitable place. Hence the name." *And I will not be there to keep you warm or protect you.*

"The land had been uninhabitable before the horses came, but afterwards, it blossomed, and the people prospered. The goddess smiled upon us. Peace prevailed for many, many generations. Eventually, though, people grew restless, and they ventured outside the borders of our realm, which the first Horsecaller had cautioned against, and they learned the horses were unique to Cirq."

"Seriously? Are you sure this place didn't used to be called Eden? Was there a snake involved?"

Leinos had never questioned their history, and he did not understand the ironic note of skepticism in the Horsecaller's voice. "You wanted to know what happened."

"Yes. I'm sorry. Do go on."

"Going outside our borders was not exactly the downfall, but it was the beginning. Those in other countries quickly understood the power of the horses and wanted it for themselves. But they—the horses—could not be made to go. Even though the then Horsecaller tried. The first had always said the horses were for Cirq only."

"Greed and envy. It's the same everywhere. Let me guess, if the others couldn't have the horses, then they wanted to destroy them. To destroy Cirq."

She gazed into the fire as if seeing something else there, something from her own history, perhaps. He waited, knowing questions were forming in her mind—as they continued to do in his own—expecting her to land on the most difficult one.

"Does the Horsecaller somehow control the horses?"

Like a punch to the gut, his doubts returned. If she were the Horsecaller, she would know this. He needed to talk to Vraz. But the sage had gone to ground for the night so Leinos only nodded, hoping she would not ask how the Horsecaller controlled the horses. If he knew the answer to that, he would have succeeded in his own attempt to call them.

"Why did the Horsecaller try to make them go?"

Leinos released a breath he hadn't realized he was holding. "We have asked this ourselves over and over. He disappeared and his entire family was murdered. We were invaded from all sides. Many died." He could not keep the bitter tone from his voice. "People and horses. One herd escaped. But we have not had a Horsecaller to call them."

Her mood had quickly turned from teasing to serious, and he didn't like being the cause of it. But she needed to know. She picked up a sliver of wood and twirled it between her fingers, stopping only long enough to finish her tea.

"How long ago was this?" she asked.

"Over two hundred courses." As he said the words, the Crone Prophecy struck him like a thunderbolt.

She nodded and leaned out of the fur to pour more tea into her cup. A hank of her dark hair spilled over her shoulder and swung toward the flames. He grabbed it before it could catch. She turned quickly and regarded him with wide eyes, lips slightly parted. He could cup her cheek, run the pad of his thumb over its rise to feel the softness of her skin. Her glance flicked to where his palm still hovered beside her face, and she smiled. A cautious smile, fleeting but genuine. The tingling returned to his chest as it had when the Ravery opened, right before she appeared. They both sat back.

"And you're sure there are horses in the Bitter Reaches?"

Leinos gathered the fur around them again before

answering, still stuck on the prophecy. "The High Crone has been close enough to sense their presence."

"But not close enough to see them?"

"No. But she sensed your presence. Through the Ravery. And here you are."

"*Indeed*," she said, with more of her earlier mocking tone. "Here I am."

Leinos poked the fire, and they sat quietly for a time, the only sound the crackling and popping of the burning wood punctuated by a cutting snore from Pheeso. And the rapid tapping of her sliver of wood against the ground.

"Where did you get your Horsecallers before? Surely you're not in the habit of shopping the universe and snatching people from their homes for your own purposes?"

"No, my lady. We have never done this before. All Horsecallers descend directly from the first."

He didn't add that many believed the first Horsecaller was also a Raver, like Lauren. Vraz had not wanted her to know, and it could be that he was right. There was a growing faction who believed the Horsecaller and horses were the cause of all their troubles rather than their salvation. A faction who also believed anything or anyone to do with the Ravery to be evil. Surely the portal must also be the *dark, unused path* of the prophecy?

Their new Horsecaller was a woman. Many concluded their goddess had turned her back to them, and that was why the horses stayed away. But he often wondered if it was the people who had turned their backs on the goddess, and that was why everything had gone to ruin. Either way, Lauren was a gift in their time of greatest need.

Nothing anyone had done or tried had turned around Cirq's decline. While he lived, he would not allow its people to be overrun and absorbed by other countries, countries that waited patiently just outside their borders for Cirq's death rattle. Why waste resources on a campaign to finish them off when it would be over soon anyway? He studied Lauren's profile in renewed wonder. There were many empty bellies crying out for surrender. When the horses returned—when the land returned to its former splendor—they would see that he had been right.

"What did you mean when you said you needed the horses to live?"

Leinos took a deep breath, forcing his mind to the present. How to explain something he knew without reason?

"Since the horses have gone, the land has lost its plenty. Slowly but surely, the ground produced less and less. Flowers stopped blooming, then didn't grow at all. No fish in the streams. No birds in the sky. Drought for seasons or downpours that washed away what was left of the soil. Then, people began to succumb to the slumbering sickness. They do not eat or care about anything and eventually they simply fade and...die."

He stopped. His voice had begun to shake, and she had stilled, her cup poised at her lips. Again, he breathed deeply, this time pushing away the images of his family. She put her tea down and turned to him, lightly laying her hand on his arm, her touch all at once a brand and a balm.

"I'm so sorry," she said. "If I made light—"

"No—"

"Let me finish. It's just that this is a lot for me to take in. I was dreaming earlier, when you jumped on me—"

"Apologies, my lady. You needed to be quiet at that moment or I would never—"

"It's okay. But the dream…it was more of a nightmare…of horses being attacked by those flying things…if it's anything to do with what you're telling me…" she paused and looked at him, the firelight casting stark shadows under her eyes.

"It was terrible. Terrible. Sometimes when I'm scared or nervous, I use humor to deflect that. I mean, when I confronted my husband about his affair, I couldn't keep a straight face. Giggling and crying at the same time." An indelicate snort of laughter escaped her throat. "See?" She squeezed his arm. "I'll do what I can, but—"

"That is all we ask." He laid his hand over hers.

Again, she gifted him with that smile, a little less tentative this time. He found himself smiling in return, the pain of the past dulled, if only for a moment.

"You owe me, though," she said as she eased into their sleeping bag. "I have tickets to the Yankees game Friday night."

... 11 ...

ARGUING. LAUREN must have set her alarm to radio again. She reached for the snooze button and froze.

Again, she'd forgotten where she was, what had happened. She sighed. The fur still smelled of him, of pine and leather and sweat, but he was gone. Better. It was bad enough sleeping with him. Waking up together like they had yesterday was too intimate. She heard his voice mixed with the others.

"We can not send the boy back on his own and we do not have time to take him back."

"It is too dangerous, Leinos." This from Artepa. "He is one of the only children in all of Cirq. We can not risk him."

"I can keep up," Malek said. "I found you by myself in the dark."

Lauren pictured the boy's stubborn face. He couldn't be more than ten or eleven years old. How had he traveled the same path they had the day before on foot, alone, in the dark? Much of the way had been over bare, hard ground. There had been no obvious trail, and they'd left almost no marks in their wake.

"We have no choice," Leinos insisted.

"We have waited this long," Artepa argued.

Lauren stretched, knuckled her eyes, pushed her tangled hair back, and rose—against the wishes of her body. It creaked and groaned like an old sailing ship leaving port for the first time in years. The others hushed when they saw her. They stood in a tight knot just beyond the fire.

She nodded to them and went to Pindar, noting that most of the camp had already been packed. He whinnied. It must be morning because it was no longer dark, but it wasn't particularly light. Wind howled outside their shelter, and she hoped they would be done with the mountain today.

"My decision is made," Leinos said. His tone brooked no argument. "We will leave him in Steepside and send a messenger to Ramela. She can fetch him later."

Pindar pushed his nose into Lauren's chest like always. He probably missed his paddock and the other horses. She stroked his long face and rubbed one of his favorite spots—his ears—then hugged his neck. He tilted his head against her, returning the gesture.

He must be tired. Climbing mountains wasn't what he was used to, either. She felt his legs and picked up each hoof. No swelling or heat to indicate inflammation.

She poured grain into his feed bowl and went in search of something for her own rumbling stomach.

"Perhaps the queen can leave the city and meet you somewhere instead of dragging the Horsecaller all the way down there?" she heard Vraz suggest.

The pot sat in a pile of glowing coals. Would it be more of the same from the night before? She hoped not. The watery broth hardly qualified as soup let alone enough to sustain them through another day's trek. She lifted the heavy lid. Happy surprise, the pot contained hot cereal, and she ladled a small portion into a bowl, unsure whether the others had eaten yet.

They returned to the relative warmth of what was left of the fire looking in turns downcast, determined, distressed, and delighted. This last emotion belonged to the boy, of course, who probably thought this was all very exciting. Lauren wished she shared his enthusiasm. If nothing else, having him along would lighten the mood. He dropped cross-legged to the ground with a little bounce. The others sat or crouched more slowly. They were all old and creaky, she thought. Malek was one of the only children, Artepa had said. This must also be part of the land 'losing its plenty.' How awful it would be to see everything and everyone you loved collapse and disintegrate.

"Please, Horsecaller, help yourself to more," Artepa said, gesturing at the pot of cereal. "We have taken our fill."

"Thank you," Lauren said. But the avid look on Malek's face as she swallowed another spoonful told her that he had not taken his fill. "So, what's our itinerary?"

"Today we travel down the southeast side of this range," Leinos said. "We will pass through Steepside where we will restock our provisions."

Pheeso grunted. "If they have anything to spare."

Lauren filled another bowl from the pot. "I don't like to eat alone, do you?" She handed the bowl to Malek. "Would you mind? Just to keep me company."

The boy's bright blue eyes nearly popped from his head. He tucked his blonde waves behind his ears, took the bowl without a word, and began shoveling its contents into his mouth so fast she was sure he'd choke.

Leinos, meanwhile, had glared at Pheeso and continued. "From there, it is two more nights to the Inn at the Crossroads. If my message made it to the queen, we will be met by the Horseguard."

Pheeso grunted again, undaunted by the look from the Guardian. "If she deigns to send them."

"She will send them."

Lauren could see Vraz had something to say and was getting impatient. Over time, she would understand their hierarchy and relationships and where she—or the Horsecaller—fit, but she had a bone to pick with the sage, saw no need to allow him to get a word in edgewise. She turned to the boy.

"How did you find us, Malek?"

He looked up from licking his bowl clean, startled. She scraped the bottom of the pot to give him another helping and plopped a half scoop into her own dish.

"I…" He flicked his eyes around the circle, his jumpy gaze lighting on Artepa.

"The Horsecaller asked you a question," the woman said, but with kindness. "Answer her."

He swallowed hard. "I followed the flowers. Right pretty. Like none I ever saw." He set down his bowl. "Forgot. Brought you some." He dug in his pack and shyly passed a few wilted white blooms to Lauren.

She took them. Tiny and delicate, like Star of Bethlehem, one of her favorites. "They're beautiful." Limp as they were, they glowed in the pale morning light.

"Easy to see even without the full moons," Malek added. "Like bits of them come down from the sky in little drops."

"Thank you. But..." It was her turn to sweep the small group. Each of them stared at the flowers with a different version of shock. "I don't remember seeing any flowers. I think I would have noticed." The landscape had been so gray and raw.

She would have noticed.

They all stared at Malek. He squirmed under their scrutiny. They all stared at Lauren. She lifted her shoulders in a helpless shrug.

Vraz stood and grabbed the boy's arm, hauling him to his feet. "Show me."

They all got up. Lauren started to follow. Leinos touched her arm. "No." He pointed his chin at Pheeso. "Go with them. We will finish striking camp."

Pheeso nodded and loped after the sage and the boy.

Lauren helped Artepa roll up their sleeping bag. "What does it mean?"

Artepa didn't answer right away but there was a glint of anticipation in her eyes. "Let us wait for them to return.

Then we will know."

Lauren busied herself packing the grooming supplies and getting Pindar ready. She dipped her hands in his chilly drinking bowl and scrubbed them over her face thinking she must look a fright. The inn Leinos had mentioned would have a tub. It had to. And a bed. Two more nights sleeping on the ground. Would her body hold up? Chiropractors were probably few and far between in Cirq. Yet, now that she had gotten warmed up, she didn't feel too bad. She just had to keep moving and not think too much.

Something new in the air buoyed her steps, something brought by a boy with a fistful of limp flowers. She'd seen it in Artepa's face. Felt it when Leinos touched her arm. He stood at the edge of their camp, staring in the direction Vraz, Pheeso, and Malek had gone. Even with his back to her, she could sense his excitement.

The uplifted sensation expanded her, created an opening for…expectation, an eagerness pulling her forward. She hadn't felt this way since a child. Christmas Eve, a big horse show, her first date.

The common thread stitching these events together was not only the anticipation, but their singularity. The freedom of giving that one thing her full focus. She could worry about her dentist appointment next week, or that she was low on cat food, not to mention how everyone was handling her disappearance or whether Steven was feeding her cats. He was. But there was nothing to do about any of it. Worrying only wasted precious energy.

What she could do was give the situation here in Cirq

her full attention, allow that eagerness to pull her forward. They needed their horses. She was a horsewoman. She might not have given her entire life to it until now, but she could trace her lineage back through generations of horse people all the way to Enzo who brought only his prized stallion and a dream with him from Italy.

Come to think of it, Pindar descended from that magnificent horse. The thought froze her momentarily, then she slowly straightened from brushing the horse's foreleg and looked him in the eye. His return gaze held a hint of smugness, as if he were thinking, "Really, you just remembered that?"

"Lady Horsecaller!" Vraz sounded out of breath.

They gathered around her and the big gray, looking... well, they looked like kids on Christmas morning who'd just discovered under the tree the very thing they'd dreamed of.

They stared at her, goggle eyed, until it became ridiculous. Their joy was contagious, but caution was Lauren's nature. Their reaction to the flowers had been electric. She kept one hand on Pindar's side to steady herself as she faced them.

"Yes?"

Then they all started talking at once. *Pindar's footsteps... the flowers...the land awakening...the prophecy...*

Above them, the air grew dense. It pressed behind Lauren's eyes like a sinus headache. The density took shape then brightened, and High Crone Sebira gradually touched down, her tunic and long wispy hair blown flowing about her.

87

The others quieted and looked from Lauren to the crone.

"The prophecy is fulfilled, my lady," Sebira said. "By your arrival. This we knew. The land recognizes her own and is refreshed. Our Lady is grateful." She bowed.

"I didn't do anything."

"The land recognizes her own," Sebira repeated, as if that explained.

"You mean him?" She patted Pindar's rump, and he snorted, sounding as disbelieving as she felt. She looked at Vraz. "So, you needed a horse, not me?"

Before he could answer, Sebira spoke again. "The land needs her horses. The horses need you. You must make haste." She directed this last to Leinos.

"We go to Lerom, to the queen," he said.

Sebira squinted and her brow puckered, then she all but dismissed the Supreme Guardian of Cirq by flicking her gaze back to Lauren. "The horses are dying, my lady. As surely as is their land and their people. They have been separated too long. All is in your hands."

"No pressure," Lauren quipped, feeling anything but amused. The eagerness she'd felt tightened into full-blown urgency. Horses dying? This, she had to stop.

"You're not making this up just to get me to help, are you?"

Sebira's knee-length hair billowed around her shoulders like angel's wings. "How dare you," she hissed.

Lauren hurtled backward into the stall as if she'd run headlong into an electric fence, and landed on her rear beneath Pindar's head, unable to breathe, a wave a nausea leaving her reeling.

Vraz started forward then stopped.

"By the goddess," Leinos said, and also took a step then halted.

Lauren sucked in air. Pindar's ears lay flat against his head, his lip curled into a snarl, he held one back leg up with ominous intention, and his tail swishing angrily from side to side.

The others stood, unsure of what to do, but sure getting past the horse to reach Lauren wasn't an option. She almost laughed. Almost. Instead, she patted Pindar's leg, and he relaxed, lowering his head to snuffle her ear. She pulled herself up and Leinos reached for her but stayed clear of the powerful animal's back end.

"Forgive me, Horsecaller," Sebira said, also coming to her side. "A regrettable loss of control. It will not happen again."

Lauren leaned away from the crone, still feeling woozy, unsure whom to trust. Clearly, from the appalled expression on everyone's faces, Sebira's outburst was unusual. The high crone had powers and was revered, but not infallible. Also clear was the level of emotion surrounding the horses and the fate of Cirq, which was understandable. But to succeed, Lauren would need a cool head.

"Can you tell me exactly what you mean when you say the horses are dying?" An absurd question, maybe, but nothing was what it seemed in this place. "Have you seen dead horses?"

For an instant, the crone looked like she might fling another thunderbolt, but Lauren didn't duck, even though every molecule of her being—still vibrating from the first shock—screamed for just that. Instead, she eased away from Leinos and stood on her own. Sebira ran long fingers over the top of her head, settling her thin silver hair, or soothing herself, Lauren wasn't sure which.

"I have seen…" The crone's gaze wandered into the middle distance.

Ah, Lauren thought, the old gal wasn't used to explaining herself. She decided to help her along. "You've been to the Bitter Reaches and seen the dead bodies of horses."

The crone's head snapped around. "No," she answered quickly, then looked surprised. "Not precisely."

Lauren tried not to roll her eyes. Vraz's head swiveled so he could gaze into the middle distance just as Sebira had. But he was trying to hide a smile. She resisted the urge to look where they had because she knew perfectly well there were no answers in thin air.

"Then what, precisely?"

"I saw them in a vision."

If Lauren hadn't had the vivid dream, she might have scoffed. It didn't matter, really. Even if there were only a chance that the horses were sickening as the people had, she would do everything in her power to help.

"All righty then." She turned to Leinos. "Which way is Lerom?"

"South."

"And the Bitter Reaches?"

"North," he answered.

She crossed her arms and took a moment to look at each of them.

"Then, shouldn't we be going north?"

~~~

They moved out quickly. Sebira left the way she'd come, and Lauren figured that if the woman could beam herself to and fro at will, then maybe her visions could be trusted. Her party wasn't traveling north or south at the moment, but more-or-less east, using the only path down the mountainside. Weak sunshine and a light breeze greeted them as soon as they reached the tree line and the going was much more pleasant than the day before. Even though cold still bit her cheeks and numbed her feet.

Occasionally, she glanced behind to see if she could catch sight of tiny white flowers magically popping up from of Pindar's hoof prints, but she never did. She still didn't know what it meant, but the others plainly believed it demonstrated the connection between land and horse, but she didn't assume it meant that she was, indeed, the prophesied Horsecaller.

She turned her attention forward, to finding those pesky horses. To "calling" them. She expected there was a difference. That if she found them didn't mean she had called them. There was deeper meaning there she didn't grasp. And that worried her. Because she couldn't beam herself to and fro at will; she didn't have magical powers. She wasn't the prophesied Horsecaller, no matter what they believed.

Artepa had said they would reach Steepside at the middle of the day, and there they would leave Malek with relatives. The boy walked beside Pindar whenever the path allowed. At a particularly sheer and rocky passage, she had suggested he hold on to her stirrup to keep from slipping, and now he continued to hang on regardless of the footing. Sweet.

The trail switched back down the mountain, and every now and then provided a tantalizing glimpse of a distant plain, but most of the time the view was blocked by craggy, white peaks covered in dense brush and weathered evergreens. All of it old and dry. The only place she'd seen any sign of life had been at the Ravery, where the magnificent trees had been covered with fragile green buds.

Long after her stomach said it was lunchtime, Pindar stopped. She had nearly toppled off. The smell of smoke reached her, making her stomach growl. Where there was smoke, there was fire, and where there was fire, there was food. Pindar's nostrils flared and ears pricked. He made a half-whinny, half-grunt deep in his throat, then tossed his head. Whatever scent he caught, he didn't like.

The air carried something else to their nostrils.

Leinos knew what it was. Foreboding slid into his empty belly. He stretched his senses outward, stealing his way through the sparse trees to the village.

Death.

The immediate danger, gone. Everything, gone. Artepa and Pheeso, who had been bringing up the rear, came alongside him. Without looking, he knew Malek stayed at the Horsecaller's side. The sage had his own way of traveling and did not walk with them. But he was never far away.

"Steepside?" Artepa whispered, and the note of despair in her voice echoed what he feared.

Vraz came toward them from the direction of the village. When his eyes met Leinos's, he confirmed what the Supreme Guardian already knew.

Vraz glanced at the Horsecaller before speaking. "It would be best to go around."

"No," Leinos said.

He began to run. The closer he came to the village, the thicker the smoke, and the smell…he knew it too well. Smoldering corpses. As he broke into the clearing that marked the outer fringe of the once quaint, lake-hugging hamlet, he took in what was left. Nothing but the charred foundations of small homes and workshops, and at the far end of what had been the main street, the pile of smoking bodies.

Vraz caught up. "I bade the others remain. One woman was hunting in the forest when it started and returned in time to see the attack. She wisely stayed hidden. After they were gone, she worked all night to drag the bodies into a pile. Her parents—"

Leinos brought his hand up sharply to silence the sage. Impotent fury surged through his entire body as fiercely as the fire that had ripped through the ancient village. He needed to hit something, or someone, but not Vraz.

"Yekerk?" He could smell them still, their foul stench lingered along with the smoke.

Vraz nodded. None of their enemies had penetrated this far inside their borders since the war. Whoever sent the wicked flying creatures had no doubt also sent the ones that attacked them at the Ravery.

The Ravery was near the river that divided Cirq from her nearest neighbor. Derr's queen was an ally, but she had been overthrown by lords united with King Rast of Tinnis, and no one knew where she was or if she lived. Derr, though not deteriorating in the same way as Cirq, had known nothing but civil war ever since the revolt. They were too busy with their own problems to have sent the yekerk.

That meant they had to come from Tinnis, but this was far beyond their normal range.

"Why now?" Leinos asked, not expecting an answer. If they had only been faster, they might have prevented this. This complete destruction. There was nothing here to take, no reason to attack except to terrorize. If they had their horses—

"I have convened the sage council in Elaz," Vraz said. "I must leave to join them. One of our own may be behind these attacks. He may also be aware the Ravery opened, and even that someone has come through."

"A sage?" Leinos's mind raced with the implications. Long ago, Cirq had welcomed the sages and given them safe haven when they were driven out of the other nations. Same with the crones. They were allies, not adversaries. If a sage were in league with their enemies—

"The Horsecaller is in danger," Vraz said. "You must protect her above all else."

At the sound of movement behind them, they turned. Lauren and the others emerged from the trees. The look on her face spoke of the horror she saw. The boy sat behind her, and she helped him down before dismounting, never taking her eyes from the remains of Steepside and its people.

She wrinkled her nose, then turned to him, eyes glittering with unshed tears.

"Are those—?" She coughed to clear her throat. "What happened here?"

Leinos moved to block her view. He knew nothing of her world but suspected this was not something she was used to. No one could be used to it. "A yekerk attack," he said softly.

Her face lost all color, her lower lip trembled, and she crumpled in on herself. He grasped her upper arms so she wouldn't fall. Closing her eyes, she gulped several breaths in an obvious attempt to will herself under control.

He added a small amount of his own power to shore her up, but she needed to do this on her own. Slowly, her color returned. She squared her shoulders and met his gaze. The compassion remained but had been joined by grim determination. Good. She would need this and more.

A keening sound pierced the air. The lone survivor knelt near the blaze and wailed again, hands raised in supplication, then slumped to the ground, her slight body wracked with sobs.

"My God," Lauren said, her voice strong again. "We have to help her."

Leinos signaled for Artepa and Pheeso to go. They and Malek went to the woman. Vraz said he would search the area for signs that might confirm the origin of the attack, but then he must be on his way.

Leinos still held the Horsecaller's arms. Even through the thick leather cloak, she felt bound to him, as if they had been connected long before Vraz and Sebira brought her through the Ravery. His bones recognized her as if her sinews twined with his. This was neither time nor place, but he couldn't prevent the surge of exhilaration that thrummed through him. Every time he touched her. He tamped it down. Being near her would have to be enough.

He must have allowed some of this to seep beyond his skin, for she squinted, bringing him into sharper focus, and tilted her head to one side regarding him for all the world like he was an unknown but unexceptionable bug.

Indeed.

"Vraz told you to stay back and you did not," he said more harshly than intended. No reason to release his anguish on her. "I want you to wait here."

Truly, the Supreme Guardian of Cirq did not outrank Horsecaller, but he hadn't yet reconciled himself to this new order.

"I couldn't," she said. Bending sideways, she peered around him. "And I won't now." She stepped out of his hold. "Does the Horsecaller take orders from sages and guardians?"

He studied her for a long moment. It was a guileless question. She might be an unknown—he suspected as much to herself as to him—but she was far from unexceptionable.

This, and more.

In answer, he moved to her side and they walked down Steepside's rutted main road together, in silence.

Artepa and Pheeso had the woman on her feet, steadying her between them, and she had her arms wrapped around Malek. As they drew closer, Leinos realized she was Malek's older cousin, Armody.

She turned. Her face was streaked with tears and soot, eyes red rimmed, swollen, and wild. She gripped Malek as if she swam with the dead like the rest of her village and the boy her only lifeline.

At first, it appeared she did not recognize the Supreme Guardian. Her gaze swung blindly from him to the horse and back. Then, she released Malek and fell against Leinos, crying soundlessly into his chest.

Lauren felt their agony as if it were her own. Leinos squeezed his eyes shut, and she couldn't bare to look at him in this moment of extreme misery. He had been strong for her a few minutes ago. But these were his people, and hard as this was for her, she couldn't imagine his heartache.

She took Pindar a little ways off, toward the bank of the lake, where he drank. He had followed her toward the mound of burning bodies, but was jumpy from the roiling smoke and and stench.

Death.

She'd never seen so much of it.

The big gray's ears flicked back and forth and his nostrils flared. He drank for a moment, then jerked his head up and looked intently over the calm surface of the water, moisture dripping from his chin. She followed his gaze but couldn't see anything on the far bank. He put his nose to the water again, and she rested her forehead against his strong shoulder, swallowing hard against fear, sobbing, nausea.

She would stay strong. For herself, for Pindar, for the horses, for Cirq. Could she withstand what this place demanded? Her main concern had been keeping up physically. She'd thought her ability to analyze and quickly solve problems would help her navigate this new territory.

How naïve.

Artepa came over. "Are you well, my lady?"

"Yes." Lauren shrugged and turned. "No. Are you?"

The older woman shook her head and studied the dirt around her feet, her straight white-blonde hair falling around her like a curtain. After a few moments, she lifted her gaze to Lauren's. In the pale light reflecting off the glassy surface of the lake, her eyes were the color of newly baled hay.

"We have fought battles," she said. "People die. There has been a truce since we were young. But only because the sport had gone out of attacking us. We are too weak to bother with. King Rast of Tinnis has been waiting for us to simply die off."

The elder woman plainly needed to get this off her chest so Lauren just listened.

"He doesn't want the land, just to be rid of all potential

threat to his power. We have never threatened him or anyone. Cirq always upheld the tenets of the balance of power until his great-grandfather tried to take the horses for himself. Then we defended ourselves. But this.." She cast her eyes around Steepside. "I do not know why they have attacked like this, now. This is senseless and barbaric."

She glanced over her shoulder. Leinos stroked the young woman's hair and talked to her. The girl nodded.

"He was born here," Artepa said.

"The Supreme Guardian?"

"Yes. Was there when Armody was born. He was very close to her parents. Once, he was joined with Armody's aunt."

"Joined, like married?"

"If that is what you call it when two become one, share one fur, one roof."

"Yes, that's what we call it."

Lauren watched Leinos comfort the young woman. She'd known the people of this village were his countrymen, but not his family. She'd considered herself a master of hiding her true feelings, but she was a rank amateur compared to him. He and his wife had probably known each other from childhood.

"Was she—?" Lauren gestured helplessly at the ruin of the village, trying to imagine what it had been like before.

"Oh, no. Not here. No. She died long ago."

"Does he have children?"

"They did. A boy and a girl. Both died at the same time

as their mother." Artepa shook her head again. "All had the slumbering sickness. He tried to save them, but…" Her voice cracked. "Not even the Guardian of all…no one survives it."

At that, Lauren's throat tightened painfully and the tears she'd been holding back escaped, stinging her cheeks.

... 12 ...

LAUREN HOPED they would be gone from Steepside quickly, but it was not so simple. The names of the dead needed to be spoken.

Three times.

Once to acknowledge the person's life, once as a promise to remember, and once more to release them from the physical plane. The more people who participated in the ritual, the better. She untacked Pindar and let him loose. Traces of grass clung to the edges of the lake, and she didn't think the horse would stray.

She resigned herself to join the ceremony and felt relieved to make this gesture for the people of the tiny village. Armody had been too distraught to remember everyone's name, even though she had lived in Steepside her entire life and there were fewer than one hundred people. She had tried, but kept getting mixed up, and had become paralyzed with fear that their souls would go to the sea if she didn't do it right.

Those with no one to say their name got forever stuck under water, evidently. Unless someone came along to speak for them. Lauren figured it was no weirder than many superstitions of her own world.

Leinos knew everyone's name. And their ages. And their relationships to one another. He added this information as he recited the roll of freshly dead. Lauren stood with the others in a circle. Armody had found a bell in the rubble. She rang it after each name had been invoked three times.

"Erranor, son of Erran, life-mate of Arrala, father of Erranorla, seventy-five." Leinos said.

"We thank you."

"Erranor."

"We remember you."

"Erranor."

"We release you."

The bell clanged, echoing over the lake.

The recitation became a chant, an incantation to stir the soul, prodding hot grief to the surface where it could be released.

Lauren cried and didn't try to stop it or hide it. Armody had to hand the bell to Malek who looked proud to be entrusted with the task. Artepa and Pheeso held hands. Leinos closed his eyes and stayed steady. Lauren imagined him picturing each person, etching them in his memory. His voice was beautiful. Deep and rich and filled with love for the people he'd known and whom he hadn't been present to save.

The wind picked up, swirling smoke and ash in a dense cloud over the lake. Pindar huffed his displeasure, but didn't stop cropping grass sprigs down to their roots. The air currents shifted. A cloud billowed around them, pushing cinders into their eyes and making their cloaks flutter and snap like flags. Lauren felt she was being buffeted by the spirits of the dead taking a final turn around their village, caressing the warm flesh of the living one last time.

An hour later they were on their way with no new provisions and another mouth to feed, headed for a sacred spring that might yield fish to fill the hollows of their bellies if not the craters in their hearts.

~ ~ ~

The afternoon blurred into sensation—the cadence of Pindar's stride and the matching swing of her hips, the squeak of saddle leather and glide of reins along his neck, the wanton grumbling of her stomach and the plod, plod, plod, plod of everyone's even footfalls punctuated by the occasional slip on loose gravel followed by muted curse. Lauren let her eyes close and kept her ears open. Goddess blood…frit dung…frit spit…son of a frit. Later, she'd ask what a frit was. Pheeso either missed his footing more often or simply liked to complain, but he swore the most.

When she thought—which she resisted but couldn't help—she tried out arguments against sleeping with Leinos again. A frivolous thing to ponder compared with the implications of flowers sprouting in their wake, a whole town incinerated by flying bird-men, and reviving an entire country. Exactly why she stuck with this subject. The other topics were beyond big. They were huge.

Her attraction to Supreme Guardian Leinos, on the

other hand, was of immediate concern.

She was fairly certain he wouldn't be able to use the cold in his favor tonight. The temperature rose as they descended, and while it was by no means hot, she didn't think they'd have to share body heat to stay alive, or give their cloaks to Pindar to keep him from freezing.

She slept better alone, that's what she'd say. They were so respectful of her, surely he would acquiesce to this simple request without challenge.

And if he didn't? Could she tell him the truth? What was the truth? She was terrified of him, although she couldn't justify the word *terrified* in this context anymore, not after today.

Scared.

Afraid.

His strength and kindness, that rare smile, pulled her to him as surely as gravity kept her feet on the ground. She shook her head. It was too much. She already felt a part of this place, as if she'd always been here. As if this were where she belonged, just as he'd said.

If she worked at it, she could conjure up her daily routine at home, but it seemed less distinct—less real—by the minute.

She'd been here, what, *two days*?

Pindar's stride changed as if he'd stepped in a hole, and the sharp scent of pine filled her nose. She opened her eyes. They were strung along a narrow path, deep in needles, surrounded by dense blue-green branches and quiet. Lauren inhaled to her toes and sighed.

Artepa walked a little ways ahead of her, no one behind, and the others were farther up the trail, so Lauren decided this might be a good time to broach the subject of their sleeping arrangements. Scaredy-cat that she was, raising the question with another woman was easier than confronting Leinos. She hopped down, slid up her stirrups, and jogged to catch the other woman. Pindar trotted along as well, snorting into Artepa's hair when they stopped at her side.

Artepa jumped.

"Sorry!" Lauren brushed ineffectually at the thousand specks of wet dirt clinging to the woman's sleek hair.

Artepa stepped away and kept a wary eye on the horse looming over her shoulder. The wariness wasn't born of fear, though. Longing and reverence flitted across the woman's features, and the desire to do right without being sure what that entailed.

Suddenly, Lauren felt overwhelmed with the task before her. She couldn't very well call the horses, then leave these people to their own devices. Who would train them?

"Hey, there's nothing to be afraid of." Thankfully, it had grown warm enough to shed their gloves. She raised the woman's hand to the stallion's soft muzzle. "Just let him sniff you."

Artepa looked unsure, but held her palm where the horse could smell it. He sniffed and licked her fingers. She jerked away, then giggled like a girl and put her hand out again.

"He's looking for treats," Lauren said. "Wait a sec." She

went to her pack, scooped out a handful of grain, and transferred it to Artepa's cupped hands. "Hold it near his mouth. Keep your fingers together and flat…"

She watched as Pindar's whiskers tickled Artepa and delighted wonder crept over her face. A smile transformed the woman, erasing years of care and thwarted hope. This was a start. Lauren would do what she could, one person at a time until she could return home.

A belligerent voice in her head asked, *And return to what?*

Lauren didn't have a ready answer.

Artepa waited until the horse had licked her hands clean, then brought them to her nose, inhaling deeply. "Sweet horse breath," she said. "Just as in the prophecy."

"What does that prophecy say exactly?"

"The ground will not shake from sacred hooves, nor the wind carry a proud whinny, nor warriors smell sweet horse breath for two-hundred and twenty-two courses," Artepa recited. "But before the horses leave forever, a new Horsecaller will come along dark, unused paths." She sniffed her hands with a smile.

"And here you are."

Up ahead, Leinos had stopped to wait for them.

"And here I am," Lauren said. But she didn't want to discuss prophecies. "More importantly, are we there yet?"

"Where?"

"Wherever we're going to camp tonight."

"Ah, yes. The spring. I have not been there in so long." She rubbed her abdomen. "I hope the fish are willing."

"Willing?"

"It is said that if you are true, and you immerse yourself in the spring's water, fish will jump out onto the ground for you."

"Really. And you've experienced this?"

Artepa lifted her shoulders in an apologetic shrug. "Only one fish offered itself, but he made a fine supper. And the water is hot."

Interesting and a little crazy, but she needed to steer the conversation back before they caught up with Leinos. "It's not as cold here as it was on top of the mountain."

"True, but the water will feel good just the same."

"Right. But we won't need all those furs for Pindar because it's not cold out."

"That is up to you, Lady Horsecaller."

"I'm thinking not." Now that it came to it, she couldn't find the needed words. Then, inspiration struck. "Is there a place for horses at the spring like there was last night?"

"I do not think so."

"Then I'd better sleep near him." She pointed over her shoulder at Pindar. He swiveled his ears to attention and looked like he might snort again at this absurd suggestion.

Artepa hesitated a moment, then said, "Of course, my lady. As you wish." She didn't sound convinced.

"Alone," Lauren added, wanting to make sure this was clear. Leinos was striding toward them, his long legs closing the distance too quickly.

"Alone, my lady?"

"I sleep better that way."

The Supreme Guardian came abreast. Lauren kept forgetting how big he was until they were side-by-side again. The top of her head barely reached his collar bones. She tried to forget how her stomach did happy little backflips whenever he came near, but that didn't stop it from happening.

"Is something wrong?" he asked.

"No—" Lauren started.

"The Lady Horsecaller does not wish for the comfort of another tonight," Artepa supplied helpfully.

*Un*helpfully. The Supreme Guardian's eyebrows drew together, deepening the crease between them.

"Perhaps you prefer someone else's comfort?"

Oh, brother, she hadn't expected he would take it personally. Lauren forced a laugh and began walking to cover her chagrin. "You want to talk about comfort?"

Leinos kept pace and Artepa fell back.

"I'll tell you what comfort is," Lauren continued. "It's a pillow-top mattress and Egyptian cotton sheets. A coffee machine that brews to my exact specifications at the exact moment I want it in the morning. It's central heat and air-conditioning and hot and cold running water with lots and lots of hot. A pantry full, *full* of food." She paused and pointed at Leinos. "Especially chocolate. And fresh raspberries. In season, of course. A toilet. God, I never appreciated what a luxury that is. Lip balm." She ticked items off on her fingers. "Red wine. Shelves of books. Thick towels. Soap…"

At the expression on his face, she heard herself for the spoiled brat she sounded like. He looked a little bemused and a little indulgent and a lot...disappointed. Hurt, even. She shouldn't care what he felt. She'd kept her emotions in check for some time. Since long before the divorce. She never got pulled into anyone else's drama. If she didn't get involved, she couldn't get hurt. Or upset others. Life stayed small that way. Safe.

Images from Steepside slammed into her. "Oh, God, I'm an idiot, I didn't mean—"

"Of course," he said, cutting her off.

Leinos was master of his feelings as well. He'd revealed his inner world only briefly, but now had arranged his features into cool indifference.

"We will do what we can to accommodate your... comfort, my lady."

Terse. Formal. Restraining anger.

No, Lauren wanted to scream. *I take it back*. But it was too late.

Artepa circled behind the Supreme Guardian. Her eyes were round, her lips pulled in nervously as she stared at them with a shake of her head. Leinos turned from Lauren. Artepa froze in her tracks. He walked up the trail without glancing at either of them.

His withdrawal clouted her like a punch to the gut. "What have I done? What does it mean, *the comfort of another?*"

They watched Leinos stalk away, then Artepa appeared to gather her thoughts. "It means simply that all a warrior's glory—all the things you listed—mean nothing without the comfort of another to rest with, to be easy with, to hold you if you need holding, or simply to be present so you know you are not alone."

Lauren had only been venting. Hadn't she? Three days ago, all those things did matter. She knew they weren't really important. She remembered the emptiness when she first moved out of the house she'd shared with Darren. She didn't want Darren or anyone like him. That didn't mean she preferred being solitary or didn't need… *comfort*.

"The Supreme Guardian sees to the needs of Cirq," Artepa continued. "He gives comfort when needed, as he did today for Armody."

"And doesn't ask it for himself."

"Never."

He probably needed it after today. So did she. They began walking again. "It's just that…"

Lauren'd been about to describe the tingly frisson of awareness every time the man came within a few feet, the shock of want at his touch, the fear of losing herself, then remembered Artepa and Pheeso were Leinos's guardians. Probably anything she said would go straight from her mouth to his ears. She'd keep her feelings to herself, like she always did.

"Are we almost there?"

"It is ahead. Perhaps the spring's warm waters will bring you comfort."

Great. She'd alienated Artepa as well. When Lauren decided to stay in Cirq—as if there'd been a choice— she'd blithely thought she could do what they needed and leave. Quickly. Without getting *involved*. How wrong she'd been. Foolish, really.

As foolish as when she'd married Darren thinking he would change.

He didn't.

As foolish as she'd been when she accepted her brother's invitation to move back home, thinking it would fix everything for her.

It didn't.

She continued to berate herself as she followed Artepa, leading Pindar along a widening path that muffled their footfalls with layers upon layers of pine needles. The deeper into the grove they went, the larger the trees. Taller and thicker and farther apart with few lower branches to obstruct the view. Yet all that could be seen to either side was an increasing density of trunks until they blended into darkness. It was getting toward evening and not much light penetrated the thick canopy from the cloudy sky above. Did the sun ever shine in this place?

Still, their steps churned scents of fresh and decaying pine into the air and this reminded Lauren of one of her favorite places to ride. But picturing it didn't bring any measure of peace to her agitated thoughts.

By the time they reached the gate to the sacred spring, she had solved nothing nor drawn any helpful conclusions. Instead, she merely plowed the same furrow over and over—how stupid and insensitive she was, and, if she were completely honest—how apathetic she had become long before arriving in Cirq.

As they approached, two guards snapped a smart salute. Leinos nodded, but did not return the gesture. The man and woman assessed the rest of the group and exchanged nods with Artepa and Pheeso. Then, their gazes landed on Lauren and Pindar.

"Any activity?" Leinos asked.

"None, Guardian."

"Steepside has been destroyed by yekerk."

Both guards blanched and looked up sharply.

Leinos moved closer to them. "They will not enter here."

"They penetrated Raverwood," Pheeso said.

Without moving, Leinos said, "It is impossible for them to enter the sacred grove of the goddess."

"It should have been impossible for them to enter Raverwood," Pheeso said. "But they did."

Leinos turned slowly and stared at Pheeso, silencing him with a look as icy and bitter as the mountain's wind. Everyone took a breath and held it. Pheeso either hadn't gauged the Guardian's mood or didn't care. Lauren suspected this wouldn't end well.

"Vraz said the aegis over Raverwood had been broken," Pheeso continued. An apprehensive note in his voice. "That it could be removed by another powerful sage. If he did it once—"

"The aegis that protects this grove is not made by sages or crones or any mortal," Leinos said, his tone clipped and icy. "But by the goddess herself."

He appeared to expand as he spoke. The air around him vibrated. He looked younger for a moment, the creases of his face eased, the hollows in his cheeks filled out.

Around his shoulders, sparkling golden light glowed as if a beam of sunshine had escaped the clouds. Lauren looked up. No, the light emanated from him. She took a step back, deeply regretting her earlier flippancy if it had any part in bringing on whatever this was.

Shock waves drummed through her chest like thunder rattling windows. Next to her, Artepa muttered something under her breath that sounded an awful lot like *uh oh*.

"Yekerk. Will. Not. Enter. Here."

The words resonated from every direction as if projected by huge concert speakers. Everyone stepped back. Pindar shook his head, pranced and shook again. His hearing was so sensitive. Lauren stroked his neck but he wouldn't be soothed. She reached up and grabbed his ears, trying to gently close them, but he tossed her away with a swing of his head. The noise reverberated through his entire body just at it did hers. She understood its source—sort of—the horse could only feel and react. He tried to escape—side-stepping, backing, lunging forward —she stayed at his shoulder and moved with him as if they were dancing a tango.

Whatever it was, it ended quickly. The light around Leinos dimmed. The air stilled. Pindar settled with one last shake of his big body. And a little ball of annoyance lodged halfway between Lauren's chest and belly. Was the Supreme Guardian put out because his guardian had challenged him? That's what it looked like. And because she had rejected the comfort of another. What were these Guardians, anyway? She needed to educate herself. Her life might depend on it.

Leinos—tall, broad, a little gaunt and frayed around the edges—held himself erect but met her gaze with apology in his copper eyes. The last of the sparkling light radiated from them and filled her with peace. For a breath, she felt the weight he carried as Supreme Guardian of Cirq, the compassion and love he had for his country and its remaining people, the fierce demand to save them. She forgave him instantly even without fully understanding what was happening. The knot under her ribs unraveled.

Her mother swore by forgiveness. Lauren, not so much. Her mother also believed each person had a mission in life, something to learn, something to teach. She couldn't help wondering what her mother would say about the turn her daughter's life had taken a couple of days ago.

She pushed away thoughts of home before they undid her. She missed her family.

"I believe," Leinos said, sounding weary, "we would all benefit from whatever succor the spring has to offer today. We will go one at a time. Our Lady Horsecaller first."

The day's events—especially the past five minutes—and an empty stomach had Lauren on edge. The momentary peace evaporated. Danger or something supernatural lurked around every corner. Someone else could experience the spring's succor and leaping fish first.

"Thank you, but that isn't necessary, really. You go ahead."

He reached a hand toward her. "Come. We will go together. Bring Pindar."

Just like that, she yielded. Ping-ponging emotions always had addled her good sense. She'd removed Pindar's bridle earlier when she'd shown Artepa how to feed him. Quickly, she got his saddle off and set it on the ground without knowing why that was necessary. In the past, she always had to understand *why*. Despite her reluctance of a moment ago, letting Leinos lead her felt natural now. Vraz had left earlier, so she knew she wasn't being swayed by some sage trick. She trusted Leinos wouldn't do that, although he probably could if needed.

She put her hand in his and let him tug her forward.

The gate was nothing more than a break in a dense, tangled hedgerow. Once through, the air instantly felt different—lighter, cleaner, fresher. She inhaled deeply, feeling as renewed as if she'd had a nap, a good meal, and a cool drink. If nothing else, the spring promised a hot soak. She hoped he didn't expect they would enjoy the water together, but at this point, she wasn't sure she really cared so long as she could get her body clean and warm.

The same tall pines lined the way, larger than the ones outside, like still sentinels frozen in time. Here and there was a lower bush with dark, shiny leaves. Holly? She couldn't tell, but there were more the farther they went.

Overhead, a rustling flutter, wings against branches. She flung her body into his. He easily enfolded her in his arms, as if it was exactly where she belonged.

"What is it, my lady?"

They were being attacked and he wasn't reacting.

"Didn't you hear that?" Her voice squeaked as she peered up through the branches. Her heart rapped against her ribs like a farrier's hammer shaping a horseshoe. He tightened his arms around her. She tucked her head under his chin.

"I heard nothing," he said.

But he was shaking, too. Wait, was he *laughing?*

After stroking her back a few more times, clearly taking the time to get his voice under control before speaking, he said, "You are safe, *k'varo risa.*"

Oh, right. *Yekerk. Will. Not. Enter. Here.* Damned if she didn't feel comforted.

"I thought I heard birds or something." Comforted and foolish.

Whether he took her seriously or just wanted to make her feel better, he scanned the area above them. It was too dark to see anything. And he'd already told her there hadn't been birds in Cirq for many years.

"You are tired, but you will feel better after soaking in the spring."

That seemed to be their cue to get going, and surely the others were eager to take a turn, but he didn't let her go. Instead, he took a deep, sighing breath and pulled her tighter to him, fitting her bones to his, resting his cheek on the top of her head. Oh, lordy he felt good. Could she do it? Could she comfort him? Is this how one derived comfort, by giving it to another? Maybe he didn't have to ask because that's how it worked. She thought of his losses—today in Steepside and long ago when his wife and children had died—how had he survived?

She had miscarried a baby early in her marriage, and the grief had been overwhelming. For months afterward, she could barely pick her head up off the pillow some mornings. Darren had been no help. He hadn't wanted a family, and she'd been too afraid to try again.

She'd let it go.

Just let it go.

The day had stripped them raw, and she was lightheaded from the swirling turmoil. Later, she would find the courage to lie next to him and try to learn about the comfort of another. It was the least she could do. For both of them.

By some unspoken mutual accord, they separated and continued in silence. She heard the fluttering once again, as if something followed them.

"You don't hear that?"

"No, but the grove of the goddess is a strange and wondrous place. Most fear to enter, but those who do report seeing and hearing things that others do not. Do not be afraid. Nothing can harm you here."

Soon, a steamy glimmer of light heralded the edge of the spring and she forgot about whatever it was that might be following them. The spring was more like a pond, about twenty-five feet across. Dark, flat stones formed a walkway around the edge, and the surface was glassy as black ice. She'd been picturing a hot tub. Several feet of lush grass ringed it before meeting the soaring pines. The sky was clear, just as above Raverwood. One moon had risen over the tree tops and the water mirrored it. A soft, mysterious light suffused the area. It was beautiful as a postcard.

The scenery left Pindar unmoved. He already had his

nose in the grass. Lauren unbuckled his halter and let him go. She walked to the water's edge.

"What do I do? Is there a protocol?" She was eager to be immersed.

Leinos chuckled, and she turned at the sound, glad to see him smile. It intensified the lines around his eyes, and she wondered if they'd been made by laughter or a long life spent mostly outdoors. She hoped there had been laughter, and that there would be more in the future.

She put her hands on her hips. "Are you laughing at me again?"

He shook his head. "No, my lady. Merely appreciating your discovery of this place. There is no right or wrong way. I will leave you to enjoy the spring."

He had laughed, but was back to calling her "my lady" again. She didn't like.

And no mention of towels. The implication being she could drip dry. At night. Alone. In the sacred grove of the goddess.

She didn't mind.

He began to go, then stopped. "We will hear if you need anything. Trust in the goddess." He made a bow and disappeared in a swirl of mist.

Lauren slowly counted to ten, then stripped and eased herself into the inky pool. The water was warm and soothing and smelled faintly of just-bit apple. She found a small ledge where she could sit. Water reached her chin.

"Oh my God, this feels good," she said after a moment. "Goddess," she amended in case anyone was listening.

Sore muscles stretched and relaxed. Layers of fretful sweat and tears slipped away. She pushed off from the wall and floated on her back, looking up at the sky. The second moon had followed the first, slightly smaller and the palest shade of pink. Their light polished her curves with rosy gilding. She closed her eyes and let the bellows of her lungs buoy her up. She was aware of gentle eddies here and there and wondered if it was the magical fish testing her trueness. She doubted any would offer themselves to her. She could think of many words to describe herself but true wouldn't be on the list.

If, as her mother believed, she was here to learn something, perhaps that was it. How to be true. First, she'd have to understand what it meant.

She took a deep breath, flipped over and dove, rubbing stiff fingers through her hair and scrubbing her face before surfacing. When she did, everything had changed.

Not everything. She was still in the spring, it was still dark, and the straight, straight trunks of the ancient pines still stood guard. But the water had brightened. Pinprick-sized orbs twinkled in a rising cloud of luminescence at the other end of the pool. The water billowed and bent as if being pushed up from below. Lauren paddled back to the side where she had entered, unsure, but trying to trust as she'd been told.

Nothing can harm me here. Nothing can harm me here. Nothing can harm me here.

The radiant cloud, pulling water with it, rose over the opposite bank, sparkling brighter and growing more dense. It began to take on a roughly triangular shape with edges that blended with the background. Lauren's breath and heart quickened.

Details came into focus. Leaves of all sizes and shape and shades from red to gold to brown and a few that were green. Where could they have come from? There was nothing but evergreens as far as she could see. At the apex of the triangle strands of thick hair waved and waved then cascaded into the water flowing into the spring with the sound of a tinkling brook purling over rocks. Small, smooth stones mixed with the leaves—brown, gray, purple—like looking into a vertical stream. Iridescent fish swam in the depths. The leaves were everywhere on what now appeared to be a garment made of surging ocean and starlit sky. An arm took shape beneath a sheer belled sleeve. A shoulder, slightly bent. Slender neck.

A face. A woman. Beyond beautiful. Ethereal. Serene. Young. Old. Skin of alabaster and obsidian and suffused with light from within. Eyes that were blue, green, brown, clear and exuded kindness, compassion, love, mercy. Lauren could neither grasp nor describe that face, but she knew she was in the presence of something—someone—supernal and unknowable.

Despite the warm water, she shivered. All she could think was, *and I'm naked as Eve.*

"Good evening, blessed Horsecaller."

Did the vision speak? Lauren couldn't tell if the voice was inside or outside her head. She nodded. Maybe. Maybe she only thought she nodded.

"Good evening," she croaked. Good evening, what?

Your highness? My Lady? Your Goddessship?

As if reading her thoughts–of course she could read her thoughts—the woman said, "I am The All."

... 13 ...

THE ALL stood yet remained in perpetual motion, and Lauren sat, transfixed. Water continued to flow up and down into the spring, stars flickered, fish jumped, leaves whirled, and The All's hair lifted on a breeze Lauren didn't feel. She wouldn't blink. She didn't want to miss anything. Yet, part of her knew understanding of this—if any was to be had—would not come through sight alone. She tried to formulate a question, but so many whirred about her brain, she couldn't catch hold of one. Finally, she blurted her mantra from the past couple of days.

"I'm not the Horsecaller."

And regretted the moment it left her lips. If The All addressed her as such, surely it must be true? She didn't want to come across as impertinent, but what, or who, exactly, was *The All?*

"Words do not matter," the glowing presence said. As before, the sound of her voice came from everywhere at once. "They have worshiped and cursed what I am with many names over numerous millennia in your counting."

The woman, or goddess, sat on a rock at the water's

edge, the leaves rustling, a hint of murmuring rippling the water. She laughed, a peal that could have been a bell, the wind, a wave, and casually rested her elbows on her knees. Lauren realized it was the items on her back that made The All's shoulders slump.

"The leaves..." Lauren whispered. "Are they heavy?"

"They are prayers." Her smile was brief. "Carried to me on the wind, brought with sweet horse breath. Laden with longing and sadness. Heavy, yes, but not burdensome." She plucked a yellow ash leaf from her sleeve and gently set it on the water. It floated toward Lauren.

When the leaf reached her, she cupped her hand beneath it. And could not lift it. The leaf followed a current back to the All and disappeared into the stream.

"Even I cannot answer these prayers. Not without the horses."

"But aren't you—"

"Passion and Neglect. Promise and Betrayal. Naught and All."

Whatever the heck that meant. Nothing like ending an eventful day in conversation with a cryptic deity. Lauren tried to muffle her uncertainty. Her skin tingled, and she registered—somewhat belatedly—that the water circulating through The All also flowed around her.

"Yes, we are connected, as is everything. People have forgotten the dance. They must remember before it is too late. Soon, the blight will spread beyond Cirq's borders. These orisons rode to me upon the horses' breath, and that is the only way to clear them from my back."

Pindar, nonchalantly chewing a mouthful of grass,

walked up behind The All. He paused to sniff the woman's hair. Lauren stopped breathing, but he didn't choose this moment to blow his nose. The All put her hand up, and he nuzzled her palm, bringing his face close to hers. They inhaled and exhaled together for several minutes. Lauren knew he smelled sweet, and she frequently did the same thing. Did he listen to prayers? Did he send them to a higher power? Or was it only the horses of Cirq that had this ability, this responsibility?

A rapturous smile suffused The All's face with light. She sat a little straighter.

"The prophecy…?" Lauren asked.

"Is merely potential."

Which could mean she wasn't necessarily destined to call the horses. Even if she accepted that she was the prophesied Horsecaller, it didn't guarantee success.

If she did call them, the leaves—the impossible weight —on the All's back would blow away. Thousands of prayers would be answered. She'd never wanted to do something more in her life.

"How can I do this? How can I call the horses?"

"You must choose between love and fear. Between allowing the light or being swallowed by dark. That is all there is."

Great. More mumbo-jumbo. Still, she didn't want to appear disrespectful.

Should she meet The All's gaze? She'd been looking at the leaves and the flowing water, and only sideways at the woman's face. Memories of bible stories with people bursting into flames or turning into salt flashed in her mind, but she could be mixing that up with some horror flick. Her religious education was sketchy at best.

It scarcely mattered.

The most thorough training wouldn't have prepared her for floating naked in a spring talking to an otherworldly being. She felt nothing but a humbling compassion from the woman, though, so she lifted her eyes, hoping to gain some understanding of what it meant to choose between love and fear, of allowing the light. Sudden brightness blinded her, and she lost track of time.

~~~

The moment Leinos returned from escorting Lauren to the spring, he went to Pheeso. The older man sat hunched at the base of an ancient, gnarled tree, looking equally aged and wizened. He studied his hands, which lay open on his lap. The Supreme Guardian crouched and took them in his.

"My friend, will you accept my apology? There is no excuse for speaking to you as I did. You were right to voice your concerns—"

Pheeso snatched his hands away. "This is a fool's errand," he hissed. "You know it. You think you can make the queen see reason. But even if you do, it will be too late."

In the warm glow cast by the fire, his eyes were red-rimmed and stark. Artepa stopped brushing Armody's hair and came over. The girl stared blankly into the flames. Malek kept his eyes on the entrance to the grove, and one of the guards stood watch.

Artepa put her hand on Leinos's shoulder.

125

"We are all tired," she said.

"Indeed." Leinos stood, brushing his hands together. "Some more than others." He looked at Artepa, and her hand slid away. "As I have told you many times, you and Pheeso need not delay retiring. I would miss you both, but if that is your desire, then I release you."

"Pheeso and I will not be disrequired so easily. Even you cannot change the law, Leinos. We are bound as Guardians until you die."

His gaze slid to the flames. "Or you die."

"Or *you* are disrequired." Pheeso jumped to his feet, new energy in his movements. "Have you thought of that? The queen may disrequire you for this. Do not deny you have considered transitioning away from your pledge."

"I made a vow."

"In a time of great sorrow," Artepa said gently.

"How or when I took it neither diminishes my commitment nor alters my obligation." He felt the heat rising in him again, the power of Supreme Guardian that was both honor and bane. Giving it up had never occurred to him, not until holding the Horsecaller. From the moment he had caught her in his arms, he had thought of little else. Pheeso knew him too well. He changed the subject. "The queen will see reason. She will see that it is right to call the horses."

Artepa and Pheeso exchanged a look. "Perhaps," Artepa said.

Pheeso jerked his head to the side and spat.

"That woman would not see reason if you slapped her with it." He stalked off in the direction of the latrine.

Leinos started after him, but Artepa held him back.

"Let him go." She sighed. "He's afraid to hope after all this time." She squeezed his arm, glanced at Armody, and moved them a few steps farther from the fire.

"You have been Supreme Guardian of Cirq for most of your life. But that is not all you are. You are still a man. Surely you desire to join again. She is well formed and strong, the right age, with the heart of a warrior whether she realizes or not."

Leinos almost laughed. "Armody?"

Artepa shushed him. "Of course not. I mean Lauren."

"She wishes to return to her home."

"If you two joined, she would stay. Have you thought of that?"

"If she chooses to stay, it must be her own decision."

"How you look at her. This has crossed your mind, I know. I see the pain in your heart."

"As I see the pain in you when you look at Malek." He set his jaw. "My pain is not your concern. I will speak to Queen Naele about disrequiring you both."

He began to walk away, but she stopped him again, speaking more sharply. "Do not dismiss me. It is my concern. I practically raised you and could not love you more if you were my own." She paused, softened, tamped her own internal blaze. "You are my concern. Our queen will not release you easily, no, but if this is what you desire—what you need—then you must request it."

"What I need is what we all need—for our Lady Horsecaller to call the horses."

"Stubborn man. Search your heart." She laid her palm against his chest. "I know it is in there. Battered, but…" She cocked her head as if listening, then said, "Yes, still beating."

He covered her hand with his. True, his heart still pushed blood through his body. But it had been hardened so long, it scarcely knew how to feel. How welcome it would be to sink into the comfort of another. To forget for a while. And in that forgetting, strike flint against steel and catch the spark of remembrance. But Artepa's familiar touch, tender and caring though it was, would not do it.

"She returns!" Malek called from the entrance to the grove.

Leinos turned his head toward Lauren like a sage drawn to ground. She carried her cloak over her arm and her boots in her hand. He had seen her frightened and angry, troubled, tired. She had smiled and even laughed, but he would never have described her in those moments as happy. Nor would he use that word now. She looked thoughtful, calm, nonplussed.

The horse followed closely, but when they reached the entrance, he wheeled and tore back into the dark of the grove with a high-pitched noise that echoed through the wood. The Horsecaller did not notice or did not mind. She walked straight up to the Supreme Guardian.

"Where is our fur? I need to lie down."

He heard what she said, but the word *our* struck him

mute. He had built a fire a little ways from the others and put a fur there for her, knowing she wished to be alone. Or had wished to be alone. He would not question this now. Her demeanor was distracted. Whatever she experienced at the spring had turned her inward, and she clearly needed to rest. She might not notice at the moment, but she would soon be chilled. Her bare feet were pink with the cold.

"This way," was all he could manage. Her toenails were red. She asked for their fur as if she expected to share it with him. The notion of sleeping without her had unsettled him. He had not realized how much. He could not remember ever feeling this…uncertain.

"There are fish," she said. "Lots. I couldn't carry them."

He signaled and all but one guard took off for the spring and the promise of full bellies. He relieved her of her boots, slung her cloak around her shoulders and led the way. Tucked her in when they reached the site. Stoked the fire. Intended to return to the others.

"Stay," she said, a thready whisper. "If you don't mind."

Mind? He lay beside her. She rooted under his arm and he put it around her and she rested her head on his shoulder. Could it be that she had encountered the goddess?

Her body gave off nearly as much heat as the fire. She placed her hand over his heart as Artepa had earlier. The sensation was completely different. He inhaled deeply just to feel the weight of it rise and fall with his chest. To be sure she was really here, cradled against him. He had not missed the comfort of another. That was part of being Supreme Guardian—relinquishing his needs to care for everyone else.

This had never been a burden, but now his senses spun with the rightness of her muscles and bones relaxed against his, the scent of spring water in her hair, her breath against his neck, the steady rhythm of her heart. With fear of his growing need for her. He could pretend he was providing her comfort and nothing more. It would be a lie.

"Should I tell you what happened?" she asked.

He took another deep breath and tightened his hold on her. "Only if you need to."

"You want to know."

"I know it was more than a cleansing soak in the spring. That much is evident in your manner."

"And my manner is what?"

"Distant. Lit from within. As if you soared beyond the worries of your world and mine in this life and the next."

She nodded. "I think I did."

"Yet you chose to return to us."

"I…I'm not sure I had a choice."

She bent her knee and drew her thigh along his, nearly lifting him off the ground. It was as if his body recognized a missing piece and rejoiced. This, he was certain, was not her intent. He did not think she even noticed him as a person just then. As a man. He tried to push away thoughts of lying like this without layers of fabric separating them, the soft soft skin of her inner thigh against him. To be accurate, when he pledged to become Supreme Guardian of Cirq, he had only relinquished *satisfying* his needs.

He had seen her favor that leg, though, particularly in the morning, suspected stiffness in her hip. Most likely, she was merely easing that achy joint. He would give his attention to it later, while she slept.

"You would choose to return to your world if you could."

She neither confirmed nor denied that for some time. Finally, she said, "I don't know," and gave a startled laugh. "This will sound a little crazy, but I'm not sure where home is or what's real."

"This moment is real, my lady. And this." He covered her delicate hand with his, pressing it to his pounding heart.

"Please just call me Lauren."

They stayed that way for some time, their hands clasped over his heart, their breaths aligning. He felt her relax deeper into him, dozing.

He did neither.

~~~

Rezol's band of yekerk returned from their foray. Raver's keep had yielded nothing. They had penetrated deeper, destroyed a village, and seen nothing unusual. But he did not feed them so they would think. Something was happening in Cirq, he could feel it, and he would not take any chances.

On the southeast face of the mountain, the side that

Candace Carrabus

looked toward Cirq, Rezol prepared them. Sending so many again constituted high risk, but he must smash whatever resistance the Cirqians mounted before it grew. They were a highly independent people, well trained to wage war, even if they chose not to.

"Go slowly. Look for anything odd," he ordered, and set in their minds images of horses.

As these visions took hold, the yekerk flapped their stubby wings, hopped up and down, and squawked. Their collective memory remembered the taste of horse blood.

Rezol watched them with disgust. He disliked using them, but it was necessary. Images of the horses flashed before his eyes. He knew little of them, and yet...

"No horse killing," he commanded.

He had begun to think he could make use of their strength, if he could find a way to bring them to Tinnis. A Horsecaller might turn up eventually. If he already had the horses, the Horsecaller would have to come to him.

"Kill the people around the horses, except—"

How to make them distinguish a Horsecaller if there was one? No, had a Horsecaller surfaced, he would know. The sages and crones would be too excited. One would let a thought escape.

"Kill them all."

Red feathers floated through the air as more than a score of yekerk took to the sky.

... 14 ...

BY LUNCHTIME, Lauren and her escort made their way to the base of the mountains. As they descended, a headache drove deep roots into Lauren's skull. It grew worse the closer they came to their next landmark—the Resting Plains—and an inexplicable grief enveloped her. She rubbed her temples and eyes and let Pindar pick his own way. The fragments of peace and confidence she'd grasped the night before turned to vapor, slipped her hold. Pindar grew restive as well, swishing his tail and grinding his teeth.

The ever-present overcast didn't help. Although they'd left behind the bitter cold of high altitude, spring had not sprung. Gray sky, gray soil. What small amounts of vegetation grew…also gray.

Her mood…blacker by the moment.

The way widened as they traveled through shallow foothills. Malek had been at Pindar's side whenever he could, but had skipped forward to walk with Armody for a time. Artepa stayed at Leinos's side. Lauren found herself with Pheeso for company.

"Why do you do this?" the old man asked.

He kept his gaze forward, so all she could see was the top of his head through thinning gray hair.

"What do you mean?"

"You give false hope to him."

"The Supreme Guardian?"

"All of them."

She really was not in the mood. "But not to you."

"This cannot work."

He carried on as if he'd been thinking about this for a while and didn't care if or how she responded. It hadn't occurred to her that some in their party might not be on the same page.

"You don't know that," she said. After meeting The All, she had to admit that anything was possible, and there was much—so much—she didn't know.

"Queen Naele will not allow it," he said.

"I guess we have to try."

He stopped and finally looked up at her, confusion and fear contorting his broad face. "But why? Why do you go along with it? Why do you want to try?"

The last was a fair question. "I don't see how I have any choice. He wouldn't let me leave the first time, and you blocked my way the second time I tried to get away. So, don't blame me. It's not as if I came here on my own and told you all it was time to find your horses."

She huffed, had not realized that beneath her own fear and confusion, there was also anger. It was her turn to carry on, not caring if or how he responded.

"In case you've forgotten, I was brought here against my will."

"You should fight harder."

"What do you mean?"

"If you don't believe in calling the horses, tell him. Do not go on letting him think you can do it."

"I don't believe I can. I think I've made that clear."

"Yet, you insist on trying."

"I—"

Did she? Had she insisted? No. But she did want to try. Holy hell.

She wanted to call the horses.

She wanted to please Leinos, to see him smile.

She wanted to do something good in her life for a change.

To be the hero.

Pheeso shook his head. "You do not have much longer. Once we meet up with the Horseguard, it will be too late to turn back."

He stalked off. Was he right? Lauren glanced behind, imagining traversing the mountain alone. Should she make a run for it? Would Pindar allow it? The others were ahead. She tested her horse, taking one rein out to the side, guiding him around.

He jerked it out of her hand.

Her group stopped. Leinos watched her with narrowed eyes and slightly set jaw. That look had become too familiar. It was no small measure suspicion but largely curiosity mixed with annoyance at another delay. It imparted a clear understanding of her own thought process. It also conveyed a limit on his patience. She gave Pindar his head and he took them forward.

A little while later, they stopped to cook more fish, and she offered to take Malek for a ride. Pheeso's accusations had unsettled her. A good gallop always cleared her head. Pindar needed to stretch his legs into something faster than walk, too. The boy hadn't asked, but she knew he'd been itching to get on again. She'd give Armody a chance later.

The girl had been quiet and withdrawn, had just lost everyone and everything she'd known. Oh, yeah, so had Lauren. Almost. At least she had Pindar, even if he, too, seemed to have his own agenda. She would talk to the girl later. Perhaps their common plight would provide them both solace.

She dropped her heavy cloak and the awkward stave. After a couple of tries, Malek grabbed her arm and swung up to the horse's broad back behind her. He adjusted the crossbow at his belt to hang to the side. He didn't carry one of the long sticks.

"We won't go far," she told Leinos. Because she knew he was about to give her a warning of some kind.

There was the faintest twitch at one corner of his mouth. "Stay in sight," he said. He laid his hand over Malek's bony knee. "Take care of our Horsecaller."

Malek slapped the back of his hand to his forehead in salute. Leinos saluted back.

"And you," he said to Lauren, handing her the stave. "Keep this with you at all times."

She stifled an annoyed sigh, took it, and squeezed Pindar's sides with her legs, balancing the stick on her saddle's pommel.

They walked for a minute. Dead grass stubble stretched as far as she could see. As if the entire land was dormant, just as Leinos had said. Would the horses really turn this around? She pushed thought away. They needed to move. She turned to Malek.

"We're going to run. You need to hold on. Ready?"

He put his arms around her and nodded. She clucked and Pindar swung into a canter. He gave his head a playful toss and picked up speed.

Low brush along the foot of the mountains whizzed by. Lauren leaned low, gave the horse his head, and gave herself over to it. To cold wind squeezing water from her eyes, to Pindar's mane lashing her chin, to the mundane meter of his bunching muscles, the cadence of pounding hooves. Sacred hooves, according to the prophecy.

Malek lay his cheek against her back and sank into the ride as if born to it.

Her headache fled, her body relaxed, she let go of the conversation with Pheeso.

He was afraid. She understood.

Pindar flattened his stride and stretched his neck and Lauren let an exuberant "woohoo!" escape. Malek giggled. She yelled to him not to fall off. He laughed harder. She joined in and had to slow the horse to a walk to catch her breath.

"You can't laugh and ride at the same time." She tried to sound stern, but her own laughter prevented it. She patted Pindar's neck. He snorted a couple of times to clear out the cobwebs. They both felt better.

"We just did." The boy's laughter gradually subsided to snorts and hiccups.

Lauren blotted her eyes and nose on her sleeve.

"What is it like where you come from?" Malek asked.

Lifting her gaze from Pindar's ears to look at their surroundings, she said, "It's kind of like this in some places. Many, many more people. Lots of horses." And dogs and cats. She missed her cats. And Steven's dog, Jack. And her brother. And…she stopped herself. There was no point in wallowing in it. As Pindar had made clear, they were continuing forward.

She wanted to call the horses.

"No flying bird-men, thank goodness."

They had traveled down an incline and lost sight of the others. She turned Pindar. And stopped. There, in their wake, the tiny white flowers, fully formed, as if they'd been there all along. But they hadn't. She'd wondered but been afraid to backtrack in case it wasn't true. In case it was true. She wasn't sure which she feared more. But there they were. Glowing in the dull light. Impossible.

They walked on, following the trail of bright blossoms back the way they'd come.

After a bit, Malek whispered, "Will I have my own horse someday?"

She patted his leg. "I'm sure you will."

"You are going to call the horses, then?" He sat up straight.

She cursed herself for the glib answer. It was ridiculous to think she would be able to lure back the mysterious horses. Yet, she had resigned herself to staying in Cirq and doing what she could. It was this small hope she gave Malek.

"I'll do my best."

He hugged her tighter.

Her stomach did a flip. How she had longed to feel a child's arms around her, to hold her own. Never would she have guessed how sweet it would be, even though Malek was not hers.

She tried to empty her mind of all except images she could not banish—more dreams the night before of wild horses, running, a great cloud of dust around them—scenes accompanied by a yearning she couldn't fathom. Early on in her life, she'd learned to stifle longing. It had started when her father left them when she was five. Her mother fell apart for a while. For a while, she'd had no one but her little brother. A three-year-old just wasn't much help.

By the time she'd married a man who didn't like horses and didn't want children, she'd mastered the fine art of locking away her own needs and wants. But the burning ache in her dreams refused to be ignored or put away. What to do about it, how to satisfy it, that was another question.

Malek bobbed up and down behind her. "Let's run again!"

Lauren had accomplished her goal—her headache was all but gone and her horse walked easily, head down and back long. "I think that's enough for now."

The boy deflated like a popped balloon.

Pindar came to an abrupt halt, pitching her and Malek forward. A large animal blocked their way, the size of a lion with a short, golden coat. A spiky rough tipped in black edged its thick neck.

"What the—" Lauren shortened the reins to back Pindar up. "What is that?"

Malek had turned to stone behind her. He gave his head a little shake. Not good.

Pindar lowered his head for a closer look and sniffed. The animal flinched but held its ground. It looked dangerous, but its body language spoke otherwise. It crept closer, belly to the ground. She pulled the big gray around and gestured sharply.

"Shoo!" she shouted as if it were a troublesome dog.

But it had eyes only for the horse and stayed put, wagging its short, stubby tail. Pindar took a step, stretched his neck, and the dog-lion licked the stallion's nose then rolled over on its back. Everything about it gave the appearance of submission, but then it hopped to all fours, spun, and growled. An odd smell filled Lauren's nostrils.

The unmistakable howl of a yekerk, a sound etched in memory, turned her blood to ice. Before she had time to think, one dropped in front of them. Pindar started backing. Another passed overhead. The dog-lion snarled, stole behind the flying demon and clamped powerful jaws on its leg.

"Hang on!" She wheeled Pindar then pulled up short.

Three stood behind them. A hiss sounded near her ear. Malek's arrow hit one in the chest.

She dug in her heels, turned Pindar toward camp, and fumbled for her stave. Malek let go another shot. How many were there? Four more soared over a foothill.

Too many.

Pindar swerved around those in front and flattened his ears. He bit a bird-man on the shoulder and flung it to the ground. Lauren dropped the reins and slammed her stave into one with a sickening crack. The dog-lion kept pace, dragging them out of the air and ripping their throats.

"We're going to run for it."

Pindar didn't need to be told twice. Malek held tight as the big horse jumped forward into gallop. The high *keeeyerr* of the yekerk sounded all around them. Flying bird-men swooped in like hunting hawks.

Leinos, Pheeso, Artepa, and Armody sprinted toward them. For a moment, she thought they'd make it, but more of the attackers flew in front of the others, cutting them off.

Leinos thrust his palm forward and a bright flash of light brought a dozen yekerk flopping to the ground.

Wing beats shuddered over her shoulder. Pindar scooted sideways to get out from under the thing and Malek tumbled to the ground. She grabbed a handful of mane and spun the horse. A yekerk lunged for the boy a few strides back. She kicked Pindar, trampling the monster under his sharp hooves.

She circled Malek. "Grab my hand!"

He reached.

She overshot.

"Come *on*." She made another pass, leaned down, caught Malek's collar, and flung him behind her. She'd lost track of the dog-lion, the creature that was helping.

The others engaged the flying creatures. Without losing momentum, she rushed into the fray. Talons raked at them. She let go of the reins again and swung her stave like a baseball bat. It connected and a monster dropped. On the other side, Pindar lashed out with a lightening kick, breaking another in half. Still, more came.

Red feathers drifted through the air. And blood. So much blood. The others fought through, staves swinging. A few bird-men began flying up the mountainside.

Leinos pursued them. "They must not escape!"

Pheeso grabbed Malek's crossbow, and dropped a bird into the brush. Leinos and Artepa continued running.

"Stay with the Horsecaller," someone yelled to Armody.

Lauren clung to Pindar's neck and forced him away from the fight. He struggled with her, then faltered and stumbled. Before she knew what was happening, his legs buckled, and they were all on the ground. He rolled with a groan. Malek jumped clear but Lauren's foot caught. She swore and yanked it out of her boot before fifteen hundred pounds of thrashing horse came to rest on it.

"Pindar? What's wrong?" She shouted past her own ragged breaths. Three bloody gashes across his flank. *No.* She tore off her over-shirt and pressed it against the bleeding.

"Malek!" The boy picked himself up and rushed over. "Keep pressure on this."

She jerked at the girth, threw the saddle to the side, knelt by Pindar's head, and rubbed his face and ears. "He's so cold."

The others were in the foothills. Shouting. Yekerk screeching. More flashes.

Silence.

Malek asked, "Shall I rub his legs?"

What good would it do? It couldn't hurt. She nodded and watched the boy slowly, gently, stroke the horse down the length of one leg. She gestured Armody over. The girl took over rubbing the horse's ears. Lauren removed the makeshift bandage. The cuts oozed a blackish liquid that smelled of yekerk—that gagging scent of burning rubber. They needed water, antiseptic, anything to make this better. She'd even welcome Vraz. But he had left them for a big sage meeting in Elaz, the place they called home.

She breathed deeply and worked to control herself, trying to focus, wiping tears from her face and waiting. And praying. To God. To The All. To anyone listening. Pindar had to be okay. What would happen if he wasn't okay? He *would* be okay.

Love or fear. No fear during the attack. Her body had acted without the aid of her mind and in perfect sync with the horse. That's what it seemed like, anyway. He had been fearless, too. She didn't like to hurt anything and had never killed more than an insect before. Surely she wasn't expected to love the yekerk? No. What she felt for them was something else entirely.

What was taking the others so long? Had it been a minute? Fifteen? She couldn't tell. Pindar coughed. Armody lifted her hands. The horse folded his legs as though he might get up, then shook his head, flopping his mane from side to side.

Thank you, Goddess. Lauren went limp with relief.

"He needs to sit for a moment," Malek said.

So did she.

Artepa returned at a run.

"Are you are all right, Horsecaller?" she asked, struggling to catch her breath.

"Pindar is hurt." She turned to the boy, not sure what she expected from him. "Malek?"

He lifted his eyes, but they were unfocused, the usual sky blue of them turned to cobalt. "He will be all right."

Lauren caught Artepa's eye. Clearly the older woman thought the boy's behavior unusual as well.

"Do you mean Pindar?" Lauren asked. She wanted to believe him, but... "How do you know?"

He blinked, looked fully at her. "I know."

And then he went back to stroking the horse. The wounds had stopped oozing and the smell had gone. There was no swelling. Had Malek done this? He must have, but...were they all healers?

While they waited for Pindar to recover, Pheeso returned and built a fire. He gave Lauren one dark look that spoke volumes. This was her fault.

Soon, Leinos returned, smeared with blood.

"Well?" Pheeso and Artepa both asked.

Leinos didn't answer them. He turned to Lauren. "Are you and Pindar all right?"

"He will be fine," Malek reiterated.

Leinos studied the boy for a long moment, then returned his gaze to Lauren.

She shrugged. "He's right. I don't know how, but Pindar seems to be recovering quickly."

"One yekerk might have escaped," Leinos said, his voice weary.

"Meaning?" Lauren asked.

"Meaning," he explained, "someone seeking evidence of your existence will soon have it."

... 15 ...

LEINOS HAD to get Lauren away from here, and fast. He turned to the others including the boy in the sweep of his gaze. "See to the bodies."

They did his bidding without comment. Lauren knelt at Pindar's side and busied herself undoing the bridle. Her hands trembled. Leinos knew the import of the attack was settling over her. The horse got to his feet.

"You defended yourself well, Pindar." Leinos stroked the gray's neck. "And you, too," he added, putting a hand on her shoulder.

Shaking racked her body. He pulled her to him, eased out of his shirt and wrapped her in it. How long she leaned against his chest and sobbed, he did not know. He could hold her forever. Once calm, he took her face and brushed away her tears.

"What do they want?" she asked.

"They are said to have a taste for horse blood and take orders from anyone who feeds them. Vraz believes a sage named Rezol sent them looking for you. Rezol serves

King Rast and no longer abides by the code set out by the first-degree sage. King Rast would see Cirq vanquished for good."

She nodded. "They want to kill me so I can't call the horses."

He expected to see fear in her eyes, but the knowledge instead seemed to arouse her commitment. He could see some internal decision being made as she nodded.

"You have the right of it," he said. The others had finished their work. "We must move on."

She changed into her spare shirt and returned his, and they were on their way. Lauren saddled Pindar, but led him instead of riding.

They moved quickly, but not quickly enough. The plain left them exposed. He did not want to push her or the horse. If she would mount, they could move faster, but Lauren had turned within, so for now, he would leave her be. Malek had healed the horse. He would need training, but this would have to wait.

They followed an unseen path, one he could traverse in his sleep. Artepa and Pheeso bickered, as was their way. It almost made him smile. He loved them but wished for quiet. Dipping into the deepest reservoir of his power to fight the yekerk had depleted even him, and he looked forward to reaching the inn and a real bed. They should have been able to stop that last yekerk. Perhaps they were getting old. Perhaps he should request to be disrequired.

"The Horseguard should have been here," Artepa insisted for the fourth time from his left. "Why did you have them stop at the inn? With twenty more warriors we could have prevented the last one from escaping."

From his right, also for the fourth time, Pheeso muttered, "That useless bunch of over-soft warriors—"

"They will barely make it to the inn before us as it is," Leinos said. He didn't want Lauren to hear anything bad about the people she would command. He had yet to fully explain the power and importance of her position.

"Ordering the Horseguard to the inn for a meeting will not raise suspicions. Having them continue north to an unknown destination risked too much speculation."

Leinos glanced over his shoulder. Lauren's face held nothing of the radiance from the night before when she returned from the spring. If she heard their conversation, she did not show it. He should have told her more before now. The sooner they arrived at the inn and met with the Horseguard, the better. He dropped back to walk beside her, but did not speak, hoping his silence would draw her out. It took some time, but worked.

"Right before the attack," she said. "There was something—an animal—big and gold colored. I don't know what it was, but I think it was friendly. It killed a few yekerk before you got there."

Artepa stopped. "That sounds like a frit."

"A frit?" Pheeso said. "No such thing."

They fell to arguing about the existence of the legendary creature, and Leinos feared his head would explode. He hoped when they reached the ancient Inn of the Crossroads, that his old friend, innkeeper Belenn, still had masava in stock, the brew he saved for special occasions.

"I saw it," Lauren said. "Malek did, too." She turned to the boy who had been walking behind Pindar with Armody. "Tell them."

"Never seen one, but that is how my mam described them when she told stories."

"It had to be a frit," Artepa said. "Nothing else fits. Bands of them used to protect the horses."

"And where were they when the army of Tinnis attacked ours?" Pheeso demanded. "It is also said frits hunt yekerk. Why did they let the yekerk all but destroy our herds?"

Leinos could no longer take the squabbling. "It is said the frits thought they were no longer needed because people were caring for the horses."

"People did not like frits," Malek said. "They chased them away."

They all stared at the boy.

"It is what my mam always said."

"Pah," Pheeso grumbled. "They never existed."

"They exist," Lauren said. "And they want the horses' forgiveness."

They all stared at her.

She lifted her shoulders, dropped them heavily. "I saw what I saw."

Leinos directed a stern look at Pheeso, and the older man did not further gainsay the Horsecaller. They continued in silence until it grew dark, their slow pace across the open plain and the constant watchfulness for more yekerk making him want to strangle someone. They would not camp in the open. Not after this second—third, counting Steepside—attack. They would push on until they reached the inn.

It seemed the horse shared his uneasiness and impatience because he had been increasingly twitchy the farther they went. Lauren tried to calm the big animal, but her heart wasn't in it. Her eyes were half closed, and she fidgeted as well, as if the touch of her clothing irritated her skin. Finally, she stopped.

"I have to see what's bothering him."

Leinos and the others stood well back as she removed the saddle to check underneath. Pindar could not keep still. She ran her hand over his back and sides. He swung his haunches, nearly stomping the saddle.

"I can't find anything wrong." She removed his halter and let him go.

She was letting him go in the Resting Plains in the dark?

Pindar circled them once, then tore off, whinnying as he went. Malek ran to follow, but stopped a little way along, gaze remaining on the horse until he disappeared.

Lauren watched too, then dropped the halter and lead rope with a gasp and pressed the heels of her hands deep into her eye sockets. "Nooooo." She moaned. "There is great suffering here," she cried. "What is this place?"

Leinos caught her before she fell flat. She drew her knees into her chest with a sob. Fear shot through him, and he looked to Artepa and Pheeso while he held the Horsecaller and summoned his power again.

"It hurts," she rasped. "What's wrong with me?"

... 16 ...

LEINOS CAST his gaze around, alert for threats, and the others took up defensive positions, staves and crossbows ready.

"Lauren! What is it?" He turned her toward him.

"Get away." She swung wildly, landing a loose punch to his jaw.

He grabbed her wrists, gently restrained her arms, and she went limp. *What, in the name of Goddess?*

With a growing sense of unease, he slipped his arms beneath her shoulders and knees, picked her up, and began walking. What could they do except keep moving toward the inn?

"No," she said again, then arched in his arms. She shook her head, opened her eyes, squeezed them shut. He lowered her to the ground.

"Here," she whispered. "It happened here."

Sorrow etched her face, shadows gathered behind her eyes as she searched for answers. She knew, but how she had felt or seen, he could not fathom.

"The horses died here," she said. She let tears flow, then rolled away, shakily getting to hands and knees. "Thousands of yekerk. My God." She tenderly patted the ground that had absorbed the life of the horses, soothing their pain, wiping away the stains of history. Then, she sat back on her heels, wiped her face, and looked at her companions with desolate expectation.

"Yes," Leinos said. "Here is where the horses lived, where many died, and where they are buried." He pointed east, into the dark, where he knew a large mound softened the plain's flat profile.

"I must go there," she said.

Going to the resting place would take time they could ill afford. Each delay cost more horse's lives. But she was the Horsecaller, and she knew this as well as he.

"As you wish," he said. "I believe Pindar may already be there."

She gazed in the direction he had pointed and nodded. "He feels it too."

For long moments, she said nothing.

"It was as if I was here when it happened," she began.

Her chin trembled and her voice quivered. Leinos almost ordered her to stop, almost took her in his arms but sensed she would push him away. But she gathered her strength and resolve.

This, and more.

"I heard their screams. Felt fear and pain, saw them stumbling, mothers trying to help babies—"

She slumped and buried her face in her hands.

"I watched…the blood…I didn't help," she sobbed. "I didn't do anything."

"You could do nothing, *k'varo risa*. This happened long ago."

After a moment, she used her stave to pull herself up, retrieved Pindar's tack, and began walking toward the burial mound. Leinos hesitated, thinking again of the urgency of their mission.

To the others, he said in a low voice, "Go to the inn. If we are not there by morning, bring the Horseguard."

They had to drag Malek away, but they went, and picked up a slow run, a gait they could maintain all night across the edge of the flat plain. He followed Lauren, their packs and a fur slung over his shoulder.

They walked without a break, even when freezing rain stung their skin with needle-sharp pricks. He let her set the pace and the tone, leaving her to her thoughts. Sometimes, the white flowers left behind by the horse led the way, sometimes, their path veered from his.

The air warmed and rain soaked them, then the storm blew away and the moons rose, the first time the skies had cleared in this area for many seasons.

On the horizon, Leinos could make out the soft outline of the burial place, growing larger with each step. And on the ground, white flowers glowed, illuminating a corona of green encircling each stem. The closer they came to the mound, the larger these circles grew, until some even connected.

The land here, here where the horses lived and died… would it be the first to recover?

They all knew stories of the war. But how had Lauren seen it? Lived it? Even he could not relieve her of the terrifying thoughts and images, but he would make sure she understood what happened in this place so long ago had nothing to do with her.

When they reached the final resting place, she dropped her things, walked a short way up the slope and knelt, then lay down and put her heart and one cheek against the ground. He followed.

She closed her eyes. "The horses. So angry. Who could blame them? Murdered or sent away and uncalled for so long. They loved Cirq. And no one spoke their names. Many are at sea."

Leinos stretched his energy into the ground but heard nothing. He extended his energy toward her but was repelled. Did she even realize she had drawn a protective shield around herself?

"Can you feel it?" she asked

"Only more cold and wet seeping through to my skin."

"Are their names listed somewhere? I must speak them so they can rest."

"There are record books in Lerom."

She nodded. "Good."

The horses were not speaking to him, so he stood. He could not tell if she communed with dead or living horses, or both, but the fell bearing of a warrior ready for battle wrapped her like a hauberk.

"We can still reach the inn tonight—"

"I must stay here."

Leinos set to ordering their things, started a fire, and brewed a strong pot of tea. The chilly wind that had driven rain and sleet in their faces had eased, but the rest of the night would be cold if they did not get dry.

"Are you not worried about Pindar?"

She stood, wiping her hands together. "He's near." She whistled. A single answering whinny floated eerily on the damp breeze. She nodded as if this was exactly what she expected.

They ate in silence. He kept a wary eye on her, but she appeared to be absorbed with the visions within and only stared into the flames, her deep, brown eyes luminous. He spread their sleeping furs and noticed part of the seam holding them together had split. Whether they slept on the plain or continued to the inn, he could take a few moments to repair it.

"When Pindar returns and eats some grain, we can continue," she said.

He didn't bother wondering when she thought the horse might return, for it did not matter. They would wait. She started to hum. He could not decide whether she was recovered or only hiding her distress. For a change, her hands were still. She held nothing, did not fidget, had not picked up a piece of wood to tap while she thought.

With the fur across his lap, he began to sew.

From across the fire, she observed him for a time, her gaze slowly becoming more focused. "I'm curious, Supreme Guardian," she said. "You cook, sew, save lives with aplomb, wield crossbow and stave equally well, and have some other hidden power I don't understand. You make a good pot of tea. You'd be quite a catch where I come from. Is there anything you can't do?"

He stabbed himself with the needle. "Ebro's blood!"

"Perhaps I spoke to soon? Who is Ebro?"

An unfamiliar feeling of pleasure laced with annoyance made him cross. He did not get cross. And that vexed him even more.

"Indeed, my lady, there are many things I am incapable of." He sucked his injured finger, then added. "Ebro was the first Horsecaller."

Her brows drew together, and she looked at him very hard for a long moment, then smiled a small and enigmatic smile, and turned to stare into the middle distance. He finished the tight, even stitches with a knot, and asked, "What do you see?"

Without turning back to him, she said, "I met The All at the spring."

He had suspected as much. An uncharitable stab of envy caught him unaware, but he resisted the urge to deny the possibility. His emotions had never been so close to the surface as they had since Lauren's arrival.

"If I were in my own world," she continued, "I would be drinking a glass of wine and reading a book. My cats would be snuggled up with me." She pulled her knees to her chest and hugged them.

"Tell me about your life there."

She sipped tea. Her eyes held a hint of bitter amusement. "It was small," she said.

"Small?"

"Um-hm. I made sure it was. Safe. Small was…right. Big was wrong."

He did not pretend to understand, but nodded.

"My mother always said that my father liked to 'live big,'" she explained. "That's why he left us. She was so sad and lonely. I concluded that big was wrong and vowed to live small."

She shivered. He lifted the fur, she got next to him, and he draped it around them.

"I was five," she said. "I remember him as joyful and exuberant. He was big, in his way, and he loved us—in his way. Leaving wasn't right, but I missed him. Missed his bigness, but swore to stay small so I could never hurt anyone like that."

Another shiver took her, and he put his arm around her. He understood how children could get things wrong and carry those ideas all their lives.

"And now?" he asked.

"I'm not so sure. There were good things about him. All of a sudden, my whole life is big. Really, really big."

"And frightening?"

"Yes, but that doesn't make it wrong."

"Nothing is either all good or all bad."

She leaned against him. He had not spoken the truth, he realized. Some things were all good.

"But I was so convinced," she said. "So sure."

She sighed and relaxed more deeply into the safe—and very big—embrace of the Supreme Guardian.

Lauren wanted to stay exactly where she was. Just the two of them and the fire. No flying bird-men, no sages or crones, no desperate need to find a missing herd before everyone died, and no goddess who might sink under the weight of unanswered prayers. Just the two of them and Pindar, who was drawing near.

He'd become an extension of herself in the last couple of days. Or maybe she was an extension of him. Either way, their connection, which she had always thought strong, had become something much, much more powerful.

This was big, all right. But it felt more right with each passing moment.

She hoped Steven would understand.

"I lived my fear," she said, thinking out loud. It would take a while to tease meaning from all she felt. "Never engaged life." Now, life had taken her by the throat and nearly strangled her. It had her attention.

Pindar strolled into their camp, a blade of grass hanging out one side of his mouth, a white blossom from the other. She laughed and offered him water collected from a puddle, then grain. And tucked herself next to Leinos again to wait.

"He is so magnificent," he said. "And also so…"

"Mysterious?"

"Yes. That is the right word. How do you understand him?"

"I don't pretend to. I try to keep in mind the words of our God in a book called the Bible. In one part, there's this guy named Job, and God decides to tell him a thing or two about how things are. 'Do you give the horse his strength, and endow his neck with splendor?' He asks."

"Sounds like the goddess. What else did He say?"

She took a deep breath and recited with all the gravitas she could muster. "'Do you make the steed to quiver while his thunderous snorting spreads terror?'" Lauren stopped, thinking how Pindar had participated in the fight, not just carried her through it.

Leinos watched the horse peacefully munching grain. "'Thunderous snorting,'" he said. "I like that. Is there more?"

She summoned the rest of the verses. It was the only part of the Good Book she knew. "He goes on to say, 'He jubilantly paws the plain and rushes in his might against the weapons.'" She pictured Pindar rushing across the Resting Plains into the dark unknown. He'd known what he was doing.

"I don't remember all of it," she lied.

She knew it by heart. The visions of the war that had dropped her to her knees came back full force like a gut-punch. Sights, sounds, and smells. She took a calming breath. The All's counsel to choose love or fear echoed. She considered mystery like she never had before.

And looked at Pindar with new eyes, recalling how he'd stomped the bird-men, and reciting to herself the next line God spoke of the horse:

He laughs at fear and cannot be deterred…

... 17 ...

A LONE, welcoming torch beckoned out of the dark and wet of a muddy crossroads, swinging and guttering in the wind. Gentle rain had started again when they reached the edge of the plain, and the bare trees to either side of the dirt road did nothing to slow its descent. Leinos strode unerringly through the night. She couldn't see her feet let alone the way but liked being cocooned in the dark with him, soft drops pattering around them. She trusted him.

The thought startled her.

She hadn't trusted a man in…she didn't trust men, period, the only exceptions being her brother and his sons. She had trusted Darren, and that had been a colossal mistake. Was she making another? Did she have a choice? No. Despite what Pheeso had said, she couldn't turn away. Not now.

They made their way slowly but steadily. Lauren didn't want to risk Pindar slipping in the deep footing. Even though he didn't appear to suffer any ill effects from the attack, there was no point taking chances. Her own body, however, was beginning to complain. She'd wrenched her back whacking at the flying bird-men, and most of her muscles felt pulled, overworked, bruised.

She walked, Leinos beside her, and the continuous movement helped postpone the inevitable stiffness and pain that would set in after she'd slept. She also postponed examining the idea that someone was out to get her.

It didn't matter whether she believed. Someone wanted the Horsecaller dead and that meant someone wanted her dead.

If Leinos felt anxious about their pace, he hid it well. For a change, she was the one who was impatient, frustrated with each step farther from the Bitter Reaches. They were now traveling south, directly away from the troubled herd.

The talk with the horses had galvanized her resolve. Their essence, or spirits, or souls pulled at her, demanding justice, peace, reunion. They called her as surely as she must call them. The need to do this had become as essential as eating and sleeping. More so, for she would do without both to find Cirq's horses. After that, well, someone had to train the people. That someone would be her.

Her old life, all aspects of which she had considered important, if not necessary, four short days ago faded moment by moment, becoming the dream. Despite deprivation, uncertainty, fear, and fatigue, she didn't miss it. Surely there was something wrong with her. For a while, she recited numbers to herself. Phone numbers, accounts, passcodes. Remembering them didn't make the old more real than what was right in front of her.

A certain grim satisfaction came to her, though, imagining Darren, baffled by her disappearance. He'd always accused her of being predictable. Visualizing the look on his face made her smile.

Leinos told her about the Horseguard, who should already be at the inn, how a small contingent had always been retained, secret from their enemies. They spent their days keeping up the royal stables and cleaning tack, making Cirq's saddles and bridles the most well-oiled leather in all the universe.

He never offered anything of himself or his family except to explain that Guardians were chosen or could volunteer. He had picked his words carefully, reluctant or unsure how much to disclose. She grasped at any crumbs that would reveal his inner workings to her, to show what he hoped for besides finding Cirq's horses and returning plenty to the land and its people.

After Guardians completed their training in a distant place maintained by the sages and crones, they received their powers in a ceremony—secret of course—and took certain vows. She'd been about to encourage him to elaborate on that when the solitary light appeared, casting a golden glow into the damp air.

It turned out to be a lantern held by a man peering into the darkness from beneath a dripping cloak. She thought it was Pheeso at first, but this man wore a stained apron dragging in the mud, and the rest of his threadbare clothes hung loosely from a small, bony frame.

Leinos's grasped the man's wrist. "Belenn, old friend."

Belenn dipped his head. "Too long, Supreme Guardian, too long since we shared a cup." His bald pate bobbed up and down in the wobbly light.

"The Horsecaller," Leinos said, inclining his head toward her.

Belenn released Leinos and dropped to his knees in the mud.

"My lady." He looked as if he wanted to say more, but was at a loss, overcome. Instead, he smiled crookedly at her and Pindar, revealing uneven, yellow teeth.

Lauren took him by the elbow and encouraged him to stand. "Nice to meet you," she said.

Belenn returned his attention to Leinos, but the smile remained. "Everything is as you requested. Follow me."

He started off, holding the lantern high for them to see. "The stable is ready," he said over his shoulder. "Long it has been since anyone stayed there. Except, of course, when guests sleep there, for a reduced rate, of course. But we have had no guests since, well, since the last time you were here. And that has been too long." He hopped over a puddle. "Too long."

He led the way around the side of the inn, across a cobbled courtyard, and into a cozy barn.

She untacked Pindar, put him in a large, well-bedded stall next to what looked like an ordinary cow. Such relief to see a familiar creature. The cow lifted her head and she and Pindar sniffed each other.

Lauren inhaled deeply the homey and heady scents of hay, straw, and manure. Leinos and Belenn watched while she pushed the worst of the wet out of the horse's coat with a brush. A bucket of fresh water took his attention. She poked around the dark recesses of the low-ceilinged building to find something for the horse's back while he dried, Belenn skipping to keep up and hold the lantern so she could see.

Another stall had been converted into a chicken coop where a few scrawny birds roosted.

She grabbed a dusty blanket to shake it out and dropped it with a yelp. Two bodies—no. Malek and Armody jumped up, rubbing sleep from their eyes and blinking in the light. Malek saluted and swayed sleepily before the girl propped him up with a steadying hand.

"What are you two doing here?" Lauren asked.

"My little cousin insisted we wait for you," Armody said around a yawn, "And I could not let him stay out here alone."

"A fine welcoming committee," Belenn said.

"Indeed," Leinos breathed on a tired sigh, but she could hear the smile in his voice.

"Thank you," Lauren said. "It's good to see you. And look," she pointed at the big gray hanging his head over the stall door. "Pindar is happy to see you, too."

They both went to the horse. Armody stayed back, but Malek put his hand on Pindar's cheek.

"You missed me, did you not, big one?"

He let himself into the stall and examined the horse's flank, running his fingers over the ridges left by the yekerk. Watching the boy with Pindar, something soft welled up in her chest, one part tenderness, one part contentment, and mostly, if she were honest, exhaustion, but a lovely feeling just the same.

Belenn handed her a different blanket and she billowed it up and over the big horse's back. Malek helped her pat it around him as if they were tucking him in for the night.

"Will you take refreshment, Lady Horsecaller?" Belenn asked.

Lauren shook her head. "I can sleep here. That's all I want right now."

"He will be safe," Leinos said, "I promise. I will put the Horseguard on watch once you are settled. And..." He tilted his head toward the inn. "There is a room upstairs with a bed."

"And a fire," Belenn added.

She could easily sink down right there and curl up in the corner to sleep. But if there was a bed available, who was she to argue? Still, she was nervous about leaving Pindar. Odd—she hadn't worried about him running loose out on the rain-soaked plain in the dark. She put her hand on his neck. He wuffled softly, tossing hay from side to side, finding the best bits.

"We will stay with him," Armody said.

Malek nodded eager agreement.

"And take care of his needs in the morning. I know what to do," the boy added. "You showed me. You should rest."

"That's tempting," Lauren said, "but I'll be fine, really. You kids go inside."

Leinos studied her, his look measured, giving nothing

away, and she realized that if she didn't go, neither would he. He'd never complain or admonish her. He'd stay with her, damn him. Which was exactly what she wanted—his arm around her, his warmth, his comfort—more. She had a sneaking suspicion the bed upstairs would be hers, and hers alone. She would be apart from her horse and her... Guardian.

Oh, but a bed, what luxury. Sheets. A pillow. It would be dry and soft. Even if she could deny herself, she couldn't do it to him. His joints creaked as much as hers in the morning, and she'd caught him kneading and rolling his right shoulder more than once, working out the kinks after rising, when she suspected he thought no one was looking. She was aware of him every moment, tasted him on her tongue like bittersweet chocolate, couldn't shake him if she tried.

She hadn't.

She sighed and gave a tired nod and followed them through a back door and up three flights of stairs to the top of the building where two rooms were tucked beneath the sloping roof. Hers was in the front, the larger of the two, the best in the house, she guessed. There was a fire and bed with a quilt, and suddenly getting into it was all that mattered.

Leinos stared at his bed from a chair by the fire. Belenn had provided a flask of masava. Not his best vintage, but it burned a satisfying trail from lips to stomach and served to take the edge off his ill temper.

He had successfully hidden his mood from Lauren, but Belenn left quickly, all too familiar with the result of provoking the Supreme Guardian when he took to drink, rare as that was. Then again, the innkeeper should be eager to grab what sleep he could. His day would start soon enough.

He could not pinpoint the exact source of his dark thoughts. They had started the day before and been fueled by the yekerk attack and their detour out into the middle of the Resting Plains. After seeing Lauren to her quarters, he had roused the snoring Horse Guard. There had been a great deal of grousing until they saw who disturbed their precious rest. Pheeso was right. They had grown oversoft.

Even that did not fully explain why he was on edge, more wary than usual.

He could blame the Horsecaller. How her generous mouth quivered when she tried not to laugh and trembled when she was afraid. It always gave her away. The silver threads in her hair, and the web of wisdom around her eyes…when she smiled. Or her quiet acceptance of their demands. Her clumsy—and effective—attempt to provide comfort to him simply by staying near. The curve of her hip against his. The way her breathing fell into perfect time with his when she slept. Comfort. There would be none for him in what was left of this night.

He could not allow himself to become used to her. To depend on her. To expect anything.

His hand curled around the glass. He downed the rest of the masava in one gulp, closed his eyes and savored the smoky flavor. He needed to concentrate, but his senses kept circling to her. To the angle of her jaw and how she squared her shoulders with determination when faced with difficulty. The way she lost herself around the horse, became one with him, like two fluids combined. The way he wished to be with her but never could.

That was a problem but not *the* problem.

He extended his awareness, lightly caressing Lauren's still form burrowed beneath the quilt, through the barn and around the horse, Armody, and Malek, and the Horseguard, making sure they remained alert. Then, into the village surrounding the inn, over the rock encrusted hills to the south, and beyond.

Something was coming. And it was not good.

... 18 ...

A HERD of horses surrounded her, just out of reach. They were large, their manes and forelocks long and wavy, their eyes dark, luminous, beseeching. She put her hand out. They stepped back. She tried to get closer, they turned and moved away, then stopped. She hesitated to follow, knowing from experience how this game was played. All horses used the same strategy when they didn't want to be caught. They would let her get close, but never close enough. Still, she couldn't keep from pursuing them. They trotted, she ran. They stopped, she closed the distance, breathing hard. If only she had carrots or corn. But she was empty-handed, without even a halter or lead rope should she get next to one.

She stretched forward again and the wisp of a tail slipped between her fingers. Off they went, this time picking up gallop and disappearing into a cloud of dust. She stumbled to her knees, unequal to the task, unable to stop.

Lauren rolled over, half awake, half still in the dream. The fire had burned down and the dark room had grown stuffy. She rose and fumbled with the front window until she found the catch and it swung out. A gust of fresh air blew her hair back from her face, and she sucked it in,

169

shaking off the last of the dream. Damned horses. Why did they run away?

The twin moons hung high in a clear sky, waning now, now, not quite full. A few stars as well. Oh, sure, it cleared after she was inside.

In the yard below stood a man with his back to her, scanning the area like he was listening keenly, a hunting dog who'd just scented his prey. Straight and still, one hand grasping a staff, the other resting on the stock of his crossbow. Wavy blond hair cascaded past his shoulders, reminding her of the horses in the dream. Snug leather pants, a sleeveless tunic, moonlight bouncing dully off wide metal bands at his wrists.

He turned his head just enough for her to see his right ear and a short, tawny beard. She was sure he could hear her breathing. He continued the circle. She took a quick step back, then dove under the covers, afraid to move, wondering if it would be improper to run to Leinos. She held her breath, listening hard, just like the warrior below. And finally returned to sleep as dawn suffused the room with ivory light.

The horses were coming. She could hear them.

Clack, clack, clack, clack.

Trotting on the pavement, not far from Steven's barn.

She wasn't ready. The stalls weren't clean and no matter how many loads she ran to the manure pile, there was more when she returned. Or the wheelbarrow was empty when she got to the dumping place.

Clack, clack, clack.

Closer now. Usually, she loved the sound, but it was so loud, they were so close, and she was so unprepared. There were too many. Where would she put them?

Now she couldn't find the pitchfork. Call someone. Get help. The phone in the office had no dial tone. She upended her purse on the desk and her cell landed with a clunk, but it was a complicated piece of equipment she'd never seen. She threw it down in frustration.

They were at the gate.

She ran outside.

And woke swimming in tangled sheets. Someone was coming through the door. She snatched the covers up. Evidently, she'd managed to strip to her skin the night before. It was daytime. How late? Sunshine flooded the room. Sun? Full sun? A gift.

Clack, clack.

That annoying sound was not horses. It drifted through the open window.

She watched a woman around her own age drag a large tub in and position it in front of the fireplace. Another followed with buckets of steaming water. Still another stoked the fire. They left and returned with more hot water and other supplies. Then, a tray of tea. And more hot water.

Lots and lots of hot water she'd said when lecturing about the meaning of comfort. And here it was. Her eyes drifted to the window. She'd opened it and stood there. Naked. Oh, God. And there'd been a man. But he hadn't seen her, she was sure of that.

Fairly sure.

She wrapped the quilt around herself and tiptoed over.

Below, Leinos swung his staff and connected hard with the shoulder of another man. The other hadn't gotten his own stick up fast enough to block the blow. His hair was slicked back with sweat, he bled from various small cuts, and he grunted with the effort of parrying a thrust to his midsection.

The insistent rapping had been their sticks clacking together. Leinos was shirtless, and her breath caught at seeing his bare torso. She'd sensed his strength beneath the thick clothes they wore, saw it in the way he moved, and felt it when he held her. But none of that compared to seeing the taut muscles of arms, shoulders, and chest bunching and rippling, the focused power. He looked ferocious. Had the other done something wrong?

"My lady?"

Lauren didn't turn right away. She still didn't always realize they meant her when they said that. And, she was mesmerized by the scene in the yard. Twenty or so others stood around, watching. To one side, Pheeso and Artepa sat on a bench. Artepa glanced up, saw Lauren, smiled, and winked. Lauren gave a little wave.

With a loud whack, the man's staff flew through the air and clattered to the ground. Leinos stepped back and gave a curt nod. Another came forward, looking nervous. Leinos plunged in, spinning and whipping the long stick around. The other man's feet flew out from under him and he landed hard on his back.

"Goodness," Lauren breathed.

The woman cleared her throat. "Been at it since sunup. We have more bruises than salve today."

Lauren turned. "The sun's out," she said, as if that naturally followed the woman's comment.

"And too long has it been." She joined Lauren at the window. "I am Jana, sister to Belenn."

Jana's light-brown hair was tied back, but frizzy tendrils curled against her forehead and at the nape of neck. She stood a couple of inches above Lauren's five-foot-six. Her slight build resembled Belenn's, but she had more meat on her bones. Lauren wondered if he went without so others in his family could eat.

She returned her attention to the window, wanting, just for a while, to focus only on sunshine and a tub full of hot water.

Just for a while.

"I'm Lauren. It's good to meet you. Thank you for bringing the bath."

"Of course, my lady."

Lauren sighed. "Please call me Lauren."

"Yes, my—of course."

With a shake of her head, Lauren changed the subject. "Why are they fighting?"

"No reason. Practice. Because they like it."

A surprised "ooff" flew up from outside, followed by groaning. "Doesn't sound like they're enjoying it."

"The Supreme Guardian ordered it. And if the Supreme Guardian—"

"—orders something, it is done."

They shared a smile. "Right you are, my lady...Lauren. Now, speaking of the Supreme Guardian, he was most insistent about your bath here. Will you have a look and see if you need anything?"

Lauren moved toward the items laid out on a table. Hairbrush, comb, toothbrush, soap, oil, thick towels, a jar of cream. She opened it and sniffed. Faintly cucumber.

"That is for your skin after you are done, if you are troubled by dryness."

Jana walked over and pointed to the slab of soap. "You can wash your hair with that, but you will want to use this after." She indicated a bottle with a stopper.

"Do you leave it in or wash it out?"

"It is oily. I would wash it out."

A veritable spa. "Perfect."

The woman looked satisfied. "And about your tea here," she said, touching the lid of a blue teapot. "Not many like it. But Supreme Guardian suggests you try it."

Lauren smiled wryly. "Suggests or orders?"

Jana laughed, a tinkling sound. "He does not order anything of the Horsecaller, that I know."

"Ah, so everyone has heard, then?"

"That you are the Horsecaller? I think not. Belenn told me but said to keep it quiet for now. Orders of…" she caught herself.

They both laughed and happy tears filled Lauren's eyes. It was good to laugh.

Jana smoothed her damp curls. "You should get in that bath before it cools. Supreme Guardian wants you to join him in his room to break your fast proper like as soon as you can."

"But he's down there beating the crap out of everyone." Lauren hitched her thumb over her shoulder in the general direction of outside.

"He is about done with them. Belenn says he will be in a right better mind when he has. Oh, I was to keep that quiet as well. You will not—"

"Mum's the word."

Jana looked confused, probably not understanding the expression, but she went out without saying more.

And every fiber of Lauren's body sang *hallelujah* as she sank into the hot water, soap in hand.

She soaked, scrubbed, rinsed, repeated. The tub had been placed precisely over a drain in the floor, so she yanked the plug, emptied it halfway, filled it again. Her sore back, stiff muscles, tension, and trepidation flowed out along with the dirty water. The edge of the tub held a stand that supported a bucket. Pull a chain and water flowed down. Shower and tub combined. Very ingenious and helpful for getting the soap out of her hair.

The angle of the sun indicated late morning. She should check on her horse, but knew he was in good hands. Though only a young boy, Malek had proved a quick study, and Pindar liked him

Pindar never minded being in a stall or a strange place. They hauled him to show after show, and he always behaved. An exceptionally well-mannered stallion. Although he always knew if a nearby mare was in heat. His nostrils flared, his head went up, occasionally he let out a soft whicker, but unless you knew him, you'd never suspect he wasn't a gelding.

Yet, she couldn't ignore the new side of him she'd seen the past few days. The side that stomped flying bird-men to death, calmly communed with the divine one day and thousands of dead horses the next. Was it a new side or simply an aspect unneeded in their world? Or had he decided, as her friend Carol always advised, to take the opportunity to reinvent himself?

Lauren drained the tub, sat on the bed, and combed out her hair. The tea Leinos had sent for her to try was a revelation. Dark and bitter with hints of chicory. Not quite freshly roasted and ground coffee, but close. Without milk or sweetener, it was almost too strong. The more she drank, the more she liked it.

Drinking the brew reminded her of long nights studying for exams. She and Carol had met in college. Not long after graduation, Carol took a job across the country. She'd been a good friend and confidant, but when she returned, just a couple of years later, she was different. Not changed exactly, but…more. As if she'd shed her skin, like a snake, and uncovered a brighter version of herself.

Carol had been encouraging Lauren to do the same ever since. They had remained friends, and Lauren had always harbored the wish to go where no one knew her history, where she could explore aspects of herself that never got a chance when surrounded by routine and habit, family and friends who expected her to always be the same.

Her wish had been granted. She'd traveled through a portal, fought monsters, had a conversation with a goddess, known the feelings of Cirq's lost horses.

How could she not be transformed? She smoothed the greasy cucumber-scented cream over every inch of parched, new skin. She smelled good. Today held promise.

There were new clothes folded neatly on a side table. Lighter-weight, loose trousers, an oatmeal-colored overshirt similar to the one she'd been wearing, but with a more open weave. What she supposed was an undershirt had laces—whether they went up the back or front, she couldn't be sure. It would provide support, but if it was made for a woman, she was flat-chested. It didn't look comfortable. She'd stick to her bra, knowing it wouldn't last forever, and chose her own shirt and breeches to meet the Horseguard. These had been cleaned for her after she first arrived, but since then, she'd been living in the serviceable garments they provided.

The top she'd been wearing the day she came through the Ravery was new, a rare splurge at the tack shop to celebrate being single again. It was snow white, long-sleeved, with a small horse embroidered on one shoulder and a zipper at the neck which she left open. Made of some high-tech wicking material, it fit snugly, flattered her figure, and gave her a boost of confidence.

The breeches weren't new, but still held their shape, and their color was cinnamon, which matched the plain brown of the majority of Cirqian clothing she'd seen so far. Like all English riding pants, they weren't much more than heavy tights, leaving little to the imagination, but making riding so much more comfortable than jeans or anything else.

She wished for her own boots, shiny, black calf-huggers that reached her knees and looked so elegant. The shorter brown ones would have to do. They listed together near the door like drunken sailors but were freshly cleaned and brushed. Someone had been busy overnight.

By the time she ventured out, a hard little nugget of joy had lodged beneath her breastbone. Sense of purpose, happiness, and anticipation had condensed right there. Unfamiliar but welcome.

Jana sat on a stool against the wall. She rose, her eyes widened, then blinked several times as if the sun had suddenly blinded her. But there were no windows in the small hallway. Lauren realized she must have been a fright earlier to elicit such a response.

"You look…"

"Better?"

Jana only nodded. "You are to go right in."

Lauren stopped and put her hand out. One of the many little ways she'd kept her old life small and safe was by never extending herself to others. She patted Jana's arm. A small gesture, maybe, but she tried to infuse it with as much warmth and gratitude as possible.

"Thank you again for the bath. It…" She didn't know the language of big living. "…made all the difference," she finished lamely, wishing for more.

Jana put her hand on the door latch, keeping her eyes on Lauren. Lauren hesitated. Did she have soap stuck in her hair or what? She ran her fingers through a few strands, and whispered, "Is something wrong? Do I look funny?"

"No, my lady. You are…different from before."

"Is that good?"

"You startled me." Jana patted her own hair. "You look…fierce. And, and serene. How I picture The All." Her eyes darted away. "I should not have said—"

"It's okay. I've met The All. She is fierce and serene… and so much more."

Lauren pushed the door open, and stopped.

Leinos had his back to the door. His bare back. A scar traced his ribs on the left side, a straight, dark welt. And a red mark, fresh, on the other. Someone had gotten past his reflexes. It would be a nasty bruise in a few hours. He splashed water on his face and shoulders from a basin on the dresser, turned when he heard her sharp intake of breath, and froze, staring.

All Lauren could think was *beautiful, he's so beautiful*. She'd spent nearly every moment of the past few days with him, slept next to him every night, yet felt she was seeing him for the first time. By the look on his face, he felt as stunned as she.

"Is ought amiss, my lady?" Jana murmured from the hallway.

"Yes. No." She didn't glance at Jana but whispered, "I think I'm having a hot flash."

Jana pulled the door softly closed.

Lauren's hand had gone to her chest. Beneath it, she felt the accelerated beat of her heart, and prickly heat rising to the surface. She couldn't take her eyes from the man before her.

Strong muscles tapered from neck to shoulder to corded arms and across the flat planes of his chest to a six-pack that would have been the envy of most twenty-year-olds. Not an ounce of give to him. The thick ridges dipped into the low-slung waistband of his leather pants. Her fingers twitched to glide over every bulge and explore every valley. But it was the way he looked at her that made her chest explode like fireworks sending hot sparks of desire arcing along her skin.

His gaze brushed her from head to foot and back and searched her eyes as if for answers to questions he didn't even know he had. He, too, seemed to see something different, something new. Every part of her came to attention. His eyes darkened.

Before she could regain her senses, she crossed the small space separating them. He could have been a statue. Only his eyes moved, watching. She stood on her toes and kissed him on the mouth.

For a moment, he didn't react. Then, his hands came up and his fingers curled into her shoulders and moved her away, just enough to study her face again. Too many different emotions flicked across his features for her to know what he felt.

He plowed one hand into her hair, tilted her head back, and kissed her. Hard. His other hand hunted her back until he found the edge of her shirt and slipped beneath to scorch her skin, to pull her tight against him.

He might have dropped a match in a hay loft. She swayed beneath the onslaught, beneath the weight of instant, precipitous want, threw her arms around his neck

Raver

for support. His heart pounded hers, his shallow, quick breaths matched hers. He moved them against the wall—not rough, not gentle—and dived deeper, tongue exploring the inside of her mouth.

Was this kissing? No. This was searing possession, an explosion of primal force she'd never known. *Danger, danger,* she heard distantly. She ignored the voice and gave in to the drowning, tangled her tongue with his, molded herself to him, swam deeper than ever before, let him take what he needed, give what she needed.

Sensations came fast. The shock of velvety skin against her belly where her shirt had ridden up. The heat of his mouth. The taste of summer. He hoisted her against the wall, cupped her bottom. She lifted one knee and opened to him, the hard ridge of his arousal a sharp pain against that most tender place at the juncture of her thighs. The rush of desire hit her everywhere at once. She was drunk on need. His and her own. Dizziness made her cling to him, but her body knew what to do—it exulted in nearly climbing him to get closer still.

Never had she known fear and jubilation in equal measure. She'd meant only to thank him. Now, with her blood thudding in her ears, her skin on fire, her heart screaming yes, yes, yes, she knew this wasn't only what she wanted. It was what she was made for.

She broke the kiss, could scarcely breathe. He plunged down her throat, leaving a trail of wet heat, plundered the vee of her shirt, nipped her collar bone on the way. He lifted her other knee and rocked his hips against her. She cried out, an urgent noise she didn't recognize somewhere between a whimper and a groan. Her hands scrambled down his back, over the scar. His pants were too tight, she couldn't get under them. She needed him closer.

Leinos's hands stilled on her hips. He buried his face in her neck, panting. Both of them panting. Slowly, slowly, he lowered her legs. He mumbled what sounded suspiciously like a plea for forgiveness. Blood still rushed too loudly for her to hear.

"We can not," he rasped between breaths. "I cannot be like this."

We can, we are.

"What?" was the only thing she could say.

He gripped her face between his hands. His eyes were wild, hungry. "Try to understand."

"I don't."

He growled and tore himself from her, leaving her trembling, suddenly cold. No, no, no. Her legs couldn't hold her. She slid down the wall and sat on the floor.

Silence stretched as their breathing returned to normal. Her heart slowed, but her lips still tingled, felt swollen. All of her was swollen, expanded, damp. Leinos found a shirt, dropped it over his head, faced away from her.

"I gave this up when I became Supreme Guardian." His voice sounded choked, anguished. He scrubbed his hands through his hair. "Everyone who becomes a guardian must give up the one thing that matters most to them."

Lauren's brain had gone off line the moment their mouths connected, and she was having a hard time getting it to reboot.

"Kissing was the thing that mattered most to you?"

He whirled, anger glinting in his coppery eyes. It was gone quickly, replaced by something far worse—grim resignation. He crouched before her, took her hands. His thumbs moved restlessly over her knuckles while he looked to the side for a moment, obviously having as much difficulty herding his thoughts as she was having with hers.

"Passion," he said. "Love. That is what I gave up."

Lauren's brain flickered. Had he just said he loved her? He stroked her hair away from her forehead, tucked it behind her ear so gently. A new pain in her chest. Shards of glass. Tears threatened. He had to stop. This gentleness was too much.

"It was after my family died," he continued, his voice raw and subdued. "They were all I cared about. What had brought me the most happiness, fulfillment, and eventually, a pain so deep, I never thought to recover."

She got the pain part. Too bad she'd missed out on her portion of happiness and fulfillment.

"Until now, it has not been a difficult vow to keep."

"What about Pheeso and Artepa? They're joined, aren't they? A couple?"

"Yes." He cradled her cheek with his palm. "Yes, but they, too, gave up what mattered most to them both."

She edged her chin away from his hand, cast her gaze over his shoulder. "Which was?"

"Having children." He noted an infinitesimal wince in response to this and stored it away to examine later. "It is different for each prospective guardian. I knew a woman who carved the most exquisite figures from wood. She gave that up."

Leinos was not sure Lauren heard him. He recognized the flat look in her eyes, like shutters slammed against a storm, and hated that he had caused it.

She let him help her up. She felt weightless, empty, looked like she wanted to run, and jerked her arm from his grip as soon as she gained her feet. He started to say more, but her hand came up, a small, eloquent gesture fraught with misery.

"I need to go check on my horse."

He should have told her. He knew his feelings, had seen the same longing in her eyes. This should not have happened. By The All. He was Supreme Guardian.

"Wait," he said, knowing the request to be futile. "Eat."

"I'll find something downstairs."

She spun on her heel and retreated.

The moment the door closed behind her, Leinos turned and attacked the wall.

He thought running drills with the Horseguard had been enough. He had convinced himself escorting her to the Bitter Reaches would be enough. He had always believed serving as Supreme Guardian was enough.

Arrogance. He still had not told her everything. Humility was what a prospective guardian was supposed to gain by giving up what was most important. His wood-carving friend had learned quickly and requested to be disrequired. She had gone back to sculpting because in that way she served better, more completely. He, however, had never overcome his pride. He had merely channeled it into his work.

He flexed his abused fist, forced himself to sit, poured tea, and stared out the window.

To all of Cirq, and beyond, he was known as the self-sacrificing, the un-presuming, even the wise Supreme Guardian, who thought of everyone but himself, who put everyone before himself. And so he had for most of his life. But he had also taken refuge in his position. When he made his vow, he had already lost that which he valued above all else. It was nothing to give it up because he no longer possessed it, could not go back to it.

Leinos sipped the tea. Gone lukewarm. He ate, because he must, but the food had little taste. Slowly, agonizingly, he retraced his steps from solitary, starving orphan to young man with a family and hope for the future. He allowed himself to dwell in the beauty and warmth of those few seasons for a time, but not long enough to grow melancholy. He did not linger over their deaths, but did visit with the grief-stricken rage that had driven him to seek out Vraz, which led to Marzak, sage of Lerom, the queen, the proffer of a new rank—Supreme Guardian—and his acceptance of this elevated role and the power that went with it. The place where he had hidden until now. What a sham his self-conceit had been.

He must thank Lauren.

Later.

For Lauren, Raver and Horsecaller, had just shown him to be a fool.

... 19 ...

THE SUN shifted while Leinos sat, and no longer angled through his single window. How he had missed its warmth and always knowing how early or late it was. He must find Lauren now, find a way past the shutters she had battened around her heart, and introduce her to the Horseguard. He rose to complete his ablutions with cold water.

A short time later, he found her in the barn. He deceived himself yet again if he thought she might one day seek refuge in him. Her horse would always hold that place. He who most assuredly was the source of the sun shining this day. Lauren brushed Pindar's gleaming coat with such force he thought she would rub the hair away altogether.

Jana leaned on the stall door watching. Behind her on a stool, the remains of a meal, empty tea cups. She turned, the sister of his heart, and gave him a narrow, accusing look. So, the Horsecaller had already gained an ally here. Good. She would need all the friends she could muster. And, the more relationships Lauren formed, the harder it would be for her to return to her own world. Selfish, yes. Self-serving, absolutely. His true nature seemed determined to assert itself today. This Raver had stormed his own battened heart and torn away its heavy shields.

So be it.

"The Horseguard is assembled," he said.

Lauren spun to face him, her skin shimmering with sweat, hair tied back but flying loose, eyes red-rimmed. The excited sparkle of anticipation he had seen in her soft, brown eyes just a short time ago had been replaced by cold determination.

He had done this to her. The knowledge hit him in the belly like a stave thrust.

"Very well," she said. She put the brushes down, skimmed her hair back, and wiped her face on her sleeve, leaving a faint smudge on the immaculate garment. She stiffened her spine, squared her shoulders and said, "I'm ready."

She secured the stall door and strode out of the building without a backward glance.

"I am not sure they are ready for you," he muttered.

She stopped and waited for him to catch up. "Is there a problem?"

Leinos took a deep breath, glanced at Jana, but could see no reinforcements would come from that quarter. She spared him only a speaking glance and a you-made-this-mess-you-clean-it-up shrug. He let out a sigh, resigned to whatever came.

"Yes," Lauren said. "Jana kindly filled me in on certain

details you have neglected. Specifically, the one about Horsecaller being second only to your queen in authority. Above even you, Supreme Guardian. What were you afraid of? That it would go to my head? That my ego would get out of control? Because I'm thinking you are an expert on that subject."

She did not wait for him to answer but walked on. He deserved to be flogged by her words. He was relieved to see her calm response to this new information. Although *calm* was perhaps not entirely the right word. In any case, she was right. And magnificent in her outrage.

He must tell her.

Later.

"Indeed," he said to her back, knowing the word vexed her. And was rewarded by a slight hitch in her stride.

Pheeso and Artepa had gathered the Horseguard in the common room of the inn as Leinos requested. There, they enthusiastically ate what the inn staff put in front of them, nursing their bruised bodies and egos over the watery brew that passed for ale anymore. Getting out of Lerom was cause for celebration. The queen kept them tethered tight. Even facing the Supreme Guardian over short staves did little to dampen their spirits.

Leinos and Lauren entered from the kitchen unnoticed by all but Geed, Captain of the Horseguard. The man's head came up and his eyes unerringly fixed on them, or, more precisely, Lauren, and followed their weaving progress through the long tables to his.

Most Cirqians took after Geed—large and light of hair and eye with freckled skin prone to burning—not that it had been a concern for most of their lives—faces more round than long with soft features. Hair tended toward thick and wavy. A handful resembled himself, tall and darker, but not as broad, with more prominent bones.

None looked like Lauren. Compact in build, wiry strong with dark eyes and sleek hair, she had high cheekbones, a long, razor-straight nose, a stubborn chin, and superbly drawn mouth that still looked freshly kissed. Her skin was almost as tanned as his but finer. His fingertips tingled thinking of how soft she had been. And he knew that a delicious blush rose to fan her cheeks when she caught him looking at her with undisguised want. He had witnessed this just a little while ago.

Geed stared at her now the same way, as she swung first one leg, then the other, over the bench across from the captain. By all that was holy, those pants she wore should be outlawed. Leinos took the place at the end of the table, glad they had it to themselves, his back to the wall where he could keep an eye on the captain as well as the rest of the room.

He was deeply gratified to see Lauren did not respond to Geed's blatantly salacious regard. She did not appear to notice him at all, purposely avoiding eye contact, instead looking out over the heads of those at the next table.

Belenn put a mug in front of Leinos.

"For you, my lady?"

Lauren smiled at the innkeeper, thinking he looked harried and tired. Probably the Horseguard kept him hopping. "I can get myself some water, Belenn, thank you." She began to rise.

Belenn put his hand on her shoulder. "Do not think of it. I will be right back."

She wanted to get up, to get out from under the lewd scrutiny of the man across from her.

Leinos nodded acknowledgment to the bearded man. "Captain Geed, you son of a frit, good of you to come on such short notice."

And finally, finally, the blond man took his eyes from her. He'd been about to bore two holes where her nipples were, and that was after he'd nearly burned the breeches off her while she crossed the room. She began to regret her wardrobe choices. If she'd known they would incite testosterone overload everywhere she went...no, she didn't regret what happened with Leinos, even if, well, she would deal with all that later.

This other man, though, Captain Geed, he was the one she'd seen in the inn yard when she woke early that morning, between dreams. Had he seen her at the window? She didn't think so. There was nothing of recognition in his heavy-lidded perusal of her. He looked every bit the fierce warrior of Gaul that nearly drove Rome out of western Europe. All he needed was a kilt and he could walk through the mists of time. Her time, anyway. She wouldn't mind if he went right now. She didn't enjoy him examining her the way he did.

"At your order, Supreme Guardian," the captain said. "Why the urgency?"

"This is Lauren," Leinos said.

Geed turned a puzzled glance to her, this time looking at her face, probably wondering how the introduction answered his question. Belenn put a mug in front of her. She thanked him and drank gratefully.

"You bring me a gift, Supreme Guardian?" Geed said with a sly smile.

Lauren stiffened. Leinos pressed two fingers to her wrist. *Stay calm.*

"Lauren," Leinos said, "This is Geed, Captain of the Horseguard."

"Captain," Lauren gritted out. "Pleased to meet you." She clunked her mug against his, and his puzzlement grew into confusion. "Are you the one who put that bruise on the Supreme Guardian's back?"

Geed's eyes—hazel, she decided—flew wide, and he looked from her to Leinos and back. She knew the question was risky, implying inappropriate intimacy with the Supreme Guardian. Although, she could not profess knowledge of their social mores. She wasn't quite sure what made her do it other than being angry and upset— and genuine possessiveness toward the bloody man, even if only as friends. A stab of guilt hit her. What if there was punishment for breaking his vow? He was like a priest.

The bloody man in question had tipped his chair back and stifled a smile, his eyes dancing. Not upset. She'd read the relationship between the two men correctly. Because while Geed had been stripping her with his eyes, Leinos had been shredding the captain with his. She didn't want a quarrel, but she did want to establish where her loyalties lay right from the start.

"Well?" she prompted Geed.

He took a long drink and wiped his mouth with the

back of his hand. Stalling. A smile was beginning to force its way onto her face as well, Leinos's mirth spreading to her. If Geed didn't come up with an answer soon, the jig would be up.

"Is it my fault he reacted too slowly? He does not forgive if we hold back." He turned to Leinos, his brows drawing together at what he saw in the other man's face. "Who is this woman?"

Leinos lowered his chair and became serious. "This woman, Captain, is the Horsecaller."

If Geed had been confounded before, this news hit him like a thunderbolt. He jumped to his feet, the bench careening into the next row, startling those seated there.

"Horsecaller!" He slapped his hand up in salute.

A ripple went through the crowd.

Horsecaller? The Horsecaller!

Everyone in the room stood with a whoosh, and she was met with a cloud of browns and grays, like a flock of sparrows taking flight. Men and women, some young, mostly older, turned to her and saluted, shock and wonderment on their faces.

She eased herself up, heart jarring her ribs. "Should I say something?" she whispered.

Leinos stood and crossed his arms, taking in the assemblage. "They live to do your bidding, Lady Horsecaller, and long have they waited for the honor."

Why, why, why hadn't she asked more questions when she'd had the chance? Yes, there was the small matter of flying bird-men, and guardians, a dog-lion, sages, crones, and the not-so-small-matter of The All—she'd been distracted. Still, she wanted to get off on the right foot. She squared her shoulders and made eye contact with as many individuals as she could, then saluted, retaining it a long moment, keeping them in her thrall. When she lowered her arm, they all exhaled.

An invigorating heat washed her from head to toe. She sucked in a deep breath and sat, lightheadedness sweeping over her as if she had drunk down a glass of scotch. Something she could do with just then. She sat down too hard, held up her empty mug, and Jana brought her another water.

Leinos sat as well, leaned close, gave her arm a reassuring squeeze, and spoke close to her ear. He suggested she order Geed to send half the guard on patrol to the same positions they had held the night before. She had to start giving orders? Not something she was good at, having people looking to her for leadership. But he was making it as easy as possible; this was an innocuous way to begin.

Captain Geed righted the bench and slowly lowered himself to it as if he feared the thing on fire. Served him right. Lauren cleared her throat.

"Captain, do forgive me for having some fun at your expense." She offered her winningest smile.

"Certainly, Horsecaller. Naturally." He dipped his chin several times. "No harm done, to be sure."

She didn't like directing people but had observed the best—Darren. One thing he was good at was managing people. He said it was simple. Be direct, specific, and clear, and give subordinates their own authority where possible. Too bad he'd never been direct with her.

"Now," she said. "Half the Horseguard must go on patrol to the same positions they held last night. I leave it to you to decide which half and when they should rotate."

"Yes, Lady Horsecaller." He scrambled to his feet, careful of the bench. "Right away, Lady Horsecaller." He saluted.

"I would like a list of the current Horseguard, names, ages, length of service and experience prior to joining. Can you get that to me by the end of this evening's meal?"

He nodded, holding the salute.

"I will meet with you and the rest in the courtyard shortly."

Another crisp nod.

"Dismissed, Captain."

He turned smartly. Lauren let out her breath. As he called out names for sentry duty, she tried to commit them to memory but lost track.

He delegated the list making to a Lieutenant Enaid, saying she had the best handwriting. Thoughtful. He might be oversexed and presumptuous, but he took and executed orders well.

Lauren would study the list tonight and conduct individual interviews tomorrow to get to know them. Things to do that she could control. Daily responsibilities. She hadn't realized how much she missed that.

But the overriding goal—finding the horses—still hung

over her head. She hadn't forgotten what the crone, Sebira, had said. That the horses were dying. Hadn't forgotten what she'd felt at the burial mound.

After the room emptied, she turned to Leinos. He grinned at her, a rare, full-on smile. "Well done."

She wasn't sure if he meant the order giving or the fun with Geed. "I'm sorry. What I said about your bruise was inappropriate."

His smile faded. "I am honored by your concern, my lady. You gave the good captain...pause. And he has most likely already forgotten that."

She hated the formality. Is that how it was to be between them? Perhaps it was for the best, but she didn't want to lose his friendship. She'd been hurt and upset to find out there could be nothing more between them, but she had kissed him because she wanted to and wouldn't change that.

Then, his eyes glinted wickedly. "I think I saw steam coming out of his ears. And thought I would burst a blood vessel trying not to laugh."

Relieved, she made a clumsy grab for his hand and missed. He saved her by taking hers in both of his.

"I'm sorry about before, too," she said in a rush. "I never meant to make you do...do something... improper."

He rested his elbows on his knees and focused on their clasped hands, massaging her palm and between her fingers, sending little waves of pleasure to her belly. She breathed deeply, wishing they were someplace private, knowing they couldn't, shouldn't, needing him to stop, wanting him to continue. What happened between them earlier was just an inkling, she knew, of what could be.

And so much more than she had ever dreamed of at this point in her life. Nor would she allow herself to dream of it now.

"Do you think you could make me do something I do not want?" The words came out low and husky.

The inn was silent. It was late afternoon. The lull between cleaning up from lunch and getting dinner started. Either that or everyone within earshot was holding their breath, straining to listen.

She bent and touched her forehead to his. "I guess not," she said on a sigh.

"It is I who must apologize, *k'varo risa*. I should have told you before."

She couldn't help it. She melted a little when he called her that. "Yes, you should have."

She could feel his smile without having to see his face.

"You did nothing wrong," he assured her. "My behavior was dishonest and dishonorable." He lifted her chin to look her in the eye. "I beg your forgiveness."

"I..." Oh, he looked as desolate as she felt. Since she'd arrived, he'd been committed to her protection, comfort, and assistance. This diffident humility threw her off. She'd never seen him so exposed.

Because she'd lived small for over forty years, keeping in the background, rarely speaking up let alone complaining, no one had ever asked for absolution from her. If her feelings were hurt, she just let it go.

"Of course," she said. "There's really nothing—"

"Shhh." He touched her lips. "Thank you."

She sat back, confused and light-headed again and needing to change the subject. "How long are we staying here?"

"The sooner we leave, the sooner we get to the Bitter Reaches."

She wouldn't mind sleeping in that bed a few more nights, but they really did have to go.

"But we're still going to Lerom first? To the queen?" Lauren didn't like the queen. That wasn't fair since they hadn't met. But the woman was a barrier to the horses.

"We must."

"Why? Why can't we just get the horses and then go to Lerom?"

"It will take more than you and the Horseguard if there are any number of horses left to call. We must recruit more guards and secure supplies to feed them. The only place to do that is Lerom. Without the queen's order, you will have recruits but no supplies will be released."

"The battle is won or lost by the quartermasters."

"Quartermasters?"

"The people responsible for procuring and distributing everything the troops need."

"Exactly so."

Gently, she extricated her hand. "I'm going to introduce Captain Geed and the rest of them to Pindar. Come with me?"

"If it is your command."

"I will not order you."

"It is your right, Horsecaller."

"Well, I won't be exercising that right, Supreme Guardian. It's your choice. But it's getting dark, so I'm going to do it now."

She walked out to where the Horseguard waited in a straight line. Each had a staff, crossbow, and quiver of arrows. She'd gotten used to carrying the staff but doubted the rest would become part of her kit. The stick was clumsy enough when she was mounted. How they would manage when they had horses to ride, she didn't know. And they couldn't eat weapons. That wasn't a particularly original thought, but she understood better now why some made that argument. How did Belenn keep their bellies full?

The sun had been out all day, and she'd barely caught a ray. Maybe it would shine again tomorrow. She corralled her thoughts. *Focus, Lauren.* She faced them, started to chew her lip, caught herself, stopped. They looked as nervous as she.

Chickens clucked and scratched in the awkward silence.

"Permission to speak, Horsecaller?"

Lauren followed the voice, male, to the end of the line. Slim—they were all slim—reddish hair, blue eyes, on the younger side. Perhaps in his early thirties. "Yes? Your name, please?"

"Dosin, Horsecaller."

"Thank you, Dosin. What is it you need?"

"I am wondering where you hail from. We have been

waiting our whole lives for the Horsecaller, and our parents and grandparents before."

"Longer still," a woman said without asking permission.

The captain rebuked her for speaking out of turn.

"Meaning no disrespect," Dosin said. "But where have you been?"

She should have been ready for this. "I—"

"The Horsecaller was detained," Leinos said. He had hung back, leaning in the inn's doorway, but now he stood beside her. "That is all you need to know."

Dosin made a brisk nod. "Yes, Supreme Guardian."

Lauren schooled her features into pleasant nonchalance, a well-practiced, almost reflexive state for her, in her old life. "Yes. I have indeed been detained," she said, making a mental note to find out why Leinos had cut her off. "Now, would you like to meet my horse?"

Astonishment flashed. Hope surged through the group, excited whispers—a horse!

They formed a rough semicircle around the door to the stable. Inside, Pindar stood with a hind leg cocked, dozing. He lifted his head and blinked as she approached.

My horse, she'd said. But he wasn't. In that moment, she realized no one could ever own him. If he chose to allow her to ride him, if he chose to carry her where they needed to go, she would be grateful. But hers? Never.

Malek and Armody sat in a pile of straw. Malek dozed, Armody read a book. A book! What a welcome sight.

"Is all well?" Armody asked.

"Yes. I'm taking Pindar out to meet the Horseguard.

You guys okay? Did you get enough to eat?"

"Oh, yes, my lady. Do not worry over us. We are content to keep him company." She looked at Pindar.

"Good. Thank you." Armody looked better every day. Paling around with Malek and sharing Pindar's care agreed with her. "I appreciate your help. Pindar likes company."

She picked straw from his mane and tail and smoothed the hair along his back.

"Don't be surprised when we go out," she said to him. "There are a bunch of people waiting to meet you." He nudged her side, looking for treats. "I'll try to find carrots for you, later."

She put his bridle on, the heavy metal bit clinking against his teeth. "Sorry. Good boy," she crooned as she buckled the noseband and throatlatch. Pindar nodded. "Yes, you're a good boy. Ready?"

She pushed on the heavy door. There was a collective gasp as the soldiers of the Horseguard looked upon their first horse.

Pindar lifted his head, ears flicking back and forth, awake now, nostrils flared as he assayed the group. She thought all horses beautiful, but knew him to be particularly impressive. His coat was a dappled mix of white, black, and gray, giving him the luster of moonlight on water. He had large, intelligent, wide-set eyes, a mane of white, and a sumptuous tail shot with silver. Looking at him brought a small hitch to her chest. They would face Cirq's challenges together—already had.

The Horseguard inched forward, murmuring—

magnificent…incredible…beautiful. She tried to imagine never seeing a horse when your entire world revolved around them.

"Who wants to touch him?"

They stood transfixed, rooted, silent. She picked out the woman Geed had told to make the list. "How about you? Enaid?"

Enaid stumbled as if being pushed from behind. Pindar stood quietly as Lauren guided the woman's hand to his neck. The rest of the group edged closer. Enaid smiled. She was tall and thin, like Artepa, with the same stick-straight blonde hair. Lauren knew what the horse felt like. Smooth, warm, with hard muscles flexing just under the surface; power encased in satin.

Everyone had to touch him now. She couldn't be happier than to be with a group who loved and respected horses as much as she. One at a time, each received a quick summary of how to approach a horse—not tentatively, but firmly. Pindar leaned his chin on her shoulder, bored.

Geed put hands on hips and looked Pindar in the eye.

"What are you doing, Captain?" she asked.

Geed didn't look away from the horse. "Apologizing to him for my rudeness to you, Horsecaller." He shifted his gaze to her. "I would not want him sneaking up on me."

"I don't think you have to worry."

Geed patted Pindar's cheek, making a dull slapping sound. The horse blinked and jerked his head back.

"The paintings and statues in Lerom do not compare

with seeing one in the flesh."

Pindar sniffed Geed, and she kept tight hold of the reins, just in case the big gray decided to take a taste, too. The captain smiled as the horse snuffled his belly. She was about to warn him not to be too trusting when Pindar swung his head and butted the big man hard in the stomach.

With a grunt, Geed fell backwards and tumbled into a puddle. She put her hand over her mouth to keep control, but no one else felt the need. The rest of the Horseguard burst out laughing.

Astonishment swept Geed's features, then a raucous, howling guffaw erupted from him, ending in a loud snort, which continued as he picked himself up off the ground but remained doubled over with mirth.

She looked at Leinos. He mouthed, "thunderous snorting," quoting from the book of Job. She buried her face in Pindar's mane and laughed until tears streamed down her face, a much-needed release.

"Well," Geed said after he could stand straight again, addressing Pindar. "I guess you showed me who is boss after all. I give you my oath I will never insult the Horsecaller again. I will never let anyone else do it, either. If they do, I will cut out their tongue."

Leinos clapped Geed on the back. "A good oath, Captain. For now, Pindar and the Horsecaller need rest. We leave for Lerom tomorrow."

"I think Belenn still has some ale left," Geed suggested, and the Horseguard followed him back to the inn.

Inside the barn, Leinos addressed Pindar as Geed had.

"You have good instincts. I wish I could be so direct myself." To Lauren, he said, "You will have no trouble with them."

Lauren narrowed her eyes at him, giving him the same look he often gave her. She even felt her back teeth grinding together, just as his must when she did something annoying or suspicious. Did he really think she hadn't noticed how he'd stepped in to answer Dosin's question?

"Why don't you want them to know I'm a Raver?" When he didn't answer right away, she added, "Try being direct."

"I suppose it is time you know."

"I suppose it is past time."

He turned to Armody and Malek. "You two, go wash up and get something to eat."

Armody closed her book and elbowed Malek. He yawned but got up and trudged out. Lauren put Pindar in his stall and removed the bridle. His lower legs were a little filled from standing all day. She would walk him around the courtyard later, after the guard rotated and the other half returned. Leinos waited for the kids to leave.

"There are some in Cirq, including Queen Naele, who believe nothing good comes from the Ravery. Although legend has it the first Horsecaller was a Raver."

She absorbed this, liking the queen even less than she already did.

"If you can't say I'm a Raver, what will you say? That a horse and rider magically appeared out of thin air?"

She came out of the stall, closed the door and leaned against it. "I'm good with that, you know, because from my perspective, that is what happened."

The comment was flippant, but her mind raced with the implications of the first Horsecaller coming through the Ravery, the portal having an opening on their farm, and the long-ago disappearance of her family ancestor, Enzo, with his prized stallion—forebear to Pindar. The parallels were almost too neat. And what had Leinos called the first Horsecaller? Ebro?

"If the first Horsecaller came through the Ravery, that's a good thing, right?" Lauren asked. "There would be no Cirq without the horses."

"True, but Naele would argue they were also the cause of Cirq's ruin."

Just as Pheeso had said. She'd hoped he'd been wrong, speaking from fear rather than any real understanding. "Are you saying the queen doesn't want the horses?"

"She is ambivalent, at best. And not all that has come through the Ravery is good."

"Such as?"

"Such as yekerk."

"Oh." She swallowed a moment of panic thinking of the vicious creatures. "That is bad. They didn't come from my world." She added quickly while filling Pindar's water pail from a pump near the door and giving him a ration of grain. "But I'm glad you told me. Forewarned is forearmed."

Without doubt there was more, such as precisely how he intended to get supplies out of a queen who didn't want the horses found, or if he thought that job belonged to the Horsecaller. She had enough for one night, and her stomach was growling.

"Is there anything else?"

"No," he said.

A flat-out lie told with a straight face. Well. She reminded herself that regardless of what had happened between them that morning, he was the Supreme Guardian of Cirq. As such, he would do whatever it took to save his country.

"Okay, then. Let's eat."

They went in through the kitchen, Lauren realizing he hadn't answered her question. How *would* they explain her origins? Human nature being what it was—and Cirqians were as human as she—if they didn't tell the truth, then it would be decided for them by someone else, and rumors would fly.

She reined in the worry and stopped to see if she could get enough hot water to freshen up. She had decided to change and retire her old clothes. Perhaps looking Cirqian would bend the queen more favorably in her direction.

Belenn sweated over a large pot on the stove, and the two women who had helped Jana bring water upstairs earlier chopped vegetables. Another man cut slices from a large block of yellow cheese. Jana kneaded dough. The smells were mouth-wateringly familiar, and she longed to jump in and help, to do something so ordinary as cook a meal. She wondered where all the food came from if there were shortages, supposing that supply and demand ebbed and flowed everywhere.

Jana looked up and blew a strand of frizzy hair out of her eye. Lauren went over to her just as the woman punched the dough and folded it under.

"I wouldn't mind doing that," Lauren said.

Jana smiled. "It is good for frustration, that is for sure."

"That obvious?"

"Oh, no, my lady. I mean, Lauren. It is a chronic problem around here what with trying to coax healthy plants from the soil and people up and dying. We are luckier than most. This close to the Resting Plains, things have never as bad as other places."

Said so matter-of-factly, a lump formed in Lauren's chest. She cleared her throat, suddenly feeling very tired. Perhaps she would take her meal alone in her room.

Jana turned the dough and pressed it with the heels of her hands. "But it will be better soon, thanks to you and Pindar."

Lauren felt the weight of an entire country's hope. She checked her concerns, trying to take it one step at a time. "I won't keep you from your work. How do I get a half-bucket of hot water? I'll take it up myself."

Jana gestured over her shoulder with her chin. "That barrel by the stove keeps the water hot. There are pails there as well. Jek, get a bucket of water for the Horsecaller."

The man slicing cheese looked up.

"No, really," Lauren said. "I insist on doing it myself. Please."

She went to the barrel, put an empty metal pail beneath

the spigot and turned it on. The containers were large, more like old-fashioned milk cans with lids. She filled it only halfway, but it was still heavier than expected when she picked it up and faced three flights of narrow stairs. Taking a deep breath, she rallied her strength and hoisted. And then, it weighed nothing.

"I need water as well, if you do not mind sharing, my lady."

Leinos took the can from her. She thought he'd gone into the common room, but here he was, shadowing her, aware of her needs before she was. Weird, the way he did that. She could argue, but there was no point. She only nodded and followed him up.

He first poured a small amount into the basin in his room. Being alone with him again forced a flotilla of butterflies from groin to chest. She was weak, and knowing there would be sustained contact with him going forward didn't make it any easier. When they were on the road again, she would insist on her own fur.

In her room, the tub had been removed, the bed made, and only embers burned in the fireplace. Leinos filled her basin and put the can on the hearth.

She stood by the window, as far from him as she could, with the bed between. Not the best of defenses under the circumstances, to be sure. Each move he made stroked her skin as if they were touching.

"Tell me," he said. "Are you joined with another in your world?"

"You might have wondered about that sooner." Sharper than she intended.

"We have established that I made mistakes."

He took a step toward her but stopped when he saw her flinch. She wanted to run.

Right. Into. His. Arms.

She gripped the windowsill and fought for a measure of restraint.

"I was married," she said, still feeling the sting of bitterness whenever she thought of her ex. "Joined. The dissolution of our marriage was finalized the same day Vraz came to get me."

"Dissolution?"

"I divorced him. Because he was unfaithful. We unjoined."

He nodded and came closer. "Unfaithful?"

"He slept with another woman. Had…" She waved her hand, as if that would fill in the blank, not wanting to ignite the very air with the word sex. "…you know. There was at least one. Maybe more."

"So, you take a vow when you join, to be only with each other."

"Is it the same here?"

Again, he only nodded. Again, he came closer. If she pulled back any farther, she'd fall out the window. She heard movement below, voices floating up from outside. The Horseguard rotating patrol so soon?

"Do you have children?"

She shook her head. "We tried in the beginning, but he didn't really want them."

His eyes hardened, glittering with instant condemnation

of this man he didn't know. Much as she had already written off the queen for not wanting the horses.

"I got pregnant, but miscarried at fourteen weeks." She took a shuddering breath. This was why she had worked so hard to closet her feelings. They swamped her. "I was scared to try again for a while. Then, he went and got a vasectomy without even telling me—got fixed so he couldn't make babies anymore—"

"And that is when he became unfaithful."

She squeezed her eyes shut and nodded. His breath was on her forehead, his warm hand reaching for her cheek, and she was in agony. Why was he doing this? God help her, she turned her face into his palm, and he brushed a tear away.

Footsteps pounded up the stairs, someone bellowed, "Leinos!"

Pheeso, she thought. In the next second, he ran through the doorway and stopped.

"The queen," he wheezed. "Queen Naele is here."

··· 20 ···

A YEKERK unrolled itself at King Rast's feet. Rast tucked his boots under the throne and glared at Rezol.

"It will not bite you," Rezol said.

"Do not let it get so close," Rast replied. "Find what it knows, and get rid of it. And step off the dais. I hate the way you tower over me."

Rezol relished Rast's uneasiness for a few moments before moving to the yekerk's level and concentrated on its small brain. He gleaned it had seen a horse and a rider —two riders, though that part was confused—there had been a fight, the riders and others killed the rest of the yekerk. This one thought he had clawed the horse. Yekerk were easily flustered—once sidetracked, they had to start over.

That did not matter. What mattered was there was a Horsecaller in Cirq.

He could put a Horsecaller to good use.

He calculated the meaning swiftly, considered withholding this from the king. "They were attacked, the others were killed." For now, he needed Rast's army to bring the Horsecaller and horses. He would let Rast draw the obvious conclusion. "They saw a horse and rider."

"Ah!" Rast exclaimed.

To keep Rast off balance, he said, "It does not mean there is a Horsecaller."

Rast looked annoyed. "What else could it mean?"

"I see your point, my lord. Indeed, what else could it mean? There must be a Horsecaller." And right on time, he thought, considering the prophecy. Had that goddess-forsaken crone been right?

The king sprang up to stand behind the throne, his favorite place for thinking. "That means they will call the horses soon. We cannot allow them to regain their power. I have waited too long for the collapse of that cursed queendom to allow it to resurge now, just when we are on the brink of victory!"

Rast underlined the point by bringing his closed fist down hard on the back of his throne. He grimaced and cradled the injured hand with his other. Rezol kept his face straight, just.

"I will send troops to kill the Horsecaller."

"An excellent strategy, my lord." Rezol did not mention he had a well-placed spy in Cirq, one he had engaged nearly ten courses before. With luck, a report about the Horsecaller's whereabouts would arrive soon.

Rezol had no intention of allowing Rast's shortsighted idiocy to destroy the Horsecaller. He had other plans for

Cirq's horses. The King could not invade, not yet. Even though Tinnis did not allow Cirq to billet a fighting force, Rezol had no doubt they would guard their Horsecaller with all they had. Every last one of Cirq's citizens was a well-trained warrior. He would suggest his alternate strategy when the king's failed.

"You have not forgotten your arrangement with Cirq's Chancellor?"

"What of it?"

Rezol suppressed a sigh. One thing he missed about the company of other sages was intelligent conversation. "She is your ally now. No doubt it would please her to help you in this matter."

The King scraped one of his long incisors with a gray fingernail and fluffed his thick beard from underneath. Then, he returned to his throne. Clearly he did not know how to make use of his new associate.

"Yes," he answered slowly. "It would please her to please me and also prove her loyalty. I will send word." Rast swung a stubby leg at the yekerk. "Get this thing out of my sight."

Rezol scrambled the yekerk's brain with a concentrated stare. A perplexed expression spread over its ugly features, it collapsed, shook for a moment, then went limp. Rezol frowned. The procedure should have worked faster, but he had few to practice on. He could not do it to people, not yet, so he turned his ever-more powerful mind to the cows already slated for slaughter, which he could drop with a glance. Perhaps the yekerk were more advanced than he thought.

"Did you have to do that?" The King snapped his fingers for the guards to take the yekerk remains away.

"I am sorry it disturbed you, my lord." Rezol bowed. "In future, I will confine my efforts to my tower."

~~~

As Queen Naele stepped over the threshold of The Inn at the Crossroads, she noted it had changed not at all. She could not remember how long it had been since she last visited, but it had been many, many seasons.

She stood inside the doorway for a moment flanked by two of her guardians. The common area was smaller than she recalled. That was always the way. Their favorite room, the one on the third floor she and Pirron had always used, would probably not be as cozy as she pictured in her memory.

Beldon scuttled toward her. No, Beldon was long gone. This was his son…Belenn, who favored his father down to the stained apron with frayed hem.

"Your majesty, you honor us." He bowed.

"Do you mean *surprise* us, Belenn?"

The following moment of silence spoke loudly. He recovered quickly and spit out the expected platitude.

"Too long has it been since you visited our lowly establishment, my queen. Shall I prepare your usual room?"

He glanced at the ceiling as though he could see the roof rafters. Obsequious, but guarded, even nervous. Well, she should expect nothing more, nothing less.

"I have no wish to climb three flights of cramped

stairs." Better to not visit the one place she had known true joy. It could never be again. "You still have the private room off this area?"

"Yes, your majesty."

"Have it made up for me. The common room is not to be used while I am in residence."

"Of course, your majesty." He gestured over his shoulder to what she assumed were people in his employ hiding just out of sight. "And how long can we expect to enjoy your presence, my queen?"

As if they *would* enjoy her presence. "As long as necessary, Belenn. No more, no less."

As the innkeeper backed away, Naele felt the Supreme Guardian approach. She always knew when he was near, the way one knew the sun had risen even with eyes closed. She sensed his light before he entered the room. Which he did now at the base of the stairs.

He was different. She had not seen him in nearly three-hundred days, and then he had been as always: powerful, composed, inaccessible. Something—or someone—had disturbed his self-possession, and it was not the sudden appearance of his queen. Every hair perfect, clothing immaculate, deferential smile in place, yet he looked... disheveled.

"My queen," he said. "How glad I am to see you." He came toward her, hands extended. "You look very well for having walked here from Lerom so quickly."

She took his hands. It was his eyes, she decided. Oh, they were the same color as usual—the sunset reflected by the sea—but there were depths and shades of warmth she had never before seen. "My guardians help keep my steps light."

"Even so, will you sit and take tea?"

He led her to the nearest table, and a woman rushed forward to wipe it while another set down a tray with a pot, cups, and a plate of dried fruit and nuts. The first women then dusted a chair before pulling it out. Naele sank into it gratefully. Her guardians helped, but she was tired. Leinos could see it when no one else did. Oddly enough, he had this ability before having the powers of Supreme Guardian bestowed upon him. Keenly observant, unfailingly kind, endlessly compassionate, unless the situation called for force. Then, he could be stealthy, swift, and deadly as a sage.

If she were younger, if he were older...but no. No one could replace her consort, her one love, Pirron.

"Thank you for sending the Horseguard so quickly." Leinos poured her a cup of tea, then one for himself. "Had I thought you would leave the capitol, I would have requested that as well."

He was right, as usual. She had isolated herself ever since Pirron's death. "It was time."

Leinos's guardians, the old ones he insisted on keeping, clattered down the stairs, he smoothing his hair, she straightening her overshirt as if she had just thrown it on. Well. They never failed to make good use of a bed when one was available. Naele envied them. They took positions at a discreet distance.

"Tell me of this hope you mentioned and for which you needed the Horseguard."

"Did the sun shine during your journey today?"

He never idly sat and chatted. "I beg your pardon, Supreme Guardian. I am not sure I heard you right."

His smile was fleeting and patient. Arrogant man.

"Indulge me a moment, my queen."

"No. The sun did not shine on my journey," she said, sounding more cross than intended. "But as we came farther north, I could see that it was clear in this area. What of it?"

His eyes danced with excitement, and apprehension suddenly gagged her throat.

"We have a Horsecaller."

Four simple words.

Correction.

Three simple words and one outrageous, complicated unnerving word. She stared at him, waiting for more, wishing the sentence back in to his mouth. *Not now. Not now.*

"Did you hear me? A Horsecaller! And a horse. A magnificent horse. You must see him."

Naele was aware her hand had flown to cover her throat. She forced it back to the handle of her teacup, willed it to be still, compelled her pulse to stop fluttering like dry leaves on a windy day, and managed to make her voice steady. Even though she felt as though he had just taken his stave to the back of her head.

"How can this be?"

He pulled back, his enthusiasm drained away. His eyes, so animated a moment before, became flatter than a becalmed lake. He knew she did not welcome this news.

"We had help from Sage Vraz and High Crone Sebira."

"The only help that comes from sages and crones is sorcery. Did they conjure a Horsecaller from thin air?"

A nearly imperceptible startled blink. She did not relish mocking him, but this, this *Horsecaller*, could not be allowed.

"No, although it seems so. They brought her through the Ravery."

His voice carried a rare—no, an unprecedented—note of wonder.

"The Ravery?" *Her?* Naele now understood what had disturbed his self-possession. "Have you gone mad?"

Belenn's people had carried carpets, chairs, tables, and now a bed through to the private sitting room that would be hers for the coming days. She already longed for the ordered austerity of her tower in Lerom.

"It seems impossible after all this time," Leinos said. "But consider the prophecy. *A new Horsecaller will come along dark, unused paths.*"

"Crone gibberish?" Naele rubbed her temples, feeling the beginnings of a headache. "This is what I am to base the future of our country on? A Raver? A female Horsecaller?"

"Let me bring her down to meet you. You will like her."

Naele stared at him, leaned closer and looked deeply into his eyes. "She has enthralled you, this Raver, and you do not even realize. You know nothing of where she comes from or what awful power she might own."

His narrowed and his face hardened. As if she, Queen Naele of Cirq, were the one without her wits.

"I am retiring for the evening." She downed the last of her tea. "As are you. I suggest you use the time to think on this. We will meet again in the morning."

Naele drew cool dignity around herself like a protective cloak, and rose.

"Marzak should be here then as well. I will have him remove whatever glamour this Raver placed on you. Then, when your head is clear once more, we will talk."

She turned and walked to her quarters without a backward glance.

~~~

Upstairs, Lauren had been pacing. After Leinos left, she had tried sitting, but there was nothing to occupy her restless hands, let alone her mind. She desperately wanted to know what Leinos and the queen were talking about, how it was going. She longed to go to Pindar and immerse herself in grooming him. That was how she handled stress. With activity. Leinos had told her to stay put, but she was losing it.

If she used the back stairs and returned quickly, no one would be the wiser. As she grasped the door handle, though, a soft knock sounded from the other side. Finally. News. She pulled the door open, expecting Leinos, or maybe Artepa or Pheeso, though she'd scarcely seen them since arriving. Instead, filling the doorway was a man, a very large man with white hair and beard. If not for the long, shiny cloak that she recognized as similar to the one Vraz wore, she would have thought Santa Claus had come to town.

"A very jolly good evening to you, Lady Horsecaller," he said, his voice a deep rumble. "I am Second-Degree Sage, Marzak. I bring greetings and the kind regard of Vraz and High Crone Sebira."

Lauren gaped at him. His long, bushy eyebrows nearly hid a pair of piercing blue eyes that glowed like little neon lights. He glanced over his shoulder, then whispered, "Do ask me in, if you please. I must speak to you before Queen Naele knows of my presence."

Based on her experience with Vraz, Lauren could think of many reasons not to be alone with a sage, but she stepped back. Help was not far away if needed. He turned sideways to enter, and took a seat by the fire, warming his hands.

"The ground is cold. Will you ring for tea?"

Lauren yanked the bell rope near the door. Jana had told her how to use it earlier. Just like in an old English manor house.

A few moments later, Jana poked her head in, saw the sage, and said, "I suppose he wants tea?"

Jana went out after Lauren nodded. She sat in the chair opposite Marzak. "The ground?"

"Yes. Sages travel through the soil. You did not know?"

She shook her head.

"Vraz did not educate you as he should have. I have already taken him to task for it. And crones use the air. You saw Sebira, I believe?"

Lauren confirmed she had seen the woman materialize out of nothing, like smoke. The light faded from Marzak's eyes. As though an artifact from his method of getting around that dimmed once he was above ground. She was fascinated by his looks and the familiar way he had launched into conversation, as though they were old friends. He probably knew all about her, while she knew nothing of him.

"Now, I have advised Queen Naele for most of her life. At one time, all monarchs made use of our wise and unbiased council. That changed after the horse wars. Ah, we do not have enough time for history. What was Vraz thinking?"

Jana brought in a tray with tea and snacks.

"Beautiful," Marzak said, addressing Jana. "You are the goddess incarnate." He rubbed his hands together while she poured. He took the cup, drank down the hot liquid, then held it out. "Again." She refilled; he drained the cup once more. "Much better. Is Leinos still with the queen?"

"No. He has gone out," Jana said

"Out?" Lauren and Marzak repeated in unison.

"He met with the queen. She has retired. He left. His guardians went with him."

Marzak nodded. "Thank you…?"

"Jana," Lauren and Jana said together.

"Thank you, Jana. Please ask him to join us as soon as he returns."

Jana inclined her head and went out.

"No doubt he needed a walk after meeting with Queen

Naele," Marzak said. "She has that effect."

Nervous tension tightened Lauren's gut. Leinos had gone out? That couldn't be good. Out where? To the nearest pub?

"Now, where were we?"

Marzak was trying to smooth over it, keep her distracted. She would go along, for now.

"The horse wars," she said. "Or, after."

"Yes, yes. We were released from service. And that is putting it too nicely."

"You were kicked out?"

"Precisely. Unwelcome we were," he said with a gusty sigh. "The queen of Cirq gave us refuge, and the crones, too. Not Queen Naele. This was long ago, you understand. Before my time." He paused long enough to note he still had her attention. "No, the new world order did not allow for he old, the mysterious. Much wisdom was lost. The All was forgotten."

"She might have been forgotten, but she's still around."

Marzak poked her knee with one finger. "I know. And envious I am. She has never seen fit to reveal herself to me. Then, that would be counted as a blessing by some. Did you know Sebira had a dream she believes was inspired by The All? It is what led us to you."

"I see." What else was there to say?

"Are you not curious, Horsecaller? There are connections everywhere, if you only look. Too many have been blinded by fear. Surely you are not one of them."

"I don't know about that."

The All had said she must choose love or fear, between allowing the light or losing herself to darkness. Was it love that opened the eyes to see, that shed light? Nothing was that simple. She was so far out of her depth, she didn't know what to think, or even how to think. Her world was code. Cool, consistent computer code that either worked or not. Code didn't have feelings. It wasn't concerned with shades of meaning, philosophical theories, or deciphering abstract concepts like love and fear.

Marzak patted his body, clearly looking for something. "I brought you a gift from Sebira. She was quite adamant about its importance. Ah, here it is."

With a flourish, he presented her a rectangular bundle the size of a small book, wrapped in very fine, faded blue cloth, and tied with braided…hair? She angled it toward the fire and ran her fingers over it. Horse hair? The fabric had a faint sheen to it, like silk. She held it on her lap, not sure this was a gift she wanted.

"What is it?" she asked.

Marzak busied himself inserting a taper into the flames, lighting two torches on either side of the fireplace, and a candle on the table by the window. The room brightened considerably. She'd been so preoccupied worrying about the queen, she hadn't even noticed how dark it was with only the fire. He picked up the table, brought it over, and put it in front of her.

"Should I know what it is?" he asked. "She gave it to me just as you see it and bade me deliver it. Said it belonged to the first Horsecaller. The world has come to a very bad end when sages are reduced to delivering packages for crones."

He smiled when he said it, and there was no rancor in his tone. If anything, he sounded amused, like it was a private joke. Lauren smiled also, but she still didn't open the package. She put it on the table and rubbed her damp palms against her thighs, nerves twisting her gut like a plate of live eels.

Fear had ruled her life.

She was damned tired of it.

Fortifying herself with a gulp of tea, and taking a deep breath, she picked apart the knot. The blue material slithered aside to reveal a narrow black book and a strand of dark, dull beads. But it was the book that riveted her attention. She glared at it, commanding it with her thoughts to be something else.

Anything else.

Marzak seated himself across from her and peered at the contents of the package as well, then into her face expectantly. "Well?"

The book was an old, leather-bound diary. She was sure of this without picking it up, without opening it. She knew this because she had once held one just like it and turned its fragile pages. A slim journal identical to the volume before her sat in Steven's safe at home.

And that one had belonged to her great-great-grandfather, Enzo.

... 21 ...

THREE THINGS happened at once. Someone entered the room, Marzak disappeared, Lauren shoved the journal and beads in her pocket.

She jumped to her feet and turned to the door. Leinos stood there, the planes of his face stark in the dim light. Her stomach grew queasy. Things had not gone well.

Out of the corner of her eye, a swift movement made her swivel back around. There, in the middle of her bed, stood her cat, Jester. It couldn't be. No, this cat was too large to be Jester, but his markings were the same—mostly white with one black and one tawny ear.

He walked to the edge of the mattress, jumped to the table and sat, purring. She rubbed his head. He lifted his back into her hand, and she ran her fingers along his silky coat, lightly grasped his tail and tugged gently, just as he liked. Tears sprang to her eyes.

Marzak's cloak as well as the rest of his clothes puddled on and around the chair where he'd been sitting. Had he turned himself into her cat?

Leinos came closer and pointed at the creature. "What is that?"

Somehow, Lauren maintained composure. "I think it's Marzak, masquerading as my cat, Jester. He's a pet of mine, at home."

Leinos reached for Jester, who'd begun to wash himself, but the cat leapt to the chair, vanished inside Marzak's cloak, and before their eyes, the sage materialized as himself. Lauren thought she'd ceased to be surprised by anything in this place, but she couldn't stifle a startled jerk as the sage popped into view.

They waited while he made sure everything was in place. "My," he said. "That was…interesting." He used his napkin to wipe cat hair off his tongue. "Apologies. Not often does anyone sneak up on me, but if anyone could, it would be you, Leinos."

"How—" Lauren sat down again. "Why my cat?"

Marzak patted her hand. "Cat," he said, filling both their cups with tea. "Intriguing creature. I am afraid you have caught me out, Lady Horsecaller. Ethically speaking, that is. Had it not been for the precipitous arrival of the Supreme Guardian, you would not have known."

"Known what?"

"That he was probing your mind without first asking permission," Leinos explained. "Or at the least, warning you."

"Precisely. Your cat was at the forefront of your thoughts when Leinos startled me. Because I prefer to control who knows my whereabouts, I reshaped into it."

Marzak emptied his cup, looking sheepish at getting caught. "Now, having discharged my duty, I leave you in the Supreme Guardian's capable hands." He rose and gave a small bow. "A jolly good evening to you both."

As he walked past Lauren, he hesitated, then put his hand on her shoulder. "Dwell in your heart. Do not fear who you are." He tightened his grip. "Lady Horsecaller."

Lauren didn't watch him go. If he used the door, he did it silently. Leinos took the chair the sage had vacated.

"You met with the queen."

"Yes."

"And?" She wasn't sure she wanted to hear, couldn't contain her curiosity.

"And…it did not go as I had hoped. I told her about you too quickly. Eagerness overrode caution. I truly believed that the promise of Cirq's horses would more than compensate for any other concerns."

"That I'm a Raver."

"That you are a Raver, a woman, and the Horsecaller."

"I'd have to be the Horsecaller to return the horses. The rest is irrelevant."

"Not to her. She dreads a repeat of the past. When the power of the Horsecaller threatened to overthrow the queen."

Ah. That was what he'd lied about earlier. "I don't want to be queen."

"She is afraid. Fear makes her irrational."

Lauren gestured helplessly. "But Cirq is falling down around her ears anyway, if I understand things correctly."

"You do. And it will be up to you to convince her of what is right when you meet with her tomorrow."

"I have no chance if she won't listen to you."

"She believes me to be...compromised."

"Compromised?"

"By my feelings for you."

Lauren stared at him. She had no response for that. She crossed her arms and felt the edge of the journal where she had tucked it into her pocket. Perhaps it held the answer. But she was afraid to open it. To see irrefutable proof that her great-great-grandfather had ridden through the Ravery just as she had. And established a new country wholly dependent on horses.

The timing was off, though. For Cirq, the first Horsecaller was ancient history. Much, much farther in the past than the hundred-and-thirty-some years ago that Enzo had disappeared. It had been longer than that since they lost the horses.

She corralled her thoughts to the present.

"You told the queen how you feel about me?" Lauren didn't understood his feelings for her, let alone her own.

"No. But she is sharp as ever."

"I see." Lauren fidgeted with her tea cup, smoothed her napkin flat. "Well. I need to go check on Pindar. Has the other half of the Horseguard returned?"

"Yes. And they are eager to meet their first horse."

In the barn, Lauren repeated the earlier session, teaching them how to approach the horse, where to touch him. Being with Pindar and sharing him with others calmed her rattled nerves. He was as restless as she, but patient with the questions and petting and oohs and ahhs.

Leinos ushered them out, and she took the big gray for a stretch of the legs down the long aisle of the dark barn. There were twenty stalls, all empty save for the lone cow quietly chewing her cud just like cows back home, and the chickens who had settled into their roosts for the night.

In the morning, she would meet with the queen. Somehow, she would convince the stubborn woman that calling the horses was in everyone's best interest, and they would be on their way to the Bitter Reaches. They must go soon. Or there would be no horses to call. Cirq would cease to exist.

The adament pull toward the Bitter Reaches she had felt after visiting the Resting Plains returned. What would happen to her if Cirq ceased to exist?

Pindar's hooves made soft thuds on the packed dirt of the passageway, a rhythm as familiar to her as breathing. Glancing into the vacant stalls they passed, wondering about the horses who had stayed there, she could feel their presence, as she had on the Resting Plains. They were restive, anxious.

She and Pindar made the turn at the far end of the building. The only light came from a lantern near the door, filtered through a thin haze of dust, casting Malek's and Armody's shadows toward her. Leinos leaned against the wall, watching, always watching.

She stopped to etch the sight into her memory. Everything up until this moment had been fear, learning, anticipation. Tomorrow, the whole of it would change.

Lauren closed her eyes. She would choose love—as The All had advised—trust that she knew enough, and pursue the horses with conviction.

There was a slight rustling to her left, the sound of a horse moving through straw. Pindar let out a soft wuffle and received an answering snort, a sigh, the stamp of a foot. She looked. Horses. One in each stall, heads out, ears pricked, greeting her, blinking as if just waking up, nostrils flaring to know her with every sense. Dusky and pale, solid and paint, long, wavy manes, forelocks sweeping down over noble profiles.

Lauren's breath caught in her chest. A quick glance to the others told her they did not see them, but Malek had perked up and looked from her to the stalls as if he suspected something. Pindar whinnied and tugged on the lead line, trying to reach the nearest nose.

Then they were gone, leaving her wondering if she'd imagined them. But Pindar had seen them, so she wasn't crazy. Not yet.

Malek stared at her as she walked the big gray back toward his stall. The boy rushed into her arms.

"Did you see them?" he whispered.

"Did you?"

He shook his head. "No, but I could feel them, could tell you saw them."

She hugged the boy. More than anything, she wanted him to have his own horse. He would, and soon.

After taking Pindar up and down the long aisle a few more times, she returned him to his stall and the vigilent, loving gazes of Malek and Armody. How these two had become the big gray's guardians, she didn't know, but she was glad.

Outside, several of the Horseguard kept an eye on things, and she felt safe heading to bed. Sleep? She didn't expect much of that, but she'd need rest before facing the queen.

As usual, Leinos anticipated her needs and sent her to her room while he made a pot of tea that would help her relax. He brought it up a few minutes later, poured a cup and brought it to her where she sat on the bed, propped up by plump pillows. She sipped the tea. It tasted faintly of licorice. He turned to go.

"Can you stay?"

Selfish. But she couldn't ask Jana. She and the rest of the inn's staff were working all night in the kitchen to create meals fit for a queen out of their meager stores. Malek and Armody were with Pindar. Artepa and Pheeso were with each other. She didn't want to be alone. Yet, was it too much to ask of the Supreme Guardian?

He regarded her, his face unreadable, his mind elsewhere. That was just as well.

"I'm sorry. I shouldn't have asked. Only...I miss you." She groaned inwardly. The tea had already relaxed her quite enough.

"Are you requesting the comfort of another, Lady Horsecaller?" He asked this quietly, barely more than a whisper. The hint of a smile played at the corner of his mouth.

"Yes, Supreme Guardian, I am."

"Then, I cannot refuse."

He climbed onto the bed and put his arm around her. No more than a few seconds passed before her head nestled into the contours of his shoulder, and she found blessed, dreamless sleep.

Early morning found her under her blankets—alone— the fire burning brightly, a container of hot water on the hearth. A covered tray on the table smelled of warm bread. Today, they would all eat like royalty. Today, she would face Queen Naele. Today, she would officially become the Horsecaller of Cirq.

She washed and dressed carefully, braided her hair back. In the light from the window, she examined the strand of beads Marzak had brought. It looked to be made from tiny hunks of hoof left over from a trimming, polished and strung together on a metal chain. Sacred hooves.

What was the significance? Marzak had said the package he'd been told to deliver was something of the first Horsecaller's.

She fastened the strand around her neck hoping a bolt out of the blue would infuse her with the secret to calling the horses. She held her breath.

Nothing.

She kept it on anyway.

Leinos arrived shortly, knocking this time, and waiting for her response before entering. She grabbed the journal and tucked it inside her shirt before telling him to enter.

"You look born and bred Cirqian," he said.

"Maybe that will take her mind off the Raver thing."

"Indeed."

She released a nervous laugh. "What should I say?"

"Say as little as possible. She will ask questions."

"I will be demure and unthreatening—" He cut her off with a look. She shrugged. "So it's a bit of a stretch."

"You have from now until we reach the bottom of the stairs to practice."

They exchanged a smile.

"Will you be there?"

He took a breath before answering. "Her mood is hard to read. She may wish this interview to be very public or entirely private. Either way, she will be ready soon."

"And we mustn't keep her waiting."

She followed him down the stairs, forcing air in and out of her lungs, promising herself she wouldn't fidget. But her hand strayed to the necklace. She traced the beads with her fingertips.

The common room had been cleared of all but a small, freshly constructed dais with a large, cushioned chair on it. One table and stool were nearby. Of course, the monarch would be elevated above the riffraff. Why should it be any different here?

As soon as they entered, Artepa and Pheeso stepped from the shadowed corners. In the courtyard, most of the Horseguard stood in small groups, trying to look casual, but there was too much foot tapping, uniform adjusting, and shifting of weapons from one hand to the other. She was reminded that the fate of many hung in the balance.

Minutes ticked by. There was no clock, but Lauren felt

a second hand tap, tap, tapping inside her head.

Soon, a door opened and people filed in. Guards—guardians—first, then a tall woman who had to be the queen, more guardians, Marzak, and a small man with a stiff-legged limp. Queen Naele sat and her cadre took up position in a line behind her. The sage stayed near the wall. He winked at Lauren, and she tried to smile but was afraid what she produced was more of a grimace. The man with the limp lowered himself slowly to the stool, stretching his leg to the side. He put a sheaf of paper, ink bottle, and pen on the table in front of him.

Unlike the muted, natural hues on everyone else, iceberg blue draped the queen from throat to toe. Lauren judged her to be in her late seventies. She wore her white hair slicked back on the sides and teased very high on top. A regular beehive. Her cheekbones were sharp as frozen mountain peaks, her eyes could have been cut from ice, and her mouth etched a bleak and bitter line beneath an aquiline nose.

Lauren's barely maintained confidence evaporated.

"Will the pretender step forward?"

Naele's voice sliced like wind off a glacier, numbing Lauren's brain. She knew what the woman meant, but would not respond to *pretender*, knowing a loaded question when she heard one. Even if she felt like a phony on the inside, she wouldn't give the queen the satisfaction.

"I see," Queen Naele said. "Who claims to be Horsecaller?"

How Lauren responded to this meant everything. She reminded herself that the queen might appear intimidating, but she was still just a woman, an ordinary person, like herself. She summoned her self-possession and stepped forward.

"I am the Horsecaller." Said quietly but with assurance.

Naele turned her diamond-sharp gaze on Lauren and stared without blinking for some moments. She rose, slowly, slowly stepped off the dais, and approached, circled like a gyrafalcon, measuring, calculating, *examining*, before returning to her makeshift throne. If a bucket of freezing water had been dumped over her head, Lauren couldn't feel more cold.

"Belenn?" the queen called.

The innkeeper trotted out of the kitchen. "Yes, my lady?"

"You have a secure room in the cellar, do you not?"

Belenn glanced uneasily at Lauren. "Yes."

Naele gestured over her shoulder to the guards.

"Take this…*Raver* there to await execution."

... 22 ...

AN INSTANT of staggered silence.

Then, an anguished *No* from nearby.

Several voices at once. Leinos, Artepa and Pheeso, perhaps Marzak. Maybe even Jana. Sound came as if through thick ear muffs. Images fractured in a kaleidoscope, frosty blue at center, periphery, and back to the middle of Lauren's field of vision.

Someone seized her arm, but she wouldn't let the strange guards drag her off. She pulled away, he kept hold —Leinos—tugging her into the shelter of his side.

"No," he said.

One by one, her senses registered. She could feel his heart beating, hard and quick. Hear the silence of a roomful of people holding their breath. Smell the aroma of simmering stew wafting from the kitchen. The blue queen stood frozen in sharp relief against the drab gray and brown background. Her guards had begun to come forward, but stood frozen mid-step.

The Supreme Guardian had spoken in that voice that rumbled from the earth and boomed from the sky.

But he'd said it himself. He was compromised by his feelings for her. She would like nothing more than to stay forever in the safety of his embrace. That is, the old Lauren would have liked nothing better. But she had changed since traversing a universe to come to this place. Not Cirq, but a place within herself wide open and full of love and intention and mystery. Why she had journeyed so far to find everything she wanted in a man only to have him denied, she couldn't guess. Why she had journeyed so far to find purpose only to have this woman try to yank it away, didn't matter. She knew only that she would not go down without a fight. And the fight was hers alone.

Gently, she withdrew from the sanctuary of Leinos's arm. When he reached for her, she put her fingertips against his, tender as a lover's kiss. The loss in his eyes nearly crushed her, but she forced a reassuring smile, drew a heartening breath, and faced Queen Naele.

Demure and unthreatening be damned.

"You are making a grave mistake," she said.

"Do you speak to me, Raver?" The queen infused her voice with the haughty tone of one grievously insulted, but she hadn't completely hidden the growing alarm in her eyes.

"I do. And you had better listen. Your country is nearly dead, in case you haven't noticed. Your people die of starvation or for no particular reason, your fields have withered, even the birds and fish have fled. All because you do not have horses. I don't pretend to understand this, but I believe you do. The horses are your only chance—"

"How dare you?" Queen Naele's hands tightened into fists at her sides and Lauren thought she might stamp her foot. If the situation wasn't so serious, she'd laugh.

"How dare *you*?" Lauren countered, taking a step closer. "How dare you deny your people their only chance at salvation? I might not succeed, but right now, I'm all you've got."

"The queen does not tolerate insolence. Guards!" Naele snapped her fingers. "Take her away."

"My queen," Leinos said, "please consider her words."

What little color remaining in Naele's face drained away. "By The All, such defiance must be punished."

Lauren slapped her hands up to the guards approaching from either side. They hesitated. "Don't even think about invoking The All to me, Queen of Cirq. I have met The All. Spoken with her. She has heard the prayers of your people. I am her answer."

Another shocked silence fell over the room.

Naele launched off her dais and came nose-to-nose with Lauren. "I will throttle you with my bare hands if need be," she hissed. "I do not know what sorcery you used to enthrall these others, but it is wasted on me."

Lauren leaned into the woman. "No magic, only something sorely lacking here. Good sense."

Queen Naele pulled away and slapped her, knocking Lauren back a couple of feet. "Get her out of my sight."

She stalked back to her chair, then whipped around and directed her words to the rest of the room. "Those who interfere will share the Raver's fate."

The guards surrounded Lauren. Still reeling from the slap, she didn't react. People started shouting. What would happen to Leinos and Malek? What would happen to Pindar? Strong hands yanked her arms. She thrashed against their hold. Their grips tightened. They began to drag her away. A strangled *no* burst from deep inside.

She should go quietly, for the sake of her friends, but she couldn't help fighting. More guards appeared to hold Leinos, Artepa, and Pheeso.

In the distance, she heard banging, realized this racket had been in the background for the past couple of minutes.

A shrill noise pierced the air—one not heard in Cirq for a long time—the enraged bellow of a battle-ready stallion, followed by the swift and loud clopping of steel shoes on cobblestones. A gray streak flashed past the front windows. The inn door crashed open, blew off its hinges, and showered the room with splinters.

The queen's guardians released Lauren and blanched.

Pindar filled the doorway, eyes white-rimmed, nostrils flared, coat sweat-darkened. Cuts dripped blood down his chest and legs. He loosed another ear-splitting stallion roar, searched the room until he found Lauren. He rushed forward, ears flat against his head, lashing out at a man who didn't move out of his way, biting his shoulder and flinging him to the side. The rest pointed their staves at the horse, but didn't try to come closer.

The big gray looked fully six inches taller than usual, and the primal glint in his eyes bespoke eons of survival against more intimating odds than a few peasants armed with sticks.

She put her arms around his neck, felt the powerful bellows of his lungs working, knew a twinge of fear to see him like this. "Whoa, now. Good boy," she murmured.

Pindar snorted. Everyone jumped. They stared. On their faces, in their eyes, disbelief warred with long-forgotten hope. All at once, it dawned on her the hold horses had on these people, the power she possessed by her knowledge. She'd always known she and Pindar had a connection, but could it be the same mysterious link between Horsecaller and horses?

She wanted to swing to his back and take off. Get away. Her gaze found Leinos. And Malek and Armody, who had come in behind the horse. Love had grown unbidden in her heart. Now, it pierced her soul. Running was not the answer. And where would she go? No, she had to play this out, protect them. Surely Leinos would find a way around his obdurate queen.

She ran shaky fingers through her precious steed's mane, repressed stinging tears, turned to the queen. "What will happen to him when I'm gone?"

If Queen Naele had been colorless before, her skin had gone chalky when the horse burst in. She lowered herself to her seat and took a moment to regain her composure, peering at nothing for some time. "You will release him," she said quietly. "On the Resting Plains. Now."

Leinos moved close to Queen Naele, knelt before her.

"Already, the land awakens with only one horse in our midst. See how magnificent he is! So shall Cirq be again."

"Flowers and grass spring up from his sacred hooves," Pheeso said.

"A frit helped fight off the yekerk," Artepa added as if remembering a dream. "The frits still live."

Naele sprang to her feet. "Enough. I have proclaimed my will." She faced Leinos. "If you interfere, you will be disrequired. *Permanently*." She turned abruptly and walked out the front of the inn, head high, spine stiff.

The scribe scrambled to collect his notes, knocking over the ink bottle. He left it to try and catch his monarch. From outside, Lauren heard her tell him, "Leave me." He staggered back in, papers clutched to his chest, looking lost and confused.

Everyone turned to Lauren. She tried to keep the soul-stealing fear she felt off her face. With one hand on Pindar's withers, they walked out together.

The Horseguard made way, then fell into step behind. Queen Naele strode up the road at a brisk pace. Her guardians jogged past the Horseguard to catch her.

Leinos came alongside Lauren, Pheeso and Artepa positioned themselves in front, and Malek and Armody got on the other side of the horse, each keeping one hand on the big gray's side.

"I will talk to the queen again," Leinos said. "She will see reason."

"That hasn't exactly worked so far." Lauren kept her eyes straight ahead."She wouldn't know reason if it smacked her in the face." If she looked at Leinos, she might lose her resolve. "I'm going to let Pindar go because no matter what else happens, it's important to me that he is safe. Maybe he'll find the other horses."

She stroked his shoulder, willing herself to keep putting one foot in front of the other. She would see him again. Ride him again. Somehow. "I don't want any of you to do anything to endanger yourselves." She directed this especially over Pindar's back to Malek and Armody.

She realized how ridiculous that sounded the moment the words left her mouth. If *danger* could be a middle name, they all shared it.

Leinos took her hand, his touch the comfort of a tranquil lake, a peaceful sunset, an ocean breeze. Silence kept them company the rest of the way. By the time they reached the edge of the plains, their procession had become a parade.

Everyone had piled out of the inn, and it looked like the entire village had joined in as well. No one spoke, but everyone could see the patches of soft, green grass stretching away into the distance.

Pindar's attention went to the mound barely visible against the horizon. *You will be all right*, Lauren repeated to herself. If she let any other thoughts intrude, she would falter, and she would not, could not. Not in front of the queen, not in front of the Horseguard, not in front of Malek.

Pindar stood next to her when they stopped at the edge of the plain. Seventeen hands and fifteen-hundred pounds of spectacular horse flesh that was so much more than muscle, sinew, bone. He didn't nudge her side for treats, stamp his foot, swish his tail, or nod his big head.

Leinos gave her hand a final reassuring squeeze and stepped back. She urged Pindar forward with a pat on the hip. "Go on," she said, and clucked for good measure.

He took a step, and another, then turned his huge brown eyes on her.

Lauren squeezed her eyes tightly closed. *Please, just go.*

He did not. Again, he emitted that huge stallion whinny that came from deep in his chest and shook his entire body. He turned so that he circled her, began to trot, and slowly spiraled away. Others had to move or be run over. Queen Naele fell backwards in her hast to avoid being trampled. Within his circuit, every blade of grass turned green before their eyes, and here and there, the tiny white flowers popped up.

The audience had been quiet, but they began to murmur now and point.

Pindar picked up canter, tossing his head and whipping his tail from side to side. His sacred hooves churned the soil. A couple of people exclaimed and clapped their hands as clods of dirt flew through the air.

And all the while, Queen Naele's face grew thunderously, dangerously furious.

Lauren could not suppress a smile as she watched her horse. Not her *horse*...her—*what?* By The All, she couldn't think what to call him any more. Whatever their relationship had been, it had inexorably changed.

Just when she thought the queen might burst a blood vessel, Pindar wheeled and halted in front of Lauren. He lowered his velvety muzzle to her face and they breathed together. She put her hands on his cheeks and pressed her forehead to his. In a flash, she saw him sprinting across an endless grassland, feet not touching the ground. A huge herd joined him. The horses of Cirq, moving together in boundless joy.

She kissed him between the eyes, not trying to understand what passed between them. And not allowing herself to believe this would be the last time she saw him. He spun away. Within a few strides he flattened into a ground-eating gallop, and soon, all they could see was the rising cloud of dust in his wake.

~~~

A short while later, Lauren was shoved into a dark, dank room. The heavy door slammed shut, the outside bolt thrown. She tumbled down a few steps and landed in a heap at the bottom, where she stayed. There was no point in getting up. The dirt floor was cool against her cheek, a musty tang sharp in her nose.

Finally, in the blackness, she allowed her tears to fall.

... 23 ...

THIS, LAUREN thought, was what waiting to be executed felt like. Wild imaginings, sickening dread, bone-shaking terror.

She cried until her very being leaked out, and her body wilted against the floor. But eventually, because she never could stay still for long, she picked herself up and explored the storeroom.

She groped forward from the base of the steps until she reached a stone wall, and followed the seam of grainy dirt and smooth slab from corner to corner. In the third, an obstruction. Lightly, she ran her hands over its contours. An empty wooden cask. She found the spout and sniffed. Wine, or brandy. Which she would love a glass of right now. Or two, Or ten. Insensible would be good.

At the steps again, she gradually stood, keeping one hand over her head until it touched the low ceiling. She followed a timber back to the wall and investigated from ceiling to floor, searching for openings. None. Nor on the other three, except for the door. And quiet. This room was below the cellar, and clearly unused for some time.

Once familiar with the basic dimensions and obstacles, she stepped off the distance to the corner opposite the door, put her back to the wall and slid down to sit.

Eerie calm after weathering the most crushing storm of emotion she'd ever known. She'd lost a baby and withstood a nasty divorce, both times thinking it couldn't be worse. All that propped her up now was simmering anger.

She hadn't seen this coming.

Not. At. All.

To keep her too-vivid imagination at bay, she tapped out songs with her fingertips and played an endless loop of the little-traveled road near her brother's house in her mind. Driving at night in early summer. When swarms of bugs pattered the windshield like rain.

They could have given her a chamber pot. And a candle.

A few hours in, the silent darkness took on a life of its own, humming with texture and color. But not light. Perhaps they intended to let her wither and die here in the dark. Just as Cirq had withered and would soon die without her horses.

Exhaustion. She put her head back and slept.

Insects pelted the windows of her dreams.

~~~

Sound jolted her awake, it took a moment for her to remember, and in that moment, her heart rate shot up and she started to shake. They were coming for her. The door opened and Jana entered with a lantern that circled the blackness like the beam from a lighthouse. Welcome as it was, Lauren put her hand up to block it until her eyes adjusted, and her pulse settled.

The dismal room looked just as she had imagined except that the cask and steps both were decoratively carved, a remnant of better times, merrier times. Jana came down the steps with a large basket hooked over one elbow, and a can of hot water over the other. Clutched to her side—bless her—a pot to pee in. She knelt in front of Lauren and offered a wobbly smile.

"You are to tidy up as best you can. The queen's scribe will be here shortly."

"Why?"

Jana paused in setting down the lamp and other things. She glanced over her shoulder. A guard kept close eye on them. "Do you not wish to tidy up?"

"I don't see the point." Lauren lifted her shoulders and rolled her head around, trying to release the tension. Her body ached. "But I meant why is the scribe coming?"

Keeping her back to the door, Jana slid a short knife from her sleeve and stabbed it inside a small loaf of dark bread.

"They did not tell me. Here, eat. I will brush your hair."

"I'm not really hungry," Lauren said, keeping her expression downcast. "I'll save this for later."

She wrapped the bread in a napkin. While Jana fussed with her hair—and blocked the guard's view—Lauren worked the knife free and into her pocket. She used the hot water to clean her face and hands, and dutifully drank a cup of tea.

Jana pretended to wipe dirt off the shoulder of Lauren's shirt, leaned close, and whispered, "Supreme Guardian Leinos is with the queen. No one has seen either of them all the day."

"Is it night?"

"Nearly. Now, eat."

"That is enough," the guard said from the doorway.

"Coming." She pressed the bread and a tiny wedge of cheese into Lauren's hand. "You need your strength." She began to go, then added, "We all do."

Lauren grabbed her hand and squeezed. "Thank you."

Jana nodded, left the lantern and pot and hurried out.

Again, the door shut and the bolt was thrown. Lauren would find that amusing if the situation weren't so dire. The queen must really think she had some magical power. She quickly made use of her new facilities, making sure she didn't stab herself with the knife. Was it for self-defense? To slit her wrists? Take out the guard and escape? Or simply to slice the bread? Whatever the reason, she felt less helpless with its chunky weight against her hip.

Soon, a table and two chairs were carried down, followed closely by the scribe, who made his way one step at a time, keeping a hand on the wall for balance. Watching him, Lauren's steamy anger began to roil, then, just as quickly, it cooled and dissipated, to be replaced by sadness. Sadness for Cirq's people and all they had lost, and for how close they were to salvation.

She hated big swings of emotion, or more precisely, events that elicited the feelings. In her previous life, she had purposely lived small to avoid this exact experience. Her time in Cirq had been a lot like watching a hard-played tennis match, only this time, she was the tennis ball, battered and bruised from being slammed back and forth. She'd opened herself to living bigger, thinking she was ready, and look where it got her.

Lauren took a seat, wary of this latest distraction, and watched the scribe lower himself into the opposite chair with a grimace. Yes, her situation was dire, and yes, fear clawed her belly, yet her mind still functioned, and her natural curiosity got the better of her.

"What's your name?" she asked.

He looked up from organizing his writing utensils, his fingers twitching as if needing constant employment. She knew that feeling.

His eyes were gray-blue, like the sky after a downpour. He was younger than she'd first thought, perhaps not even thirty. The constant pain of his leg had scored his face prematurely.

"Gr—Greff. Greffer," he said, shyly.

"Greffer," she repeated. "I'm Lauren."

"Yes. Yes, of course." He dipped his quill in the ink bottle and began to write, squinting hard at the paper.

Lauren nudged the lantern closer to him, overwhelmed by motherly compassion.

"From where did you come?" he asked.

"You want my life story?"

He paused and blinked. Once, twice. Did no one ever talk directly to him? She leaned back in her chair. "I'll tell you about me if you tell me about you. What happened to your leg?"

Greffer rolled the quill between thumb and forefinger. "That...does not matter," he said slowly. He considered the stalled pen for several moments. "Why do you wish to know?"

"I'm curious. Are we in a hurry?" She hadn't meant to delay, to keep him with her longer, but all at once, it was all that mattered in this dark and stale hole. She didn't fool herself into thinking that befriending the queen's scribe would make any difference to her fate. She genuinely wanted to know more about him.

"I'll start," she said. "I come from Earth."

He began to write, then stopped. She spelled it. "Another planet," she said. "I came through the Ravery. Was brought through the Ravery, to be specific."

"Brought?"

Lauren didn't really enjoy being a never-ending source of wonder. "Let's get some tea." She hopped up with a growing sense of purpose, took the steps in two strides, and pounded the door with her fist. "A tray of tea, please," she said when it opened.

The guard considered her, his lips drawn into a tight line, then shut the door. She went back to the table to wait. Greffer gaped at her.

"Now, tell me about your leg."

He considered the offending appendage for several moments before answering. "It was an accident" he said slowly. "When I was a child. I climbed up on the roof of our barn."

When he didn't continue, Lauren prompted him. "For the view?"

"What? No. No, indeed. I intended to jump off. To… to fly."

He sounded amazed. At what, his own temerity? That he had once been a boy who entertained the thought?

"The roof caved in. And the upper level."

"You crashed through two stories? Sounds like you're lucky to be alive."

He nodded, but she wasn't convinced he agreed. They were quiet a moment. Jana brought a pot of tea and a plate of dried fruit and a few nuts. She gave nothing away, but a certain gleam in her eye suggested she'd had everything to do with the success of Lauren's request.

When Greffer poured tea for them both, Lauren noted that his hand trembled. Was this a vestige of the accident or was he nervous?

"Your horse is glorious," he whispered as though afraid someone might hear. "The queen requested a drink for her head. He can be heard from upstairs."

"Heard?" Whatever could he mean? Pindar was long gone, wasn't he?

"The boy—"

"Malek?"

"He remained out there on the plain, until he was

forced to come back. And your horse has stayed near." Greffer took a sip of tea. "Calling for you."

Lauren's stomach did a flip. She wanted Pindar to go far away. To be safe. Why was he hanging around? For that matter, what had made him break out of his stall and come to her in the common room? Was he calling her? Had she called him? The implications…

Greffer set the tea tray on the floor and once more picked up his papers and stacked them together, neatening the edges. "Now, please tell me how it is you were *brought* here."

Lauren gathered her thoughts and began to tell him about that day. He stayed her with his hand and pulled a small miracle from his pocket. A pair of eyeglasses. "Do you mind?" he asked before putting them on.

"Mind? Are you kidding? I've been wondering if I could get a pair. May I?" She held out her hand and he placed the spectacles in it. She put them on. They weren't the right magnification for her, but if she squinted, they helped. She could read the journal Marzak had brought her if she had a pair.

"You need help to see?" he asked, a note of awe in his voice.

"Just up close. Lots of people do. I use them for reading and when I'm at the computer—" At his quizzical look she waved her hand, as much to brush away his question as to quell a wave of nausea. "Never mind." She gave him back his glasses.

Casting around for anything to take her mind off the inevitable, she asked, "Why hasn't Marzak healed your leg?" She didn't appreciate the full extent of a sage's power, but given what Vraz had been able to do with her ankles, surely something could be done for Greffer's leg. The oversight—if that's what it was—bothered her.

A lengthy silence followed. Clouds blew through his eyes. At first, it was as though she'd spoken another language—no comprehension at all. Then, bit by bit, he pieced together a puzzle that had long eluded him. Awareness, hurt, betrayal. Somehow, she understood at the same time as he that a remedy had purposely been denied him. But he'd never realized. Until now.

"Please," he said stiffly after a prolonged silence. "Continue your story."

She continued. He wrote it all down. For what? Posterity? Cirq wouldn't be having any posterity if they didn't get their horses back. Her voice grew hoarse as they finished.

Greffer collected his notes and stashed his glasses. "Thank you," he said with a small bow. "They will come for you at daybreak."

"How will it be done?" Lauren blurted. She'd tried to put it out of her mind, but it was there, front and center.

"It?"

"The ex…" Her voice faltered. "The exec—"

"I do not know," he answered quickly.

Perhaps so she wouldn't have to force out the word.

"There has never been one in Cirq."

... 24 ...

IT HAD been her turn to blink stupidly at him.

Never?

With Greffer and the table gone and the candle burned out, and tired of pacing, she'd curled up under the steps, feeling a half portion safer there than out in the open. She didn't think she would sleep, tried not to think at all, but before long, her eyes dropped closed.

Again, she drove that empty back road, grass waist high to either side, where moths and lightning bugs and mosquitoes pinged her windshield. Soon, she would find her way home.

But after a time, the road became pot-holed, and the jarring banged her head.

Lauren woke confused, being lifted from below. A flash of light—there, and gone. She scrambled back. A square of the floor heaved again, an inch. Dazzling light poured in. Someone said her name, a barely audible exhale. Still dreaming? She rubbed her eyes. There, a straight crack in the floor. A trapdoor, buried by dirt. The light receded. A hand reached through.

She grabbed it, put her face close and whispered, "Pheeso?"

He lifted the trapdoor, tugged her through the opening, set her on her feet, awkwardly patted her cheek, then pulled her along, saying only one word. "Hurry!"

A long, dark tunnel. He extinguished the torch, but emanated a glow of his own, enough to light their way. They ran uphill for several minutes. Lauren lagged behind, gasping for breath, her legs like leaden noodles, a stitch stabbing her side. Pheeso lifted her as if she were no heavier than a bouquet of flowers, and continued moving swiftly upward. If his feet touched the floor, she couldn't tell.

She heard Pheeso's fist against a wooden barrier, another opening, more light.

A cottage. Jana's house.

"We have all your things," she said. "We must go before first light."

"Pindar is close by," Artepa said.

They moved swiftly.

She imagined hoofbeats nearby, and that was all that mattered.

~~~

Lauren woke from a dream of Pindar. She snuggled down in the fur, imagining his warm breath fanning her cheek. Sweet horse breath. It was so real, she could smell the rich, earthy scent of him. She opened her eyes. And met his. Large, brown, and liquid. He made the soft wuffling that sounded like someone chuckling. She laughed and stroked his cheek.

Happiness rose in her chest. Sweet and painful as an icy drink of heavenly nectar. She squinted at the bright sunlight, looked around, didn't know where they were, didn't care, except that she was free and alive. And Pindar was next to her. Pheeso sitting on one side, staring into the distance. Artepa to the other, busy with a pot of something that smelled good. Armody and Jana were nearby, but they watched her rather than talking to each other. Not far away, Captain Geed and the Horseguard, at attention and alert. Others she did not recognize milled around, waiting. For what?

"Where's Lei—"

"Shhhhh," Artepa soothed. "Have a bit of soup." She ladled a serving into a bowl and handed it to her.

Lauren did as she was told, knowing it was the only way. She scooted herself to a sitting position and began to eat, Pindar nuzzling her hair and rooting in her neck, tickling her with his whiskers. After one bite, she realized how hungry she was and began to shovel in spoonfuls as fast as she could swallow.

Pheeso crouched before her, drawing a stem of green grass through his teeth. "Easy now," he said. "Do not make yourself sick."

He waited while she slowed, compassion in his eyes and a bittersweet smile curving one side of his mouth. She'd never seen any hint of vulnerability in him, toward anyone let alone her, and that scared her.

"What?" Lauren sputtered. "What's wrong? Where's Leinos?" Her eyes searched the area again, this time with more purpose. "And Malek?"

Pheeso and Artepa exchanged a look. Lauren caught a glimpse of Jana and Armody. They, too, shared a speaking glance. Captain Geed was within hearing distance but kept his back to them. Her stomach began to cramp, and it wasn't from the soup.

"Leinos bartered for your life," Artepa said gently.

"And to give you a chance to find the horses," Pheeso added, his tone flat and gaze far away. "In exchange for being disrequired."

Her mind seized on what that meant for them. "Okay, so he isn't Supreme Guardian. So?"

"She has taken him," Artepa said, nearly choking on the words. "As her consort."

"And Malek as her son," Pheeso added with disgust. "To complete the family she never had."

The empty bowl slipped away. Lauren lurched sideways like she'd been slammed in the head with a bat. If possible, she felt more stupefied than after receiving the death sentence.

Before she could form words, Artepa said, "The order of execution still stands. Unless…"

"Unless?"

"You deliver Cirq's horses in twenty days…from yesterday."

Lauren pressed the heels of her hands deep into her eye sockets to quash the intense emotions erupting inside.

Rage propelled her to her feet.

"That bitch!"

She kicked the fur, strode a short distance away and bellowed incoherently at the sky, not caring what anyone thought. Her fingers pushed into her hair, whether to tear it out or keep her head from exploding, she didn't know.

"I'll…I'll…" She stormed back to the others.

"Goddess help that woman when I get my hands on her."

Her eyes darted about frantically until she spied her saddle partially covered by a fur. She snatched it up and stalked over to Pindar who moved sideways, away from her. Firmly, she told him to halt, and he stood for her to heave the saddle to his back and tighten the girth.

"My lady—" Artepa started.

"*Don't* call me that."

She ignored the alarm that passed between the dear woman and Pheeso, and Jana and Armody getting to their feet, and Captain Geed's open scrutiny, and rummaged through the area where she'd found the saddle, heedlessly flinging supplies. Nothing would get in her way.

"*Where* is my bridle?"

She finally found it at the bottom of a bag, got it untangled and on Pindar, and mounted, clenching her teeth against a moment of dizziness and grabbing his mane to steady herself. She hadn't eaten or rested enough and didn't care.

"Which way did they go? Lerom? That's south, right?" She had no idea which direction that was, had no bearings. It was midday, the sun high above, no help.

Captain Geed, Captain of Cirq's Horseguard, her Captain, positioned himself in front of her. What nonsense. What utter and complete nonsense this entire business was. She had to get Leinos and Malek away from that spiteful, vengeful, hateful woman.

She pulled Pindar right. Geed cut her off. With very little guidance, the horse parried left. But Geed was quick on his feet for such a big man. Even loaded down as he was with weapons, he moved nimbly. Technically, though, he took orders from her.

"Get. Out. Of. My. Way." She kept her gaze over his head.

Geed moved to her side, and cautiously put one hand on the rein and one on the saddle in front of her knee. It wouldn't stop her. Pindar's ears were up, his energy coiled. One signal from her, and he'd spring away.

"You cannot go against all of the queen's guards and guardians alone," he said reasonably, almost matter-of-factly, but quietly, for her ears only.

"Then, you will come with me." Still, she didn't look at him.

He appeared to give this serious consideration. The rest —Pheeso and Artepa, Jana, Armody, some of the Horseguard, Greffer...*Greffer*—what the hell?—gathered at a polite distance.

"We are already nearly two days north of the crossroads," Geed said, his voice neutral, simply stating facts. "The queen will be at least that far south. It would take us five, maybe six days to catch them."

Pheeso moved into the intimacy of their conversation. "And as many to return."

Lauren exhaled loudly. Pindar, sensing the urgency of the situation waning, cocked a hind leg and relaxed. She shifted to one side to stay balanced in the saddle, lowered her eyes to the faces of the people around her. Some of them must have come from the village. All of them anxiously waited to see what she would do. Twelve days out of the eighteen she had left. To accomplish…maybe nothing. There would be a fight. People would get hurt. Because she was angry and upset.

And selfish.

Leinos had made a deal. He knew what he was doing. She had to believe this. She had to trust.

She took a deep, deep breath, blew it out, more slowly this time. And sat, gathering her thoughts. She'd let fear take control when she'd been alone in the dark. But she couldn't allow it continued rule over her. If she loved them, she must capitalize on the opportunity Leinos had provided.

Loved them?

She let this concept sink in. The notion wasn't one she could grasp with her mind, but it raced along with her blood into every fiber and tissue of her being, to be absorbed on a deeper level entirely. Her skin prickled with comprehension as if feeling a breeze for the first time. Little by little, her muscles loosened, her bones settled more deeply into their joints. Air moved in and out of her lungs with new ease, and upon each exhalation, her heart expanded a touch. Even her eyes softened.

Pindar balanced on all four legs again, coming to attention and tossing his head as if in agreement with this latest adjustment. Absently, Lauren stroked his neck and shoulder, delighting in his smooth silkiness, his warmth and strength, grateful to be reunited with him.

The best thing she could do for Leinos and Malek—the only thing—was to call Cirq's horses and take them to Lerom. And be quick about it. Twenty days? With two already gone? To get to the mountains, find the herd, call them, and then shepherd them all to the capital. With not one other experienced horse person to help.

No problem.

Finally, shaking her head slightly, she asked, "Which way to the Bitter Reaches?

... 25 ...

GEED POINTED in the direction she faced.

Convenient.

"Let's get going, then."

The woods they had sheltered in gave way to open ground. They were northeast of the Resting Plains in what looked to Lauren like high desert. Low brush covered the dry ground in clumps. Here and there a stunted tree broke the monotony. There might be hills on the horizon, but clouds and haze blended with the skyline in the distance.

The afternoon wore on until the sun began to sink into a cloud bank to their left. Pheeso and Artepa led the way, and she trusted they knew where they were going. Geed positioned half the Horseguard to either side, although what they might be guarding against in this barren landscape, she didn't know. She supposed there was always the chance of yekerk finding them. A shudder took her at the thought. Behind, the villagers who tagged along—about thirty more men and women of various ages—stayed together and matched pace. Armody and Jana were right behind her, but she couldn't see Greffer. How would he keep up? Why had he come? Had he been sent?

These and other questions swirled around her tired brain, such as, how the heck were they going to feed all these people? And where would they find water in this landscape? Everyone carried provisions of some sort, but would it be enough? Geed marched at Pindar's shoulder, using his stave as a walking stick. His other weapons—crossbow, various knives, quiver of blue-fletched arrows—clanked in rhythm with his strides.

Admiring the captain's Golidlocks hair, she couldn't help thinking it should be Leinos walking at her side. Sadness speared her from belly to chest, and she found her fingers first splayed over her heart, then fisted across her mouth to keep a sob from escaping.

She had to get Cirq's horses. *Had* to. But there was so little time, and too many things to go wrong. She might not find them at all. If she did, she mightn't be able to call them. That was her greatest fear.

Geed must have felt her scrutinizing the top of his head.

"What is it like?" he asked without turning.

Lauren squelched a stab of annoyance that he wasn't Leinos and forced a smile into her voice. "What is *what* like?"

He stopped and faced her. "Being up there." He gestured at the saddle. "Riding."

How to answer such a question? They walked on before everyone behind them had to stop. She should have an answer for he surely wasn't the only one with that question. But then, soon they would know for themselves.

"It's like flying," she said after a few strides, then wondered if that was a good analogy given that few Cirqians had ever seen a bird and the only other thing around with wings were yekerk.

He nodded and kept walking.

If only she *could* fly.

A short time later, he said, "I imagine this is difficult for you, as a Raver. Coming to a strange place and making your way among strangers."

"You don't know the half of it," she groused.

He shortened his stride until he walked at her right knee, too close for her liking. With a slight squeeze of her leg, Pindar shifted in the opposite direction. She patted his neck.

"Should you have need of comfort of any kind, Lady Horsecaller," Geed said, "do not hesitate to ask. I would be honored to provide such."

I bet you would.

"Thanks," she ground out. "I'll keep that in mind." *Don't hold her breath.*

Then, to move to a more neutral subject, she asked, "How long until we get there?"

"Three days," Geed answered without turning.

"And how long back to Lerom?"

"It is at least ten days' march from the mountains to the capitol."

Which left five days for her to find and call the horses. "Can we go faster?"

He looked behind them to the camp followers, and if he didn't exactly roll his eyes, he came close. "We can, but they cannot."

"Why are they here?"

He shrugged. "I expect they believe their prospects better with you than in the village."

She'd been afraid of that. "Not concerned that I'm a Raver?"

Geed tilted his head to one side like her brother's Labrador Retriever. "In truth, some of them fear you. But they are more afraid of doing nothing more than waiting to run out of food or die from the slumbering sickness."

Not quite a ringing endorsement. She sighed. "You keep going. I'll ride to the back, then catch up."

"I will go with you."

"That isn't necessary."

"Orders of the Supreme Guardian, my lady. Even if he has been disrequired from that station, I ignore his command at my peril."

Leinos *would* find a way to watch over her, even if he couldn't be here in person.

The road they followed was barely a dirt path winding through the scrub, and the way mostly flat. She turned Pindar and took him to the side so they could walk around the outside of the group. She wanted to look into the faces of these people who had put their faith in her—however reluctantly—and make sure Greffer was all right.

She smiled and nodded at each person she passed, saying hello to quite a few. Some returned the gesture, some quickly averted their eyes when caught looking.

All righty then.

They found the scribe at the very back, his face grimed with sweat and dust. He moved at a good clip despite his handicap, but she could tell it took everything he had.

Lauren jumped to the ground and led Pindar alongside, deliberately slowing the pace.

"Can you bend that leg at all?" she asked.

He shook his head. "A bit."

"I'd like you to ride with me, if you think you can."

"Oh, no, my lady. I could never. Do not fret over me, and do not alter your progress on my behalf. This was my choice, and I fully understand the urgent nature of the journey. If I fall behind, I will catch up. Do not waste time looking for me. You must succeed in what you came here to do. What you were brought here to do."

Clearly, he had given this some thought. "Why did you choose to come?"

A crooked smile lit his strained features. "When I explained to Queen Naele that you had been brought here against your will, and therefore had no designs on her seat, she said that if I were so enamored of you, then I could walk your path."

Greffer wiped his glistening forehead on his sleeve. "I do not believe she expected me to accept her…offer. In the past, I have always done as she wished without question."

And the queen knew full well that the scribe would slow them down. Lauren couldn't let that happen. She would leave him behind if she had to. But for now...

"I need your assistance. A lot of people need to be trained. It would help if you made notes for me."

"I am at your disposal, Lady Horsecaller."

"You'll have to ride."

The young man blanched, then appeared to gather his courage as he looked up at Pindar's back. Up and up. Lauren mounted, and nodded to Geed, who took Greffer by the waist and hoisted him into position. The scribe let out a grunt of surprise. It took a moment for him to settle and find a comfortable position for his bad leg. This required Lauren to give up her right stirrup for him to rest his foot in. And they were once again on their way.

But not before Lauren saw a flash of something on a small rise to the south.

"Captain Geed," she said. "Did you see that?"

He nodded. "It is a contingent of the queen's guard. She ordered them to give chase."

By this time, their entire party had ground to a halt. Pheeso and Artepa had come to the back to see what was going on.

"They're chasing us? Surely they could have caught us already if that was their intention."

"Indeed," the Captain said.

Lauren's stomach did a flip. But the comment lacked

the rich layers of patient forbearing, gentle self-mockery, and intrigued musing that Leinos managed to infuse that one word with. She missed him.

"What are you saying?" she asked.

"They are following, but will not interfere," Pheeso said.

Lauren looked at the older man. He had aged. Quick on that awareness came the thought that he and Artepa had to have been disrequired as well. Being separated from Leinos would be even harder on them than it was on her.

"Was my rescue staged?" When Artepa nodded, Lauren asked, "Is there anything else you haven't told me?"

The two old guardians exchanged one of those looks she was learning to dread.

"It is nearly time to stop for the night," Artepa said. "Let us make camp, and I will explain."

Lauren didn't want to stop. She wanted to gallop Pindar north, keep going until she reached the mountain and the herd. And then she wanted to run them all the way to Lerom. The persistent longing she felt grew stronger with each stride nearer the Bitter Reaches, like a craving that could be satisfied by only one thing. And that thing was Cirq's horses.

They made camp, even though Lauren thought they could continue for another hour or so at least. Her body ached, and her head felt fuzzy, but that hardly mattered. While Pheeso put together a pot of soup, Artepa led her a short distance away from the rest.

"I have known Leinos for most of his life," Artepa said. "Watched him grow from a quiet and thoughtful boy into a strong, courageous man who cares deeply for family and country. I have seen him killing fierce and been frightened by the ferocity in his eyes. And watched those same eyes shed tears over the dead."

Lauren nodded.

"Yes," Artepa said. "In only a few days, you have come to know this man."

A week, Lauren thought. They'd lived a lifetime in a week.

Artepa brushed a strand of Lauren's hair out of her eyes, tucked it behind her ear. "In only a few days, you have come to esteem him very highly."

Not quite a question, not quite a statement.

"I love him." Lauren hadn't thought it possible to feel so deeply for someone in so short a time, but there it was.

"Good," Artepa said. "Know that with every fiber of his being, he fought. He argued and reasoned and pleaded. We had only moments when he came out of that room. He could not reveal all they had discussed. Unbeknownst to us, our queen has been negotiating with the rebel lords of Derr. They want access to our southern ports in exchange for taking in the last of our people. The queen believed it to be her only recourse."

Artepa stared in the direction of the Bitter Reaches. "Everyone would have enough food and shelter." Her eyes met Lauren's. "It was a concession to *allow* you to escape. Do you understand?"

"Is that why she sent some of her guards after us? So it would look like she was trying to capture me?"

"Yes. To assuage her keen sense of pride and also for the benefit of any Derriens who might hear."

"We call it plausible deniability where I come from. Why did she have to take Leinos and Malek?"

The older woman gave a delicate one-shouldered shrug. "Control. You had a better chance of succeeding with his aid. In her heart of hearts, I believe she wants what is best for Cirq. But she is also…"

"Afraid."

"Yes. Because one Horsecaller long ago developed a following, and this threatened the throne. That division created the weakness that eventually led to our downfall. She also recognized that Leinos's devotion to country no longer aligned solely with blind fidelity to her ideals."

"By controlling him, she controls me."

"Yes. If you do not deliver the horses before the Derrien lords arrive in Lerom, she will relinquish control of the ports to them. It is not what she wants. Who knows what it will lead to? If you do deliver the horses, you will be escorted to the Ravery and sent back to your world. If twenty days pass without success, her guards will execute you."

"They'll have to catch me, first," Lauren said with more bravado than she felt.

Artepa smiled and hugged her. "That is the Horsecaller I have come to know and love."

Lauren should have been relieved to hear she would return home, especially with a death sentence hanging over her head. But she was having a hell of a time mustering enthusiasm for the trip. And that's when it hit her. She didn't have to reinvent herself or learn to live big. This place had already molded her into someone who cared about more substantial things than hot running water and dark chocolate. Passion and willingness were all that were required.

And the truth was, she'd never give up on dark chocolate.

"I'm sorry you and Pheeso have been separated from Leinos," she said.

"We are your guardians, now. It is all he asked."

"But—weren't you disrequired when he was?"

Again, the exquisitely dainty and expressive lift of one shoulder, this time accompanied by a sly smile. "Unfortunately, the sage had to leave for Elaz before he could extract our guardian faculties." She put her arm around Lauren's shoulders. "Come, let us go and taste what magic my Pheeso has made of grass and water."

Lauren didn't know if the soup really was made from only grass and water, but it filled the empty spaces, and she felt fortified. Pindar wandered freely and cropped grass of his own making. That was real magic.

Or so she thought.

She was about to borrow Greffer's glasses and settle in to tackle the notebook, when she saw Pindar pawing a sandy patch. Thinking he was getting ready to roll, she walked closer. She never tired of watching him fold his seemingly too-fragile legs, lower his big body to the ground, and revel in rocking and wriggling from side to side to scratch his broad back.

But he didn't lie down. He dug deeper, with a look of

intense concentration in his eyes, like a dog burying a bone. Flinging dirt. And then mud. Then water poured out of the dry ground, quickly forming a puddle. Pindar slapped the surface with one hoof a couple of times, splashing them both.

He shook himself, then looked at her. If horses smiled, he was grinning. If he could speak, he was saying, "Cool, huh?"

Lauren walked through the growing pool and patted his wet shoulder. "Very cool, my friend. Very cool indeed."

... 26 ...

FROM THE single window in his tower, Rezol watched the latest group of workers being herded in to the courtyard below. They looked frightened and travel worn and hungry, as they always did. This group included a few light-haired Cirqians and a few of the darker Derrians, but altogether only a handful.

Never enough. There would never be enough of them to dig as far into the mountain as he needed them to and also bring out the mined rock. He needed the horses. Had allowed himself to become obsessed with them. As it was, only his power enabled the workers to assail the mountain at all, so strong was the spell put on it long ago.

Wheedling his away under the ancient aegis had taken too much time. He had known it would not be easy, yet the mountain's defense had yielded, though the protection endured. Keeping the mines accessible required constant concentration, but even he had to rest. Then, the curtain descended, and whoever was inside stayed until he returned his attention to the mountain. Progress was slow.

Cirq's horses would change that. With their strength to pull wagons of stone out of the deep shaft, he could put more to work digging. And, if what he had read about the combined power of Horsecaller and horses was true, they could do even more. He would have The Absolute. Then, woe to Elaz for what they had done to his family. But before he exacted his revenge on the other sages, he would find his daughter and protect her.

The Horsecaller had to live. He knew her name now—Lauren—knew she had come through the Ravery with a horse when Vraz and that ancient hag had opened it. How well Lauren fulfilled the prophecy.

She would call the horses. Then, he would pounce.

A scrap of vellum slid beneath the heavy door barring entrance to his refuge. He stared at it for a moment. His agents knew better than to risk speaking directly to him. Coming to his tower thusly to deliver a missive could be deathly hazardous. The contents must be momentous. And that gave Rezol a rare moment of apprehension.

He crossed the room and snatched the slip of paper from the floor, then sat at his desk before unfolding it.

A few coded words conveyed the blow. Rast had done the worst possible thing—sent a sortie into Cirq to look for the Horsecaller. He was overeager for conquest, and destroying the Horsecaller qualified.

Rast had also sent a message to Cirq's Chancellor commanding her to stop the Horsecaller if this attack failed. Rezol closed his hand around the note and crushed it, then dropped it in the fire and watched it turn to ash.

He left his tower, considering how best to thwart this scheme, but every time he turned his thoughts to Lerom, he found himself searching for his daughter's spirit. He could not let himself be distracted and risk Marzak learning his intent.

Rezol invaded Rast's private rooms without knocking. "What have you done?"

A young woman perched on Rast's lap slid to the floor as the King rose. She gathered her things and slipped past Rezol, looking relieved.

"How dare you!" Rast fumed. "You cannot barge in here. Guards!"

No response. Rast blustered past Rezol to look outside his door. The guards were there, they were standing, their eyes were open, but they neither heard nor saw him.

"You will regain their full attention soon," Rezol said. "Now, tell me what disaster you have invoked in Cirq."

Rast moved to a window before speaking. He tucked in his shirt with jerky movements. "What do you mean? We needed to get rid of the threat. I have taken steps to do so. That is all you need to know."

Before moving toward Rast, Rezol pulled in a deep, sustaining breath. Otherwise, he would fly across the room and strangle the squat monarch or simply toss him through the window. Better not to put his hands on the man. He stalked up to the king and hissed in his ear.

"You need the Horsecaller, you idiot. We need the horses. It will not avail us to have her harmed before she calls them. Do you understand?" He infused his tone with sage persuasion. Not enough to take over Rast's mind, as he had with the guards, but sufficient to make him think the idea his own.

"I understand we must not allow Cirq the slightest advantage," Rast persisted. "Give them the tiniest opening and they will swarm through. Before we know it, the very foundation of our country will be undermined beyond repair."

That Cirq still represented a threat, Rezol would not argue, but where this unreasoned fear came from, he could not fathom. Still, feeding it and stroking Rast's ego at the same time could work to his advantage.

"You are right, my King, they are a blight. Think what we could do if we had Cirq's horses. Imagine how powerful you would be, how weak they would become. Taking the horses would suck the last breath from Cirq."

"If only there were a way to get the horses here," the king said.

"Yes, my liege. You should wait until the horses are called. Then, with my help, you can bring horses and Horsecaller here."

"That would crush them completely," Rast said, waving a fist. "Why have I not thought of this before?" He spun on Rezol. "Why have you not advised me on this? You should have known—never mind that." Suddenly officious, he summoned a scribe. "I must withdraw the attack and stop Cirq's Chancellor before she ruins everything. Get out of my way."

Rezol bowed as Rast rushed out. "As you wish, my King."

It was too late to withdraw the attack, but even over distance, the sage could countermand the king's orders to the small brigade of soldiers. Rezol placed in their minds the belief that hurting a horse or Horsecaller would anger the king. All knew the risk of provoking Rast. They would still attack. If they killed any of Cirq's remaining military or her famed Supreme Guardian, he would be pleased.

As for the message already sent to Cirq's chancellor, in the days it would take it to reach Lerom, much could go wrong. Hampered as he was by the risk of discovery, he could not change that. Tense with anger and frustration, he made his way back to his tower. If he could go to Cirq, he would surround the Horsecaller with an aegis for protection. Would Marzak think of that? He might, but do it? Never. Too unethical, too interfering.

If he did go to Cirq, he might find his daughter. Had he known about the aegis when younger, had he suspected what the sages of Elaz would do to his family, he would have wrapped his mate so solidly not even the great Lanizrac could have harmed her. Too late, always too late.

He knew little of Cirq's Chancellor except that she sought the throne. With Rast's help, she would be queen of Cirq. How quickly she might kill the Horsecaller was what worried him.

His gaze fell on a small stone statue of a horse, a spoil from the war waged by Tinnis two-hundred-and-two courses before. Would he be too late to save the Horsecaller and his own hopes for the future? After a moment, the horse began to glow, then burst into a thousand shards.

... 27 ...

UNDER COVER of night, Lauren stuffed her pack with everything she could think of. There wasn't much. She didn't know exactly what she would need or for how long. She only knew she had to go. The twin moons had already set, and she stumbled more than once trying not to wake anyone. An unfamiliar combination of nerves and excitement made her legs jerk and wobble as if she walked on a trampoline.

To make it worse, Pindar stalked her like a curious cat, nudging her shoulder, nibbling her shirt and picking up the odd length of rope or scrap of cloth. He chewed each briefly as if to discern its worth, then dropped it.

His muzzle and lips were delicate tools, flexible as rubber and able to nose through weeds and brush to locate the tiniest clump of clover. Then, he could delicately nip off every stem at the base with his sharp front teeth. He could find her bra strap through her shirt and snap it without pinching her skin. There was no ignoring him when he wanted attention. Gently, she elbowed him back, then wondered if he was trying to tell her something.

Ever since jumping through the Ravery, the horse had become increasingly…aware, was the only word she could think of. Of himself, of her, of the environment— in the way all horses were—but more so. All horses were mindful of their surroundings, mainly to suss out threats. Survival demanded it. Thousands of years of domestication had changed nothing in that regard. What had changed was the way he used his awareness now, and how he communicated with her. Or tried.

Lauren tied a fur to the back of her saddle, then pressed her fists into her lower back to ease tight muscles. She paused, breathing and listening, trying to settle both mind and stomach. What she was about to do was either unbelievably foolish or incredibly brilliant. Pindar turned his head and touched her hip. She moved to his shoulder and rested her forehead there.

Somewhere in the darkness surrounding the camp, several of the Horseguard stood watch. She wasn't sure how she'd get past them. Everyone else slept. After the evening meal, she'd burned through two and a half candles reading the journal. Upon turning the first page, she'd known it was her great-great-grandfather's. There was no mistaking his spidery hand, careful attention to detail, and deft segues from English to Italian and back.

A thrill of excitement had vibrated her from the inside out. She couldn't always read his writing, nor did she have any useful Italian, so at least a third of it was lost to her.

But she had the gist of it. And it came down to going into the Bitter Reaches alone. Only she could call the horses, and they would answer only if she went solo—she and a horse.

Great-great-grandfather Enzo, who had to be the Ebro Leinos referred to, had drawn a map of the range and the pass she needed to use. He'd added illustrations of the landmarks and vegetation she could expect to encounter as she crossed the mountains. Almost as if he'd known she'd need it. She was confident that within a few days, food would not be a concern.

If enough horses still lived.

The alternative didn't bear consideration, so she halted thinking there.

Instead, she'd borrowed Greffer's ink and paper, made notes of the details she needed to remember, writing large enough to read without glasses, because she wouldn't deprive him of his.

She rubbed the big gray's neck. "Are we ready?" she whispered, feeling silly and hopeful. "Have I forgotten anything?"

Pindar nodded his head as was his habit. He might be answering; he might simply be eager to go. They would have plenty of time in the next few days to work on their communication skills. Although there could be no doubt it was the human side of the equation that needed work, not the equine.

After checking the girth once more, Lauren gathered the reins, thrust her foot into the stirrup, and climbed to Pindar's back. Once there, it took a moment to settle pack and stave. Leaving the weapon behind had crossed her mind, but in deference to Leinos, it was duly strapped to her back. Much good it did in her hands.

But then, she had acquitted herself surprisingly well when the flying bird-men had attacked them at the edge of the Resting Plains. She remembered those moments frequently, trying to understand the intense focus that had possessed her, the consummate connection she had attained with Pindar. She only hoped that if the situation demanded, she would again enter that same trance-like state.

They stayed for a moment near the edge of camp. The eastern sky hinted at dawn, and the slight glimmer limned the soft mounds of her friends' sleeping forms. She whispered an apology and turned Pindar north.

Soon enough, a shadow emerged from the dusty twilight. As they drew near, she recognized Enaid. The woman stood at attention and did not make eye contact but kept her gaze straight north. Yet, everything about the soldier's eager stance cried out for contact with the horse. They halted next to her.

"Good morning," Lauren said. "Enaid, right?"

"Yes, Horsecaller."

After that cheery start, Lauren drew a blank, an awkward lump lodging in her throat. Enaid's long, white-blonde hair hung down her back in a tight braid. Lauren focused on the intricate weave and swallowed hard a few times, trying to think what to say. Neither command nor deception came naturally to her. "All quiet?"

"Yes, Horsecaller."

"Very good." Pindar pawed the ground, impatient.

Enaid took a cautious half-step to the side, her eyes briefly flicking up. Just as quickly, she moved toward the horse again, as if he were a magnet. Lauren let out her breath. She was impatient too, but could no more deny the soldier's urge to touch Pindar than halt her own breathing. She doubted it differed very much from her own need to call the horses.

"Can you do me a big favor and make sure Pindar doesn't have any brambles stuck in his tail?"

"Of course, my lady." Under Lauren's watchful gaze, Enaid made her way along Pindar's side. "Run your hand over his hip so he knows you're there." Enaid did as she was told. "Now, comb your fingers through his tail and shake it out."

"Yes, Horsecaller." After a moment, she continued, "It appears to be clean."

As Lauren already knew. "Great. Thanks."

Enaid took up her former position, the muscles of her face working hard to contain a broad grin. "We are getting an early start, Lady Horsecaller?"

"On the contrary, everyone should sleep in today. I'm going to scout ahead. We'll meet for the midday meal." By then, there was no chance anyone would catch up.

"Yes, Horsecaller."

An excellent soldier. "Good job. Carry on."

Enaid nodded smartly, and Lauren and Pindar jogged away. Within a few minutes, she'd lost sight of the camp, and although the sun still hid beneath the horizon, there was enough light to be sure of the footing. She relaxed her grip on the reins, and Pindar sprang into canter.

~~~

Leinos had been stewing in a deep kettle of self-recrimination since leaving the inn. Walking had always been his method when he needed to think, but for the past few days it had not yielded its usual clarity. As Supreme Guardian, he thought well ahead and was never surprised. To others, he always knew what to do, but that was because he had already considered all the possibilities. This turn of events, however, had never occurred to him.

And he was no longer Supreme Guardian.

Yet, what else could he have done? Securing Lauren's freedom so she could fulfill her destiny as Horsecaller was all that mattered. Negotiations had failed. Acquiescence to Queen Naele's demands had been the only way. He had profoundly misjudged the depth of her fear. Pheeso had been right all along. She had refused to see reason.

They were a quiet group, moving swiftly toward Lerom. The queen's guards and guardians never spoke unless spoken to. Naele, well, he would not guess what went on behind her cool gaze. She did not offer conversation. Nor did he.

Malek grew more pale and withdrawn as if each step farther from Lauren and Pindar drained the blood from his body. Without Guardian powers, there was nothing Leinos could do.

He would not be shocked to learn that he, too, had become colorless, fading into the background. There was no self-pity in him, only a hollow helplessness. He had mastered the anger. But not the sickening worry. Pheeso and Artepa, Captain Geed and the Horseguard would watch over Lauren. But wondering exactly where she was, how she was sleeping, if she was afraid, gnawed at him. He needed to see her smile for himself. He needed the reassurance of her body against his.

He needed her.

These thoughts, and more, made an endless circle in his mind. That, and the inability to simultaneously cast his senses ahead, was why he never saw the attack coming.

The men were already past the outer guards before he even realized they were in a fight. He saw the queen being swept to safety by her guardians. He spun to protect Malek, but the boy had disappeared from his side.

In less time than it took to inhale, he had loosed two arrows, each piercing the chest of Tinnisian warriors.

As always happened in battle, sound was lost to him, and time slowed. He tried to fight in the direction the queen had gone, but he was surrounded. They were heavily outnumbered.

Where was Malek? He could not locate the boy in the fray or amongst those already struck down.

He blocked a thrusting sword with his stave and ducked to avoid another. Thought flew. His body took over, welcoming the clear purpose of kill or be killed, even while a part of him recognized that only a couple of the queen's guards still stood.

More attackers rushed at him. He fought until he could barely lift his arms, his feet braced against bodies instead of the ground.

Then came a flash of light and crashing pain to the back of his skull. He saw Lauren on Pindar. Alone.

Anguish.

Darkness.

~ ~ ~

Lauren let Pindar set the pace and choose their path. Whether he worked on instinct or had somehow intuited their destination, she didn't know. He had been drawn to the missing horses as much as she ever since they'd arrived. She trusted him more than herself.

And so they jogged, and sometimes cantered, for hours. Toward midday she forced him to stop, even though he wasn't winded. She was. She needed to put her feet on the ground, stretch, and have a drink, even if he didn't.

Pindar rolled and shook when Lauren removed his tack. He nibbled on the soft grass that sprung up around him, and once again, he dug a quick hole and found water for them both. To do this once had been magic. Twice. Well. It wasn't a fluke. It was deliberate. He knew exactly what he was doing.

And the water! It was clear and cold, refreshing and revitalizing. Lauren splashed her face, and on impulse, used her bowl to scoop it over Pindar's neck, back, and sides. He stood for this bath and used his nose to point to different parts of his body for her to rub it in to.At least, that's what she thought he was doing, and she could tell by his response that it was right. He had a way of sticking his head out, half-closing his eyes, and curling his lip that communicated what she was doing felt good.

She laughed. A sense of freedom unfolded inside her,

an expansiveness that lifted her to her toes. She'd never felt more right, more connected, more purposeful. In the next moment, she sank to the ground, momentarily off balance, feeling like she'd been punched in the gut. How would the people she left behind find water without Pindar? If they stayed put, they would have enough. The hole he'd dug at their camp had showed no signs of drying up. Maybe they would stay there. Maybe they would find this new watering hole. Maybe only the Horseguard would follow.

She could hope.

On that thought, she readied Pindar again so they could be on their way. Nothing and no one would slow them down. She grabbed a handful of nuts and dried fruit to eat as she rode.

Still, a small ball of worry rolled around her belly. Pindar didn't act tired, and his legs looked strong and healthy. There was no swelling to indicate inflammation or tendonitis. He was fit, but was she pushing him too hard? Her own body clamored to lie on a bed, for another long, hot bath, to not be in perpetual motion for a while. Their time at the inn had been too short.

Soon. In just a couple of days they would have the horses. Then, they could rest.

... 28 ...

LAUREN WOKE in the murky pre-dawn to what had become a familiar sound—one she had missed the night before—a crackling fire. And to an equally well known, but not quite as welcome, scent—the ubiquitous pot of porridge—and knew a few moments of disorientation while she dragged herself up to full consciousness.

She wasn't in her brother's house. No. And…she'd been alone when she'd collapsed into an exhausted and heavy sleep the night before. Pindar's new abilities notwithstanding, it was doubtful he was cooking breakfast.

He was, however, lying nearby, feet tucked beneath his body, head up. The intruder must be someone they knew. Her heart leapt in her chest. Leinos? She lifted onto one elbow.

Pheeso and Artepa watched her from the other side of a steaming pot. Lauren dropped back to hide her disappointment. Of course it wasn't Leinos. He was far to

286

the south, maybe already in Lerom, fulfilling who-knew-what duties as queen's consort.

Pindar rolled flat, stretching his neck until his muzzle rested on her shoulder, breath fanning her face. Sweet horse breath, full of prayers and hope. She enfolded his head in her arms and stroked him, seeking—and finding—comfort.

"How did you find me?" she asked the others without rising. She and Pindar had ridden into the night until the need for sleep had so dulled her senses she feared she might topple off his undulating back. But putting as much distance between herself and the rest of them had seemed imperative.

"We are your guardians now," Artepa said gently, as if this explained.

"I have to go alone and quickly. The others were slowing us down."

"We can keep up with you," Pheeso said. "With Pindar."

"And save you time by building the fire and preparing meals," Artepa added. "At least until you reach the pass. We know you must go alone from there."

"I wish someone had told me that a little sooner in this whole enterprise," Lauren groused, mostly to herself and Pindar.

She eased his big head to the side and sat, knuckling the last vestiges of sleep from her eyes. Truthfully, she was glad for their company. If she hadn't already been dead on her feet when they stopped the night before, she would have been afraid. With a jaw-cracking yawn, she rolled up the fur. Pindar got to his feet. They were right. She could get everything ready while they made food—a much better meal than she would have made for herself —and set off sooner than if she were alone.

"Thank you. I'm glad you're here. And I'm sorry I took off without telling anyone."

She got a brush from her pack and applied it to Pindar's coat while he browsed for grass.

The corners of Artepa's eyes crinkled as she let out a soft laugh. "You said enough to Enaid for us to know what you were thinking."

A murky haze had surrounded them during the night, and it muffled their voices, making Lauren feel like they were all in a safe cocoon. "Was Captain Geed upset?"

Pheeso snorted. "When is that overblown son of a frit not upset about something?"

Something had changed in Pheeso. He had softened toward her. Perhaps Leinos had ordered it.

"Is the Captain always upset about something? I haven't seen that side of him."

Artepa filled three bowls from the pot and brought one to Lauren. "That is lucky for you. No doubt he has shown you only his best side."

"And that is no broader than one of Pindar's whiskers," Pheeso said. "You will see the rest of him before long."

Great. A moody *and* horny captain was exactly what she wouldn't need with hundreds of horses to care for and only a handful of inexperienced people to do it.

One step at a time, she reminded herself. She ate the

hot cereal standing while Pheeso and Artepa filled water skins and struck the camp. After cleaning her bowl and putting it with the others, she tacked up Pindar and mounted.

And froze. The morning mist parted. Her breath hitched in her throat. Before them rose the Bitter Reaches. The rising sun illuminated sharp, bare peaks stabbing the still-dark sky. Craggy. Imposing. Terrifying.

Bitter, indeed.

Lauren forced air into her lungs. Small wonder the horses stayed on the other side. There was no way she could get over those mountains, find and call the horses, and deliver them to Lerom in the fifteen days she had left.

A new wave of anger washed through her. The queen had known all along this was a fool's errand. The queen had her own agenda. The queen wanted her, along with whatever imaginary threat she represented, dead.

Pindar strained at the bit. He lifted his head and whinnied. She could feel his energy building, his powerful muscles bunching. She patted his neck. "You're right. We have to try."

The big gray shook and pranced. Lauren restrained him with a gentle tweak to the reins as she turned to Pheeso and Artepa. "We're going—"

Pindar launched into gallop, nearly dumping her right over his tail. She grabbed mane and pulled herself into the saddle. Her last word, *now*, was taken by the wind. She figured her new guardians got the picture.

~~~

Leinos first became aware of throbbing pain. Mostly in

his head. But there was little to distinguish it from the burning soreness of his stiff arms and shoulders, or the stabbing sensation on his left side when he breathed, or the tender ache of what must be bruises down the length of both legs. He was lying on a hard surface but something soft cradled the back of his head, the locus of the most severe discomfort.

How he had come to be so thoroughly thrashed, he did not know.

Then, the smell hit him. Death. All around. He struggled to his hands and knees and vomited. And immediately collapsed to the side again, dizziness making sparks swirl in his vision and the pounding in his head worse.

He had survived a fight. Others had not.

Perhaps he slept. He would like to sleep until the pain receded and someone else had come for the bodies. Next, he heard a voice nearby.

"Are you awake again? Thank the goddess."

Awake *again*? He did not remember. A soggy rag trailed over his forehead. The voice, familiar. "Malek?" The sound a strange croak.

"Yessir."

Leinos started to clear his throat, but the effort rebounded in his skull, so he stopped. Still, when he spoke, he sounded more like himself. "What happened?"

"We were attacked. I ran away. They left you for dead. I waited. You came to, but not for long. After you fell asleep, I thought you would never wake up."

He could not put the pieces together. The last he remembered was walking beside Malek. "How long?"

"Since the attack?" Malek asked slowly. "A day."

"Who else was here? Who attacked?"

When no answer came, he slowly lifted one arm to shield his eyes before opening them. He could not quite make the boy come into focus, but Malek knelt beside him, blinking, fear pinching his brows together. Leinos let his hand drop to the boy's knee with a sigh.

"It will be all right. I was hit in the head. I have seen this before. It is usual to be confused and forgetful for a time. Do we have water?" His throat felt like charred parchment.

The boy scrambled up and came back with a skin. Leinos fought down the nausea and drank. He needed time to recover, but a sense of urgency clawed at him. If only he could remember what he needed to do.

No matter what it was, they first had to care for the bodies of the fallen. He lifted his head and probed the back. A lump and dried blood. After a while, he sat up, drank more water and looked around. The dead were the queen's guard.

The queen. They were traveling together to Lerom. He looked about wildly, causing the throbbing, which had eased, to begin anew.

"Is the queen unharmed?"

"I saw her guardians take her away, and I do not think anyone went after them. But I…"

"You kept yourself safe. That is good. And I bet a

clever boy like you scrounged some food for us, yes?"

Malek smiled and nodded. "Yessir."

Leinos ate and began to feel stronger. The lightheadedness lessened. By nightfall, they had stacked the bodies, called out the names of the dead, and set them alight. The attackers had removed their own. Over the course of the day, most of his memory returned.

So much, he thought ruefully, for any privilege accorded queen's consort. She and her guardians had left without a glance behind, he was quite sure. But he had never intended to be more than her mate in name, and Naele's retreat now provided him an advantage.

There could be no doubt the attack had been ordered by King Rast. If what Vraz and Marzak feared was true, the Tinnisians were looking for the Horsecaller. Whether to kill her or use her for their own purposes hardly mattered.

As far as the queen knew, neither counterfeit consort nor sham son had survived the battle. They took what weapons and provisions they could carry and headed north at a run.

Lauren was in danger.

... 29 ...

IF PINDAR'S hooves touched the ground, Lauren couldn't tell. She gave him his head, closed her eyes, and relaxed into the mesmerizing cadence of flat-out gallop, trusting him to safely get them where she needed to be. Where he needed to be.

She'd ridden many horses at many speeds but never experienced this, this joyful melding of heart and soul and body with another. They whipped across the dry plain like a scirrocco in the desert, ripping a path through what remained of the morning haze and leaving a spiraling plume in their wake. She hunkered low, opening her hands flat to his surging neck, giving herself over to him, to the wisdom of ancient blood and bone.

And felt them. Knew the presence of Cirq's horses alongside, buoying them up, pressing them on, tugging them forward. Up into the foothills without slowing. Silent now, as if the world held its breath and they rode over clouds instead of solid ground.

By nightfall, they were well into the mountains, and she was equal parts elated and exhausted, though the big gray was fresh as he'd been in the morning, as if every breath closer to the herd sent new energy pulsing through his vessels. But Lauren had to rest.

She pulled off Pindar's bridle, and the saddle and fur, left it all in a heap, and leaned against a wall of rock, knowing, somehow, that despite the arguments of her guardians, they would not catch her tonight. Even they could not keep up with a galloping horse. Which meant a cold meal of the few bits of trail mix she hoped were still rattling around the bottom of her pack. And no fire to ease her sore muscles. Nor any breakfast.

All day, they had curved steadily upward along a path strewn with humped slabs of rock. Pindar eased the pace enough to place his feet carefully, but wasted no time. His metal shoes sparked tiny bursts of rock dust that winnowed up to catch in her dry throat.

When they reached a level patch, they stopped. Pindar nibbled grass, and she chewed her last piece of dried meat. She checked his feet for stones, then they continued.

During the day, the trail had switched back on itself between two peaks, providing her last view of the desolate valley below. The place where her guardians and probably all of the Horseguard and camp followers raced to the foothills, to catch a glimpse of her before she disappeared into the mountain mists. And the place they would wait for her to emerge, as though coming through the Ravery again, but this time with their horses.

She'd give anything to have their faith. Even the ones who cast sidelong glances because she was a Raver. If only they knew their first Horsecaller had come along the same *dark, unused paths*, they would change their tune.

And what of the queen's guards who followed at a not-so-discreet distance? What did they think of this duty? Did they hope for her success or failure? Surely, as Cirqians, they must want the horses as much as anyone. Were they absolutely loyal to Queen Naele? *Would* they execute her if she didn't find the horses?

With a sigh, she'd booted Pindar on up the trail. There was nothing to be gained from that line of thinking.

Toward night, they found a small cave that accommodated them both, and she'd called a halt to the ceaseless climbing. The air had grown increasingly dry as they ascended, and a chill clung to the tawny walls.

With unerring ease, her horse tapped the stone and brought a gush of water from a crevice. After it overflowed a natural depression in the stone floor he could use as a trough, she filled her skin and drank deeply, then, ignoring the gnawing of her stomach, spread the fur and slept.

Pindar woke her in the morning with a gentle nibble to her ear, his warm breath tickling along her neck. She opened her eyes to a pile of green leaves, their color so vibrant against the dull rock, they seemed to glow. He wuffled and pushed them toward her. She looked at him.

"Are these for me?" He only pushed them at her again. "I'll take that as a yes."

She sat and took a bite. Tough and bitter, then, as she

chewed, a pleasant mint flavor filled her mouth. "Yum," she said with a nod. "Thanks."

Several handfuls later, Lauren paused long enough to wonder if she should be eating a strange plant brought to her by a horse. He lay before her with his front legs tucked beneath his chest, and she ruffled his forelock and stroked his ears. "You wouldn't poison me, would you?"

In the past, she'd often imagined a horse laughing at her. Now, Pindar fairly rolled his eyes at her question. Of course she could trust him.

"Remember when—just last week—I took care of you? You depended on me to look after your needs." She stroked his flat cheek and scratched a speck of sweat away with a dirty and ragged fingernail. "Your world consisted of your stall and paddock, a once-a-week trail ride over familiar ground, and the occasional horse show." He leaned into her touch, and she rubbed around his eyelid. "Now, you're taking care of me. But then, I always knew you were smarter than the average horse."

He snorted at that, and she laughed, surprised she still could. Exhaustion, she reflected, could be a good thing. The night before, she'd been too tired to worry about being alone, but then—she tilted her head to one side, considering the amazing creature before her—she wasn't alone at all.

The plant Pindar had brought revived her aching joints. She rose, and he got to his feet.

She could sense that he was eager to move quickly again, but she made him walk for a time while she consulted her notes. There was nothing about the sustaining leaves she'd had for breakfast, but if her calculations were right, they should make the pass today, and soon after, come to a glacial lake hidden deep in a pine forest. And there, there the horses would be. She sucked in an excited breath, and just as quickly, let it out. Maybe. Part of her still doubted. But she forced that part into the closet and slammed the door.

Heavy clouds soon brought a cold drizzle, and she fanned her cloak over Pindar's back to keep him dry. The narrow track, now more gravel than solid stone, turned into a sluiceway. Pindar calmly continued, unconcerned, on his own mission. She thanked the goddess for his sturdy, sacred hooves.

The gray light gave no indication of whether it was morning or afternoon, but soon, the rain stopped, and the ground leveled off. The sky cleared. The air grew clean and sharp, clear light etching details of tone and texture, picking out a few blades of grass and their attendant shadows drawn with razor-like precision against the stippled gray and tan faces of boulders.

All afternoon they walked and trotted, picking their way through the tight and twisting cleft marking the pass. Precisely carved pillars shorn from the walls by freezing and thawing sprinkled the canyon floor. Water seeped between the vertical cracks, steadily winning its way. After exiting the pass, they stopped. Anticipation tightened her chest, and Pindar could not keep still. They must be close.

Over another rise and below stretched a pine forest. But it was mostly brown, dotted here and there with a greener tree stubbornly clinging to life. She refused to consider the implications and urged Pindar into the shadows and quiet beneath, walking again, and she held her breath as the trees thinned up ahead. They should hear them, or smell them. Something.

They came into the clearing.

Nothing. A cracked dry bowl where a lake had once been, and nothing more. No horse tracks marred the porous soil, no droppings warmed the frost-heaved roots. The herd had not been here in a long time.

Hot tears welled up and spilled over Lauren's cheeks.

"Goddammit," she muttered with a swipe at her face.

Should they turn around? Had the crone spoken the truth about there still being horses up here? The ancient woman had no reason to lie. In a change from his usual keen determination, Pindar stood quietly, waiting. His nostrils flared and his ears flicked back, then forward again, testing the air, listening. He shook his head, flopping his mane from side to side. His self-assurance had kept her going. Was he hesitating now? What would she do if he lost his confidence?

Menacing clouds bunched behind a row of saw-toothed peaks. An unsure wind gusted. Typical mountain weather. Clear one moment and stormy the next. Dry grass and leaves and dust swirled into a mini tornado that twisted out of sight. A cross breeze sent loose strands of hair lashing into her eyes. Pindar's forelock flipped up once then down. Still, they sat. Lauren tamed her hair behind her ears.

She had taken Pindar's elevated mental capacity for granted as a side effect of coming through the Ravery.

Somehow, they had both connected with the collective unconscious of Cirq's horses. Or the horses had connected with them. Either way, it had been easier to let him do all the heavy lifting while she stood by and watched. Maybe the problem wasn't with him, but with her. She had been trying to trust him—as if she had a choice—but fear always managed to overtake her effort.

Fear, The All had said. Or Love. She must choose to allow the light or plunge into darkness

She still didn't know what that meant.

Maybe Pindar needed to know that she was truly with him, that they were in this together. Lauren closed her eyes and breathed deeply, trying to open herself to her horse, to all the horses, seeking guidance, offering faith. She did not need certainty, only willingness. And love. She felt warmth around her heart and allowed this to expand until it radiated through her body and out her fingertips. Her skin, especially that of her face and hands, tingled with new awareness, as if each fine hair had stood up and reached outward. Beneath her and against the insides of her legs, Pindar trembled, but not with cold.

Without opening her eyes, she felt heat all around them, as if the sun had broken through the clouds to put a comforting hand on her shoulder. She inhaled the hot light and let it pool once more in her chest. She felt weightless. She felt love.

There was nothing for it but to keep going. Pindar stepped forward without any physical signal from her, and they trotted through the broad trough that had once held water, between the two tree-fringed ridges, heading up again. She wondered a little about getting lost, but consoled herself with something her mother was fond of saying: *You can't be lost if you don't know where you were in the first place.*

There was no other path, anyway, no turns or forks, just the one slender trail, beckoning them forward like a crooked finger.

Something else her mother had been saying lately came to mind. *You have to let love in, Lauren girl. Make space for it. Let it in.*

But there had been no love after she lost her baby and then Darren's betrayal. She had not allowed it.

A little while later, thunder shook the air. Pindar didn't need to be told. He ran toward a line of evergreens as the first streak of lightening flashed.

Rain and hail pelted them, and the wind threatened to rip her cloak from her shoulders. He tossed his head and flicked his tail, digging in for more speed. Heavy clouds turned the day dark, and lightening lit the unfamiliar landscape with a brilliant strobe. They were almost to the trees.

Somewhere in her mind it registered that this forest was green and lush. Pindar scrambled up a steep embankment, as anxious as she to find protection.

She hugged his neck and lifted her eyes in time to see a thick branch coming straight for them.

He slid under.

She leaned sideways, but the branch banged her shoulder, and stiff needles scraped her face. His wet mane slipped through her fingers.

She hit the ground, landing hard on her hip and blindly grabbing for reins, stirrup, tail, anything, anything to stay with him.

~~~

Each jogging step brought a new pulse of pain to Leinos' head. Next to him, Malek looked like he dragged his feet through mud. They could not keep on like this. They would not gain the Bitter Reaches in enough time at this rate. They needed a faster mode of travel. A sage could take them. But contacting a sage demanded the powers of a guardian. He had not thought to regret the loss of his abilities so soon.

He called a halt and assessed their position. They had left the road and struck out cross country, the most direct route. But if they cut east now, they would soon come to the dry riverbed that would lead them to Siblan.

"Why did I not think of this sooner?"

Malek gave him a curious look, but did not bother to try and answer.

Leinos turned them, and soon they found the going easier. By nightfall, they would reach the city.

"Why do we go this way and not north?" Malek asked. "We must find the Horsecaller."

"You are right, but a slight detour is necessary so that we can reach her sooner. We go to Siblan. You have heard of it?"

The boy's eyes grew large. His color had begun to improve, but now it drained away. "The city of the dead?"

301

"The same."

They walked in silence for several paces.

"Will we see them?"

Leinos smiled for the first time in days. "Perhaps, but I hope we are not there long enough for that. We go to visit Kadre, cousin to Queen Naele, and his guardian, Pagajera. She can help us contact the sages. If they deign to send help, we will be in the Bitter Reaches by dawn."

"But how? How can we travel so far so fast?"

Leinos put his hand on the boy's shoulder. "The sages have a way. They can take us, though it is rare. And we will need rare courage to travel with them." He ruffled Malek's hair. "But you are a young man of exceptional valor. And I know you will do anything for Lauren."

The boy's brows drew together in concentration. "And for Pindar."

"And for Pindar," he said with a final pat to Malek's back. The thought of seeing Lauren soon sent a cheerful surge through him, banishing the head pain. The boy must have felt it too.

They broke into a run.

They reached the outskirts of Siblan as the gray day dissolved into night. No torches lit the gates, nor did any guards greet them or request to know their business. Leinos hoped security had not become this lax in Lerom. A brief pang of guilt speared him. He should be in Lerom. But the queen had made her choice. She was on her own. At least until they had the horses. He shook off the regret.

Siblan was not as large as the capital, and probably too far east to worry about attack—not to mention being hard on the sea, and few wished for such proximity to the unnamed dead—but seeing it so vulnerable, especially at night, made him uneasy.

He put his arm around Malek's shoulders and drew him closer as they made their way through the quiet streets. In the past, it would have taken at least half a hand to gain the city center where Kadre lived; the streets used to be full of farmers selling food, shopkeepers hawking their wares, traders from all over. That was before the river dried up. Before the farmers had scarcely enough to feed themselves, the shopkeepers could no longer restock their shelves, and traders had nothing to trade.

The occasional murmur of hushed voices floated through upstairs windows, but otherwise, it was as though the sea itself had washed the place clean, leaving behind only whispers.

At Kadre's door, Leinos lifted the heavy knocker. Before he could let it drop, the stout door swung in, Pagajera's arm shot out, scooped them inside, stopped the knocker from falling, and silently closed the door.

The guardian pulled him into a tight hug. "Leinos, how good it is to see you!" She patted his back with a commitment that took his breath, then held him at arm's length, a wide grin splitting her ever-cheerful face.

"And who is this?" She glanced at Malek but did not wait for an answer. "Last we heard, you had gone to the Ravery with the hag of hags and one of the graybeards on some fool's desperate errand to— "

She must have finally read the pressing need in his face. It was unusual for Pags to pause for breath, let alone stop mid-sentence. Malek looked at the woman in shock. He had probably never heard sages or crones spoken of with anything but the utmost respect.

"By the goddess," she continued. "You have been disrequired. And look like you have been swimming with the dead. What has happened?"

"Malek," Leinos said. "Meet Pagajera. She believes it her job to stir the dirt at your feet until dust so clogs your nose and fills your eyes, you can neither breathe nor see."

The boy only nodded slowly, keeping his wondering gaze on the tall woman's round face.

Then, to answer her impatient look, Leinos said, "We need to talk."

Pagajera ushered them through the large house to a room at the back, where she roused Kadre from a doze before a cold fireplace. He greeted them in much the same manner as she had, but in blessed silence. Pags summoned a maid who brought them warm food and drinks, but the guardian would not allow Leinos to explain until they were alone.

Kadre commented on his condition as well. "Have you been wrestling the goddess, my friend? I have seen you bruised and cut before, but never so troubled."

Leinos started at the beginning, when Lauren burst through the Ravery, for his friends had not received any news in many days. Kadre shook his head mournfully to hear of his cousin's actions.

"She ever was more fearful than bold," he said. "But

you already know that is why, as much as anything, I left the court at Lerom."

"Cirq without Supreme Guardian. This does not bode well," Pags said.

"Cirq has a Horsecaller once again," Leinos said. "Our beloved country no longer has need of Supreme Guardian."

Pags and Kadre nodded.

"But can it be true?" Pags asked after emptying her mug of tea. "That the sage in Tinnis has turned his power to evil? This has never happened before."

"Most likely," Kadre said, "he does not think of his actions as bad, but serving a higher good."

"Bah," Pags scoffed. "This Rezol only wants power. And King Rast is merely his instrument. Surely the other gray beards can stop him?"

Leinos rested his elbows on his knees. "All the sages sit in council now at Elaz to determine the best action."

"But that could take—"

Kadre laid a gentle hand on his Guardian's arm. The gesture communicated great affection even while it stayed her enthusiasm. "Leinos needs you to summon a sage, now, Pags. He must get to the Bitter Reaches."

Less than a hand later, Pags returned from another room where she had gone for privacy. Leinos noticed a hint of apprehension in her eyes, but she schooled her features quickly, smiling reassurance.

"I do not know how long it will be. You should rest, and with your permission, I will tend your wounds. Let me take you to your rooms."

Leinos rose, feeling fatigue as he never would have when Supreme Guardian. Malek had fallen asleep against his shoulder, and he lifted the boy into his arms to carry him upstairs. He nodded to Kadre.

"Your help and hospitality are greatly appreciated, Kadre. I am sorry to have brought news that saddened you."

Kadre rose as well. "On the contrary, old friend, you bring hope to this home. Now, go. I will rouse you the moment the sage arrives."

Pags had already sprinted ahead. The woman always had energy to spare. Leinos could find his way in the dark. He knew the house well. As he turned the corner into the hall, an older man emerged from the shadows. Leinos did not recognize him, and he knew most everyone left in Cirq. But Kadre had connections in many countries, and travelers often found their way to his door. Had Kadre been female, he would be queen. It struck Leinos that if the Horsecaller could be a woman, then why could Cirq's ruler not be a man?

But this was a theory best left to an unencumbered walking day. He hoisted the boy against his chest and nodded to the stranger. He would have continued to the upper level, but there was something about the man's eyes, even in the dark, and even without the heightened senses of Supreme Guardian, that made him pause.

"My lord," the stranger said in a foreign accent, "a word if you please."

... 30 ...

QUEEN NAELE paused in her pacing. She had caught herself treading this same path in her tower more and more since returning from the Inn at the Crossroads, barely escaping death on one of her own thoroughfares. To think it had come to this. The queen not safe to travel her own land.

The hard stone floor beneath her feet showed no sign of wear, but her back ached, and her legs were tired. She allowed herself to drop into her chair in an undignified heap. A distinctly un-queen-like heap.

Perhaps she should practice this, add the frivolous and superfluous into her life. For soon, one way or the other, by design or force, she would be disrequired.

The idea thrilled and frightened her in equal measure. In thirteen days, a delegation of Derrien lords would descend upon Lerom expecting her to hand them the reins of power.

In exchange, she would have a well-deserved retirement in an obscure cottage somewhere off the southern Derrien coast. Somewhere near the place of Pirron's

307

birth, alongside the harbor and ships he loved so well. It would be quiet. And warm.

A few knew of the plan. Her chancellor, Seyah, here in Lerom, who likely saw opportunity for herself in the change. And Marzak, although he had not approved. She had told Leinos when arguing with him about the Horsecaller, and he had surely told his guardians. But she had not revealed the whole of the agreement. They thought the Derriens came to take control of Cirq's southern ports. Not the entire country.

If the horses magically appeared before then—she had made sure there was no possibility—then she had no doubt Cirq's people would gather behind the Horsecaller and rise against their faithless queen. But that was only if the Horsecaller did not kill her first. And who could blame the Raver for that?

Especially after the Tinnisian raid that deprived them both of Leinos forever. Regrettable, losing both him and the boy. She pressed her hands against her face. It was chilled. And dry. No tears for her. Yet, these losses were more than regrettable, were she honest. He had been a good man, Leinos, a dedicated guardian of Cirq, and in the end, more loyal and steadfast than she.

She had expected nothing from him as consort, they had both understood that. But she had hoped the boy would come to love her, and she would not be alone in her self-imposed exile. Futile, this line of thinking. Self-indulgent. And fantasy. Leinos would have fought the Derriens when they came, and others would have joined him. Cirqians were independent to the core. Leinos's love and loyalty lay with his country, not with her. The moment he learned she had betrayed them—even it was for the best—he would have turned against her.

Queen Naele lifted a cup of cold tea to equally cold lips. But she did not like to see how much her once-steady hands shook, so she put it down, sloshing some on the tabletop.

She could see him—Leinos—surrounded by Tinnisian warriors, fighting to the death. Saw again the blow that felled him.

It was just as well. If it took the rest of her miserable life, she would convince herself it was just as well.

~~~

Lauren rolled to her back, sharp pain shooting from her left hip over her tailbone. She was done.

How much was one not-so-young-anymore woman supposed to do? She'd tried. Tried to believe, tried to overcome her fear, tried to keep going in the face of mounting evidence that everyone in this godforsaken place was wrong. Enough was enough. Even her horse had dumped her.

But as she lay there, she realized she was comfortable, other than the throbbing pain in her hip. The rain and hail of a few moments before had stopped. And the pain, at least, was familiar. She even knew what the bruise would look like, how it would blossom over the joint like a giant chrysanthemum and spread down her thigh, first purple and blue, later green and yellow.

The injury, though not severe, would make her arthritis flare, and she wished for an ice pack. That arthritis, however, had not bothered her after the first couple of days in Cirq, probably the result of constant movement rather than sitting at a desk.

The ground beneath her was soft and dry, a deep pine needle bed that smelled like Leinos. Sweet goddess, she missed him. She would stay right here, she decided, and wallow in self pity. The trees were so dense, the storm couldn't penetrate. Thunder made itself felt, rumbling just outside her haven. Inside, the air was warm and still. She closed her eyes and slept.

Pindar hadn't abandoned her. His questing muzzle worked its way along her side, pausing at the injured hip, nostrils flaring hotly with each breath, then continuing until he found her face. He lipped her forehead and cheek, whiskers tickling. Horse kisses.

The reins were hooked over his right ear. Gently, she took them down so he wouldn't get a foot tangled, and stroked his ears, soothing herself and reassuring him she was all right. He nibbled the edge of her cloak, then carefully took it in his teeth and pulled.

"No, thank you."

He pulled again, harder, lifting her shoulders. All around, branches hemmed them tightly, yet, when they moved, there was plenty of room. She pried his teeth off her cloak.

"Easy there," she said. He peered at her, his deep brown eyes questioning. "I'm okay. Just need a few minutes."

Lauren lifted herself onto one elbow. The light inside the forest had changed slightly, and the air felt different.

It was morning, she realized. She had slept the night right where she'd fallen. Behind Pindar, large trees like those in Raverwood strode into the forest, their branches beginning high up, well over Lauren's head, even if she were in the saddle. Around her and Pindar were mostly smaller trees she could encircle with two hands, their close-set branches starting at ground level, forming an impenetrable barrier.

Absently, she waved a hand in front of her face. "I like it here." Pindar swished his tail. Then, she realized what she'd just done, what he'd done. "Was that a fly?"

She hadn't missed the irritating pests, but it wasn't normal, even in Cirq. Their presence in this sheltered place could mean only one thing. She waited, holding her breath, listening intently.

There, a buzzing past her ear. She swiped at it with a grin. Never before had she been happy for the presence of a pesky fly.

With a groan and the help of a nearby trunk, she hoisted herself up. "Let's get this show on the road."

Before mounting, she loosened the girth and checked beneath the fleece saddle pad, smoothing his coat and making sure there was nothing that would cause him discomfort, then resettled the saddle. Pindar stood while she mounted, her left hip complaining at the strain.

Trees and branches parted. She didn't see them move, they just kind of dissolved momentarily. When she looked behind, they had closed in, once again solid forms. Their path was marked by new shoots of grass and clumps of tiny white flowers with broad green leaves. These, she realized, were the leaves Pindar had brought her. How long had he spent carefully picking around the flowers?

Soon, they were away from the dense part of the wood, but the trees still stood tightly together, as if in tender embrace. Pindar walked slowly, reverently, silent on the spongey ground, and the trees opened their arms, gathering horse and rider into a warm hug.

The wood emanated its own soft light as well, for although she knew the sun was up outside the forest, its light did not penetrate the dense canopy. Yet she had no trouble seeing where they were going. Pindar had his head. The way was not obvious, but he continued as if there were an open road in front of them, and she was content to let him choose.

They walked for a long time. She felt safe, comforted, and the wood showed no signs of thinning or ending. The level of brightness never changed, and no breeze moved the stiff branches. It was as though the place were in a state of suspended animation.

Nor was there any evidence here of horses. But they had to be near for this place to be so alive. Is this what all of Cirq had once been like? Small wonder the people clung to the desperate hope of regaining their former lives and had gone so far as to send someone through the unknown of the Ravery to fetch her. Well worth the risk.

If it panned out.

She couldn't allow new doubt to creep in at this point. No, they had to keep going. As of tomorrow, she had thirteen days left to deliver Cirq's horses.

Not that anyone would come and fetch her from here

for execution. But nice as it was, she couldn't stay in this lonely place forever, either. If there was any chance of being reunited with Leinos and Malek, she had no choice. She had to press on.

But first, they needed a break. Her water skin was empty, and Pindar had to be thirsty, too. She pulled him to halt and slid to the ground, then undid the saddle, set it down, and slipped off his bridle. He nosed her side, but she hadn't had treats for him in a while. With a whispered sorry, she pulled out a brush and worked it through his coat, pushing away the damp where the saddle had left its mark, then patted him on the rump.

"Go on, find us something to drink." He walked off, and she went to pick leaves to eat.

Shortly, he dug a hole, and she went over to wash up and make a cold pack for her hip. As she wrung out her spare shirt, Pindar lifted his head and became transfixed, the only sound water dripping from his chin down to the spreading pool at their feet.

A prickle ran up Lauren's spine, and she had the distinct impression someone watched them. No underbrush impeded her view, and the steady glow didn't create shadows. Which meant something had just scooted from one giant tree to another.

To her right came a cough, like the huffing of lions at the zoo.

"Who's there?"

No answer.

They had to get the tack.

She hooked one finger under Pindar's jaw and tilted her

head to indicate that direction, and they began to move.

A form darted between two trees, a creature low to the ground, not human, not equine. She decided to make a dash for their supplies. She almost made it.

Halfway, a root caught her toe and she sprawled on the ground, flung nearly to her goal, her forehead painfully smacking a rock. Without thinking, she flipped to her back, stave at the ready, but nothing assaulted her. Moisture seeped into her eye, and she tried to flick away the nervous sweat, but it persisted. She rubbed at it, and her fingers came back bloody.

She blotted it with her sleeve, and the cough sounded again, this time near Pindar. She spun. He pricked his ears, but didn't look worried, only curious.

Not the evil flying bird-men. She forced herself to her feet, overcame a moment of dizziness, ditched the stave, grabbed the bridle, and covered the distance between her and Pindar at a sprint. She leaned against his flank, letting his steady breaths calm her.

Next to them, the surface of a fallen tree was shredded into strips, as if a very large cat had repeatedly cleaned her claws there. Lauren had no intention of waiting around to see what had made that mark. The huffing sounded again, closer, and from more than one direction. She looked longingly at her saddle and pack, hopped up on the mangled trunk and slid her leg over Pindar's bare back. He was already moving away as she gathered the reins.

A step of trot, then canter. The forest melted before them but shadows kept pace to either side. She couldn't make out what they were. Heart in her throat, Lauren sank into Pindar, her body fusing with his as again he flattened into gallop. They wove through the darkening wood like that for minutes, hours, until she no longer felt her legs. And still, the creatures stayed with them. How long could they keep this up?

Just when she thought they'd have to stop to face the threat, everything changed. The wood ended as abruptly as it had started. The ground dropped away. They hurtled into blackness.

Pindar jammed his feet into the ground and tried to halt. Momentum threw Lauren over his head. Down and down and a hard thud that knocked her breath away. Pindar scrambled above her, trying not to go over the cliff. She hung from the reins with two fingers. His feet scuffled back, kicking dirt and gravel into her face. An anguished cry, hers, or his, or both. Her feet found no purchase. His eyes—she could just see them—wild with panic. He couldn't get his balance. He couldn't pull himself back, and her too.

And she wouldn't pull him over.

"Okay. It's okay," she yelled, and hoped he understood.

Then, she let go.

~~~

Leinos assessed the stranger, still in shadow. He was neither tall nor short, heavy nor thin. The kind of man who could pass for anyone, blend into a crowd, or disappear entirely if he wished. "I am no lord," Leinos told him.

"Aye, well, you've that look about you, just the same." He stepped forward. "They call me Dan, just Dan."

"I am Leinos, Suprem—" he caught himself. "Just Leinos."

Pagajera came to the head of the stairs with the lantern. In the sudden light, the man's eyes showed clearly. Deep blue-green as the sea, heavy-lidded, with a placid surface that hid unknowns in the depths.

"I see you have met Dan," Pags said. "He likes a tall tale, and we have no time for that tonight." She came down to stand on the step above Leinos, making her seem even taller than she was.

"But I must speak to him, you great monster of a woman." Dan sliced the air with his hand. "He'll believe me where you scoff."

Pags looked thoughtful a moment. "That he might, after what he just told us."

"Didn't I already hear all that?" he asked. "It's exactly why we must talk."

"Listening at keyholes again old man?" Pags shot back.

"And how'm I to know what's going on otherwise?" He said this with a shrug and a wink that made the woman's face contort with the effort to contain her smile.

"Give me the boy," she said to Leinos, "I will put him abed." Leinos shifted Malek into her arms, and Pags returned her gaze to Dan. "If Leinos allows, you can chew his ear off, as you like to say, while I tend his wounds. You can see he is near dead on his feet."

Leinos nodded to Dan, and they went up the stairs together. Whatever else the man might be, if he could call Kadre's guardian a *great monster of a woman* without being flattened, then he must be a trusted friend. There was something about the man's speech pattern that bothered him, but he could not put his finger on it. He was tired and let it go for the time being.

"The boy," Dan asked, "is he yours?"

"No. He apprenticed himself to the Horsecaller, and I believe him to be a horse healer. I need to get him to the Bitter Reaches. His parents live at Raver's Keep."

"Ah yes, Raver's Keep. I collect this is near the place you found your Horsecaller?"

Leinos nodded.

"I have a boy, myself," Rab continued. "All grown now, he'd be. Probably with a family of his own. Not seen him for an age, though."

Leinos had traveled the far borders of Derr once, and even crossed the boundary into southern Tinnis. He did not know what lay beyond those countries, but whatever was there, it must be where this man came from, for he neither spoke nor looked like anyone he had ever met. Now he could see Dan, he knew that he would stick out in a crowd with his thick hair the color of dried blood and light, freckled complexion.

They reached the first landing where a door stood open to the room Leinos used when visiting Kadre. Pags had Malek tucked into a fur in the corner, reserving the small bed for him, and if he did not already have many reasons to be thankful to the woman, this small favor would keep him forever in her debt. But added to that, a deep, steaming tub waited in the middle of the room, and he wasted no time getting his sore bones into it.

"Ah, look at your beautiful body all banged up," Dan

said. "Your Horsecaller lady won't like to see you in such a way."

Leinos looked at the man sharply. There had been nothing in the story he told Kadre and Pagajera about his feelings for Lauren.

Pags crouched behind Leinos to inspect the head wound. "It is this vast crease a Tinnisian sword laid above your neck that worries me," she said, cleansing the cut. "You are lucky to still have all your hair, not to mention your scalp and everything else above your ears."

Leinos winced and ignored them both, too weak with relief to wonder or argue, but after a few moments' soak, he managed a tired smile. "The goddess still has use for me."

"As do I," Dan said, and then he began to explain.

A hand later, gashes and bruises bandaged and soothed, lying on the bed with a full stomach and in clean clothes, Leinos mused the world could not get any more unusual. Lauren would call it weird, and he longed to see her face when he told her. "If what you say is true—"

"Can you doubt me?"

"Your story is hard to believe, but I do not doubt you. We must find a way to bring you to the Bitter Reaches. If the sage cannot transport us all, you must leave immediately on foot. Can you do that?" Leinos looked from Dan to Pagajera who sat staring into the small fire. Kadre had joined them as well.

"We will all go," Kadre said.

Pags looked up, listening. "He is here," she said. "They are here." She ran out and down the stairs, returning shortly with not one, but two sages, one of them Vraz.

"Truly, Leinos," he said. "I hardly expected to find you lying down at this juncture."

"Leave it, Vraz," Kadre said, his voice quiet but full of warning. "Can you not see he was nearly killed by Tinnisians? And those sent by one of your own?"

Vraz turned his razor gaze to Kadre, nostrils flared, and Leinos raised a quelling hand before either of them acted. "Do not argue." They both looked startled. He may not be Supreme Guardian, but his voice still carried authority. "What news, Vraz?"

"Can you travel?" he asked by way of answer.

Leinos sat up and gave a curt nod. "Of course."

"Then we leave at once. Rezol has sent men and yekerk to the Bitter Reaches. He means to have the horses. With, or without, the Horsecaller."

... 31 ...

LAUREN FLOATED in a place of airy serenity neither light nor dark, between wakefulness and slumber, with the distant buzz of locusts, hiss of frying hamburgers, or hum of conversation sounding in her ears. Her edges felt blurry, blending with the surrounding murk and the shadows moving in the periphery.

One figure could be The All, gracefully gliding, her river hair cascading in her wake, arms outstretched, light streaming between slender fingers.

With her, a man, slight and wiry, prancing like an excited Arabian stallion. Nearby, a bent old woman watched and waited, tired, but content to bide her time.

Lauren sensed them, but could not clearly see.

All around, larger shapes moved, circling. They reminded her of something. A task to complete, a place to go, or a person who needed her, but she couldn't pin it down, rouse herself, or speak.

The shapes moved faster, creating a dizzying vortex.

The old woman nodded.

A voice came to Lauren, a whisper in her mind.

Stillness, it said, *stillness is the ultimate discipline.*

~~~

Leinos held Malek tight to his chest. The boy's lips were clamped between his teeth, and Leinos smiled assurance he did not feel.

"Close your eyes and hold on," Vraz said.

They did as the sage commanded, and he drew his cloak around them. Then, they plummeted into swift darkness like tipping head first down an endless well.

Black earth split before them, but only barely, and not without complaint. Rocks and soil scraped their elbows, accompanied by fractured groaning. The ground, used to permitting a single sage to pass did not like stretching to allow for cargo.

They moved quickly, at first, the din a roar in his ears, and he imagined this is what being dragged by a galloping horse would feel like. Clamping his jaw tight, he tried to make himself smaller, then realized it was not his will that forced the air from his lungs, but the soil around them, squeezing, hampering their progress.

He tried yelling to Vraz. "What—"

"Do not speak!"

The sage's voice came as if over great distance. But they were still chest-to-chest, and Leinos felt Vraz's expand and contract violently, like the bellows of a forge. The effort made them burst forward, but only for a moment.

They slowed again, until Leinos knew he could make

the Bitter Reaches sooner on hands and knees. He would crawl to Lauren if he had to, and, as they nearly stopped, he wished with his entire being for the chance.

~~~

Firm ground beneath her and the scent of sun-warmed earth—rich dirt and lush grass—in the air. Not the last place she'd slept, not the soft bed of dry pine needles.

Lauren wriggled shoulders and hips, testing for discomfort. She remembered her deep sleep amongst the pungent evergreens. Mentally, she retraced her steps. She'd been knocked off Pindar's back and fallen hard on her hip. She moved that part of her anatomy again, more forcefully, expecting the sharp hurt of recent injury. Instead, what she got was the slight twinge of an old, healed bruise.

Carefully, she lifted one hand to probe her forehead, recalling the frightening shadows of the wood and their mad dash to escape. There was a bump and a small, itchy scab. Again, not what she expected.

Pindar! He'd made it a habit of always being near, but— she opened her eyes and sat, all at once aware of the sound that had been niggling in the back of her mind, a sound so much a part of her that it hadn't even registered.

Horses.

They grazed peacefully, making steady tear, tear, tear sounds as they cropped grass. Hundreds—thousands— legs solid as tree trunks, bodies substantial, flowing tails swishing flies, wavy manes flouncing arched necks.

Their colors varied from the shimmering silver of dawn to the simmering blue-black of dusk, from white chocolate to dark, from new copper to rusted iron. The most stunning sight she'd ever seen.

She stared at them in wonder. She'd found them!

But where was Pindar? She tried to whistle, but her lips were too chapped. The rest of her senses came on line, and she noticed her clothes were damp, her socks squishy inside her boots. She lay next to a river under a line of white trees lining the bank, and hard on the other side, a sandy bluff rose a good seventy-five feet straight up.

Had she fallen down that? She had no memory of landing, but she must have splashed down in the river, then somehow gotten herself to the opposite bank.

Or been brought.

She scanned the herd. Could one of them have hauled her out of the drink?

She eyed the cliff again, remembering Pindar's desperate scramble to keep from going over. Nausea roiled through her. Had he slipped over the edge? Or was he still up there, battling whatever demons had been chasing them? She swallowed, fighting down the urge to be ill, and pushed to her feet.

As if one, all the horses lifted their heads to look at her.

"Pindar?" she croaked. Her throat was parched and sore. She scooted down to the water and drank, frantically searching the opposite bank for any sign of the big gray. Fear wrapped steel-banded hands around her belly. Swallowing and clearing her throat, she tried again. This time, her voice came out louder, if not clearer.

"Pindar!"

Lauren climbed the bank to the field. The horses watched, big eyes curious, downy nostrils quivering. She jumped in the air, trying to see over their backs, surprised that not one part of her body protested. How long had she been lying there? She had vague impressions of dreams. Or had it been real? Had The All been here?

A frustrated sob welled up from her depths. "Please," she yelled to whoever might hear. "Help me."

Should she look for him with the herd or try to climb the bluff and seek him up there in the dense and mysterious wood? She couldn't just stand here doing nothing. But which way? A few steps forward. The horses sidled back. Not frightened, just giving her room. She stumbled, her feet numb inside the soaking wet boots, so she took a moment to jerk them off, and her socks.

The sun warmed the air, and the sky became an unending expanse of blue. Horses milled, watchful, ready to flee if threatened. They could stampede at any moment —their energy and excitement percolated through her— but they wouldn't hurt her, of this she was sure. She reached out, and a bay mare stretched forward to sniff her fingers. They were large, most taller than Pindar by several inches and equally broad. Shaggy winter coats clung, but here and there, shiny summer color showed through.

She stepped closer to the mare, instinctively drawn to her. "Do you know where he is?" Lauren whispered. She slid her hand up the bay's neck and under her mane. The mare made a sound, a long grunt that could have meant yes or no or nothing. And yet Lauren felt reassured.

A distinctive high-pitched stallion scream echoed down the valley. She whipped around in time to see a ripple coming through the herd. Beneath her bare feet, the ground shook, drumming hoofbeats reverberating through the soles.

The herd parted, and she saw him. Pindar had shed the bridle and looked both smugly triumphant and larger then ever as he barreled straight for her, galloping playfully with his tail high and head moving from side to side like a king acknowledging his subjects.

Lauren swiped at tears she hadn't even noticed and smiled. He slid to a stop before her and immediately bent to sniff her hands, her chest, her neck and face, making soft wuffling sounds the entire time. Finally, he rested his chin on her shoulder for a few moments before swinging toward the others, moving them away from her.

She laughed at him. She had never been possessed by a horse, and she liked it.

Or perhaps it had always been so, and she'd been too dense to realize. It dawned on her that it might be she who had changed when they came through the Ravery, not Pindar. Had he always been the same, living a life that had not left open the opportunity to show his true self? Had she simply been blind to his magnificence?

It was possible. With her head down most of the time, keeping a low profile, always busy with work and in a hurry, she'd probably missed a lot. No longer. She wrapped her arms around Pindar's neck and hugged him tightly. Elation rose in her chest like an expanding balloon. She released him and walked amongst the horses, hands roving over backs and sides, down sleek necks, ruffling tangled manes, assuring herself they were real.

She assessed health and soundness. They were in good flesh—even coming off winter—and a number of bellies bulged with new life. Eyes bright, nostrils clean, coats shiny. Their feet were large and round and showed little cracking. Conformation-wise, they were all of a type—not slight animals made for racing over turf or jumping man-made obstacles—but heavy horses who's every hoof beat would draw thunder from the ground, densely-muscled horses with substantial bone and deep girths who could carry or pull significant loads.

Thick necks tied into broad chests. Sloping shoulders led to well-sprung ribcages. Short backs connected to round quarters. Yet, like all horses, they possessed an innate grace that enabled them to float over the ground when they trotted, to take a watcher's breath when they arched their necks and pranced, to shift their weight and wheel so quickly one could not be sure they moved at all.

The question remained, how to get them over the mountain? Would they follow her and Pindar?

Pindar's familiar stallion squeal reached her then, and she saw him dancing with a dun mare. The girl held her tail out, obviously in season. Lauren smiled, but a bright streak in her peripheral vision caught her attention. Another stallion galloped over with his head low, ears flat. Pindar never saw what hit him, and her warning shout dissolved in a resounding thud as the larger horse broadsided Pindar, knocking him off his feet. He recovered and sunk his teeth into the other's neck, drawing blood.

"Stop," she shouted, wondering at the same time what good it would do. The two horses circled each other for a moment, catching their breath. The bay mare had stayed at her side.

Pushing past the happy earthy scent of the horses came a smell she shuddered to recognize. Horses quieted, even the stallions, and she listened. Rocks falling, sliding. She moved to the mare's flank, crouched to look under her belly.

Through a break in the trees, she saw a group of twenty men skidding down the bluff accompanied by twice that number of yekerk, half flying, half hopping toward the river.

She kept pace with the horses as they shuffled back, her heart pummeling her ribs. Warm bodies closed around her. She clung to the mare's mane, trying to think.

"There is no need to hide, Horsecaller," yelled an unfamiliar masculine voice laced with false friendliness.

She stayed with the herd, catching a glimpse of the men as they uncoiled long ropes.

"Thank you for guiding us to the horses," the man said. "Now, you will all accompany us."

Lauren had to get to Pindar, get on him. She could see the man's legs, and he seemed to know where she was. Without taking his dark gaze from where she hid, he gestured to his men, and they to crossed the river and began shooing the herd. The horses trotted around, raising dust. She almost laughed. What made them think a handful of them could control so many horses?

What made her think she could?

"Who are you?" she yelled, thinking to buy herself time. She had no weapons, no way of defending herself, not even shoes on her feet.

"A friend of a friend, Horsecaller. A friend who needs you and your herd, and who can reward you for your help."

She didn't like the way he said her title, with a caress, as if he owned it.

"As you wish," he said, and his tone made her look. He loaded a crossbow and took aim, but not at her. "Your horse first."

She spun in fear. *Run. Run over the mountain.*

The horses didn't move, damn them. What would it take? What was the secret? She'd have to figure it out, and soon, because she'd be damned if she'd let someone take the horses from her now.

Before the man could shoot, a deep-throated horse peal came from behind her, then a shriek torn from human throat. She dove, scooted between bodies, risking a glance now and again behind her. The herd began to go the way she wanted—toward the pass through the mountains. Good, good. But bird-men flew above and landed in front, cutting off escape.

The man swore. Horses trotted in circles, reflecting her unease and confusion. Should they try to run the other way? She backed and grabbed at a tail as horses reversed, then stopped.

Men stood behind the herd unfurling ropes and swinging them toward Pindar. They were trapped. Two lassos missed, but one dropped around his neck, pulled tight. His head jerked up and swung wildly as he tried to free himself, dragging the man. Others grabbed on and one got another rope over his head. Pindar's eyes rolled, the whites showing.

They yanked him to the ground. Yekerk closed in. She pushed horses out of her way, couldn't see what was happening, only heard the men grunting and Pindar struggling, a hoof connecting with a man's skull.

"No!" she screamed.

Then, a rushing sound, growling. She got free of the horses in time to see three frits tear apart two yekerk and disappear as quickly as they had come.

She flung all her weight at the nearest man, catching him in the shoulder and knocking them both off balance. She stumbled to her knees. Someone slammed her head into the ground. She blinked, fighting to stay conscious. The man she had hit came into focus, murder in his eyes. He pinned her arms.She kicked with both legs, catching him in the knee and groin. He howled and his face contorted with anger, but he leaned close, drew a knife.

For a moment, she froze, her gaze riveted by the flashing blade. They still hadn't gotten her legs. She flailed and twisted, got one arm free, scrabbled toward horse. The ropes were too tight around his neck. He couldn't breathe. Her assailant grabbed her foot as she got her hand on a sword. He hauled her back, flipped her over, slid the knife toward her throat.

She raised the sword. With a thud, her attacker fell away. A bruising hand wrapped her upper arm and jerked her to her feet. The leader kicked the others aside.

"Fools," he said. "We need her."

With his face dark with dirt and rage, she registered only his full lips under a neat mustache. Humor might have formed the lines around his eyes, but it was a cruel humor, the brown eyes themselves cold and flat.

He pointed the loaded crossbow at Pindar, but kept his gaze on her. "Northwest," he said.

Northwest. Tinnis. King Rast and his sage, Rezol.

Not on her life. "No," she said.

He yelled orders, and the men holding Pindar moved, loosing their hold as the leader took his shot. She shoved his arms. The arrow went high, skimming the heavy muscle of Pindar's hip. She threw herself at the big gray. Horses started running. But all she could see was Pindar, on the ground, struggling, bleeding. Men rushed by her, except one still trying to hold her horse. Lauren chopped at the ropes with the sword, but Pindar caught his breath, jumped up, and bolted with the rest of the herd.

Lauren tried to keep up, but she tripped and fell, curled into a ball, and covered her head, screaming inwardly.

How could this be happening? Horses thundered by and over her, the ground shook, and dust clogged her nostrils. She realized they weren't going to hurt her, so she rolled to her feet and shot after them. Soon, the last of them passed her, entering one of the canyons on the other side of the valley. Alone, she stopped and tried to think. Where were the men? Surely, the yekerk had flown ahead with the horses, she could still hear their cries, and she remembered Leinos saying they had a taste for horse blood.

The group's leader ran along the river bank until two of the flying bird-men picked him up. They lifted him off the ground and flew on toward the horses.

Then she saw something that made her skin crawl.

"Holy hell."

One pair flew straight at her.

... 32 ...

LAUREN WHEELED and ran, blind with panic. But that direction took her from the horses—from Pindar. The fastest way to reach them was with the revolting creatures. Could she let them take her?

The stench of burning tires choked her as they got closer. She tried to remain still, but as they closed in, her heart ceased beating, and she threw herself on the ground, yelling *no no no*. Feathers brushed her skin, talons grabbed at her, orange eyes glowed. She squeezed her lids shut against the sight.

A squishy, ratchety sound made her open her eyes. One bird had retracted its wings and brought out its spindly arms. It stood on her knees and held her shoulders while the other wrapped its long toes around her upper arm. The first one's wings came out again and it, too, got hold of her arm. Her breath gusted in and out on a harsh whine. She gritted her teeth, and they lifted her off the ground.

They flapped their wings once, twice, again.

A blur of golden fur and snarling growls erupted out of the dusty haze. Three frits slammed into the yekerk, and ruddy feathers exploded into the air. They brought the birds down in a whoosh. The drop knocked the wind out of her, and she wrapped her arms around her head against the sound of breaking bones and dying shrieks and the pounding of her own heart.

Moments later, only the faint whistle of her breath and the panting of the frits. One sniffed her chin, then licked her cheek. She opened her eyes. It pricked its ears and wagged its stubby tail, but she wasn't ready to smile. Around them lay the smelly remains of the two yekerk. Their vile stink made her retch.

The dry heaves wrung her out. She flopped onto her back, the nearest frit bathing her face with a moist cloud of only marginally better smelling air. She raised her hand and patted the beast's shoulder. Its golden coat was surprisingly soft. She let her fingers comb the stiffer rough around its neck. She should be afraid, but they were so friendly, so dog-like, and she really didn't have the energy to dredge up fear at this point.

"Good job," she said. "Thanks."

It nudged her side.

"No, I'm done," she said to the sky, or the frit, or whoever might be listening. "Really done this time. I tried, I failed. Not the first time. But maybe the last."

The other two frits sat nearby. One scratched its neck. The other got up and urinated on a dead yekerk. The one nearest her poked its nose into her hip and swung its big head around to its side. It wanted her to get on?

"Nope. No way."

The bile of utter failure stung her throat. She released a blustery sigh, her heart finally slowing to a more steady tempo, and considered the frit's humped back. It watched her expectantly.

Leinos's words from their first day returned to her. What if Cirq truly was her home? Had she been born in the wrong place? No, she had to live where she had, for how else would she have learned what she needed to know about horses?

The horses needed her help. Reluctantly, resignedly, she reached for the creature's mane and pulled herself up. If nothing else, she had to find Pindar.

Without urging, the frit leapt forward. Its stubby legs and steep shoulders made for a gait that was like riding a runaway sewing machine. The other two fell in alongside. She sought the beast's rhythm, kept her fingers twined in its rough, and tried to see ahead.

They slowed as they approached the narrow entrance to a canyon. She slid off to climb up onto a ledge where she could see better, adrenaline making her legs shake. The frits scaled the steep, crumbling rock face like mountain goats, continuing to the top. Sharp stones cut into the tender bottoms of her feet, but she ignored it, drawing strength and comfort from knowing the frits were nearby. Were there more? She hoped so.

Below, the horses churned up a choking cloud of dust. She could barely make out Pindar. He stood with his back left leg off the ground, the arrow wound seeping blood.

One rope still hung around his neck. When one of Rast's men walked close, Pindar bit him on the shoulder. His unflagging spirit lifted her heart. Relief washed through her.

She tried to think. Men chased the horses toward the far side of the canyon. A tiny cleft opened at the west end.

Don't go. Fight back.

In response to her silent plea, horses returned to the canyon opening beneath her, but bird-men flew into the entrance, so the herd trotted in a circle.

A scraping sound made her whip around.

She met the menacing eyes of the attackers' leader. He stood at the other end of the ledge, a few short feet away, and looked even bigger and more dangerous than he had down on the plain. She took in more details of his appearance. A yellow and orange kilt had been smudged to brown and his leather vest and boots were scuffed. His hair lay plastered to his forehead with sweat and dirt. He leaned against the rock, smiled, and waved a sword at her.

"Who are you?" she asked again with more defiance then she felt.

"What matters," he said, "is who I represent—someone with a keen interest in the great strength of these horses. You value their lives, if not your own, so I know you will do what you must to direct them the way I order."

He moved close enough to touch her cheek with the sword point. She pulled back and felt her lip curl into a snarl. This man had shot her horse. But her effort was wasted. His attention was taken by the scene below, where bird-men howled, and horses dodged back and forth, eyes wide with fear.

Their power reverberated through the surrounding rock, their sacred hooves making the earth tremble. Stones and dirt clattered around Lauren's head. Shouts drifted up. The yekerk might frighten the horses into moving, but the men couldn't control the herd.

Could she? Maybe not. But this man didn't need to know that. He didn't need to know how close she'd just come to giving up. And he didn't know the power contained within the horses, the power to make a land live or die, to draw water from dust, or to make a mountain shake.

"I won't direct the horses anywhere but Cirq."

He tilted his head to one side, returning his gaze to her, then stepped closer. "I think you will."

The mountain vibrated. Cracks formed where ledge and canyon wall met. Better to be gutted where she stood, than give up the horses. Without her, he had nothing. Cirq wouldn't have them, but neither would Tinnis.

She backed away, feeling for anything to grab if the ground gave way. What to do? Her thoughts were as chaotic as the scene below. Then, her hand found Jana's knife tucked into the side of her pants. She forced herself to meet her assailant's cold eyes with a curious look.

"I don't know your name," she said, hoping he thought she considered his offer.

"I am Cadell." He inclined his head in a courtly bow. "Well met, Lauren Horsecaller."

Unnerving as it was that he knew her name, she gave it

scant notice, and didn't return the nicety. From below, growling and snapping preceded a strangled scream. More yells, warnings to watch out, a yelp. Either her frits had climbed down to help the horses, or others had come. More would be good. They would die along with her trying to save the horses. Bird-men swooped overhead and screamed.

"Call off your monsters and direct the horses to the western end of the canyon, Horsecaller, or I will begin shooting." As if he had all the time in the world, Cadell sheathed the sword and loaded his crossbow, but let it hang at his belt.

"I don't control the frits," she said. "They protect the horses. You should call off your monsters before—"

"I have no need of them as long as I have you."

The horses were circling now, a dizzying mass of rumbling flesh and bone, nearly obscured by the dust. Circling as they had circled her after she fell down the cliff. She understood now. They had healed her just as they would heal Cirq.

The ledge they stood on lurched. Cadell grabbed her.

Her feet started to slip. His hands closed around her throat and slammed her against the wall. She fought him, but he squeezed harder, and her breath stuck in her chest. Pressure built behind her eyes, her arms dropped. Dizzy blackness closed on all sides.

Through the fog of her pain, a whinny pierced the air. Cadell eased his grip. Her vision cleared. The dark-bay mare stood at the mouth of the canyon, twenty feet below.

A sooty cloud appeared over Cadell's shoulder.

"Call them," Sebira's voice hissed. "By the Goddess, open your heart and call them."

Lauren's mental fog ripped away like a thunderstorm cleansing a humid beach. This whole situation was her fault. She had found the horses, but not called them. She whipped out the knife and plunged it toward Cadell's neck. Uncertainty crossed his features, and he jumped away, losing his balance as another lurch shook the ledge. The knife grazed his throat and clattered down the cliff.

Sebira's shadow dissipated, swept into the air by a sudden updraft.

"I am the Horsecaller," Lauren said, undaunted by her failed attempt to stab him. She had only a few heartbeats before the ledge gave way.

Her voice echoed around the canyon. The horses stopped moving. Lauren emptied her mind as she had before with Pindar, and imagined the heat she had felt, the love that had swelled her heart. Stillness. She remembered. The ultimate discipline.

Conscious thought fled, and she felt the insistent yearning that had nagged her since arriving in Cirq, the longing that emerged from the depths of her soul. She closed her eyes and flung aside everything she thought she knew and believed.

Come to me, her heart cried.

A heavy rumble rolled up as the horses moved toward the plain.

Clearly sensing a shift in the herd, Cadell demanded,

"What are you doing?"

Summoning her loudest riding instructor's voice, and ignoring Cadell, Lauren called, "Come to me."

From below, a glimmer of light, growing brighter, emanating from the horses, turning the dust into an incandescent, billowing mantle.

Cadell lunged. Lauren leapt just as the ledge slid away, and his arms swept empty air.

She closed her eyes, said a prayer, and dropped into nothingness with a roar of falling rock and dust. She landed hard on her rear, straddling the dark-bay mare's broad back. Hundreds of horses pounded behind them. She grabbed a hunk of mane, and they galloped out of the canyon and onto a plain turned dark orange with the setting sun. The beat of thundering hooves resonated through her being. Beyond this, shouting, and shrieks of flying bird-men.

Too close.

The birds screamed and plunged. The broad plain offered no cover.

"Damn it. Faster!" She kicked the mare's sides. The horse jolted forward.

The bird-men were equally swift. Even the pairs carrying men gained on the herd. Behind her and to either side, the horses ran hard and close, forming an undulating ocean of color and foaming mane. Yekerk swooped like giant seagulls picking fish from a storm-tossed sea. Horses' squeals echoed in her ears, and she bent lower over the mare's neck, urging her on.

They dove into the river and heaved up the steep bluff.

She wove her fingers tightly into the mare's mane, closed her eyes, envisioned the pass over the mountains, and held on, letting the herd and a new, raw, faith carry her forward. They wove through the pine forest, yekerk screaming above the canopy, unable to penetrate the thick boughs. To either side, the dark shadows of frits.

Was Pindar keeping up? There was nothing she could do but ride this torrent of flesh forward and try to get her herd to safety. Neither the mare nor any of the others faltered as they broke from the forest, climbed the ridge and dashed beneath trees again.

They couldn't maintain this pace. Even if they made the next ridge, the tight, rock-strewn pass would hinder them. They swept across a shallow trough and up the next hill without slowing. When she looked back, she realized she could no longer hear the flying creature's shrieks, and began to relax. The mare checked her stride, then slowed even more as they descended toward the dry lake.

A rest would be good, and well deserved, but they needed to keep moving. As if reading her mind, the mare eased into trot. The trail funneled them into a column, five and six abreast skipping over and around the dead trees. She would stop them for a drink when they reached the dried-up lake—for surely they could pull water from the ground as easily as Pindar—and she would find her horse.

She hadn't had to assail the Bitter Reaches by herself after all. She had had Pindar's steady presence with her all along. Without him, she might not have succeeded. But she had called the horses, and they had heard. If Leinos had been there, things would have gone differently. She would be riding Pindar instead of wondering where he was and if he was okay.

She didn't like having the herd strung out over such distance. For all she knew, half the horses might not have crossed the river yet, and she worried that's where the yekerk had gone. They approached an oblique bend before the lake. She stopped the mare with a thought, but the momentum of those behind forced them past the turn and into the open.

The taste of burning rubber invaded her throat. Ahead, the ugly birds waited, and a line of men pointed crossbows at her and the horses. Cadell stood on a house-sized boulder along the dead lake's shore, his hair matted with dried blood, his face dark as a thundercloud.

... *33* ...

LAUREN CONCENTRATED with all her will to make the horses stop and turn around. Her command whispered through the herd, but they couldn't reverse in the skintight pass. If she were riding an out-of-control sled, skidding pell-mell down an icy hill, she couldn't feel more out of control.

Cadell had picked a perfect spot to ambush. But his eyes widened as the horses did the last thing expected— kept coming. When she saw the fear in his eyes, she pressed forward, and the herd bore down on the men. They scrambled up to rocks to escape. Bird-men flitted into the air, surprisingly graceful for all their awfulness.

"Stop, or I will order them to shoot you," Cadell shouted.

Lauren didn't know what to do. Before she could respond, a limp yekerk fell from the sky, an arrow protruding from under its wing.

Rast's men scattered. More arrows found targets. Another yekerk screamed and thudded to the ground nearby. She recognized the blue fletching of Cirq and

342

craned her neck to see where it came from. The Horseguard—here?

Riding in the lead and without any weapons, she could do no more than keep the horses from being caught in crossfire. She slipped from the mare to shoo them back, but found herself stuck, fingers knotted in the long mane.

From behind, a powerful pair of arms encircled her and cut her free. For a moment, she thought Captain Geed had found her. His grip tightened round her neck, and one callused hand crushed her mouth.

"This is not over, Horsecaller," Cadell rasped in her ear. He dragged her into the herd. "Rast will have these horses, yet."

She bit his hand, thrashed and kicked. He swore, but didn't release her.

"Your men are dead, or will be," she said. "My Horseguard will kill you, too."

"Not as long as I have you."

He shuffled past the horses, but she wouldn't make it easy. She hammered his shins with her bare heels and was about to scream when he clamped his hand over her mouth again. The horses closed around them. For the second time that day, and perhaps only the third time in her life, she cried out for assistance.

Help me.

Horses bumped against them. The bay mare's teeth swept by Lauren's ear and found purchase in the meat of Cadell's arm. He ducked and grunted. A flash and a spurt of red.

Blood ran down the mare's neck.

"No!"

The blade pricked Lauren's throat. "You dropped this in the canyon, Horsecaller. Stop and be quiet, or I will use it. On you or on them makes no difference."

She tried to breathe deeply, to calm herself and the horses.

From behind them, a voice, menacing, beloved. "Release her," Leinos said.

Lauren froze. Her captor froze. Cadell slowly pivoted, holding her as his shield, and faced a large and grim-looking man. The battle spark in his eyes was not the same one she had seen when the yekerk attacked them on the Resting Plains. Instead, his eyes gleamed with the reckless flash of a man prepared to die defending what was his. The sight constricted her already clenched heart.

The horses parted, and Geed and others ran up, bloodied staves at the ready. Several Horseguard crossbows pointed directly at Cadell's head.

He nicked her skin with Jana's blade. "You can kill me, but Cirq still will not have her horses," he said.

She could feel the thump of his heart against her back. He didn't want to kill her, or die, or fail, but his options were quickly narrowing. A tangled jumble of emotions seeped through, and she hadn't the strength to filter them. Beneath the chilly determination she had seen in his eyes languished other, more familiar feelings.

After a long pause, she said to Leinos, "Let him go."

Both men spoke at once. "What?"

"If he will let me go—he saved my life."

Leinos's disbelieving eyes flicked between her and Cadell. "True?"

Silence descended along with swift darkness as the sun dropped below the mountain's peaks. Enaid and others lit torches. Lauren kept her chin high and her gaze on Leinos. He looked awful—thin and dirty—and beyond wonderful, but furious, too. Whether with her or Cadell or both, she wasn't sure and didn't care.

He stared back for a long time, with that narrow-eyed look she'd come to love, his brow deeply furrowed, jaw clenched, then finally said, "As the Horsecaller orders. Drop your weapon, and let her go."

For a moment, Cadell didn't move, and she thought he would do something foolish. Then, the knife fell to the ground at her feet. He released her and stepped away. The Horseguard rushed forward. Leinos stayed them, his fists clenched at his sides as if making a monumental effort to contain himself. His face was too calm for her liking, then his nostrils flared, and he lost the battle. He stalked to Cadell and swung a lethal punch at his face. Cadell hit the ground with a thud.

Leinos hovered over him, murder lingering in his eyes. She watched, frozen, fearing he would beat the man to death, but he mastered himself and moved back.

Cadell got to hands and knees, shaking his head, then slowly stood. Blood streamed from his broken nose.

"Go. Now." Leinos pointed north. "Before she changes her mind. And thank your gods I am inclined to defer to the Horsecaller in this."

Cadell edged toward the deep pine woods.

"Not that way," Lauren said. "Through the horses. If they suffer you to pass, I will know I have judged right."

Even in the wavering torchlight, she saw his face pale, but he waded into the herd. The eyes of a large black and smaller chestnut horse gleamed with distrust as Cadell slid between them. They barely made room but didn't otherwise hinder his progress. On wobbly legs, Lauren went to the dark bay mare, feeling along her neck in the dark. Her fingers found sticky blood. The wound wasn't serious. Now, they would find Pindar.

She tried to grab the mare's mane, to pull herself up, but couldn't. Her legs gave out and she collapsed.

Leinos caught her and pulled her against him as if he might draw her within his own body. She melted against him, wishing with every fiber of her being she could recede into his warmth and strength. With one hand behind her head and one wrapped tightly around her waist, he murmured into her hair.

"*K'varo risa.* Thank the goddess and all that is holy." He pressed his cheek to the top of her head.

Tears clogged her throat—relief, exultation, worry. Horses shuffled closer, surrounding them, wuffling softly, nosing her head and shoulders, offering comfort. Leinos made to push them away.

"No," she croaked. "It's all right. I'm all right."

"Water," he ordered over his shoulder. Then, "Captain Geed, report."

"Minor injuries. One captive—"

Malek crawled beneath the nearest horse's belly and flung his arms around Lauren's neck. "Horsecaller," he cried.

The lump in her throat grew larger. She drew him into their embrace. They had the horses and now she had Leinos and Malek again. Surely Pindar was all right. She just needed to find him and make sure.

Malek made a choking sound, then said, "Artepa—"

She felt Leinos stiffen at the strangled tone in the boy's voice. "What is it?"

"She is hurt. Hurry."

Swiftly, Leinos stood, lifting Lauren into his arms, and they followed Malek across the lake bed. Above the treetops, the glow of the rising moons began to brighten the darkness.

"Put me down," Lauren insisted. She wanted to get to Artepa as quickly as he. Surely they could go faster if he weren't carrying her.

"Do not argue. You can barely stand and have no boots."

Lauren bit down on her retort. Some things never changed. Nor would she want him to. She'd thought to never see him again—or not for a while—let alone be clasped to his chest. Hope for that had been packed away. Being next to him again made her giddy and lightheaded. Or maybe that was exhaustion. She could feel his fatigue, the long-contained anxiety for his country's survival, and maybe for her. Now, new apprehension for Artepa, the woman who had raised him, the woman who had been his guardian for many years.

The woman who had become her friend.

In her head, she screamed, no, no, no. Artepa couldn't be seriously hurt. Pheeso wouldn't have allowed it. Leinos wouldn't have allowed it. But he had come to her aid. She didn't even know how he and Malek had gotten here. Maybe he hadn't even seen the guardians.

Shadows flickered around them, the Horseguard walked to either side. Horses following. For all that, quiet, except for Leinos's panting. She peered at his face. Never had she heard him struggle for air like this. Deep hollows carved shadows beneath his eyes, dried blood caked his shoulder, and dirt ground into his pores. Never had she seen him look so frayed around the edges. And never had he looked more dear. What had he been through while they were apart?

Her heart wanted to shatter. She had called the horses. They should be celebrating.

He glanced down, caught her staring and a weary smile shown from his eyes. He hefted her a little higher and she buried her face against his shoulder.

And then he put her down next to Artepa. Pheeso knelt at his lifemate's side, holding her hand, his features haggard and fixed as stone. A dark stain spread down the entire front of the woman's tunic, and there was a sound, a sucking sound, her breathing, as if she were under water.

Not far away, one of Cadell's men lay spreadeagled and motionless, a stave buried deep in his chest.

Lauren dropped to her knees and Malek sat next to her while Leinos took Artepa's other hand in his. He tried to contain an anguished cry, but it escaped from deep within, and Lauren felt it echo in her soul. There was nothing they could do. She heard it in his voice and saw it in Pheeso's stillness.

"They are here," he murmured, keeping his eyes on his lifemate.

Artepa's lids fluttered and it took her a moment to focus on Lauren's face. "Thank you," she said. "I saw them." She blinked, struggled for air. "For a moment...I saw them."

Lauren looked about her. "Back off," she said. "Let the horses through." The horses had helped her, she was sure of it. After she had fallen down the cliff and into the river, they had pulled her out and healed her wounds. Maybe—

The Horseguard moved aside, and the horses came closer.

Lauren stroked Artepa's hair. "Thank you," she whispered, though she was not sure the woman heard.

A horse the color of a faded autumn oak leaf came forward. He had long whiskers and deep indentations above his tired eyes which were ringed with gray hair. Gently, gently, he put his muzzle to Artepa's cheek and exhaled. She smiled.

"Sweet horse breath." She coughed, and then, on a sigh, "Merci...ful...Goddess."

Leinos placed Artepa's hand flat on the horse's cheek. Her face relaxed and became suffused with elation.

The horse began to glow a dark gold. The light spread to Artepa, becoming brighter. Leinos drew Lauren and

Malek back. Pheeso kept hold of Artepa's hand. Horse and woman began to shimmer. Little by little, they faded, leaving only the light, which lifted and merged and glowed even more brightly. White. Hot.

The cloud flickered like a Fourth-of-July sparkler and moved, first through Lauren, then Leinos and Malek, and finally Pheeso, who had tears streaking down his cheeks. It spiraled up, around the herd, above the trees, and blended into the night sky with the moons and stars.

Lauren stared at the spot where it vanished for a long time. No one spoke. When she looked back to where Artepa had been only moments before, there was no trace. The old horse—gone as well. The fine hairs on the back of her neck stood on end. She looked at Leinos.

"What the hell just happened?"

... 34 ...

BY THE next morning, Leinos still did not have an answer to Lauren's question. All he knew was that Artepa died a guardian, and that is what he told the Horsecaller. But Arepa's passing was nothing he had ever seen before, nothing that he knew of dying. Nearby, the Horseguard tended a cleansing fire that consumed Tinnisian and yekerk remains. That was what he knew of death—remains. But with Artepa, none, only the soaring light. And the horse—he had hoped Lauren would know, but she did not.

Most guardians were disrequired before dying. Had anyone ever witnessed a guardian passing? Did they usually leave behind a body, or was it the horse that made the difference? Had she died at all? She had been mortally wounded, of that he was sure. He disliked not knowing and could tell Pheeso pondered these questions as well, but Leinos had to put it out of his mind for now.

"Drink," he had told Lauren shortly after they had returned to themselves. After they had stared at the starry sky in silence for a long time. Not a one of them had

351

drawn breath during those moments. Perhaps it was the stars. Clouds had congested Cirq's skies for so long, he scarcely remembered the look of the night's sparkle.

She had wanted to immediately search for Pindar. He understood, but she could barely stand up or even grasp the cup. He held it so she could drink, then examined her hands. His glance found Geed, who needed no words to understand. He returned shortly with bandages. Enaid started a fire and soon brought warm water, and in short order, he had Lauren's lacerated palms cleaned and wrapped.

She looked as though she might sink into the earth, as though her bones and muscles had fused and she was no more than a lump of clay that a good rain would dissolve. He felt much the same, and if Pheeso's sluggish movements were any indication, they were not alone. Still, the ache in their hearts for Artepa had to wait.

He wanted to hold Lauren, to tell her he loved her, how afraid he had been when he and Malek were trapped underground—afraid he would never see her again. The elation that had knocked his breath away when he saw her ride out of the forest at the head of the herd. Only to have that swept by fear when Cadell and his men appeared. He wanted to take her to his fur and stay there until the ground shook with their love, to make her his, to be hers, to fall together into exhausted sleep.

But her mind was far away, not on him, not on them.

"I have to find him," she whispered. "He might not be the only one we left behind."

She meant Pindar, of course. He understood. He

crouched before her, knowing it would always be thus. The horses would ever be uppermost in her mind. As it should be. As Cirq had always been when he was Supreme Guardian.

He caressed her cheek, and she leaned into him, eyelids drooping closed. Despite that, he could see the determined set of her jaw. He kissed her forehead. "We will all go," he had told her. She started to push herself up, but he held her in place. "After you eat. That is all I ask."

She wobbled to her feet, insisting she was fine, then teetered into him.

"When was the last time you took any nourishment?"

"Don't know," she murmured against his chest. "Yesterday, I think. No, that's not right. Maybe the day before that."

His eyes found Enaid, but she was already digging in her pack.

"Do you remember," he asked as he slowly lowered them both to the ground. "Do you remember how many days you have left to deliver the horses?"

She rubbed her hand over her face then through her hair, and blew out a breath of frustrated air. "Today was thirteen days."

He shook his head. "Today was ten days."

Her brows drew together, and she blinked several times, trying to work it out. "I lost three days? But—"

Enaid handed him a plate, and he passed it to Lauren. "Eat."

Lauren had eaten, shoveling in food and washing it down like she was starved, but he knew it was so they could be away. Someone found boots for her bare feet. He had stood and moved off, rolling his shoulders, trying to keep a lid on his simmering anger. Anger that she had had to do this alone, had faced Cadell and the yekerk alone, and anger, still, at the queen, for the impossible deadline they faced.

Not, however, anger for being disrequired. No. He might wish for the power of Supreme Guardian, but he welcomed the freedom to do as he pleased, to love.

Lauren came to his side, took his arm, laid her cheek against his shoulder, and sighed. He hugged her, kissed the top of her head. "Shall we find Pindar?" he asked.

They had searched through the night.

Toward daylight, Malek found him. "Horsecaller," he shouted. "Here he is. Hurry."

The big gray stood at the bottom of a bluff, across the river at the edge of the plain, head low, one hind leg cocked, the bony protrusion above his eye cut and bleeding. Another stood behind him, a small brown horse with black mane and tail and long legs. He and Lauren skidded down the steep incline nearly tumbling over each other to reach the horse. A rope pulled tight around Pindar's neck. They found a man at the other end, or what was left of one, face down in the river.

When Lauren reached Pindar, he greeted her with a faint sound, a tremor of his nostrils. She touched his cheek and said something Leinos could not hear. The horse pressed his head against her belly, and she put her arms around his neck. Parts of his shoulder, side, and hip had been scraped clean of hair. His left hind leg bent awkwardly, and he would not put weight on it.

Gently, carefully, with tears glistening on her cheeks, Lauren examined her friend. "The tibia looks broken," she said, then pressed her fist to her mouth and choked back a sob. "He must have fallen trying to climb." She glanced up the bluff. "His back left is the worst." Barely touching, she stroked his side. "Probably broken ribs as well."

"Water," she ordered. "A bucket for him to drink from. Warm water for cleaning the wounds. We can't move him like this."

Good, Leinos thought, she is taking action. But as soon as she touched the bad leg, Pindar tried to hop away.

"Bandages," she directed over her shoulder. "And something I can use as a splint. Malek?"

Malek laid his hands on Pindar without further instruction. He shook his head. "I cannot take away all the pain, Horsecaller."

"Keep trying, okay?"

"Is he going to be all right?" Leinos asked.

She wiped her face on her shoulder and mustered a smile. "I think so, but I don't know how we're going to get him over the mountains."

Leinos studied the horse, then the terrain. "I do," he said. "Will you be all right if I leave you alone for a while?"

Lauren nodded and he left to marshal the Horseguard.

She kept busy cleaning and wrapping, not even knowing where the bandages came from. She wouldn't take her eyes from Pindar, but each time she reached, another rolled-up piece of linen landed in her hand, clearly torn from someone's shirt. "I wish we had ice to keep down the swelling," she said, mostly to herself.

Malek glanced up. "If we could get him in the river, that might help."

The river...is that what healed her? She'd thought she'd pieced together what happened. She recalled galloping through the forest, thinking they were being chased by demons, but it was just the frits running with them. Pindar had stopped at the top of the cliff, and she'd flown over his head and fallen. Then dreamed of The All, and others, and the horses, and awoken the next morning feeling refreshed, convinced the horses had healed her cuts and bruises.

Except now she knew she'd lain there for days instead of hours. And been damp still upon waking. Had she been in the river for that long? She pressed the heels of her hands into her eyes. It defied explanation. She'd been knocked out, so if she landed in the water, she surely would have drowned. Someone or something had helped her. She'd like to know who or what so she could at least give thanks, if not make use of the power again.

The waist-deep cold water would help even if it didn't have healing power. She rubbed the base of Pindar's ear. "What do you think? It's just a few steps to the river. Can you get there?"

Pindar turned and pressed into her hand, directing her

touch to his forehead. She scratched the whorl of hair between his eyes while he nodded.

"All righty then. Let's give it a shot. Malek, stay by his bad leg. Just keep your hand on his hip and let him lean into it if he wants, okay?"

Lauren put one hand on Pindar's whither, the other on his chest. "C'mon big boy. You can do it. You got this far."

Pindar shuffled forward, barely touching the toe of his left hind down, then hopping with his right.

"'Atta boy. What a good boy," Lauren murmured. "C'mon."

Together, they edged down the bank and into the water until the current swirled around his flanks, just high enough to cover the injury. The footing was sandy and sure, and Pindar sighed, his nostrils fluttering like a bird's wings.

The river was cool, but the sun warmed them. Lauren splashed his sides, especially where the flesh puckered over the ribs on his left. Dirt and gravel flowed out of his coat. Whether after she fell down the cliff, or when he tried to climb it, he must have slid down as well, forcing dirt and debris to his skin. She worked her away around, rinsing away days of sweat, more dirt, and blood. Cadell's arrow had cut away a groove of flesh over an inch deep. That would leave a scar, but it wasn't serious.

The little brown horse, a yearling stallion, had hovered near but not ventured away from the bank. She'd thought he'd purposely stayed with Pindar, but maybe he was afraid of the water.

"Who's your friend?" she asked Pindar.

He looked at the other horse, gave a snort. Not a friend, then. Youngsters could be irritating. And Pindar was in no mood to be pestered. But kids could be useful, too. She splashed Malek.

"Hey," he said.

"Hay is for horses. This water is helping Pindar. Good call. Why don't you take a break and go make friends with that guy." She pointed at the yearling who studied them curiously. "He needs help believing the water won't hurt."

Malek smiled. "Okay," he said. He waded to dry land.

Lauren held her tongue as the boy and colt fumbled around each other. She wanted to let Malek figure it out for himself, and sure enough, within a few minutes the young horse followed the young boy around like he had apples and carrots falling out of his pockets.

After a while, convinced Pindar would stay put and knowing he couldn't go anywhere very quickly anyway, she returned to the bank, and sat against the base of a tree. What were they going to do? Ten days left. She couldn't leave Pindar. How would they get the horses to Lerom in time with no equipment and untrained horses and riders? Her head hurt thinking about it. She closed her eyes and rubbed her temples, hoping for a flash of inspiration. Instead, she dozed off.

She wakened a short time later with a stiff neck to the smell of tea brewing. Leinos squeezed behind her and massaged her shoulders.

"How did you know that's exactly what I needed?" She watched Pindar. He had moved closer to the opposite side of the river. "He has to take the weight off his legs. There's no way to make him do that."

Leinos stretched his legs out to either side of hers, pulling her against his chest. He offered her a cup of tea, and she took it gratefully.

"We found a few stragglers who had been caught by the yekerk's claws," he said. "But they have recovered. Malek has seen to the other injuries which consist of cuts and bruises, a couple of arrow wounds—"

"I'll go—" She started up.

"He can do it," Leinos tugged at her sleeve, and she sat, but didn't relax.

"The Guard are cutting down trees. It took time to find the right ones."

"Whatever for?"

"A sling. We will lash furs between two poles, pass it under his belly, then carry him over the mountain. I sent others back to set up a camp by the lake and to oversee building a frame to support the poles. He can rest with the weight off his legs. Will that work?"

She pictured it and the tension flowed out of her tight muscles. "That will work." She sipped tea. "Thank you."

It didn't solve the problem of getting to Lerom, but it did relieve the immediate worry that had been gnawing at her. She leaned back against him. They both needed a bath, and she didn't care. If the hard bulge against her back was any indication, neither did he. But there was too much to do, too much to discuss. He might have been disrequired, but what of his status as queen's consort?

Leinos wrapped his arms around her waist, and said, "He ate a little grain. He approves my plan."

"Oh, really?" she teased. She jabbed him in the ribs with her elbow.

"Ow," he said, reaching under her shirt and poking her ribs in return.

"Did Pindar tell you he approves, Dr. Doolittle?"

He rooted under her hair until he could nuzzle the tender skin of her neck. "Why, yes, Horsecaller. He did."

... 35 ...

LEINOS, CAPTAIN Geed, and the others carried Pindar to the lake. No one questioned the necessity of this task. They fought over who would be on the first team to begin the journey.

The little brown hesitated when everyone else crossed the river without him, but with Malek's encouragement, he plunged in, then shook himself like a dog when he scrambled out, giving them all a much-needed laugh.

If the going had been flat, the journey would have been difficult enough, but watching wore Lauren out. She had to constantly remind herself to breathe.

At one point, one of the carriers slipped on loose rock while negotiating an especially steep ascent, nearly sending them all cascading down. They caught themselves after two fell to their knees, making Pindar scramble for his own footing.

The undertaking had tested the strength of Leinos and Geed often as they struggled to keep hold, stay on their feet, and not let anyone else lose their grip.

It was full dark by the time they made the lake. The herd had drawn water into the basin, and there was plenty for everyone to drink. Around its edges, lush grass grew, dotted with the white flowers. Most of the herd stayed near the banks, but some wandered through the pines, and Lauren wondered if the trees were coming to life again.

The frame to support the big gray was complete, and they set the long poles into it. Pindar's feet could touch dirt, but he didn't have to support all of his own weight. Perfect. The Horseguard dropped heavily to the ground, stretched aching shoulders, let loose jaw-cracking yawns, and stayed put, gazing with wonder at the horses.

Leinos put a fur near Pindar for Lauren and she sat, her knees cracking and complaining. Leinos looked like he intended to bed down elsewhere. No doubt, he was as tired as she, but she needed to know, wanted to know.

No time like the present. She snagged his pant leg before he could get away.

"Hey—"

He looked at her, but there was no fire, and the moons were behind him. She couldn't see his face or what emotion might be in his eyes. The whole time they'd been carrying Pindar she'd thought about how to approach him when she got a chance. Why couldn't he make it easy and just tell her? Now, she was too tired to find the right words, to ease into the subject.

"Are you still the queen's consort or what?"

He tensed, and she braced herself for bad news.

"The queen," Leinos started, and then his voice seemed

to fail, as if what he had to say was too terrible to voice.

He wondered at that, had puzzled over the depth of feeling, of fury, since they were attacked. Then it hit him. It was not anger he felt, but betrayal. And that changed everything. He cleared his throat and continued.

"We were attacked." His hand went to the still fresh wound at the base of his skull. "By a contingent of Tinnisian warriors."

Lauren looked like she might say something. He knelt before her and took her hands.

"It was a total rout. Naele's guardians took her to safety. We fought, and Malek, smart boy, he ran and hid."

Her eyes searched his for a long moment. *What does she see?* he wondered. What was there to see? Only a beat-up old warrior with no position, no authority, no power.

"So…"

"As far as the queen knows," he said, "her consort, and her adopted son, died with the rest."

Her face softened and she smiled.

"Will she demand you return to her side when she sees you're not quite dead?"

He pulled Lauren toward him, up to her knees. She felt stiff, hesitant. He should have told her sooner. How stupid he had been.

"She has no claim on me. Not any more."

If he had his way, he and Lauren would be joined long before the queen laid eyes on them again. If the Horsecaller would have him, now that he had nothing to offer. If she would consent to stay in Cirq.

He would not press her.

She yielded toward him, twined her arms around his neck, pulled him down to the fur, telling him more with that gesture than she could with a thousand words. Pindar swished his tail once. Twice. Shook his head. Lauren laughed, a happy sound gurgling up from deep within her.

When they were side by side on the ground, she burrowed into his shoulder. A moment later she sighed softly and began to snore.

Leinos held her, listened to Pindar's breathing and his own heart, a long absent sense of contentment settling into his bones. When Lauren first arrived, he knew that Cirq once more had a future. His own had not concerned him. Now, he had a future, too.

~~~

Morning came too soon, but Lauren was up the moment sunlight hit her, hauling water to Pindar, bringing him food, checking on the herd. Pindar was better, perkier. He whickered to her when she rose and spoke to him, and he pawed the ground when she approached with food. A good appetite was a good sign. But he wouldn't be able to walk on the leg any time soon. If there was any hope of making Lerom by the deadline, it wouldn't be done at a walk.

During their short sleep, Leinos had shifted nearly beneath the horse and there was a pile of manure awfully close to his head. She kicked it away, then stood there staring at the man, realizing she'd never been awake before him, had never been able to observe him sleeping.

Tenderness washed over her, a feeling she'd had often

enough when looking at horses, but rarely with people. The force of it made her reel, and she turned away, a little afraid, and went in search of Malek and Pheeso, hoping to find something decent to fill her empty belly. She wanted Malek to have another go at Pindar's leg, too. Maybe there was a way to get him in shape to move with the rest of the herd. She doubted it, but they had to try.

Shortly, she was back with Malek, and Leinos was gone, down washing in the lake. She struggled to pay attention to Malek rather than watch the man. Cuts and bruises marked nearly every inch of exposed flesh. Yet he never complained nor expected anything for himself. Even without being Supreme Guardian, he would probably always put the needs of others above his own.

Before the boy could lay his hands on the horse, a whirlwind whipped up grass and dirt all around. They turned to see a sooty shadow emerge from the center of the tiny tornado, and the wind died off as abruptly as it had started.

High Crone Sebira began to solidify before them, but her image never fully took shape. Instead, a larger form appeared in her place. A tall and thickset man with a short, black beard stood where the crone had been, a soft nimbus encircling him.

He wore leather leggings and jerkin and a deep blue cloak draped his shoulders. His keen, brown eyes swept over them and came to rest on the horses. The Horseguard had drawn near and now knelt and bowed.

"Ebro," she heard someone whisper in awe.

"Oh," she breathed. Then, with a jolt, realized she

gazed upon the manifestation of the first Horsecaller, her
ancestor, Enzo, and studied him more closely.

He watched the horses for some time, taking several
long inhalations of their heady scent, then walked to her
and peered deeply into her eyes. She saw herself in the
shape of his face and the tilt of his brows. A new feeling
took form within her, a sense of belonging, of being
connected as if by a long cascade of water and riding this
current into the future. Not unlike the flow of water that
had connected her to The All at the sacred spring. His
voice, when he spoke, sounded at once near and far, faint
and loud, yet as if only in her head.

Just as The All's had.

"Thank you," he said. "Come." He took her hand and
pulled her toward the horses.

His flesh upon hers was warm and solid, but his boots
made no imprint on the ground. The horses lifted their
heads, looked in their direction. A few nickered. Enzo
dropped to hands and knees, kissed the front hooves of
the first horse he reached—the dark bay mare who had
carried Lauren out of the valley—then stood and easily
clasped his arms around her neck and pressed his face to
hers.

"How I have missed you," he murmured. "All of you."
He took the horse's chin and leaned in until they were
nose to nose. "Sweet horse breath."

He released the mare and enclosed Lauren in a hug, his
chest hard against her jaw, then pressed his lips to her
forehead, held her at arm's length, looked her up and
down, smiled. She imagined that in life, he had been

boisterous and enthusiastic. Her great-great-grandfather. She had to keep telling herself that this man, or apparition, had ridden through the Ravery just as she had, then somehow stumbled upon these horses and created Cirq.

But before disappearing, he had bought a farm and built a house, began breeding horses, married and had one child—her great grandmother.

"You saved them. You saved all of Cirq. I thank you, as do the people of our country."

Our country, he said. Lauren wasn't sure how to speak to a god, or a spirit, or a vision, or if she should question him, but whatever he had become, he had once been simply a man who loved horses. She grew up in the house he built, and his journal was still in her pocket. She was blood of his blood. After a few moments, she found her voice.

"Why? Why did you come here?"

Enzo patted her shoulder. "It was an accident. We were galloping, you see. Adrianus was a fearless beast with an insatiable appetite for running and jumping." He smiled as though remembering. "What a horse he was. Pindar is much like him. Glad I am to hear you still use the Greek poets to name the bloodline."

He walked deeper into the herd. "I see Adrian here." His palm caressed the forehead of large black mare. "And here." With his other hand, he patted the deep chest of another horse.

"And here." He touched the necklace she wore. "I made those beads from his hoof trimmings." He looked lost in thought for a moment, brown eyes unfocused. But then he snapped back to his story.

"Sailed right over that embankment we did. I'm sure you know the one. Timing must have been just so. A wicked thunderstorm had blown up out of nowhere." He tipped his head back and gazed at the sky, reached his arms out to either side as though catching raindrops. "Then we were here. And there was no going back."

The shock of what he said hit Lauren like an anvil landing on her toe. "No going back?"

He looked at her sharply. "Did you think you could?"

"The sage, Vraz, told me I would be able to, after I called the horses."

His brow wrinkled with thought. "Do you want to?" he asked after a long moment.

That, Lauren thought, was the million-dollar question. "Vraz brought me through the Ravery. He and Sebira. It was no accident."

His shoulders hitched ever so slightly, and he glanced away. "You were needed."

The anvil dropped on her other toe. "You did this?"

He met her gaze but had the grace to look sheepish. He shrugged. "The horses were dying, our country was dying, and I knew—everyone knew—there was no one left in this place who could do it."

There, he said it again. *Our* country. Did he include her in this? "And who is *everyone*, exactly?"

"The All, mainly. The high crone and the first-degree sage are the liaisons between them and the people. You could say we're the ones running things. Most the time, we keep our noses out, let the story tell itself. But I could not stand by and let the horses die, let Cirq die. They're special. Different from the ones back home. Don't you feel it?"

Lauren had felt something, but she wasn't sure what it was. "I know Cirq and the horses and Horsecaller are bound together, but I don't understand this power."

"You will in time. You are bonded with them. Only one with my blood has this link. The crone, Sebira, she granted this capability." He ducked his head and lowered his voice. "I think she was sweet on me."

Lauren had a hard time imagining the old hag sweet on anyone, but it had been long ago, and everyone was young, once.

Together, they watched the herd for a time.

After a while, she asked, "So, I can't go home?"

Again, he shrugged. "Much changes with time. It has been many hundreds of years since I came through. You must tell me what the old world is like now."

"Many hundreds?" She knew that wasn't right.

"Si," he said. "We lose track on the other side, don't count it up the same way humans do, but I'd say it's been over five hundred years since I came through the Ravery. There were ten generations of Horsecallers before the last one was killed."

"No," Lauren said slowly, looking at him more closely. "It's been only about one-hundred and thirty years since you disappeared from Earth."

Enzo's forehead furrowed tightly again, making his dark brows nearly touch. He stroked his beard, staring out at the herd.

"Look," Lauren said. She pulled the slim journal from her pocket and opened it to the first page. "See, you started this in August of 1881. You disappeared in October of that same year." The same month it had been when Vraz had fetched her. But it had been springtime in Cirq. Clearly, time was not on the same calendar here as it was on Earth.

Enzo looked where she pointed, nodded. "What year was it when you left?"

"Twenty thirteen. Still is, as far as I know. But…" If over five-hundred years had passed here in one-hundred thirty years on Earth, that meant that in the nearly three weeks she'd been in Cirq, then perhaps less than one had passed at home. Later, she'd figure out the math.

He put his back to the herd, but not without difficulty, she saw.

He began to walk to Pindar with long strides. "Your horse needs help."

She followed, had to jog to keep up. "But—"

As they passed the Horseguard, all still on their knees, he said, "You may rise," without slowing his gait. To her, he continued, "You have overcome your worst fear, have you not, little Raver?"

She used to have so many fears, putting her finger on one seemed impossible. She was stronger, more whole, and more honest, even while she felt more vulnerable than ever but still did not know what he meant.

They reached Pindar. He pricked his ears as Enzo walked up to him.

"When you arrived in Cirq," he started as he put his palm flat on Pindar's forehead and concentrated for a time. "When they brought you through the Ravery," he corrected, "you did not want to need anyone or be needed by others, is that not so?"

As if he could see inside her heart. "Yes," she answered, because what he said was true, or had been. She hardly recognized herself, though, anymore.

He moved his hands over the big gray, expertly inspecting and assessing. "And now?"

While she thought how to express the vast changes she'd undergone since coming through the Ravery, he glanced over his shoulder at the crowd that stood at a respectful distance. "You," he said, pointing a long finger at Malek who stood next to Leinos. "Come here, boy."

Malek looked to her for reassurance, and she nodded, reached for him. The boy came forward.

"It is time you learned better how to use your gift," Enzo said to him.

Malek's eyes went wide.

"Don't be afraid," Lauren said and nudged him forward. Enzo tore the bandage off Pindar's broken leg and tossed aside her painstakingly wrought splint.

He took Malek's hands in his, placed them around Pindar's thigh, and closed his eyes. Malek did likewise. For a moment. Then, he lifted one lid and peeked at the big man holding his hands, but Enzo's eye's remained closed, and Malek followed suit. They stayed like that for a time, then, with care not to disturb the boy, Enzo removed his hands, sat back on his haunches, and waited.

A small smile tickled the corners of Malek's mouth. Pindar blinked, stood on the injured leg, flexed it, kicked out. Malek jumped back. Pindar bent his leg again, then put his toe to the ground. He brought his head around and nipped Enzo's arm. Enzo only smiled and patted the horse's neck.

"You went a little too far, my boy," he said. "With practice, you will get it right."

"Is it fixed?" Lauren asked, astonished.

"Not completely. He must still rest. This sling is a good idea. By tomorrow, he can begin to put weight on it again. Walking will be safe."

He stroked the horse's back, big hand coming to rest on the itchy spot at Pindar's wither and rubbing absently, something he did without even realizing, she thought.

"You brought a brave and solid horse with you," he said. "Combine his blood with those." He nodded at the herd. "He has earned that much."

He drew himself up. "Sebira grows weary of my company even though there was a time when she welcomed it. Attend me." He went to the horses again.

"Sebira?" Lauren remembered the crone had appeared momentarily before he did.

"It is because of her that I am able to be here. Continue to welcome them in Cirq—crones and sages both—for they are great allies…but formidable enemies."

They reached the edge of the herd. He touched them as

they walked into their midst, just as she had the first time, stroking their backs, fluffing manes, running his fingers through tails. She shared his bittersweet joy at this reunion with his beloved creatures, knowing he would leave them soon. The horses parted to let them through, then closed, forming a dense wall of flesh and bone between the two Horsecallers and the outside world.

The moment they reached the exact center of the herd, he stopped. The horses were full of expectation, and the nimbus around him intensified. "You comprehend the paradox of being Horsecaller?"

Did he imply she might misuse the ability to call the horses? "I accept this power—whatever it is—as a blessing, and will try to wield it wisely. But no, I don't comprehend this paradox."

"True wisdom is a virtue, my dear, but a blessing can become a curse, and virtue turn to vice." He smiled at some internal joke, leaned close. "Even divinity has drawbacks."

He put one hand on the nearest horse, the other on her head, and dizzying images swirled through her mind too swiftly to see. In an instant, she connected with the mind of each horse, knew their aches and pains and who was related to whom, felt the dust next to their skin, babies moving in mothers' wombs, and the hope in their hearts; the same hope she had seen rekindled in the eyes of Cirqians.

She longed to make everything right for them, to protect, and become one of them, not just one with them. Through Enzo, she reached out, felt her spine stretch, her hands and feet harden, and hair grow densely over her whole body. Her sacred hooves took a tentative step.

The connection broke. She collapsed and inexplicably began to sob. He gathered her to him, stroked her hair, whispered in her ear.

"My descendants of this world were trained to resist the seductive call of the horses. This secret died with the last Horsecaller. You must be wary, for you have come upon it in a manner never intended, not unlike the way I learned." His chest heaved with the memory of some deep sorrow, but he kept her close as if she were a frightened filly. "I felt it," he continued, "but did not fully discern the risk until too late. I lost my firstborn son."

She pulled away. "He became a horse?" she blurted. The sensation of growing mane and tail lingered.

"No, no."

He squeezed her shoulder, but whether to steady her, or himself, she could not be sure.

"He went with them too often, in his heart, in his mind. Finally, he never returned. His body remained, living, yet not."

They sat in the dust together, and the horses were quiet.

"You must make them one with you, Lauren, guide their sacred hooves on clear paths, but resist being one of them."

Mutely, she nodded again, too overwhelmed to think.

"I cannot always be near to help. But you are strong." He wiped her tears. "And I am never far. Come now, compose yourself," he commanded. He rose and pulled her up, smacking dust off his trousers. "Many depend upon you."

They returned to the others.

"Horseguard of Cirq," Enzo said to the assembly. "You have maintained tradition for two hundred and twenty-two courses. Now you have horses and Horsecaller again. Do not waver, always put your horses first, and above all, see to the safety of the Horsecaller."

They bowed and spoke as one. "We have so sworn, my lord."

"Horsecaller," Enzo continued, "you will need this."

From behind him, he produced a stave and handed it to her.

She took the weapon. At once, she felt the difference between it and the one she had been carrying, the one she had lost along with her saddle and bridle somewhere in the mountains. It would take flight, should she but point it, an extension of her arm, her will.

"And this," he added as he shook out a blue cloak like the one he wore.

The material was thin and supple, but she could feel its strength when he put it on her shoulders, as if silk and linen, velvet and steel had all been woven together.

He fastened the exquisite cloak under her throat. "With this, I officially welcome you to the House of Enzo. *Our* house. Live long, and," he leaned close, shot a look at Leinos, spoke so only she could hear, "make more Horsecallers."

Enzo stepped back with a wink. The air grew dense,

pressure built behind her eyes, and he began to fade. She felt herself blink like a dimwit while everything else he'd said whizzed through her brain until it connected that last comment with the bit about only one of his blood being able to bond with the herd.

"But I'm too old," she blurted.

His image solidified for a moment.

"Not here," he said.

... 36 ...

KING RAST did something he had never done before. He went to his sage's tower rather than ordering the sage come to him.

Rezol knew him to be trudging up the long, spiral stairway long before he reached the doorway, hand over heart, sucking air.

"My lord," Rezol said when he opened the door from where he sat across the room. "A matter of some import must have forced you to me. Surely you could have sent a messenger?"

"The Supreme Guardian of Cirq is dead," he gasped, dropping onto a bench. "But the Horsecaller was not with him." He raised weepy eyes to the sage. "What do I do?"

Before replying, Rezol allowed himself a moment to gloat. So, she had escaped. Good. He went to stand next to his monarch. Then, because he was happy to have succeeded thus far, he pulled a chair over to sit, rather than pose intimidatingly above the man as he usually did.

"Have you forgotten, my lord? We want the horses and Horsecaller for ourselves." It was not unusual for the recipient of sage persuasion to forget what he had been persuaded to. Rezol did not resent having to remind the man, not now. "If she goes to call the horses, then the moment of victory is upon us."

Rast mopped his brow, let his hand drop into his lap. "Yes, but how?"

"Simply intercept her before she returns them to Lerom. You must send your best men to Cirq."

"Attack them?"

"Yes. It is time."

"Of course." Rast got to his feet and toddled out, mumbling about mustering his forces.

As soon as the heavy door swung shut behind the king, Rezol sagged onto the narrow palate that served as his bed, and as he did, the ancient aegis over his mountain dropped as well. Woe to any left in the mine's depths, for he did not know if he could continue. He doubted Rast could lead his forces to Cirq fast enough to change anything.

Cadell had failed to capture the Horsecaller. He did not know where the man had gone and did not care.

All his well-laid plans slipped away. Without the horses, he might never find the Absolute. Without the Absolute, he could do little to avenge his mate's death, might never find his daughter.

He lay down and allowed himself to fully imagine his mate, to truly remember, to thoroughly look at her in his memory as he had not for a long time. Her beauty and kindness shown brightly, even after so many courses, and he willed himself to gaze at her image, even as the pain built. This crashed over him like a waterfall, and he did nothing to stop it, simply let it wash him clean. Then, for the first time, he tried to picture what his daughter might look like now, nearly grown. Did she have her mother's wispy blonde hair and deep, blue eyes?

Yes, he thought. She would take after her mother. She glided before him in his imagination, smiling.

He would find other means to achieve his goal.

He would have the Absolute.

Eventually.

And with it, absolute power.

··· 37 ···

LATER THAT day, after a numbing bath in the lake, Lauren checked on Pindar. The big gray tossed his head when she stroked his neck, impatient, now that his leg felt better, to be with the rest of the herd. She wasn't ready to let him out of the sling yet.

"But you're going to be just fine," she said, lifting a bucket of fresh water for him to drink. "And I am, too."

She admired his ears as they ticked backwards and forwards with each swallow. She still worried over what the loss of the stallion meant for her brother. The assumption would be that she stole him. They'd probably think she'd cracked and took off. Would his insurance cover the loss under the circumstances? She hoped so. There was nothing she could do about it, but she couldn't keep the niggling doubt from rising up occasionally. And now, a new concern...

"I could maybe have children," she whispered. It was hard to imagine at this point in her life, but she wasn't about to doubt her divine Great-Great-Grandpa Enzo.

She glanced over Pindar's back and zeroed in on Leinos where he stood in conversation with Captain Geed. He was clearly meant to be the father of her children. Leinos, of course, not Geed. For there could be no mistaking Enzo's intention when he included Leinos in his instructions to her.

She felt an unmistakable thrill deep in her belly, one part anticipation, one part trepidation, all desire, and pressed her hand there, quelling it for the time being. She had to be sure of the man, first. Sure that he wanted her as much as she wanted him. That is, that he wanted the same thing.

Then, she went to check on Pheeso, who sat away from everyone else, near the spot Artepa had died, staring at the placid lake surface. She couldn't imagine what he felt, what the loss of Artepa meant to him. There were no words, so she crouched beside him and tried to see what he saw in the water, balancing her new stave across her knees. Only bright sky reflected off the lake for her. Most likely, he journeyed inward and saw neither the water nor the horses.

Or her, for that matter. She didn't try to engage him in conversation, and he didn't acknowledge her. For that, she had to squelch a bubble of relief as she was more than a little afraid he blamed her for his mate's death.

Just the same, she wanted to offer what comfort she could. She'd have to check with Leinos to see if there was anything else they could do for him. After a while, she touched his shoulder lightly and rose. She stood there for a moment, wishing for inspiration, but nothing came. She kissed the top of his head and started back to the others.

Shortly, Leinos walked at her side.

"I do not know if he will recover," he said. "I do not know what bothers him more, the loss of his lifemate or the way she transitioned, but he is deeply troubled."

Lauren only nodded, lost in her own thoughts.

"What happened between you and Ebro?" Leinos asked.

He probably sensed the change in her. He was close enough for her to feel his warmth, but not touching, appeared unsure whether he should, taking in the new cloak and stave with a sideways glance and studying her face with his copper eyes.

She didn't want any distance between them, yet she was even less sure. After all, she had been conversing with a dead man. A man who had first been granted a special power, one he had used wisely, and then had a kind of divinity bestowed for his service, for creating Cirq, for maintaining peace.

She had held her great-great-grandfather's meaty hand and felt the warmth of life and kinship. The stave he had given her hung loosely in her palm, smooth, warmed by her blood, as solid and real as she. Enzo had not been carrying it at first, had pulled it out of the air. The cloak, too. She fingered its silky edge, expecting it to disintegrate, but it didn't. Delicate and unearthly, yes, but no less tangible than the staff.

"Horsecaller business," she finally answered.

Family business.

Leinos smiled broadly, a rare thing. She felt the tension ease out of him.

"I did it," she said. "I called the horses." He didn't respond right away, so she continued. "You weren't sure either, in the beginning, were you?"

"I admit, I had doubts. Every Horsecaller in history had been male. We thought—"

"Is it possible they all had sons?"

"Possible. But I do not think anyone ever thought of that. We assumed the Horsecaller must be a man." He took her hand. "Now, we know better."

With that, Lauren put concern with returning to her original home out of her mind. She had work to do here. And here felt more like home than home ever had. Even with a death sentence hanging over her head.

They had eight days to get the horses to Lerom.

If Enzo were right, it could be done.

A plan began to form.

As the sun set over the peacefully grazing horses, Lauren tugged Leinos up to a promontory where they could view the herd and be alone. The last rays of sunlight bathed them in red-gold as they stood on a spit of rock, and a light breeze ruffled the cloak away from her shoulders like ocean swells on a calm day.

Birds roosted in the trees warbling evening songs, a sound not heard in Cirq for many years. Below, campfires sprang to life and enticing scents wafted up from cook pots. Manmade music rose up, too, flutes and strings accompanied by laughter, humming, whistling.

Tomorrow, she and Leinos and half the Horseguard and herd would continue south. Pindar was stronger, but he wasn't the only one who needed to go slowly. There were mares about to give birth and others with nursing foals at their sides. She would leave Pindar and Malek with the other half of her guard to follow at their own pace. The horses wouldn't need much from the people; they knew how to take care of themselves.

They sat atop a flat rock as they had the day before with her between his legs and his arms around her. Their breathing found the same even rhythm. Leinos did not speak, but she could sense expectation in him. She felt it too—a pleasurable compulsion to continue the line of Enzo.

Somewhere between here and now and the other side of the pass, dropping down a cliff, finding the horses, she'd dashed her heart and soul against an unseen and unknown force. Instead of breaking, she'd cracked open, become softer, more vulnerable—and yet—more resilient.

A mysterious force had flowed inward. Perhaps it was the love and light The All had told her to choose. Or was it that something else had flowed away? Had she released her long-cherished doubt? Is that what had allowed her to call the horses, to make them hers?

Would she ever understand?

Did she need to?

Leinos rested his chin on Lauren's shoulder, inhaled her scent. She'd bathed after Ebro—Enzo, as she insisted—

had gone back to wherever it was the gods and goddesses resided. But she still smelled of horse, probably always would. He liked it. It was the scent of Cirq itself.

"Vraz brought us here," he told her. "Me and Malek."

She turned to him in surprise. "He did? How? Where is he?"

"Returned to Elaz. The rumblings from Tinnis are bad. The sage, Rezol, has gained control over King Rast and is working to excavate a terrible power buried long ago beneath a mountain—the Absolute. The sages in Elaz do not wish to confront him but fear waiting too long. They prefer to try and reason with him. If he recovers the Absolute…"

Lauren elbowed him in the ribs. "If he recovers the Absolute, what?"

"The sages are tight-lipped about what might happen."

Lauren sighed and settled more deeply against him. "But it won't be good. Is Tinnis far away?"

"Not far enough."

"That man, Cadell, he said he represented someone who would pay well for the horses's power."

"He wore the colors of King Rast, but it is more likely he referred to the sage, Rezol."

"I shouldn't have let him go."

"If Cadell is smart, he will disappear rather than return in shame to those who sent him."

Lauren nodded. "I hope that's true. Anyway, we have enough of our own problems."

"True. When Vraz came to get us, there was another

sage with him. He is bringing others. They should arrive soon. It is slow going, traveling the way they do. Quick when they are alone, but more difficult when towing a couple of non-sages."

She twisted to look at him again. "You came underground?"

He nodded. "It was not the most pleasant of journeys."

She touched his cheek and he warmed to her touch.

"I'm glad you're here." She faced the sunset again, hugged his arms where they held her waist. "Who are the others?"

"Kadre is a young cousin to the queen, but he left court many courses ago because he did not agree with her plans for the country. Pagajera is his guardian. They are thrilled to see the return of the horses and will be helpful when we reach Lerom."

She sighed and sank more deeply against him before saying, "I look forward to meeting them."

Her thoughts had gone elsewhere—he could tell by her distracted tone—probably worrying over what would happen when they faced the queen. Should he tell her about Dan, the stranger he met at Kadre's house? Leinos could not gauge whether she would embrace or reject the man when she saw him.

After a while, she asked, "Are you okay with being disrequired?"

He smiled at the top of her head, glad, for once, for the way her mind jumped topics.

"Yes," he said. "It was a relief. Now I can be your

unofficial guardian, so long as Pheeso does not mind sharing that duty." He pulled her tighter against his chest, took a deep breath. "Keeping you safe is the only way to keep my own heart safe. It has been so since the first night you arrived. I will be content to provide you comfort."

"Will you never let me out of your sight?"

"Never."

"Then I, too, will be content."

They were quiet for a time, watching shadows shift and deepen as the sun slipped below the western peaks of the Bitter Reaches. Leinos kept his arms locked around her waist, and she rested her hands over his, entwining their fingers together, lightly tapping one, never quite still.

"Is it enough?" she asked. "To provide comfort?"

Leinos felt his chest constrict. He knew she had been joined with a man in her own world, and then had rightly broken that covenant when her mate had lain with another. She had not been able to trust again. When she had reached out for him, he had been forced to reject her because of his Guardian vow. He worried she still wished to return to her world, even if it meant Cirq would lose her horses again. He dared not hope she might consider joining with him.

He had to clear his throat twice before answering. "Enough?"

"Pheeso and Artepa were lifemates. There more than comfort between them."

With difficulty, Leinos kept his breathing even. "They

had pledged their lives to each other for always."

For a few moments, she did nothing more than trace lazy circles on the back of his hand with her fingertip. He thought he would jump out of his skin.

"Is there a ceremony or contract?" she asked. "Or do you just agree you're joined?"

"You can agree, but here in Cirq, the covenant must eventually be formalized by a guardian, sage, or crone."

"So, Pheeso for instance, or this other sage that is coming, one of them could do it?"

Lauren held her breath. They had shared a fur, comforted one another, and both of them wanted more. That was no secret.

Leinos made her turn all the way around so they were facing. He raised one hand, barely cupping her cheek. She sensed a tremor going through him.

"Why do you ask, sweet Horsecaller?"

"Just curious," she answered quickly, suddenly taken with a case of cold feet. "You know, I guess I'm going to be here for a while, so I should know your customs."

She didn't doubt her feelings and his were plain on his face. There was no reason to dissemble.

"I'm staying here, Leinos," she whispered. "This is my home now."

He blinked once, twice, then hauled her to him so hard he knocked her breath away. His fingers threaded in her hair, cradling her head against his heart, which felt like it might come out of his chest. Her own pounded painfully against her ribs.

"Will you join with me?" he asked.

Lauren's heart had inched up into her throat, making it impossible to speak. She squeezed her eyes against sudden tears and nodded.

And then he held her at arm's length to look into her eyes. She wiped her damp cheeks. He took her face and kissed her so gently, she almost began to cry again. It was devastating, that gentleness, the gratitude and desire it held. They'd kissed before, and it had been wild, but he'd held back. She knew that now. He'd held back then even while he'd possessed her with his mouth, because he couldn't give all of himself to her.

"I love you," she said when he released her and felt the truth of that simple statement like she never had before.

He put his arm around her shoulders and held her while looking out over the lake and the herd.

"Until you appeared, like the very goddess incarnate, I thought I knew what it was to love. Believed that caring for my country to be all that was needed." He combed his fingers through her hair. "I was wrong."

"And now?"

"I feel as though I have known and loved you all of my life."

They agreed to ask Pheeso to perform the joining ceremony. Knowing she and Leinos would stay together speared through all her uncertainties.

She had a future. Of that, she was sure.

She had responsibilities to that future, too. The significance of being Horsecaller and carrying on the line truly began to permeate her consciousness. She had focused on saving the horses, not what would come after.

Before darkness made the descent dangerous, they climbed down. Perhaps she might be able to go through the Ravery eventually, to let her family know she was all right, but only if she could be sure of returning home, to Cirq.

Hand in hand, they walked to where Pindar rested. Each person they passed acknowledged her with a deferential bow. She didn't think she would ever get used to it, preferred they view her as no more than a fellow soldier. That made her laugh. She would never be like them, but could hardly deny the impact calling the horses and walking with the first Horsecaller—her great-great-grandfather—had had on her. It had certainly changed her perspective; she couldn't fight the effect it had on her Guard.

She went to Pindar and put her arms around his neck. He tucked his nose toward her, held her against his chest. Leinos stood by, then tentatively moved closer to also give the horse a hug from the opposite side.

"Should I have asked your permission to join with Lauren, first?"

Pindar turned his attention to the man, and Lauren stepped back. The horse checked around for treats, nibbling at pockets, then moved his big muzzle right into Leinos's face. The former Supreme Guardian, fearless defender of all, froze in place, eyes wide.

"Breathe with him," Lauren said.

Leinos did. They exchanged a few breaths, then Pindar

licked his cheek, and turned to her. *Took you long enough*, his eyes clearly said.

The horses of Cirq had called him long before they called her. Her fears had prevented her from hearing, kept her from believing she was the Horsecaller, that she had something to anticipate. Pindar had helped her believe, trust, and love.

Since arriving in Cirq, she'd barely been able to face each day's challenge, to keep herself and Pindar safe. She had not allowed herself to think beyond that. Now, her future unfurled, and she greeted it gladly, accompanied by a good horse and a good man.

And counsel from the ghost of a long-dead Horsecaller to make more Horsecallers.

About the Author

Candace Carrabus spent her formative years in the saddle, just imagining. She still rides horses and writes stories—frequently simultaneously—and many of these stories are imbued with the magic and mystery horses have brought to her life. She shares a farm in the midwest with her family, which also includes several four-legged critters.

She is busily working on the next book of The Horsecaller.

Candace loves to hear from readers. Connect with her today to keep up to date on her progress and upcoming releases:

Contact at candacecarrabus.com
Follow on Twitter: @CandaceCarrabus
www.facebook.com/AuthorCandaceCarrabus

Also by Candace Carrabus

The Man, The Dog, His Owner & Her Lover

A Witting Woman novella

Coming Soon

On The Buckle

A Dreamhorse Detective Agency Novel

(Contemporary romantic suspense)

Read on for a sneak peek of *On The Buckle*…

ON THE BUCKLE
Chapter 1

The truth is, my parents are alive. Pretending they're dead makes their absence in my life tolerable. When the letter came from their attorney—crap—who would have guessed they had a lawyer? Anyway, it was like they were dead because it referred to money I might receive, "amount undisclosed." That was just like them. Jesus. Amount undisclosed. What the hell was that supposed to mean? It could be five dollars for cripe's sake.

After reading what the note said, I'd needed a good gallop. I still had the stupid thing folded and in my pocket when I tightened my horse's girth and mounted. She swished her tail in irritation, tossed her head. We both needed to clear out the cobwebs.

The letter said my parents had "made arrangements." That's a thinly-veiled Dad euphemism for "Here's what I want you to do, and I've fixed it so you have to." He always gets his way. I went along like an idiot—hadn't seen or heard from them in years, and still went along.

I sent my horse, Calypso, into trot and we headed for the trails.

I'm like a dog. I can say that because I have a dog—Noire—running alongside. Doesn't matter how I treat her—and I treat her good—she'd be happy to see me.

Always hopeful. That's what it was. I was hoping this time they'd finally come through for me—this time it would be more than five dollars.

I can talk myself into anything.

This was the situation: In the next month, on May first, I would be twenty-nine years old. The letter from an attorney in Connecticut—Connecticut? Couldn't they have gotten somebody from the Island? I know it's just across the Sound. But Connecticut? Okay, so the letter said there was this trust fund for me. To get it, I had to keep a job for one year by the time I was thirty—even a job working with horses—and I had to leave with a glowing letter of recommendation. Goes to show they were still keeping tabs on me, probably through my uncle. God forbid I should know where they were or what they were doing.

We hit the straight stretch. I squeezed my legs and gave Cali her head.

Later, I'd made the mistake of telling my cousin, Penny, about the letter. She's more like my sister since my aunt and uncle raised me, and I lived with Pen and her husband, Frank. She'd shifted into gear, scoured the want ads of all my horse magazines, sent out my resume, and came up with a doozey of a job.

Penny had sat one wide hip on the edge of the bed and flipped her long, dark hair over her shoulder. "You have to do something, Vi," she'd said. "You haven't kept a job for more than a few months solid ever."

She didn't have to remind me. The truth was, the breaks between had become longer. It was getting so I could hardly keep Cali in hay. If it weren't for the tolerance of Penny and Frank, I'd have had to sell the nag.

"Penny," I'd said. "I ride horses, fancy show horses,

remember? The kind that jump really big jumps for really big money. I do not give trail rides."

"It will be a nice break for you. All the competition is stressful."

Stressful. Yeah, right. What was stressful was the owners. All they cared about was winning, not whether their horses were happy or healthy or even ready for the next level. Penny knew all about the blowup with my last client over his horse. He says he fired me, but I walked out because I wouldn't make his horse to do something that would get one or both of us hurt. And I don't mean the owner.

I tried a different tack. "Yeah, but Missouri? For cripe's sake, Pen, what do they have out there, corn fields?"

"I'm sure they do have corn fields. But St. Louis is a big city. They have baseball, museums, a good symphony . . ."

Crap. Penny is thorough. She'd done her homework, and she is always reasonable. I'm not. It's a bad habit. Can you really expect reasonableness from someone with a name like Viola? Jesus. It's the twenty-first century.

"Like I'll have time for the symphony when I'm taking care of twenty hack horses and who knows how many boarders and … I'm not teaching riding lessons, right? You told them I don't teach?"

She nodded, and I continued without taking a breath. "Anyway, you know I don't care about sports, and I'm not going to be anywhere near St. Louis. How could you do this to me?"

"I have not done it to you. I've done it for you."

She'd raised her voice. She was folding laundry and

snapped the life out of a couple of pillowcases by way of calming herself before continuing.

"You'll be a little over an hour from St. Louis. It takes that long to get to Manhattan, so don't make such a big deal about it. You hardly ever go into the city anyway. Now get going, before they change their minds or you run out of time."

I had used every excuse I could think of. Penny overrode all of them. She's not usually bossy, but had reached her limit, being pregnant. They needed my room for a nursery. I wouldn't have a home to come back to when the year was up.

So, I made plans to haul myself and Noire and Cali to Winterlight, the Malcolm family's public riding stable out in God's country, for a year of keeping their horses fit for fox hunting, giving trail rides, and "helping out around the farm." Which could be anything. They'd better not expect me to milk cows or slop hogs or anything. Working at a hack barn was low enough.

I ride jumpers, and I'm good at it. I can do things with horses others can't, like me and my mount have a psychic connection or something. Not a horse whisperer, no taming wild horses. When I get in the saddle, some channel opens, a channel closed to others. I used to get paid well to jump horses around grand-prix courses with jumps so high it would make your hair stand on end. It put me in a zone of some kind where nothing could touch us—unless I was on a horse that wasn't ready. Then, I'd get a sick feeling in my stomach and do my best to pilot him or her safely around the course.

When the unthinkable happened because I didn't listen to my gut—a deadly crash at a square oxer in the middle of a difficult triple combination which left a gelding with great heart in a heap and having to be put down—when that happened, and I went to the emergency room with a fractured sternum and more bruises and contusions and sprains than I could count, and I spent several days in intensive care on a respirator, only to hobble out to face a law suit from the irate owner who demanded I push his horse beyond his limits, I quit for a while and tried giving lessons. Made me wish they had put me down.

Maybe a year of forced trail riding would be a good break. In any case, I would do my time and get the glowing letter of recommendation. Before I left Long Island, Penny made me promise not to "smart off," drink, or get involved with my boss. Maybe she was right, but I only smarted off because the people I worked with were such idiots. The drinking thing I have under control. And Harry, well, who could resist Harry? Apparently no one, male or female. Harry didn't discriminate either. I don't like to share, so it was best to move on.

I pulled into the drive of Winterlight toward late afternoon on the last Saturday of April, and stopped. The ground rose and the road topped a hill, blocking my view of the place. A light cloud of dust hovered beyond the hilltop—probably someone riding in a dry arena. There's an easy way to avoid coating your and your horse's throat with dirt when riding. It's called water. Take a hose and spray the arena down first. Nothing to it.

I could have turned around. Nothing said I had to do it.

Nothing said I had to collect the undisclosed amount promised by the mysterious trust fund.

The problem wasn't dust with no one in Missouri smart enough to use a hose. The problem was a child. That's why I stopped with the engine idling roughly, Noire eyeing me expectantly, and Cali pawing the floor of the trailer. They wanted to get out and run. I wanted to get out and run the other way.

There was a child at Winterlight. I'd managed to avoid thinking about it all the way there. The girl of eight was just learning to ride. Penny told them I don't teach, and they said I didn't have to give her lessons. The point was, she would be around, the child and her pony. I'd have to watch her ride.

I rested my forehead against the steering wheel, but the engine jerked so bad, I feared a bruise, so I leaned back, and rubbed my hands over my face. I was road-weary and really needed to stretch my legs, take a shower, go for a ride, anything.

I didn't have to baby-sit; I would find something else to do when she rode. She wouldn't be my responsibility. No, I would not let the dangerous mix of young children and riding get in my way. I would work hard, take good care of the horses, and keep my head down.

Like I said, I can talk myself into anything.

20143160R00218

Made in the USA
Charleston, SC
29 June 2013